Carl Muller completed [illegible] in Colombo. He served in [illegible] Royal Ceylon Navy and the Ceylon Army before entering the Colombo Port Commission in 1959. He took up journalism and writing in the early sixties, working for leading newspapers in both Sri Lanka and the Middle East. His published works include *Sri Lanka—a Lyric, Father Saman and the Devil, Ranjit Discovers Where Kandy Began, A Funny Thing Happened on the Way to the Cemetery* and *Colombo: A Novel. The Jam Fruit Tree,* the first book of his Burgher trilogy, was awarded the Gratiaen Memorial Prize in 1993 for the best work of English literature in Sri Lanka. Its two sequels, *Yakada Yaká* and *Once Upon a Tender Time,* were published in 1994 and 1995 respectively. A children's book, entitled *The Python of Pura Malai and Other Stories,* was published in early 1995. *Children of the Lion,* a large historical novel, was published in 1997. Most of his works have been published by Penguin.

Carl Muller lives in Kandy, the hill capital of Sri Lanka, with his wife and four children.

Spit and Polish

Carl Muller

PENGUIN BOOKS

Penguin Books India (P) Ltd., 11 Community Centre, Panchsheel Park, New Delhi 110 017, India
Penguin Books Ltd., 80 Strand, London WC2R 0RL, UK
Penguin Group Inc., 375 Hudson Street, New York, NY 10014, USA
Penguin Books Australia Ltd., 250 Camberwell Road, Camberwell, Victoria 3124, Australia
Penguin Books Canada Ltd., 10 Alcorn Avenue, Suite 300, Toronto, Ontario, M4V 3B2, Canada
Penguin Books (NZ) Ltd., Cnr Rosedale & Airborne Roads, Albany, Auckland, New Zealand
Penguin Books (South Africa) (Pty) Ltd., 24 Sturdee Avenue, Rosebank 2196, South Africa

First published by Penguin Books India 2000

10 9 8 7 6 5

Typeset in *Palatino* by FOLIO, New Delhi
Printed at Baba Barkha Nath Printers, New Delhi

To the officers and men of Sri Lanka's armed forces and especially to the Navy. This piece of bilge is offered to all who have ever walked a deck in a running sea and in venomous monsoon weather.

You need a strong stomach for that . . . and a stronger one for this!

Contents

Foreword

This novel is a spin–off from the Penguin trilogy, *The Jam Fruit Tree, Yakada Yaká,* and *Once Upon a Tender Time.*

In straddling this particular branch, I do not wish to inconvenience readers with allusions to events or episodes in the previous books. I will try hard to make this a self–contained, self–supporting story. A different ball game, so to say.

I have threaded this story with alternating skeins of history, which are most genuine. Names and places are real, and accounts of combat true. This allows the book to be accepted with some seriousness at least. The Royal Ceylon Navy of the times may have been just a 'one–ship Navy', but a Navy all the same. And the boys were men—ready to take on the world, even if they had to paint their boots for the occasion!

I make no apologies to those who find caps that fit them. They really shouldn't get their knickers so twisted. It makes for a vile way of walking, whether they have found their sea legs or not!

Kandy 1997 *Carl Muller*

1

Of Duck Caps and Number Eights and Sick Bay Shenanigans

'God, he looks like the bloody Blessed Virgin,' said old Van Dort, and sniggered into his arrack.

Carloboy von Bloss grinned. He knew he didn't look so bad. He had looked himself over in the family wardrobe mirror and was pleased at what he saw. His singlet, with blue edged square neck, white shorts, blunt-nosed shoes and dark blue hose. He wore his cap square, decided that it made him look quite medieval, and pushed it back. The gold lettering on the black ribbon was hidden behind his hair. *HMCyS Gemunu* it said—Her Majesty's Ceylon Ship 'Gemunu'. Ship! Hah!

The flipped-back cap was much better. Not that he would wear it indoors, but it gave him a sense of belonging. Of being different.

It was the eighteenth of November, 1953, and he was exactly eighteen years and twenty-seven days old. He hadn't been home for a long time and his mother was not really overjoyed at his coming. He heard her banging in the kitchen and also heard her tell his sister, 'The damn prodigal has returned!' He told himself he couldn't care less.

His father, Sonnaboy, had slapped him on the back and insisted, 'Today we will put a drink. Here, have a Three Rose. Smoke, men. Now you're a man, no?'

So, after a lot of hurt and a long separation, father and son sat to drink a solemn arrack each, and Sonnaboy called in the neighbours and everybody trooped in to admire Carloboy in his Navy uniform and ask how he was, and the women simpered and said, 'Myeee, all this time never came home, no?'

Carloboy had a little diary. That night he made the first of many entries of his new life:

> Joined the Royal Ceylon Navy as a Signalman. Official number A-5550.

Two days later, he noted:

> Drafted to *HMCyS Rangalla* for initial training.

To those unfamiliar with the geography of Sri Lanka, let it be known that Diyatalawa is in the central hills in the island's tea country. Mountains are its main feature, as well as rolling patna and mist that puts clouds to shame. To the uninitiated, the obvious question would be: 'How the devil does one get drafted to a ship that's four thousand feet in the mountains?' But patience . . . as we become, like Carloboy, more seamanlike, and begin to think, act and behave (as Carloboy was constantly exhorted to do) in a seamanlike manner, we will understand. We hope . . .

Rather, let us reverse the tape to that blazing eighteenth of November, with the sun suffering an inflamed liver condition and being most irate. Ninety young men swaggered through the gates of the Ceylon Navy Headquarters, a shore establishment in Colombo. Nautically, this was *HMCyS Gemunu*, land-based and close enough to the sea that crashed on the shore spiritedly. The 'ship' was crewed with hundreds of duck-capped bulletheads who marched, slouched, ran or simply ambled along, performing their several shipboard tasks.

Some were flushing drains, others spreading manure on beds of doubtful-looking cannas. Some were even painting smooth round rocks. White paint. The rocks would be arranged around the flower beds. Nice touch, a chief petty officer told the duty officer. Others were sweeping dormitories and morose types carried kettles of tea to God knew where.

These were sailors? Carloboy had wondered. He watched the 'drill'. Occasionally they would transfer buckets, mops, spades, rakes or whatever they carried from right hand to left in order to salute a natty specimen who hove into view. These types walked around with the sole intent of collecting salutes. They wore peaked caps pulled down to almost cover their eyes and sported gold-banded epaulettes. They would waggle a hand in response and trot on, only to return later for another hand-wag.

Now and again, a piercing whistle would tatter eardrums and put the galley cat's fur on end. Carloboy told George Vanlangenburg, 'God, my aunty Anna screams like that. One day she saw a garandiya[1] in the firewood pile and put a yell. Whole neighbourhood came running.'

The unholy screech was followed by an amplified voice, quite hollow, demanding that Able Seaman Andare report to the quartermaster's lobby . . . at the double! This, Carloboy was told, was the wail of a bosun's pipe. It's really a sort of stubby, electroplated penis with one testicle. The bosun (who should not be confused with the bison although it has long been thought that the rudiments of the buffalo lurk in both species) is an apostrophied boatswain. It is supposed also that only a bosun of whatever stripe be allowed to use this pipe. Give it to a quartermaster and expect the worst. Later, as quartermaster (which is nothing of distinction, we assure) Carloboy tootled on it to deadly effect, making every bosun cower in his watery grave!

A burly fellow with a blue anchor patched to his sleeve, took note of Carloboy, Ronald Todwell and Ivan Sims. Three Burgher buggers, he thought, and already grouped together. He turned to a dark, barrel-chested sailor who had, Carloboy was sure, the yellowest teeth in South-east Asia. 'I say, AB, those buggers, those three there, look like troublemakers, no?'

AB Grero smirked. An AB, he told the newcomers, is an Able Seaman. 'I'm an able seaman, you understand? You are just fuckup ordinary ratings. Going to be a long time, oh yes, a fucking long time before you can become like me.' He glared at the Burgher trinity. 'You three, yes, you! I don't like the looks of you. Bloody Burgher buggers come here to give the arse! Think I don't know your type? You better watch it, you hear? I'm passing the word round. I can smell trouble with you three.'

This, the three mentally shrugged, was only to be expected. They had all spent their young lives to the utter distraction of parents, the despair of teachers, the destruction of the social order around them. The Navy, it seemed, was taking note and was convinced that there were always such pains in the butt that wouldn't take kindly to the rigours of naval discipline.

'Don't go to say anything,' Sims hissed.

'Able!' Todwell snorted, 'Not able even to brush his bloody teeth!'

'Don't worry, we'll get him later,' Carloboy soothed, 'first must sign up, no?'

The medical examination had been detailed. Quite detailed. In a tiny room, an SBA—Sick Bay Attendant—gave them a dispassionate once-over and barked, 'Strip!'

The recruits raised eyebrows.

'Oh come on, come on,' the SBA snapped, 'What's wrong? There are no women here. I'm the bloody nurse.'

'You mean all our clothes?' someone asked weakly.

'Then what? Take off, take off,' the man was rubbing his hands and growing quite excitable.

'Nothing doing,' Todwell growled, 'you're going to examine us here?'

'You'll be called, so strip.'

'So when I'm called I'll strip.'

'Strip! Strip!'

'Whose bloody orders? All of us to stand here, cocks hanging?'

'Surgeon Lieutenant's orders!'

'So where is he? He's going to come here and look?'

'Strip! Strip!'

There was a bellow from an inner room. 'What the fuck's going on there! Strip that lot and send them in one by one!'

It was the voice of authority. Clothes were peeled away and ninety young men stood in a ragged queue, inviting the purpling SBA to squat and give them the kiss of life.

'You wait,' he gritted, 'wait till the blood test.'

The Surgeon Lieutenant gave each a through going-over, sweetbreads and all. Sundry characters breezed in and out, remarking interestedly on the line of naked recruits. Cheerful snatches of this and that wafted around.

'Sha! Like the hanging gardens of Babylon . . . '

'Here, sonny, what's your name?'

George Vanlangenburg looked up. 'Me? Vanlangenburg.' Very good-looking he was, fair, fat-thighed, smooth as a Chinaman's bum.

'Vanlangenburg, eh? Nice. Buggers in *Rangalla* will have a good time.'

Vanlangenburg frowned. He thought that far too many had had far too good a time with him for far too long. When would it end?

Soon, they were dressed again and dismissed to Pathology where test tubes were distributed. 'Don't go to fill them,' a likeable fellow grinned, 'just a little will do.'

'Of what?'

'Urine. What else? Just pump a little and give.'

'How to piss like that just because you tell,' Carloboy protested, 'Have to wait till I feel like, no?'

'What, men, only a few drops I'm asking, no?'

'Few drops even, I can't now.'

'Von Bloss!' another bellow, 'you're von Bloss, no? You're trying to be funny?'

'But I can't piss now.'

'Is that so? And when can we have the pleasure?'

'I don't know. I'll drink some water and see.'

'Balls!'

'Open a tap,' someone said, 'if he hears water going he also might feel like going.'

The suggestion was welcomed. Several sick bay taps were soon in spate.

'Now how about it? See how the water is coming. You also open your tap.'

Carloboy tried and said he couldn't, to everybody's disgust. He was given more water and after a while his bladder stirred indignantly. What was deemed necessary was gratefully received.

They were then marched to the mess where oaths had to be sworn. Among other things, each had to solemnly intone his allegiance to Her Majesty Queen Elizabeth II and assure her that he was prepared to serve in any outlandish corner of the British Commonwealth, and, of course, accept that at a pinch, he could be called upon to clean sewers, unload ships in port, police the streets, fight fires, perform strike-breaking duties and provide essential services in times of national emergency including riot control, rodent extermination, house clearing, the guarding of the national transport system and shielding politicians who other political lowlife wished to get rid of.

Twelve years it was. They swore and signed away twelve years of their young lives and were then herded into a kit store where a monstrous petty officer doled out square rigs, duck caps that looked like inverted urinals, number six and number eight uniforms, bell–bottoms, silks and lanyards, boots, shoes, deck shoes, web belts and puttees and a host of odds and ends. The store became quite festive as the day progressed.

'What's your cap size?'

'I've never worn a thing like this in my bloody life. Do they come in sizes?'

'Okay, okay, try this. Find something that fits, will you . . .'

'Here, these trousers . . . nothing's fitting. All tight one place or another.'

Again, it was on the double . . .

'So you signed up,' Eardley said, 'Where, put the uniform to see.'

Carloboy ransacked the long canvas bag. Everything had to be washed, he knew. Shoes needed shining, webbing and cap pipe-clayed. But he kitted up, grimaced at himself in the mirror. Not bad.

Eardley agreed. 'Smart,' he said, poking into the bag. 'Ah, you got the ceremonial kit also, bell–bottoms, tunic and sailor collar, silk . . . wear this to see.'

Carloboy shook his head. A wild thought came into his head. 'I'll go out and come.'

'Like this?'

'So what's the harm? I'm in the Navy now.'

Eardley smiled but couldn't help firing a shot. 'With your build you would have looked really smart in Army uniform. Anyway, what to do? You'll get late?'

'Don't know. But just put a mat and pillow in the veranda.'

Carloboy bumped across the rude-planked Vihara Lane bridge, to his home across the canal. Home. To the mother who detested him, to the father who had stood, stony–faced at the door, watching him leave over a year ago.

Notes

(1) A ratsnake

2

History—The Springing Tiger

None could tell the story of Sri Lanka's fighting men better than the Indians, for it was the Indian Independence League, the old IIL that organized the first 'Lanka Unit' in Singapore during World War II. That was on March 22, 1944, and it was the beginning of Sri Lanka's involvement in the cause of India's freedom.

This 'Lanka Unit' had its parallel 'Ceylon Department' too, and both units were associated with the IIL and the Indian National Army (INA) of Subhas Chandra Bose.

Bose was *Netaji*[1] and had no qualms about what he would do or who he would use towards gaining his objectives.

It is now known that the INA and its Lanka Unit fought alongside the Japanese against the British in the cause of India's freedom, and this has been confirmed, albeit obliquely, by Indian historian Ramachandran, who dealt with the Indian Independence Movement in Malaya from 1942 to 1945.

Ramachandran has said that when the Japanese surrendered in Malaya, Bose ordered League officials to destroy all official papers. It was not advisable that any evidence of the IIL's collaboration with the Japanese fall into British hands. And Britain in turn, found the activities of Bose's INA most embarrassing.

As such, no document of the least importance has

survived, and the British, too, erased all information on the INA, its activities and its achievements.

A case in point is the story of the INA's action at the Palel airstrip in Manipur, which was the northern front of Indo-Japanese assault on British India. Gordon[2] said that the British denied that any such action had taken place and, above all, that no Indian troops ever fought alongside the Japanese.

But there is no getting away from the fact that Sri Lankans also fought for *Azad Hind*[3] and gave their lives as bravely.

Singapore was the INA's wartime rear headquarters in the Malay peninsula, and when the British re-occupied Malaya, one of their first actions was to tear down the memorial to the INA dead.

Indeed, when Pandit Jawaharlal Nehru visited Singapore in March 1946, Lord Louis Mountbatten made one request: that Nehru lay no wreath at the war memorial for the INA. This is recorded by Ziegler[4], who said that Mountbatten had reminded Nehru that the men of the INA had not only fought against the British but also against the local people of Malaya.

Even the Indian author Nirad Chaudhuri[5] suggested that the INA was never near the front.

But others differ. Durlab Singh[6] and A. Ayer[7] tell of the INA campaigns and the daring manner in which they were conducted.

Much has thus been given us of the INA's wartime activities on the Indo-Burmese border. Ayer relates how Bose trained and equipped an entire contingent of Ranis of Jhansi, his women's fighting unit, when he moved his headquarters closer to the front. Ayer was definite that the INA forces covered 150 miles within Indian territory, but, as Toye[8] said, the western world knows little of, or wishes to acknowledge any of the story. Even in India, he said, the story has received the most niggardly treatment.

The Lankans of the Malay Peninsula, who fought alongside the 'Springing Tiger' fought magnificently. Two strands of history bring the story together: the Indian struggle for an end to British rule, and Japan's aims to expand in South-east Asia.

The world will ever remember Gandhi's and Nehru's non-violent struggle, based on negotiation and compromise and non-aggressive opposition. But none can deny the armed struggle of revolutionary groups both in India and outside.

Bose was not satisfied with passive resistance. He wanted direct action against the British administrators and their institutions. And his views received support. Indians resident in the US and Canada formed the revolutionary Ghadrite movement. In Europe, the Indian Legion was formed. Bose was becoming a thorn in the British side.

In 1941, with the threat of arrest and incarceration, he made a daring escape to Germany where he organized the Indian Legion of Europe to be the nucleus of his INA. The Indian Legion comprised four battalions in 1942. In Germany, the Legion swore obedience to Hitler, as the leader of the German Armed Forces in the fight for the freedom of India.

This is probably why both Nehru and Gandhi rejected Bose and his aims, although Bose himself, as early as 1936, rejected Hitler's anti-Asian racism. And the West held firm to its convictions. Indians were collaborating with the Nazis . . . and more so, with the Japanese. Even the moderates and conservatives in India were appalled. When Bose formed the Provisional Government of Free India in Singapore, he justified the stance he had taken. He also declared that Japan had recognized his provisional government.

Perhaps Bose used Japan, took the tide at the flood. Hitherto, apart from sporadic acts of violence against British administrators and institutions, he had had no real plans for a military role in the liberation of India. Then, Japan burst upon the Pacific scene and this gave Bose the long-awaited opportunity for action through his INA force in Asia. India was included in Japan's long-range expansionist plans and Japan was keen to sponsor anti-British activities and all anti-colonial liberation armies.

As far back as 1912, Rash Behari Bose, who threw a bomb at British Viceroy Hardinge in Delhi, found safe haven in Japan. Indeed, Japan promoted the idea of 'Asia for the Asiatics' and assisted the setting up of INA branches in Kuala Lumpur, Malaya and Singapore.

When Singapore surrendered to the Japanese in 1942, thousands of Indians of the British Indian Army were recruited into the INA. Many Sri Lankans in the Malay peninsula also joined. Many question the role these Sri Lankan fighters played, but the fact of their being part of the INA is undeniable. It was time for Bose to return from Germany, take command.

The story of his journey embellished his legend. He was ready to enter into the real war against the British and he fearlessly made passage by submarine, through waters which were controlled by the Allies. Round the Cape of Good Hope, past the south of Sri Lanka, across the Bay of Bengal to Sabang, then Penang. His arrival in Singapore in July 1943 was hailed as near-miraculous.

He revitalized the IIL and the INA. He declared he Provisional Government of Free India and earned for the INA the status of an Army of a sovereign government under the Geneva Convention.

He did more. He declared war against Britain and America in October 1943!

Notes

(1) Leader
(2) Ref: *Brothers Against the Raj*, Penguin India, 1989
(3) The Free India Movement
(4) Ref: *Personal Diary of Admiral the Lord Louis Mountbatten*, London, 1988.
(5) Ref: *Thy Hand, Great Anarch: India 1921-1952*, London, 1987
(6) Ref: *The INA Heroes: Autobiographies of Maj Gen Shah Nawaz Khan, Col Prem K. Sahgal, Col Gurbax Singh Shillon*, Lahore, 1946
(7) Ref: *Selected Speeches of Subhas Chandra Bose*, New Delhi, 1983
(8) Ref: *Subhas Chandra Bose: The Springing Tiger*, London, 1959

3

Of Complying and Complaining and Dead Cats in Lavatories

The chronicler has no wish to dwell on the journey to Diyatalawa. Ninety 18-year-olds on an overnight train to the hills becomes the stuff of nightmares. Despite all strictures and the agonized yelps of petty officers at the Colombo Fort station, much good liquor was taken aboard, while Carloboy reminded all and sundry that they were now on a train, and when it came to trains he knew more than any pseudo-sailor could know about non-existent ships or ships perched upon mountains . . . 'So let's have a drink and a bloody good time!'

'Drink and be merry' is a matter of interpretation. For the boys being propelled into a life of naval discipline, into an existence quite alien, this had to be the *now* time. Nothing would matter but *now*. It was the time, then, to let it all hang out—the smuttiest language, the ripest songs, the vilest jokes, the most outrageous stories, the coarsest of laughter and, as other sleepless passengers swore, the bluest night of the calendar.

'Nobody sleeps!' Carlo Nugawira roared.

'My God,' muttered the Rodrigos in the adjoining compartment, 'what are they singing now?' while the fleeting country echoed to the rollicking strains of:

If I were a single girl, and if I were to marry,
I would marry a carpenter than any other laddie;
For he can screw and I can screw, and we can screw together,
And we'll get up in the middle of the night and screw one another.

It was only in the early hours that sleep took its toll of some and booze levelled many others, and the hills ceased to echo the ghastly uproar that had begun when the night mail groaned out of Colombo.

Arrival was as much of a shambles. They tottered out, cursing everything that moved, the short sleep, the icy chill of a new day four thousand feet over sea level, and most of all, a leading seaman who was grimly hanging on to his sanity, trying to bring some order into the whole boiling.

After much griping and sitting on or tripping over kit-bags, and after recruit Aloysius had told everyone, even the porters, that he wanted to go home, they were bundled into two trucks and taken most wheezily into *Rangalla*.

The Commanding Officer—henceforth the CO—was Lieutenant Dharamdass, the sort of name that was a cross between a grunt and a sneeze. He maintained, pleasantly enough, that sailors were made, not born.

'You're here to be trained,' he said in his deceptively musical voice, 'and this is something we are good at. Very good at. There will be parade each morning and you will learn to love your boots and your brass and look after them at all times. You may swear at anything and everything. The master-at-arms, the watch bell, the guards instructor, me, the cooks, the staff . . . ' he beamed, 'and that's all right. Everybody must swear. Gets rid of the bad feelings, I always say. And then . . . and then *I will punish you until you fall in a fucking heap and never open your dirty mouths again! Do you hear!'*

Carloboy stared. He had never seen someone so affable one minute, then go off half-cocked the next. No, Lieutenant Dharamdass' smile was a gale warning of sorts.

Led to the huts, each claimed bunk and locker. 'Get your bloody fingers out,' an able seaman said, 'collect your sheets, blankets, get shipshape!'

Sims told Aloysius, 'Once more you say you want to go home, I'll brain you!'

But the recriminations had to come. 'All this damn polishing, polishing, polishing. What the hell is this, men? Just look at that parade ground. All red dust. Polish and go and in two minutes the boots are covered in dust.'

Carloboy had a point, but there was no help to it. Boots had to be disguised as mirrors. Caps had to be Meltonian-cleaned to put Snow White's knickers to shame.

Vanlangenburg gave a superior sniff. 'One thing, I know how to do this. My uncle was in the Army and he told me how. See here, first take a little polish on the finger and rub into the leather. Then spit—' pthoo!—'and rub. All the polish gets nice and smooth . . .'

The rest watched interestedly, then put their heads together.

'*Adai*, Vanlangenburg, you like this polishing business?'

'*I* like. At home also, anyone going anywhere, asking for me to polish and give. There. How the toe cap now? Like silk, no?'

Boots sailed in from all directions. Vanlangenburg leaped off his bunk.

'You say you like,' Carloboy sang, 'then you polish.'

'What? What? You're mad! Look at the amount of boots. How to polish all this?'

'What, men, only thirty pairs.'

'You're mad. Thirty pairs! Whole day will go. You're joking or what?'

'So just do one by one. Nicely, like you did yours.'

'No! Polish your own boots!'

'Oh, all right. One thing, can't depend on anyone these days.' Carloboy picked up his boots, told Vanlangenburg, 'Anyway don't sleep in the night, you heard.'

'Huh? Why—why can't I sleep in the night?'

'Nothing. Sleep if you want, but I'm thinking, better for you if you don't.'

'You're trying to do something when I'm sleeping? You try to see. I'll make a complaint. This is a hell of a joke. I must polish everybody's boots?'

'So don't. We will polish. But we know what to do.'

'What are you going to do?'

'That's not your business.'

Vanlangenburg became quite nervous. 'But—but—this is not fair . . .'

'Fair? You're the one who started boasting. Like to polish. For the whole family, you said. But now what are you worried about? We said we'll polish—'

'But why did you say not to sleep?'

'Just.'

'Just why?'

'Why not? If we are all up, only you can sleep?'

Vanlangenburg's head swam. 'You're mad,' he repeated. It was assuring to say it. It seemed to explain all the lunacy his world was heir to. 'See, will you, even my boots, it takes about fifteen minutes to polish.'

'We know that. But if you take fifteen minutes, your boots are shining. Like straight from the shop. Look at my boots. About one hour I'm rubbing the effing things. Can you see? Like as if they have come from a monkey's arse! That's what I'm telling, you're the best man for the job.'

'But how? Thirty pairs,' Vanlangenburg wailed, 'how to do so many?'

'Why can't you? We are all in the same hut. Little co-operation, that's all we're asking. Otherwise why don't you go to the next hut? Go and tell that leading seaman fellow. I saw the way he was looking at you. You can have a good time there. Might even take you to his bunk in the night.'

Vanlangenburg looked bleakly at the pile of boots, at his tormentors. He took up a boot. 'And what about all the other work?'

'What work?'

'The webbing and the brass and all.'

'You give all that to us. We can do that. You just sit and polish. You want anything just shout. Your tea also we'll bring.'

So Vanlangenburg polished and was thanked prettily for his pains and Hut Three marched with twinkling toes until everything came apart at colour guard one morning.

Each morning, in rain or shine, the white naval ensign was hoisted and a band of recruits made up the colour guard. Colours were hoisted at eight ack emma and struck at sunset. The guard had to salute the ensign which was slowly raised by a signalman who then secured it to the butterfly clips on the mast. At sunset, usually at six pip emma, or nautically, eighteen hundred hours, the colours were brought down, just as slowly and with due solemnity. This was a daily ritual. A ship that did not fly its colours was either (a) not a ship but a sea-going washing machine, (b) under the command of a skipper who had escaped from the booby hatch or (c) had not as yet been commissioned and no one had fervently asked that God bless her and all who sail in her.

'God help us all!' screamed the Platoon Commander, 'You! Ordinary Seaman Vanlangenburg! *Fall out!*'

This manoeuvre executed, the PC called the OOD (the Officer on Duty, mind) to witness. 'Sir, look at his fingers, sir.'

Everybody looked.

On a small rise overlooking the parade ground, where another small mast and yardarm were in business, the preparatory pennant fluttered up on its halyard.

'Five minutes to colours, sir,' carolled a leading seaman.

'Fall in!' the OOD roared, 'After colours I'll make you see colours!'

Having duly presented arms, Vanlangenburg was yanked out of file again. The PC gave him a withering look. 'Tell me . . . tell me how you come on parade with some black shit all over your fingers. Stand erect! Don't fidget like you got worms in your arse! Your mother is a Kathakali dancer? Well?'

'Sir, I was polishing boots, sir.'

'Look, you bloody moron, one pair of boots to polish for morning divisions and you get polish up to your fucking elbows. Look at your fingernails!' and looking to heaven for guidance, 'is this a bloody seaman or some fucking lunatic?'

The heavens took no notice. Nobody on earth offered an opinion either, although given the choice.

'All the boots,' Vanlangenburg muttered.

'All the boots? What boots? *Are you trying to drive me mad?'*

The dam burst. 'Thirty pairs. Thirty bloody pairs every day. This is why I joined the Navy? To polish the other buggers' boots?' He thrust a hand under the PC's nose. 'See my fucking hands . . . and I have to stand here and listen to you! What the fuck do you know? I'm a bloody moron, I'm a bloody lunatic . . . Damn easy for you to stand here and say whatever comes into your head. Wearing white shoes and coming! You're not putting polish on them!'

The colour guard was in convulsions. The OOD stepped discreetly away. The PC blanched. This was a recruit!

'Fall in!' he screamed, 'Stand erect! Stand still the rest of you. Ordinary Seaman Vanlangenburg, report to the regulating office at ten hundred hours.'

Vanlangenburg didn't budge. He regarded the PC sourly. 'All cock!' he said, 'Bloody rubbish. Ten hundred hours. Why can't you say ten o'clock like other people? Calling me a lunatic. Bloody mad buggers you all are!' and he swaggered back, rifle tilted crazily on his shoulder.

'Colour guard will retire! Abaaaht—tern! Deees—miss!'

'Like hell!' Vanlangenburg snarled and, carrying his rifle like a scythe, strode to the regulating office where a fat-faced Malay quartermaster raised an eyebrow.

'Whadd'you want?'

Freezing the man with a look, Vanlangenburg shouldered past.

Nobody knew what transpired in that office. Sick Bay Attendant Winnie told Ordinary Signalman 'Daft' Fernando, 'Sin, men, now don't know what will happen. Shouldn't have made him polish like that.'

The others hung round, waiting, wondering.

'There, he's coming,' Carloboy hissed.

Vanlangenburg emerged. He carried his rifle as carelessly as ever and Sims remarked, 'have been removing the bayonet also.'

True, there was no fixed bayonet. That piece of equipment hung demurely in its 'frog' on the web belt. The others creased foreheads, trying to interpret this sign.

Vanlangenburg came up, fixed wrathful eyes on his messmates, strode into the hut and flung his rifle—*thunk*—on his bunk. Then he spun round and seized Ordinary Telegraphist Thiaga by the throat. 'Gum,' he grated, 'Gimme some gum.'

Thiaga's eyes bulged. He was a small-made, cheery little Tamil who grinned a lot and had very white teeth in a very black face. 'Here, let go,' he burbled. He was growing purple, which, on black, made him look awful.

'Gum,' Vanlangenburg growled, taking his hand away and leaving a blacker smear on a black neck.

Thiaga knew that it was not his to reason why. If gum was the need of the hour, so be it. In pots. In a barrel if desired. He opened his locker with nerveless fingers.

'Oi George,' Todwell sang out, 'what happ—'

'You shut up!' Vanlangenburg snarled, snatched at the Gripfix and extracted a sheet of paper from his pocket. Smearing glue on it, he kicked the hut door shut, slapped on the paper. Then he turned and grinned. 'If you can't shine your boots, you can go and shit in them!' he said grandly.

It was an order from the CO:

ALL RATINGS WILL POLISH THEIR OWN BOOTS OR ELSE

'Or else what?' Electrician's Mate Koelmeyer demanded.

'That you go and ask.' Vanlangenburg was relaxing in his bunk. 'Go now and ask if you like.'

Nobody wished to.

But matters did not end there, for Ordinary Telegraphist Carlo Nugawira had a brainwave when mucking about in the paint store one morning. He dabbed at his work boots . . . then gave them a gentle coating of Black Japan, and lo! they shone with a faery light. With little croaks of delight he rushed to the hut and stood before the others in twin pools of glory.

The boys gaped. 'What the fuck did you do?' someone asked with a catch in his voice.

'Painted them! Painted the bloody things. Now how? No more polishing. Just wipe. And if they get scratched or anything can put summore paint. Pukka, no?' He gave Vanlangenburg a pitying look. 'You rub,' he said patronizingly, 'one brush of paint and our job's over.'

Even Vanlangenburg took notice. 'Shine like that even I can't get,' he breathed, 'like enamel, men. What for sitting here and rubbing?'

'My mouth is also dry,' Sims said, 'spitting like this.'

The vote was unanimous. 'Let's all go and paint the fucking things.'

The Platoon Commander was in ecstasies. Why, the man actually drooled. Being at best a most sarcastic prune, he even permitted himself a little smile that touched the corner of his mouth, making it look rather like the vagina of a Shetland mare. He said feelingly that he wished to congratulate the squad on its most seamanlike turnout. He even hinted that he would be forced to wear sunglasses in future and waited for his charges to appreciate the joke. He conducted his inspection in the dreamy manner of a man, sunk in an armchair in Sun City, who suddenly found Miss World in his lap.

The boys ha-ha'd politely. They knew he was trying hard to be human and pitied him immensely. His order to dismiss was sheer saccharine. As they marched away, the sun making silver autographs on the Black Japan, they heard his small squeal of satisfaction.

It took a few days for the paint to crack. Who the devil thought it would? It began to flake off in bits and pieces and then to cobweb in hideous scrawls and wrinkles. Ordinary Telegraphist Yusuf threw up his hands and announced that the time had come to kill himself.

'Never mind all that. You can kill yourself afterwards. What are we going to do now?'

Aloysius groaned. 'Now will have to dump them in kerosene oil or something and scrape the paint off.'

'You and your paint!' Carloboy stormed, and Nugawira raised a doleful face and mumbled that it was not his fault.

'Never mind that now. What are we going to do?' Koelmeyer asked.

True, each had two pairs of boots, but one was used for everyday working parties, fatigues and general clumping around camp. Parades, divisions, colour guards and all other such ceremonial hoo-ha's required the other pair. They looked hopefully at their work boots. They closed their eyes and then looked again with hope plus imagination. The general opinion was that they looked as though they had been lain in line and sodomized by a hippopotamus. But, at least, they hadn't been encrusted in paint. They could be nursed, brought up to scratch.

They formed rank for colour guard the next morning with the distinct feeling that all would not be well.

'Von Bloss! Your boots are a bloody disgrace!'

The boy scorned reply. It would do no good to tell this excitable man that he had laboured, yes, laboured, from eight o'clock to 'lights out', grimly bringing his work boots to a semblance of the ceremonial. True, the boots were not beautiful, but quite winsome. A sort of wholesome, homely beauty. He had felt as though he had performed a major archaeological restoration.

'Answer me! Why are your boots not polished?'

Carloboy kept eyes front. 'I polished them, sir.'

'How? You rubbed them on your bum?'

'No, sir.'

'What was that?'

'No sir, I did not think of that, sir. Next time I will sir.'

'What the fuck are you talking about? Fall out! Fall out!

Fall out!'

Carloboy fell out. Most excitable, this character.

The old song of the leading seaman carried across the parade ground. 'Five minutes to colours, sir.'

The rest of the squad, also asked to fall out, were standing wherever they had fallen out and the PC was ready for a cosy session with a psychiatrist. From the quarter deck the CO looked at the most unusual formation and asked the First Lieutenant whether this was regulation procedure. The signalman on the hillock began to jiggle the preparatory pennant. One minute to eight o'clock. The PC shut his eyes in anguish, fired a mental DHL to the devas and screamed, 'What are you all doing out of rank! Fall in! Fall in! *Fall in!* Squad—hough! Slooope—arrmhz!'

Fantastic! As the white ensign climbed gracefully, they presented arms in general salute. The sound of the bosun's pipe died. Time for Act One, Scene Two.

'Will you bastards kindly tell me why you conspire *to drive me crazy at eight o'clock in the fucking morning!'*

No answer.

'You! *Yes, you!'* a quivering finger stabbed in the direction of Cook-steward Haramanis.

Haramanis was most uncomfortable with the English language. He had joined the Navy with a single intention: to sit in a galley and cook. 'Eh?' he said.

Eyes rolled. Then all the working of the face seemed to congeal. 'I suppose you all polished your boots for morning divisions?' Quite reasonable, the tone of voice.

'Yes sir.'

'I see . . . ' still the sweet tone of reason, 'You, Todwell, you did polish your little booties, didn't you? Let me see . . . you sat on your little bunk with a little boot in your hand and you polished and polished, didn't you?'

Todwell looked down hastily. He had size nine feet in size ten boots. Call those little? 'Yes sir.'

'And how long did you take to polish them?'

'Almost an hour, sir.'

'Liar!' he was off again. 'What do you take me for?

What do you take me for! One hour you polished to come on parade like this?'

Todwell believed that it always took two to tango. He held his peace.

'You know what I think? None of you polished your boots! *Isn't that so?'*

No answer.

'Right. I'll show you buggers. This is mutiny, do you hear? *Mutiny!* You all thought you could come on parade in dirty boots. That's it. That's it! Right—high port arms!

Mechanically rifles were raised over heads, held up at arms length.

'Squad will advance! Lef' tarrrn! At the double—quick—march!'

Away they went, the entire colour guard, running all over the parade ground, rifles aloft, round and round, this way, that way, any way. The PC ran behind, hooted, *'Pick your feet up there!* Hup, hup, hup, hup, hup—abaht tarn! *Hup, hup, hup, hup!'*

It was hard to tell who or what were or was more ridiculous: the squad bouncing around with rifles held up like trophies of war, or the PC who trotted behind screaming 'hup, hup, hup'.

Carloboy gasped, 'Do these buggers get as mad as this so early in the morning?' and Ordinary Seaman Jayasinghe puffed and gritted that his hands were numb.

The tragic case of the Japanned boots was finally solved with the liberal application of turpentine and much earnest cajoling to make the ill-treated leather respond. Sims was the least patient. 'This is why we joined the fucking Navy,' he intoned. He had a corn and the unscheduled morning sprint had been most unkind to it. 'To polish and pipeclay and arrange bunks . . . ' he scowled furiously and ejected a blob of spittle on a toecap.

Todwell rose, stretched wearily.

'Hup, hup, hup, hup,' sang out Koelmeyer, and they all dissolved into helpless laughter.

It was also hard for the boys to take kindly to the menial work thrust upon them. They had sniggered when they heard that nautically, lavatories were called 'heads'.

'Heads? A shit house is a head?' These Navy–wallahs were crazy.

'Maybe it's because that's where the tails are flushed,' Carloboy hazarded.

They naturally bridled when told that among their many interesting duties was heads detail. It was no earthly use telling duty officers that one came from a good family, or that never in one's delicate years had one taken a mop and bucket to a loo. Their protests went unheeded. They were told that scouring lavatories was an important part of 'wrap-up' training for shipboard duties. On board, apparently, sailors clean lavatories. Well, someone *has* to do it. 'Start now,' they were told, 'get used to it.'

'That's a load of shit.'

'Of course it is. What do you think life is?'

In *Rangalla*, the heads were, in reality, massive cesspits, dug deep and long beneath an awesome row of squatting plates. The heads were christened Cigarette City because, from days of yore, all recruits, forbidden to smoke, had done so in the privacy of the heads. Privacy? Scratch that. There were no doors to any of the privies. Yet, each was a recruit's haven. The heads . . . and a cigarette . . . ah, bliss!

Each time a recruit was detailed to clean the heads, an able seaman was sent along to supervise. The Navy had apparently reasoned that a recruit on heads detail would smoke if allowed to work unsupervised. It had never occurred to the brass that smoking is what a recruit gleefully indulges in when availing himself of the mod. cons., not when scrubbing them.

Carloboy shrugged. He disliked this detail and he didn't like the AB either. 'What do you want to come for? I'll clean the place and come.'

'You go and bring the buckets and squeegee,' the AB retorted.

'So what are you going to do? Just stand and watch?'

'That's not your business. You do what you have to do. Go on!'

It was quite nauseating to find that the pit beneath a squatting plate held a dead cat. AB Jayasena looked at it interestedly. 'Get it out,' he said.

'What?'

'That cat. How to leave a cat in the shithole? Get it out.'

Carloboy agreed. As it was, very fat, green flies were crawling over it, some supping delicately. 'Okay, I'll get a stick or something.'

The AB gave him a deadpan look. 'Just get it out now.'

'So all right. I'll get something to pull it out. How about a boat hook?'

Jayasena spat. 'No hooks and sticks. Take it out.'

'How?'

'With your fucking hand!'

Carloboy straightened up. Perhaps what the Navy so sorely wanted to do from the eighteenth November—discipline him—had reached the acid-test stage, but he thought that this was pushing things too far. 'What? Put my hand in that?'

'Yes. That's an order!'

The trouble with being a recruit was that every lowlife in uniform who wasn't, liked giving orders . . . and every recruit knew that he was knee-deep in the cranberry sauce when someone yelled, 'That's an order'. It meant, in strict naval parlance, that disobedience was tantamount to mutiny.

In the old days, mutiny merited death, yardarm hanging, or that unpleasant business of being keelhauled. The offender was tied to a long line, tossed into the sea and then dragged along the keel of the ship. In this way he would meet thousands of barnacles that resented him and gave him a most bruising welcome. The idea is that a recruit must comply, and complain.

Carloboy considered the pros and cons. If he wished to challenge this repulsive AB's attitude he would have to (a) take the dead cat out of the pit with his hand, (b) complain to the regulating petty officer who would record his statement, (c) go before the CO or the First Lieutenant at a special requestman's parade to air his grievance, and (d) abide by the CO's or Number One's decision. (By the way, First Lieutenants are also Number Ones or Jimmys).

This, to the new boys on the block, seemed and sounded most satisfactory. They felt that wherever their ship sailed, even half-way up Sri Lanka's central massif, the Geneva Convention sailed with them and the rights of all mankind and naval recruits were upheld and protected. What happens, however, is quite another ball game.

A case in point:

'Recruit Udurawana states that on the morning of November 26, he was ordered to bend over and grasp his ankles, and when in that position, Able Seaman Mendis and Able Seaman Wijesekera swatted him on the posterior—'

'On the what?'

'The posterior, sir.'

'You mean his bum?'

'Yes, sir.'

'Then say bum, man.'

'Yes sir.'

'Very well. go on.'

'Very good sir. Swatted him on the bum with a belaying pin. Recruit Udurawana states that he protested and asked why he was being so ill-treated, but he was told to shut up and bend over and that that was an order. Recruit Udurawana complied and says he was hurt and greatly humiliated. He says he received several blows on his pos—um—bum. He now makes this complaint, sir.'

'I see. Is recruit Udurawana here?'

'Yessir. Recruit Udurawana . . . two steps forward march!'

'Are the AB's here?'

'Yes sir.'

'Ummm . . . yes. Ordinary Seaman Udurawana, you are very justified in making this complaint. You claim you were assaulted. This is a serious charge. Have you any witnesses?'

'N—No sir.'

'Oh. Were you medically treated?'

'Sir?'

'Did you show your bloody arse to a doctor?'

'No—no sir.'

'Then what the devil are you wasting my time for? You, Mendis, Wijesekera, did you—'

'No sir.' (In chorus).

'There you are. Shall I tell you something, Udurawana? You come here trotting out some bloody bogus complaint to embarrass this ship and my position as CO. *Do you understand?* You come here wasting my time, and not an atom of proof! *Stop fidgeting! Stand straight!* Let me warn you—the next time you come before me I'll throw the bloody book at you! *Do you hear?'*

'Y-yer-yes sir.'

'Good! Now get out! Bum! Should have shoved the belaying pin up your bloody anus!'

It was thus seen that this comply and complain lark was a load of horse manure. Carloboy tried to reason with the AB. 'Surely you don't expect me to put my hand in that?'

'Yes, and hurry up!'

'But—'

'Look here. I won't tell you again. Get that cat out *now*! *That's an order!'*

Put like that, there was no help to it. Carloboy leaned over, held his breath, plunged a hand into the mass of excreta. Once his fingers were immersed in that foul mess, nothing else really mattered. He grasped a stiff, slimy leg and straightened up slowly. The cat dripped, stank dreadfully. Flies rose around him indignantly. His eyes blazed.

'Here's your cat,' he hissed, and swung the corpse.

It struck AB Jayasena on the chest, splattering muck on his face and neck. He howled, and then both men were racing for the taps, Jayasena squeezing the shit out of his eyes, his boots scrunching on the dead animal that had a terrible face, all drawn back, its fangs in a death-snarl.

They soused each other, then skipped to their huts for soap and sped back to strip and lather. Both thrower and throwee had been liberally daubed because the sodden corpse had exploded on Jayasena's chest to spatter Carloboy, and the wall Jayasena stood against. There was no time to start a war. They smelled. They reeked.

Buck naked, they considered each other through swirls of lather and then looked at their uniforms that lay wet, gunky, at their feet. As on signal, they kicked the clothes into the nearest pit, and Carloboy said, 'Let some other bugger come and pull them out,' and they scrubbed and scrubbed and soaped each other's backs and stood under the showers and laughed like lunatics.

They left the heads, sniffing at each other and the mountain wind raised goose pimples on their bodies.

Jayasena said, 'Never brought a towel. Now how to go to the hut?'

'Run like hell,' Carloboy advised.

'If somebody sees . . .'

'Can't be helped. My hut is nearer. Run!' and two naked sailors dashed up the concrete steps, didn't check, even to change gear, flashed past an open-mouthed Shipwright Fonseka, hurled themselves into the hut.

Jayasena clapped Carloboy on the shoulder. 'I'll put your towel and go to my hut and change.'

Carloboy was wriggling into his trousers. He grinned. 'No more dead cats, right?'

Jayasena grinned back. 'And no more shit in my face.'

It was better than an international summit!

4

History—The Kotelawala Saga

At the start, the Lankan communities in Malaya (both Ceylon Sinhalese and Ceylon Tamils) had stayed aloof from the activities of the IIL. They considered themselves Ceylonese, not Indian. But with the capture of Singapore, the Japanese began to look on the Lankans with increasing hostility.

They, the Japanese, appreciated what Bose and his Indian National Army was doing. But these Lankans? What was their role in war? For one thing, they were British subjects and they were in no way anxious to liberate Ceylon from British occupation.

The Japanese even considered the Ceylonese in the Malay peninsula hostile towards the Indian Independence Movement. They even thought it advisable to round up the Ceylonese and confine them in internment camps.

Ceylon was, to the Japanese, a thorn. Mountbatten's headquarters of the Allied South East Asia Command was located there, and the Japanese bombing of Ceylon in April 1942 had been a relatively minor, quite half-hearted action.

The Ceylonese in Malaya (the Tamils outnumbering the Sinhalese ten to one) found themselves in deeper waters than they cared to be. They were British subjects in an alien land under Japanese occupation. They had to survive deprivations caused by the war. The Japanese harassed them, sometimes tortured, even killed them.

Into this scenario came a young man who could never sit still. He was restless, full of strange dreams and intents, even as a young student in the Royal College in Colombo. He was Gladwin Kotelawala, son of Sir Henry Kotelawala and the kinsman of an ex-prime minister of Ceylon, Sir John Kotelawala.

Gladwin could never sit long enough to study, and his father, being most upset at the boy's contrary nature, took him out of the Royal College and sent him to Trinity College in Kandy, Sri Lanka's hill capital, where another kinsman, Jack Kotelawala also studied. It was hoped that Jack would 'keep an eye' on Gladwin, but when Gladwin 'disappeared', none could tell what had possessed the boy to run away as he did.

Gladwin ran far—to India—and it took time for his father to trace him and bring him back. Relief was short-lived. Gladwin disappeared again. This time he went to Singapore and resisted all attempts to be repatriated. He slipped easily into a new life there, met Muriel, the daughter of a Ceylonese in Malaya, Freddie Wettasinghe, and married her. Also, there was the outbreak of war, and Gladwin, even if he had wished it, could not return to Ceylon.

One man in Malaya held a deep fascination for Gladwin: Subhas Chandra Bose. Gladwin was vociferous in his praise and support for Bose and the way he led the INA. It was not long before these two met and a deep relationship grew between the 'Springing Tiger' and the young man who could not sit still.

Gladwin was not happy with the Japanese attitude. Also, what was the harm in the Ceylonese in Malaysia supporting the INA? India and Ceylon, he argued, was one theatre. He held frequent discussions with many prominent Sinhalese and Tamil citizens, and warned, quite rightly too, that both communities could suffer. He was spurred on by the great sympathy Bose showed for the Ceylonese. He went to Bose, seeking help, and Bose offered a way out. Form a Ceylon Department within the Indian Independence League—a civilian and administrative unit of the movement.

And so it was . . . and Jhaveri & Bhattiwala[1] made mention of the Ceylon Unit when they said that on December 2, 1943, the Ceylon Department of the IIL began work.

Next came the formation of the Lanka Unit (LU) which was the Ceylonese military arm of the INA. Kotelawala was the prime mover. He went among the Ceylonese, called for the young, the intelligent, the self-sacrificing.

'Are you willing to volunteer for the sake of your country?' he would ask, and, with other Ceylonese, began a recruitment campaign which was supported by Bose.

One Lanka Unit recruit had recollected how Kotelawala told him: 'We have formed the Lanka Unit. Do you like to fight for your country?'

'I do not know how to fight,' the recruit had replied.

'You will be trained,' Kotelawala had assured.

Suddenly, the man who had no military training himself, became a military leader. Yet, Kotelawala was no active radical. He had no political pretensions, left or right, and was no politician. All he knew was that he was deeply attracted to the manner of Bose's leadership of an Army for Indian independence. Time and again he was reputed to have said that if anyone could save India from the British, it was Bose.

He soon saw the other face of the Japanese. The image was changing. At the start the Japanese had donned the robes of the saviours of the colonially oppressed. But with occupation, the Japanese became the oppressors. This told Gladwin that there was real cause for collaboration with the Japanese Occupation Forces in Malaya. It was either that, or go under.

He had to protect his countrymen. More so, he found that although the Tamils were ten times larger in number than the Sinhalese in Malaya, the majority of the men in the Lanka Unit were Sinhalese. The Tamils showed scant interest in ousting the British from Lanka. Rather, the Tamils looked on the British as their stepping–stone to a better life and living, and kowtowed to their colonial masters most shamelessly.

The Ceylonese in Malaysia had few national political leanings. There were a few bodies like the Malayan Ceylonese Congress and the Malayan Sinhalese Association, but these were more in the nature of societies addressing themselves to parochial social problems. No national issues relating to their homeland were ever taken up. Now, suddenly, they were being asked to take a firmer view on the freedom and independence of Ceylon and an end to British rule.

Kotelawala appointed a Sinhalese, H.G. Gunapala, to be in charge of the Lanka Unit. Slowly, the unit enlarged, strengthened. Many who joined did so to escape the harassment of the Japanese. Since the Japanese had sponsored the IIL and the INA, Ceylonese participation would give the Ceylon Unit a pro-Japan pretext which would serve to protect participants as well as their property. Gladwin knew what the alternative could be—forced labour, especially on the Thailand-Burma 'Death Railway', and even internment in concentration camps.

In April 1942, even as the Japanese bombed Colombo and Trincomalee, they had also started concentration camps where men were taken for 're-education'. In Serembam, where some prisoners of war had refused to take up arms for the Japanese, machine-gun emplacements were mounted all around the camp. There was no doubt that the Japanese would cut down every man who refused to toe the line.

Also, as Kotelawala told the Ceylonese of Malaya, they would be sure of adequate food and supplies, clothing and all other things which the people of Singapore were finding very scarce. Further, there would be travel passes, freedom of movement as well as the opportunity to return as liberating heroes to Ceylon, being part of the force that would drive out the British and take power.

This last was reason enough for many young Sinhalese to join. Adventure beckoned, and soon, with the Indians, they took part in many hazardous missions including sabotage and espionage.

The Indian fighters of the INA had a bellyful of the discriminations exercised against them by many Britishers. They had smarted under many humiliations and much discourteous and contemptuous treatment. The Ceylon Unit tried to understand this. They had not been so treated, but as they were told, what was true of India was also surely true of Ceylon.

All Gladwin could infuse in them was that idealistic dream of an independent homeland. Too long had Ceylon been under foreign yoke. First the Portuguese, then the Dutch, then the British. Enlistment in the INA was to demonstrate nationalistic fervour. They had but one aim—liberate Ceylon from British rule!

But there were more telling factors, the main being the predicament of a people caught in a war. The Japanese were conscripting people to be as slaves. There was no food, no work, no schools, no correspondence from home. Many may have joined the Lanka Unit without clearly knowing what it was for. They were all educated young men and they had to undergo a two-year training. But often were they told that soon, some day, they would be marching to the front, and also that some day they would enter Ceylon as part of the force that would oust the British.

The officers of the INA maintained that there was no compulsion to join the force, and even Bose is said to have confirmed this when he wrote to Kotelawala in June 1944, stating that no Ceylonese should be compelled to join the Ceylon Unit.

But there was coercion just the same, and Bose himself insisted many a time that if any person refused to join or help the INA cause, such person was an enemy. He kept drilling it in that the INA was engaged in a life-and-death struggle for freedom, the freedom of India, and now Ceylon. He even extracted huge donations from the citizens of Malaya, hinting that they could either give to the INA or have the Japanese confiscate everything. And how would the Japanese know? Why, the INA would furnish the information.

Gladwin Kotelawala may have wished to pre-empt Japanese harassment of the Ceylonese in Malaya, but it seemed that he also had his own personal vision and ambitions. His regimental clerk in the Ceylon department, Lionel Dodampe, had said that Gladwin actually hoped to lead Ceylon after the 'liberation'. Even his wife had hinted that Bose had assured her husband of a 'much better position' in order that he could serve his country.

Who knows what dreams these men harboured? Bose and Kotelawala. And would Bose, even if he had brought about the 'liberation' of Ceylon, have planted Gladwin as the country's leader? This was most unlikely. Even if Bose had led his fighting Ceylonese into Lanka and booted out the British, it would have been a most bloody battle. And then there was every likelihood that he would have sat to discuss the future leadership of the island with those who were locally involved in the independence struggle.

It is hard to tell today, but certainly Bose was not the man to plant puppets, even though he was most attached to Gladwin.

He gave Gladwin every encouragement, and yes, he liked him. But the man remained the same dreaming spirit, the romanticist, full of smoky-eyed fervour. How could he ever be the leader of a country when he could never sit still?

Notes

(1) Ref: *The Diary of a Rebel Daughter of India with the Rani of Jhansi Regiment*, Bombay, 1945

5

Of Cowboys and Buffaloes and a Little Bit of England

Ordinary Stoker Mechanic Ronald Todwell was soon to turn the camp into shambles. There were two contributory factors: a Wild West paperback he had been reading, and buffalo.

Todwell revelled in Westerns. This book told him of how a wild and particularly woolly cowboy, who rejoiced in the name of Montana Mike, had ridden a steer bareback in a rodeo after he had gunned down three owlhoots and the town marshall (who had apparently been in his way) before breakfast.

Outside the camp, at a point where rusted barbed wire had thrown in the towel, a buffalo had decided that the clumps of watergrass within the perimeter made an excellent salad. Recruit 'Longprick' Perera was on perimeter guard duty when the buffalo had pushed its head through and sneered at him. Perera froze. Then the buffalo barged through. Talk about animal impulse. The animal broke through like a tank, and Perera shed his rifle and shot off, crying for mummy.

The confusion galvanized the camp. The buffalo, a domesticated one with a length of rope trailing at its neck, considered the fleeing recruit wonderingly and then bumbled over to taste the grass. When it looked up, there was a knot of sailors around it, all gaping, and if it were called to the stand it would have said under oath that recruit Yusuf had roared, 'Stand by to repel boarders!'

The animal bent to its breakfast. Choice stuff. Worth busting in for.

The sailors closed around. The buffalo tossed its head and showed them the whites of its eyes. Todwell inched closer. He was no longer a recruit of Her Majesty's Navy. He was Montana Mike.

Later, Carloboy said it was certainly not the buffalo's fault. 'If I were a buffalo you think I'll allow that mad bugger to jump on my back?'

Todwell did not stop to consider the buffalo-eye view. He wanted to ride this 'steer' in the best traditions of the old West. He charged, yelled, and leaped, drumming upon the animal's back. Ride 'em cowboy!

Cheers, whistles, roars of encouragement rose, bounced against the hills and rallied the men of the Army training camp hard by. Todd hung onto the beast's neck–rope and away they went, thundering across the parade ground in a smoke-scroll of red dust.

The regulating petty officer gasped and sat down heavily in a firebucket. Later he said he was sure it was the end of the world. When he was lifted up and taken into the office he kept muttering, 'The beast from the East.'

As they drummed between the cookhouse and the bosun's store, Cook-steward Haramanis, who kept complaining that life was very boring, changed his mind very suddenly and ran, screaming, to the heads. Bells were rung. Bosun's pipes were blown and two leading seamen began unrolling the big fire hose.

The buffalo pounded to the perimeter, skidded at the wire and bucked furiously. That was, for Montana Mike, the eject button. He sailed off, fell in deep, water-logged grass, rolled and rose gasping. The buffalo checked and tossed its head, saw Todwell rise and decided to put distance between them. This, thought Todwell, wasn't fair. He leaped, seized the dragging rope, hung on and began to take in the slack by looping it around his forearm.

'Let go!' Carloboy yelled, 'let go the rope!'

In Diyatalawa, buffaloes are large, well-fed, and make up their own minds. This specimen was not impressed by Todwell. It simply shifted into second gear and dragged the impudent recruit along, full forty yards, to the top of a rise. Todwell should have known better. On the rise, he grabbed at the trunk of a pine tree and hung on.

The rope snagged, then sliced into his forearm, cutting along the bone like a rotary saw. Montana Mike bit the dust. When the harassed buffalo found the break in the fence and bellowed through, nobody cheered its going. Not even 'Longprick' Perera.

They carried Todd to the regulating office. There was blood everywhere and he had passed out. Rushed to the Army hospital on the Bandarawela road, the sawbones shook his head, stanched the wounds as best he could and said that surgery was indicated. With his temporary patches, Todwell was then sent to the government hospital in Badulla, the half truck that bore him flying down the mountain roads at breakneck speed.

He wasn't very happy, even after his three-week stay. He carried back a beautiful circular pattern of stitches around his arm and a lot of fleshy discolouration where skin had been grafted, and plasters on his thighs where skin had been taken.

'So cheer up. You're okay, no?'

'Yes men, but the hospital . . .'

'Why? Public hospital, no? Saw any nice girls?'

Todwell snorted. 'Girls! Every bloody nurse was about sixty, I think,' and added that each looked like a national disaster.

He had more to sadden him, and didn't know whether to laugh or cry when he was charged with several breaches of discipline which ended with the stirring, 'whereas Ordinary Stoker Mechanic Todwell rode a dangerous animal on the deck of a ship without concern or regard for the safety of the vessel.' This, even to the Lord High Admiral, would have sounded pretty far-fetched.

CO Dharamdass reminded Todwell that he had lost valuable training time. 'If you don't pass out, you will be discharged, do you realize that?'

'Yes, sir.'

'Fourteen days number ten.'

This was, in the book, one of a numbered scale of punishments. Number ten, any Navy will tell you, is the pits. A number ten offender rises half an hour earlier than the others to be set to work; always eats half an hour later than the others; has to sign a punishment book every hour and is made to labour on, one hour after the final 'lights out, pipes down'. Also, depending on the choler of the Platoon Commander, the offender could be kept on very hard labour or be given arms drill. It was usually arms drill, and quite vicious at that.

Todwell was briefed. 'Fall in outside your hut at oh-nine hours. Number eights with pack.'

Todwell grimaced. Besides the blue number eight work uniform, he had to be togged in boots, puttees, webbing, backpack and carry his rifle. It has always been said, 'The .303 rifle weighs only nine pounds . . . but when one has to carry it over one's head and run, it becomes ninety pounds in next to no time.'

The backpack was stuffed with nice-sized rocks. The Platoon Commander eyed Todwell sourly. 'Okay? You're ready? Don't try to pretend you're going to faint or anything. No bloody nonsense with me. High port arms! Double quick—march!'

And Todwell ran and ran, and the rocks at his back made his shoulders scream and his wrists groaned and the nerves at his elbows knotted as he held up his rifle and ran and ran and ran. Behind him came the PC. Hup, hup, hup, hup. But he took it, and Nugawira said, 'They must be thinking they can drop us. We'll show these buggers.'

Todwell was a hero. He would come into the hut, the nerves on his neck swelling, face flushed red. His mates rallied round. He found that his boots had been polished, his bunk tidied. There was even a tin plate of food, smuggled out of the galley, in his locker. The days passed quickly enough and Stores Assistant Stembo was the next to wear the laurels when he crowned AB Jayasena with a bucket, and took up punishment where Todwell left off.

'You're lucky,' Todwell said, 'only ten days. I got fourteen.'

Stembo glowered. 'Never mind that, wait, will you, next time I catch that bugger . . .'

'But what, men, hit with a bucket! Lucky you didn't kill him or something.'

'And half full of caustic soda, the bucket,' Carloboy said.

Winnie cackled. 'Should have seen, men. Clouds of caustic in the corridor. Jayasena put a scream and fell. Lucky he got it on the top of the head. That bugger's head is like a coconut.'

'I told the CO the things he said,' Stembo gritted. 'I was sweeping outside the store. Bugger is coming, looking and saying, "Your sister taught you to sweep?" I said, "No, but even at home I won't sweep like this. This is for women to do." Then he's telling, "So tell your sister to come and sweep. You have only one sister?" and I said, "That's not your business." What does he care if I have a sister or not? Bloody *vul*[1] bastard. Then telling he likes to fuck my sister!'

Stembo had been beside the bucket of soda when Jayasena had stated this preference. Hence, he said, it seemed the only thing to do. He hurled the bucket.

'Relax, men, once we pass out, none of these buggers will try their nonsense. Hey, today's Wednesday. Van Dort will come.'

Van Dort, the seediest of the characters who came aboard the good ship *Rangalla*, was the civilian fruitseller. Dutch by name, a Sinhalese at heart, he revelled in telling his recruit customers of how he got his name. The boys would listen to his account of the many detours he had to take when descending the family beanstalk with chuckles. Van Dort spared no one, least of all himself.

It appeared that his father was a British sailor from

HMS Highflyer[2] who had come to Diyatalawa for two weeks rest at the Royal Naval Rest Camp, *HMS Ella*. Van Dort's mother had been quite pleased. She had brought forth a fair, mousey-haired baby that was much commented on in the village she lived.

'Years and years my mother to me name did not give,' said Van Dort expressively, 'I knowing not what to me calling. Everyone telling basket, basket and telling my mother no shame. In town when I walking, women finger pointing and asking, you also white one like your father have? My father who, I am asking. I also don't know, no? My mother, when I'm asking, father went saying. Where went? Fine thing, no? Father just going like that. To me even not telling.'

'No, men, your father put a jump and went,' Carloboy said, 'went before you were born, even.'

'That's a fine thing, no? Then father don't know I am who?'

The boys nodded. 'Daft' Fernando stuffed his pockets with the man's peaches.

'Here, here, how many took? Count and see. Ten cents each.'

'So, Van Dort, you didn't go to school?'

'What school? Birth certificate without, to school to go how? Mother said never mind, go and work in a *bangalawa*[3]. Gentleman's name Van Dort. *Lansiya*[4]. Nine years worked. One day I'm sixteen almost, Van Dort gentleman telling you buggeroff. I don't know this buggeroff is what. Afterwards to me someone telling buggeroff is *palayalla*[5]. I asking what is this buggeroff you're telling and then saying now his daughter is big and I to stay can't . . .'

'How, nice daughter?'

Van Dort creased his forehead. 'Nice I think. Now married and Bandarawela living. Children have four. When I Bandarawela go to *ali pera*[6] bring, I go to see.'

'So never mind all that, how you got the name Van Dort?'

The man chuckled. 'So I'm to my mother going. I said now for Van Dort master working can't. Money to me gave and buggeroff said. *Ammo*[7] mother very angry got. Shouted and saying you are man now, you earning how? So I this selling fruit started. Then I thought my name also Van Dort to say. How? I also white, no? Like Van Dort gentleman. *Ammo*! Van Dort master very much angry got, but now to me every one Van Dort saying.'

Ordinary Telegraphist 'Bijja' Fernando considered the man seriously. '*Adai*, Von Bloss, how if cut his hair and put him in full suit? Real Burgher, no?'

Carloboy nodded slowly. Here he was, in the mountains of an island that, for one hundred and fifty years, was under the British Raj. Around him as far as his eyes swept, were encircling peaks, their slopes upholstered with tea. The sun glinted on the silvered roofs of tea factories and blushed on the red-painted galvanized iron of planters' bungalows.

Beyond *Rangalla* was *HMS Ella*, where British seamen came to rest after their stints at sea. Yes, there were many such as Van Dort. This was the region everyone called 'Little England'. In it lived the damnedest racial concoctions—a monument to that all-important 'Service to the White Sahib'.

It may be just as well to dwell on these mountains for a while, considering the large tea estate populations and how Sri Lanka in the years past and to this day came to be stuck with what are considered 'people of recent Indian origin'.

The Dutch brought in slaves from South India, each bearing the VOC[8] brand, to work the fields of Jaffna. The British, too, found that the only way they could make this new colony pay, was to open up the mid-country forests and later, the montane jungles, first for coffee, and later, tea. They set out on a massive land-grab.

The native Sinhalese retreated, muttering darkly. Their lands were compulsorily acquired at the absurd price of a shilling an acre and that, they were told, was the law!

This meant, of course, two canny bits of legislation: one was the Crown Lands Ordinance of 1840 whereupon every square inch of unsettled land became the property of the Crown, to be parcelled out to white settlers and planters. Then came the Waste Lands Ordinance, which was worse. A white sahib could look over a Sinhalese aristocrat's ancestral property and sniff.

'You call all this your land? Rhubarb, man. This is waste land. What have you got here? Some coconut and a couple of jak trees and betel vine and what is this? Runner beans? And these things? Edible leaves! Good grief! These fellows will eat anything!'

It was hard for the avaricious British to understand the Sinhalese, who had always maintained that a man who had a jak tree and a cow was a happy man. Soon, the ancestral property was acquired. It is waste land, the British maintained, and allowed to be so, it was land going to waste!

The Sinhalese were most annoyed, and more so when they were told that they could come back as labourers and work their own lands—their lands—which were now white plantations. Those who did return to work, out of sheer economic necessity, remained ill-disposed to the white masters anyway, and it was generally opined that Something Had To Be Done.

Letters found among old estate records told of this white man's burden. The British expected docile, tractable, submissive 'coolies'. They found the Sinhalese a bunch of lotus-eaters, and belligerent to boot.

This has not changed much, and there is the favourite story of the seventies of how an UN Agency, full of pep and fizz, introduced hand-tractors to Sinhalese rice farmers. The experts demonstrated the ease with which a field could be ploughed.

'See, with this you can plough your entire field in one morning. How long does it take you with those mangy buffaloes?'

The farmer spat a stream of betel juice, examined the sky, and said, 'Two days . . . but if that Joro drinking too much toddy in the morning, sometimes three days even.'

'So there you are. Now you just hold here by the handles, and go! No more Joro, no more buffaloes and by afternoon all the work is done. Good, no?'

The farmer bobbed. 'You tell and give how to do?'

'Yes, yes. Now this is the tiller . . .'

The next afternoon the UN Agency fellow rolls up. He rubs his hands. An acre field, beautifully, near-artistically ploughed. The hand-tiller, all red and silver and knee-daubed in mud, idles beneath an Indian almond tree. And under another tree sits the farmer. Joro is with him and between them are large clay pots of foaming toddy.

They wave.

'But why aren't you working? What about the other field, and that section over there?'

'Ah, that can wait. Tomorrow—no—day after can do.'

'But why?'

'Oi, Joro, why, he's asking, hee hee hee.'

'Hee hee hee,' Joro agrees.

'Now two day's work finished, no? So after two days can do summore.'

'But—but I thought you can finish the ploughing and then do something else.'

'What else? *Ammo,* if go to work like that everything get upset. Now see, if I go and tell the woman work finished and so came home, another *kollappang*[9]. Coming home early, she will scold, not enough children we are having?'

(Exit UN Agency man, muttering brokenly.)

No, the British did not like Sinhalese labour. But over there, in India, there was an abundance of human resource. It was the simplest thing of the times to organize a system of slavery that masqueraded under the guise of 'indentured labour'.

In the mid 1800's, living conditions in south India were God-awful. And the Scots, who were predominant in the tea gardens of Ceylon, had no scruples about dragging in anybody who could do their dirty work. For the South Indians, Ceylon was 'El Dorado'. So, when the British sent agents to India to conscript labour, there were hordes of takers. The British were happy. They had cheap, very docile 'coolies'. No thank you, they told the Sinhalese, we don't want you any more. We have South Indian Tamils, and we can bring them in their thousands. Shucks to you!

It is not a pretty story. Records have it how the South Indians poured in. Little armies would trek to the south Indian coast, bearing all their earthly possessions. They were dumped into frail boats—*vallams* or *dhonies*[10]—and ferried across the Palk Strait. Many were sick, all half-starved. Those who died were fed to the sharks; and then, from Ceylon's north-north-west, the long march. An agony for flute in A minor.

Jungle footpaths, elephants, snakes, leeches, diarrhoea, malaria, foul water . . . It is said that packs of jackals followed them, waiting for the sick, the dying, who were left behind to be devoured. Many days it took: days of bleeding feet, retching, griping, dazed with fever and weariness that bored into their very bones, and then they would fall and lie, half-dead, to be borne in open railway trucks into the biting wind and the cold of the hills. The ragged disembarkation . . . the mountain trails, the ravening attacks of leopards and the blood of many in the tall grasses of the slopes.

Carloboy eyed Van Dort bleakly, and he thought, 'what the hell am I doing here?' With an excellent pass in the senior school certificate, qualified for university entrance, what the hell was he doing in this uniform, receiving a monthly pittance of fifty-two and a half rupees? And what the hell was Van Dort all about? A British father, a Sinhalese mother, a borrowed Burgher name . . . a fruit-selling bastard. . .

He shrugged. At eighteen, he had a lot to learn about life. He gave Van Dort a rupee. 'I'll take some guavas, those big yellow ones.' At least, he thought, I'm not an estate coolie.

Coolie is, the writer suspects, a word of Anglo-Chinese origin. It's a dirty word now, but the British called their labourers coolies and the word was adopted by the remnant Burghers as well. Rickshaw men were rickshaw coolies. The shit–cart men were latrine coolies. Dora Herft would accompany her husband to the Manning Market and make her month's purchases of sundry provender. 'See, child, and tell a coolie to carry all this to the buggy,' she would tell husband Rodney, who would snap his fingers and say 'Oy!' to the human packbulls who, like the latter-day DHL, carried anything anywhere.

Yes, indentured labour was the greatest evil sown by the British in Ceylon. But they had no qualms. They housed their sick, starving, shivering coolies in leaky, thatched huts and then in grimy 'coolie lines'—rows of eight-foot square rooms with corrugated roofs, where twelve were crammed into each room, huddled for warmth, and still they were content that there loomed before them a secure future.

They were each given a 'ticket' to this future—a registration slip, virtually a passport. Also, with stern reminder that the white sahib was God, a discharge ticket too. Any peralikaren[11] was simply given his DT.

Absolute power led to many evils. Pretty daughters were fair game. They were not forced. They were simply told, 'Come on, my girl, just raise that cloth and lie still . . . or do you want me to give your father his DT?'

Young bucks who vowed vengeance when they learned that the girls they wished to marry had already been raped by the white *periya dorais* and *sinna dorais* [12] were singled out for horsewhipping. The stables usually had thick iron rings fitted into the wall. Coolies were chained, wrists and ankles, and lashed, then 'sent to the coast' for a term. This meant being banished to South India, forced to leave everything behind, until bid to return. He would come back, a much changed man who would sit and watch and raise not a murmur, even as the *sinna dorai* fucked his wife and daughters.

Yes, Little England had much evidence of this Service to the White Sahib. Strange racial potpourri. Chocolate skins and grey-blue eyes; gold tints in dark-brown hair crowning swarthy faces; fair-skinned women with lustrous opalescent eyes; dusky, green-eyed girls with long black hair. They were *different* and paraded their difference—hundreds of women, faithful to tradition, plying the world's oldest trade, schooling their daughters in this art of give and take.

Later, commercialism crept in to make it take and give, and many panting males were told to pay first and then indulge. Scots blood, let it be said, is most careful blood.

Notes

(1) Sinhalese for vile, wild, vulgar.
(2) This was the Royal Navy shore establishment at Colombo.
(3) Sinhala: Bungalow.
(4) Sinhala colloquialism—Hollander (from *Holanda, Landesi*, etc.)
(5) Sinhala: Get the hell out.
(6) Sinhala: Avocado pears. Literally guavas with seeds like elephant's testicles.
(7) Sinhala: O mother!
(8) *Veeringde Oost-Indische Compagnie* (Dutch East India Company)
(9) Sinhala: Commotion
(10) *Vallam*—a fishing craft; *Dhony*—a stouter, more stable craft for passenger crossing.
(11) Tamil: Troublemaker
(12) Big and little masters—the Superintendents and Assistant Superintendents of the estates.

6

History—The Japanese-INA War Machine

Subhas Chandra Bose had much in mind for the functioning of the Ceylon Department and the Lanka Unit of the Indian National Army. He addressed many letters to Gladwin Kotelawala, especially on the Spy Training Unit in Penang, and wished the Ceylonese to be wholly involved.

Bose did not need to spell it out as far as his plans for Lanka were concerned. He made it clear that the independence of Ceylon was a logical sequel to the independence of India. India came first.

As such, there is no mention in any of the literature of the IIL or the INA on the independence of Ceylon. The primary goal was freedom of India. The Ceylonese would be required, if necessary, to fight in India for India. Every Ceylonese who enlisted had to sign a pledge. He had to solemnly swear and sincerely dedicate himself to India; pledge his life for India's freedom and promise to serve India and the Indian Independence Movement to his fullest capacity, even at the risk of his life.

The Ceylon Department was housed in Singapore's Bukit Timah road. It's aims were to (a) enlist as many Ceylonese as possible as members of the Independence League, (b) look after the interests of all who enlisted, (c) collect funds from the Ceylonese in Malaya on behalf of the

IIL, (d) impose property taxes on Ceylonese in Malaya (this was determined in consultation with the Singapore Rear Headquarters of the IIL and the Kuala Lumpur branch), and (e) select a team of Ceylonese youths for sabotage and infiltration work in Ceylon.

This latter was what many of the younger Ceylonese recruits found to be a tangible demonstration of what lay ahead. They would actually go up against the British. They were first trained by the INA and then transferred to Penang where the Japanese gave them further instructions. They were told that they would be taken to Ceylon in Japanese submarines.

The Ceylonese of Malaya were now part of the Japanese-INA war machine. The young volunteers were first trained at the Non-Commissioned Officers' Training Unit of the INA, by an Indian Tamil officer of the Madras Sappers of the British Army. This officer had stayed to join the INA when his unit had withdrawn from Malaya during the Japanese invasion.

The recruits went through it all: marching, arms drill, use of pistols, .303 rifles, sub-machine guns, Lewis guns, LMG's, anti-tank guns, grenades and explosives that were manufactured in Hindustan as well as in Japan. They also had lessons in geography and map reading. They were deemed ready and were passed out on March 22, 1944.

The Japanese also took some of the Ceylonese into their own units, the Hikari Kikan and the Iwakuro Kikan. The former served as a spy-liaison unit between the IIL, the INA and the Japanese Army. The latter was a sabotage unit on Penang island . . . and from these units did trained Ceylonese go to the east coast of Ceylon, put ashore from Japanese submarines. They went to their deaths, betrayed to the British in Ceylon by some Ceylonese in Malaya, but for a short, sharp hour, they did do what they had pledged—fired perhaps the first real shots in their island's struggle for independence!

The British had their 'moles' in the Penang Units and even in the Ceylon Department. Hundreds of Ceylon Tamils living in Malaysia did not see the worth of ousting the British from Ceylon. They, the Tamils, were well looked after. Why, the Tamils of Ceylon held more white collar jobs than the majority Sinhalese! It was easy to get word to the British that saboteurs were being sent to the east coast by the Japanese.

Corr[1] has told how the brave Sinhalese boys of the Penang units, together with some Indians, were put ashore at Trincomalee where they launched a series of acts of sabotage. But they were quickly discovered, identified and shot. Corr makes mention of four Sinhalese youths.

Bhargava & Gill[2] tell of how the Indian saboteurs fared. They, too, were executed. There is little doubt that some Ceylon Tamils in Malaya had sent information to the British in Ceylon. It told the Sinhalese men of the INA that they had to watch their backs!

In Rangoon, Burma, the Japanese launched the third component of their war machine—the broadcasting of anti-British propaganda. It was a Lankan, Dodwell Cooray, who was given the task of heading the broadcasting station. The Japanese were wrapping up their preparations for the attack of India. Gladwin Kotelawala went to Cooray's father who was Malaya's best-known journalist and on the *Malay Mail*. Kotelawala was most persuasive. He wished that a small propaganda unit accompany the Indian forces. This unit was to broadcast to Ceylon about the aims and intentions of the Japanese.

The Japanese, Gladwin insisted, were fighting to liberate all Asians who were suffering under imperialism. The Japanese would establish a Greater East Asia Co-Prosperity Sphere. Furthermore, Gladwin argued, a propaganda unit was vital. He reminded that when the first Japanese troops landed in Malaya, they had made terrible mistakes because they were ignorant of local customs. This would not happen again if the propaganda unit heralded them, paved the way.

Gladwin wanted the elder, Francis Cooray, but Cooray's wife was adamant. She would not let her husband go.

Instead, son Dodwell volunteered. From Rangoon, he broadcast daily, every evening—broadcasts in English and Sinhala. He identified his station as the Free Lanka Unit of the IIL and regaled listeners in Ceylon with the progress of the war, the many Japanese successes and of the many strides in the establishing of the Greater East Asia Co-Prosperity Sphere.

All in all, it was with this propaganda machine that the Ceylonese served the Japanese-INA war machine best. Even Bose had conveyed to Kotelawala on more than one occasion that the Lanka Unit and the Ceylon Department were simply there to show that the Ceylonese in Singapore and Malaya co-operated with the IIL.

Was all this, then, mainly propaganda? The fact is that the Lanka Unit was never sent to the front, had no active military role. In the same way, Cooray's Free Lanka Unit, which churned out anti-British, pro-Japanese propaganda, also had in the main, an obvious supportive role for military action.

Yet, Ceylonese did die. Young, inspired Sinhalese who were prepared to walk, even with the devil, to rid their country of the curse of the white sahibs.

Notes

(1) Ref: *The War of the Springing Tigers*, London, 1975
(2) Ref: *The Indian National Army—Secret Service*, New Delhi, 1988

7

Of Ghosties and Shore Brawls and the Leeches of Fox Hill

It was Van Dort who told of the ghosts of *Rangalla*. 'This place, you know? In wartime Italian prisoners had. Lot died. Somewhere, somewhere buried and put. Died in huts.'

'Huts? What huts?'

'There, where now you are. In night funny noises coming. Boot polishing noises and like pineapples swallowing.'

'Swallowing pineapples? Balls! What sort of a noise is that?'

'Ah,' said Van Dort darkly, 'pineapple if have to just swallow without even cutting, making very bad noise, no?'

'Balls!'

'Balls not. One day you will hear. I'm just telling afraid not to get.'

Carloboy got a few cronies together. If the ghosts of Italian prisoners-of-war went around *Rangalla*, polishing boots and swallowing pineapples, it was time they were revived if only for the general good of the camp. Also, there were a few soft-spoken, nervous little ticks who still missed home and kept writing to mummy and kept receiving large parcels of goodies which were quickly requisitioned and distributed to everyone.

'But that's my parcel. My mummy sent it to *me*!'

'Of course she did. Who said no? Very nice, your mummy, to send like this.'

'So why are *you* opening it? *Give it here!*'

'*Anney*, mummy's lickle boy is getting angry? See, sent you a nice pink towel and a tin of cigarettes,' (the cigarettes are carefully put aside and the towel tossed to the owner), 'ah, toothpaste . . . and a bottle of . . . hmm . . . sha! chocolate toffee. Your mummy makes chocolate toffee? Or your sister made? You have a sister?'

'*Never mind my sister! Give me my toffees!*'

'Wait, men, how to see anything when you're shouting like this . . . ah, plastic box with cake. Right. Now all can share.'

It was to the everlasting credit of the mess that distribution of all such goodies, irrespective of who the owner was, was done on a strict basis. The owner received a proprietor's share of a quarter. Nobody balked at this but the owner, of course.

'So what are you grumbling for, you cunt? You got a quarter, no? All of us have to divide the rest.'

'But that's my cake!'

'So you're going to eat the whole bloody cake and purge here? Tomorrow if I get a parcel, you also get a share, no?'

'Who wants your bloody parcel? This my mummy sent to me!'

'So you don't want? Good. Anyway my mummy never sends anything. She's got enough troubles.'

Yes, there were always a few sticky types who didn't want to be a part of the tribe. And now there was this business of ghosts (and Italian ones too) and they became quite nervous as darkness fell and refused to leave the hut as evening deepened and came to dread sentry-go, especially those night watches from 2000 to 2359 hours and 0001 to 0400 hours (this latter watch being universally referred to as the graveyard watch). They began to plead sick and this meant that others had to double on their watch turns. It was decided that, for the good of all souls, the ghosts of *Rangalla* should walk.

Strategy was plotted carefully. 'Will the buggers die or anything?'

'Can't say . . . Might get a heart attack or something . . .'

'Better if we begin slowly. Scare them a little at a time.'

That night Thiaga, gently at first, and then quite determinedly, scritched his shoebrush on the woodwork of his bunk. At half hour to midnight it sounded as if Yusuf was combing his pubic hair.

'What's that?' Nugawira barked.

'What?'

'Someone brushing something, I heard.'

'Just go to sleep. men.'

'No. I heard. There! Can hear?' Nugawira sat up. Others sat up. Thiaga scritched frantically. The mummy boys were all up.

'Wha-what is that?' one asked faintly.

'Bloody funny noise,' said Sims, 'like as if polishing boots, no?'

'Shh. Lissen,' Carloboy hissed.

Thiaga, tired of sawing away, had stuffed the end of his sheet in his mouth and begun to mumble.

Winnie, in the next bunk, squealed, 'Ca-ca-coming from near here somewhere,' and leaping to the floor, began to crawl away, seeking refuge.

'Poo-poo-put on the light,' someone chattered.

'Mad?' Roy Fernando said, 'after lights out? All will get punished tomorrow.' Thiaga bubbled on his sheet, then yanked the end out and said 'Yowk!'

'My God, what-what-what was that . . . said something, somebody said something.'

'Mus' be Italian,' said Carloboy.

Silence. Five long minutes of absolute silence. Winnie had apparently gone to sleep on the floor. Then the shoe brush symphony began again.

From under a blanket, a voice quavered, 'Our far-far-father who-who artin hay-hay-heaven . . .'

Nobody laughed, nobody stirred. The night's performance was over. Carloboy reminded that there were more nights than years and also, there was the piano accordion, and that had special potential.

Carloboy had this quite untutored ability to play any keyboard. He would perform most creditably at a piano and would make Eardley's hair stand on end with his performances on the accordion. He had picked up this old Crucianelli which he carried around, brought to *Rangalla*. Eventually, it was consigned to the Bay of Bengal, but that comes later. The conspirators decided that Thiaga should continue.

'A few more nights,' Sims said. 'Make the buggers nervous wrecks.'

Thiaga had a nerve-racking repertoire. Nights were filled with frenzied brushings, chatterings, gibberings, gulpings, groanings, gratings, yammerings. He even reached over and squeezed cold toothpaste on Winnie, who shot up with a yell and spent the rest of the night under Stembo's bunk.

'What's that? What's that? My God—what's that?'

'Shut up, Koelmeyer! Can't even sleep.'

'I-I heard.'

'Heard what?'

'The go-go-ghost!'

'I want to go hoooooome!'

Carloboy told Thiaga, 'Tonight you keep quiet. Let them sleep. But watch the fun. First we'll get that Hendricks bugger. Bloody sneak. Went and told the duty petty officer that we took the soap from the PO's bathroom.'

They slept, so soundly that it was close on three that a nagging subconscious barged through the curtains to remind Carloboy sternly that there was work to be done. He woke Sims and Nugawira with some difficulty.

Nugawira, a small, stocky fellow, swarmed up to perch on Carloboy's shoulders.

'Don't kick the bloody accordion,' Carloboy hissed, 'Sims, put the blanket nicely. Can't see a fuck. You will have to take us to Hendrick's bed, right?'

Sims slung a white Whitney blanket, draped over Nugawira, to fall in snowy folds at Carloboy's feet. The result was most gratifying. The composite was a tall, white indeterminate figure, about eight feet tall.

Sims chuckled, 'Like the bloody abominable snowman. Wait, I'll wake Todwell.'

Even Thiaga shrank into his pillow when he saw the ghost. Todd grinned.

Slowly, and with extreme caution, they shuffled to target.

Hendricks slept, dreaming of home, of chocolate toffee, of all those that made life so pleasant. The ghost stood at his bed—a white, silent mass. Sims tiptoed away and Carloboy made a wheezy sound with the bellows of the accordion, then struck a doleful bass chord that was a muffled 'veeeeoooom'. Hendricks slept on. This time it was a huffier chord, full a clashing flats, like cats in a lavatory, and Winnie stirred, opened his eyes and focussed blearily.

Carloboy and Nugawira were not aware of an audience. More rude sounds on the accordion and Nugawira began to rock and said, 'Ooooooo! Oooooooo!'

Winnie gave a strangled sob and shot out of bed as though he had just been introduced to a brood of porcupines. 'Heeee-lp! A Thing—a Thing!' he screamed; and Hendricks woke, sat bolt upright, yammered and sprawled to the floor, caught in a tangle of sheets. The sight must have been, to him, more awesome, more threatening, from floor level. He screamed. A loud, piercing scream. It woke the whole hut. It unnerved Nugawira too, who fell off Carloboy's shoulders. Outside were the sound of running feet. The camp was abroad.

Hendricks, kicking out in terror, saw a ghost topple onto him. With a rowing motion which, if his bum was a tyre, would have left three inches of rubber on the floor, he was up and away, swinging for the door. Winnie, seeing him come, dashed ahead, leading the way, and Nugawira dragged Carloboy in a tangle, both falling across the bunk with the accordion slamming into Carloboy's midriff and causing a painful 'Ooof!'

Two sentries heard the awful scream. 'My God,' one said, 'someone is fucking someone's arse! There, in the hut!' They rushed up with a clatter of boots and a swirl of Burberrys to be caught in the Winnie-Hendricks stampede. Others, too, hadn't waited for the door. Many had leaped windows and were putting much distance from the hut.

Todwell pointed at the sentries and howled, 'Italian ghosts! Run!' and the sentries did just that.

It all ended with half the hut running after the other, and in freezing cold at that. Hendricks and Winnie were finally seized and sat upon while the whole camp came awake. They were allowed to sleep in the regulating office for the next two hours (with a light on, mind) and were read the riot act in the morning. The quartermaster almost tore out his hair, trying to restore order. The duty officer was hopping mad. He should have been in camp, but he would usually spend his night-duty hours in the married quarters beyond the perimeter, where he busily screwed a petty officer's wife.

At five, the bosun's pipe screeched. 'Clear lower decks!' It brought the whole camp tumbling out again. The duty officer was furious. He wished to know how an otherwise stable camp could go haywire at three in the morning.

He was told it was ghosts.

'Rubbish! Indigestion! These bastard are eating too much!'

Hendricks and Winnie were produced.

'Ah, so these are the two? You saw ghosts? You are bloody idiots, you heard! *Idiots!*' He elaborated, of course. He said they were not fit for man or beast, that they were stark staring and obviously the runts of their mothers' litters. 'QM,' he said testily, 'place these two under close arrest!' and he went away, rather moodily. No sense going back to the PO's quarters now . . .

As the weeks crawled by, it was decided that the recruits were 'disciplined' enough to 'go ashore'. The duty officer would descend to the liberty parade and cluck, and remind Sims that he had to see a barber and tell 'Dizzy' Wise that his cap was not as white as desired.

'One thing,' he later told the CO, 'our Burghers always look well when they're kitted out. Carry themselves well.'

The CO nodded. Somehow, the Navy took pride in its Burghers. In Carloboy's time, there were lots of Burghers in the Navy and Air Force. Not many in the Army, because somehow the Burghers scorned the Army, especially the lower ranks which they thought were too lowlife even for their expansive tastes.

Burgher parents were quite proud that their sons were in the Navy. To them, the Navy as a fighting force, came first; then the Air Force, and finally (as a last resort) the Army. Why, this could be so to this day, but by the seventies the armed forces of Sri Lanka saw very few Burghers. Many had emigrated, true, but the forces, too, went ape. Commands are given today in Sinhala and drill instructors jabber in Sinhala and a Burgher recruit would find himself plunged, uncomfortably, in a world where ships sail in Sinhala and an Army fights in Sinhala and planes fly in Sinhala and signals become, to Burgher eyes and ears, as complicated as Rubik's cube.

Carloboy's time saw Burghers 'carry themselves well'. In the mid-fifties, even the Captain of the Navy—the big cheese with Rear Admiral status—was a Burgher, and ranging from lower deck to wardroom were Burghers of every calling.

Yes, the Navy was proud of its Burghers who looked good in white and blue and looked even better when full-trimmed, swinging confidently in public parade or at a guard rail when stations were called for leaving harbour.

Also, the Navy forgave a lot. Burghers, especially of the lower deck were the hellions of the fleet. They got into incredible scrapes, thumbed noses at authority, flouted regulations cheerfully and had little regard for the QR&AI which was the manual of Queens Regulations and Admiralty Instructions, the equivalent of the Navy Bible. The trouble was, all agreed, that the Burghers did not know the meaning of reverence!

In Diyatalawa, there was no place for a recruit on liberty to go. The whole territory was a vast training establishment for the Army, Navy and Air Force. The only bright spot was the old Regal Cinema which used to be wrecked regularly between 2 p.m. on Saturdays and 11 a.m. on Sundays, when recruits of the Navy and the Army met in the darkened hall to pour scorn on each other's merits as a fighting force.

The Navy referred to the Army as a bunch of coconut-tree climbers—a direct hit on the largely village type who enlisted because the Army was not over-particular about the type of yokel it took in. The Army in turn called the naval recruits *puk-kollo*[1] which, once said, was sufficient cause to start all manner of anguish of a most extreme kind.

The recruits strolled out, and once past the Army camp where, the law of uniformed etiquette demanded that they salute any Army officer they chanced upon, they flipped their caps back and looked around for trouble. Navy regulations decreed that caps should be worn square—plunked down to completely obliterate the forehead, making the most serious face quite clownish. This was always ignored.

Liberty for the Navy soon became a matter for serious review and debate. The CO *Rangalla* told the Officer Commanding, Army, that Diyatalawa lacked the facilities to keep the recruits entertained.

'You want to entertain them?' the OC had barked, 'if they have nothing to do, give them extra work. See what I do . . . send all the *yakos*[2] to Fox Hill[3] and make them dig trenches.'

'Yes, yes, that's good. But sailors dodn't need trenches. That's for you fellows.'

'Pah! Your fellows, my fellows, what's the difference? Here all are recruits! Get them to do anything!'

'Yes,' said Lieutenant Dharamdass wisely, 'But you want me to send my buggers to dig with your buggers? Will kill each other with the spades and we'll have to bury them in the bloody trenches.'

'That's also true,' the Army OC said gloomily.

'Only thing is to say that Bandarawela is a red light area.'

'And if go to Haputale or somewhere . . .'

Eventually, a happy thought struck the officers. It needed Air Force co-ordination too, and after much discussion and lots of wardroom whisky, liberty days were rotated. Let the Navy out on Wednesdays and Saturdays, the Army on Mondays and Fridays, the Air Force on Thursdays and Sundays.

The trouble was Bandarawela, the nearby town where bars, booze and girls were found in liberal quantity. Recruits would take a bus or hire a car and these excursions would always end in running street battles between Army and Navy while the Air Force milled around and punched anyone handy; or between Navy and Air Force with the Army cheering throatily; or between the Army and the Air Force, with the Navy leaping in at twenty-second intervals just to keep the tempo.

Every now and then, the forces would combine to take on gangs of civilian toughs, and the local constabulary and the military police would rush in. The shambles would leave a pale-faced Bandarawela to pick up the pieces. It was not surprising to learn, later, that when the Navy recruits were drafted to Colombo, a Thanksgiving Mass was said in the Bandarawela Church and harassed parishioners considered their daughters with much misgivings, certain beyond doubt that they were no longer in that desired state of *hymen intacta*.

Before this blessed day, however, Lieutenant Dharamdass had much to say to the Army OC. 'You and your bloody trenches. Nearly killed my buggers!'

'So if they were drunk or something, why go to walk all over the hills? Should have come on the road. That way even if a truck ran over them, would have brought the bodies to the camp.'

It had been, as Army doctor Kramer said, a close shave. Carloboy and Ordinary Seaman Caldera had been carried in, covered with leeches, bleeding from innumerable leech bites and in that pleasant state when life is ready to tiptoe away and there is a kind of hush while a tally clerk up there reaches for his slate.

The boys had been on a Bandarawela binge. First, Carloboy had scouted the Welimada Road, telling Caldera, 'My uncle is living somewhere here. Shall we go and see him?'

Caldera said no. He detested families. Families meant questions and how is so-and-so and heard about so-and-so and this is my son's girlfriend.

'But can have some fun, men. This uncle is a Pentecostalist. Will pray for us, sure.'

Caldera shuddered. 'You're mad? I know those buggers. Will tell to bow the head and go on the whole bloody evening. Come, go to a bar.'

So they turned into a bar which proclaimed ARRACK in large red letters and WINES AND SPIRITS in smaller white letters, and were soon wolfing devilled potatoes and boiled eggs and squinting at the arrack which diminished rapidly.

By eight Caldera solemnly proposed that the rest house would be a nice place to visit. 'Nice girl in the reception also. Can put beer there.'

So they swayed out, tottered up the rest house steps and sank into armchairs and called for beer. Caldera said he was going to the toilet, lost his way, stumbled into a side garden and urinated on a clump of fireballs. He told the flowers that he was in no condition to go anywhere, least of all back to camp.

It was late. They were, at the moment, in that happy state of being absent without leave. Their red liberty cards would be surrendered to the duty officer. Von Bloss, Caldera hadn't returned for supper. Therefore, they had 'jumped ship'!

When Carloboy and Caldera found that they had no more money, were very drunk and far from home, they had only one course of action. Walk, if they could, back to

Rangalla. They agreed after some consultation with the gatepost, that this was the only thing to do.

'We'll go shot—short cut,' Carloboy mumbled.

'Wha' shor'cut?'

'I'll sho—you come.'

They weaved through rear gardens, roused sleeping dogs, plodded on. As a game plan it was good. Rather than the winding mountain road which, if followed, added miles to the journey, they followed the Fox Hill track. The idea was to cross its shoulders, then drop down to where, beyond the checkpoint and sentry box of the Army camp, lay *Rangalla.*

The wind snapped at the sides of the hill and it made their heads swim. They had stumbled most erratically, this way and that, and their uniforms were studded with burrs, and they wanted, desperately, to sleep. And then, they fell into a trench and the soil was quite warm. They decided that if they closed their eyes, Diyatalawa would stop turning. They did. They slept.

It was fortunate in the extreme that Army recruits had been sent to dig another trench. That was at five-thirty in the morning. The staff sergeant who took physical training and hated standing on the parade ground at dawn, packed his charges off to Fox Hill. 'Go and dig,' he said. 'Nothing like a good dig. Good for the back and shoulders.' He told Corporal Silva to tag along, keep an eye. He blew on his hands. It was bloody cold and all he wanted was to go to the kitchen and drink a mug of steaming tea.

The Army was in the nick of time. The recruits didn't bargain on having to carry two leech-encrusted sailors—at the double—to the medical reception station. Physical training was becoming quite diverting.

At the station, blood transfusions were in order and fat, blood-gorged leeches removed from practically every part of the boys' bodies. Smelling of antiseptic, a yellow salve on hundreds of bites, pale as death and too sober for words, they lay, half-dead while grape-sugar solution was pumped into their veins and orderlies insisted that there must be a lot of inebriated leeches on Fox Hill.

In two days they were discharged and prescribed iron pills and lots of fluids and Vitamin A, and Lieutenant Dharamdass lowered the boom on them. Liberty, he said, was one thing. These buggers were like—who's that fellow who said, 'give me liberty or give me death?' —Yes, that's it. 'Gave liberty and what happened?' he glowered, 'Nearly died! No more bloody liberty!' and he then went to talk about trenches, which he told the Army OC were an impediment to the progress of drunken sailors.

'At least my buggers can navigate. Drunk or not drunk, they were coming straight home. Trouble is your damn trenches.'

'Yes, but if my buggers didn't go to dig a trench, your buggers might be still there.'

'Yes, that's true.'

'Fine bunch you got this time.'

'You're telling me!'

Notes

(1) Literally 'arse-boys' or boys who were unmindful of any indignity perpetrated on their backsides, actually welcoming such attentions.

(2) Literally devils. Used here in the loose sense of meaning 'all the useless clodhoppers the Army has the doubtful honour to train'

(3) Fox Hill was a Diyatalawa landmark. Long ago, the British sailors of *HMS Fox* had decided to perpetuate their ship. They chose a hill and, with white granite and shiny quartz and chalk boulders, made a representation of a large fox, embedded into the slope.

8

History—'Chalo Delhi' and the End of the INA

Japan was finalizing preparations for the attack of India. Muller & Bhattacharjee[1] told of the INA march with the Japanese, through Burma, across the Indo-Burmese frontier, penetrating 150 miles into Indian territory. It was an incredible feat. Everywhere the cry resounded: 'Chalo Delhi'—On, on to Delhi!—and when Kohima was captured, everybody expected Manipur to soon be in Japanese-INA. hands. All they had to do was to take the capital, Imphal.

The Ceylonese fighters were infused with the Japanese promise of *Daitoa Kyoeiken*—the planned Greater East Asia Co-Prosperity Sphere. This was a concept which came under the larger rubric of a 'New Order'. It would consist, Japan said, of some parts of China, Manchuria and Japan and all British and Western colonies in south-east Asia. It would be a self-sufficient economic bloc, based on 'co-existence and co-prosperity' and free of Western imperialism.

No one heeded the reality. The concept was a camouflage to provide Japan with raw materials to support its war effort. It fell to pieces with the close of the war.

But it was very real to Gladwin Kotelawala and the men of the Lanka Unit. The Japanese were masters. They held Guadalcanal, the largest of the Solomon Islands in the south-western Pacific. From the capital, Honiara, the Japanese received ample supplies of fish, timber, copra and palm oil.

They invaded and held Guam, the largest of the Mariana Islands in the western Pacific. That was indeed a triumph. Guam had been ceded to America by Spain in 1899. That the Japanese could boldly seize US territory in 1941 did much to bolster their image, make the Ceylonese of Malaya acknowledge that the Japanese were on a winning streak; that resistance would be futile and disastrous.

There was also the charismatic Tun Hussein Onn, the Johor-born veteran who hated the British. Hussein joined the INA and was a leading figure in the sweep into India. His father, too, organized the United Malaya National Organization (UNMO) to galvanize Malayan nationalism and fight the British proposal for a Malayan Union that, he said, was a threat to the political interests of indigenous Malays.

Hussein was to eventually become the third Prime Minister of Malaysia. Truly did the British never know how much they were resented and despised.

The INA failed. Imphal stood firm, and the British poured everything into its defence. The Japanese, too, had their problems. America was swarming into the Pacific and suddenly, all occupied Japanese territories were threatened. The war swung around, destroying all INA hopes of liberating India. The cry for the surge towards Delhi died. Indeed, for the INA everything seemed to die. Even as they retreated, and were killed, captured, few of the British Indian government displayed any real interest in these 'adventurers'. Even in Burma, the Japanese and the Indians were being pushed back. America was regaining the Pacific islands and sea battles caused immense Japanese losses. The Japanese had no longer any use for the INA or its Ceylon units. They were redundant, an embarrassment actually, as the Japanese retreated.

Then, in August 1945, Bose was killed in an air crash. It was the end of the INA and the IIL. And the fighting Ceylonese? There they were, literally up the creek, and with no paddles. True, the campaign had been a sound one. The Ceylonese would play a supportive role of paving the way for the Japanese invasion of Ceylon. The combination of the land drive from Burma and a sea-borne invasion through Ceylon would have surely subdued India.

But now . . . the Japanese were gone, and the British poured back and again, it was a time of reckoning. The British Military Administration began to round up all those who had served the IIL and the INA.

Many of the Ceylonese were interrogated, then jailed. Gladwin Kotelawala also, but cannily, he let it be known that the Ceylonese in Malaya had to choose between two evils: death at the hands of the Japanese or the acceptance of billets in the INA. It was, he insisted, a means of self-preservation.

The British were inclined to believe this. They were aware of the character of Japanese rule and accepted that the Ceylonese, as British subjects, had been indeed between a rock and a hard place.

But the treason trials in India of INA officers was another matter. Staged in Delhi's Red Fort in December 1945, it was an effective tool wielded by the British Indian government in the reconstruction of the post-war Indian Army. The British deplored the manner in which discipline and loyalty had been eroded, especially in the large-scale defections of soldiers to the INA. But the fierce spirit of nationalism could not be quelled. The trials sparked off country-wide disturbances, frenzied anti-British rioting and a naval mutiny.

In post-war Ceylon, too, Gladwin Kotelawala was ignored. The bourgeois press clamped down on any reports of Ceylon's involvement with Bose. It found no reason to glorify anti-British freedom fighters. Gladwin, too, held his peace. He did not wish to antagonize his old father any more. Rather, he pitched in with the island's ruling political party, entered politics and, peculiarly enough, the ruling party, the United National Party, actually recommended him for British government honours. At that time, all such awards were always made on the recommendation of the country's ruling party.

The restless soul of Gladwin Kotelawala was stilled. He had become a military leader. He had been a major in Bose's Army. He had organized the Lanka Unit and the Ceylon Department. He treasured the picture he had to himself with other officers of the INA. He had shared Bose's distrust and hatred of the British and spent many years of his life, planning, scheming, preparing to drive them out of Ceylon and India. For all this did the British honour him! He was made a Member of the British Empire!

What is the worth and value of the MBE one could well ask. How lightly and with what political deviousness are such honours bestowed!

Notes

(1) Ref: *Subhas Chandra Bose and Indian Freedom Struggle*, New Delhi, 1985.

9

Of Rifle Drill and Sundry Convulsions and Sex on the Never Never

Time moved on, and rifle drill took up much of it in passage. This was viewed by the recruits as the vilest way to pass the precious hours of one's young life. It was an eternal round of slope arms, order arms, shoulder arms and present arms, accompanied by the old, old song: 'Hup, two, three, over, two three . . .' which began to get on everyone's nerves.

Koelmeyer was skinny and knobby at the shoulders. Sloping arms was something he dreaded because he was expected to slam his rifle down on his left shoulder. It had to be a most satisfactory smack. It hurt him.

The guards instructor was quite uncaring. 'Now look here. I want to hear that rifle come down hard on your shoulders! Right? Squad! Ser-looope—arms! Hup, two three, ovah, two three . . . smack it down!'

Koelmeyer went about it with the best will in the world. He set his teeth, plunked the rifle down hard, and his knobby shoulder couldn't take it. It jarred the bone and he would whistle through his teeth. Sometimes, in an unguarded movement, he would gasp, '*Ammo*!'

The GI would erupt. 'You! What was that? Yes, you!

Koelmeyer! Every time you slope arms you want your bloody mother?'

Carloboy would tell him later, 'Yes men, I know, your shoulder is paining. But don't go to say anything. Where's your bloody self-control?'

'Self-control? You saw this?' showing a very red and inflamed shoulder. 'See, will you.'

Carloboy hauled the sufferer to the sick bay, where a petty officer looked at the shoulder and clucked.

'If it's like this now, how will it be tomorrow after some more rifle drill?' Carloboy asked.

'Shit!' said the PO, 'You have knobs on your shoulders. How did they pass you in Colombo? Best thing I think is to break and re-set the bones. What do you say?'

Koelmeyer blanched. 'Here, you can't just break my bones like that!'

'Oh, we can't? Why not? Knobs on the shoulders! Who told you you could join the Navy with knobs on the shoulders? Fine thing this is, sending deformed buggers here.'

Koelmeyer was given 'ex rifle drill' and then a stout shoulder pad. He was Knobby and the mess always sang 'Knobby-all' in his honour.

'They call him Knobby-all, Knobby-all,
They call him Knobby-all, Knobby-all,
They call him Knobby-all
'Cause his shoulders have big balls,
So they call him Knobby-all, Knobby-all.'

Four years later, when Carloboy quit the Navy, Koelmeyer was till Knobby to all. He had graduated to a leather shoulder pad which was his prized possession.

Pay days saw the little canteen burst into life. It was a parade, even for the pay packet, with the boys stepping smartly up to off caps and extend them to the paymaster petty officer who would place the creamy envelope on their caps. They would then each make a smart right turn, step away to cram the envelope in their pockets and don caps. Then they would scoot, for money meant a booze-up and since the canteen served only beer to recruits, beer it was, consumed in alarming quantities.

The staff would come in too, and soon the roof would ring with lots of atrocious songs, all exceedingly vile, many rumbustious and raunchy parodies, the bluest of limericks and it was also a crying shame if someone did not get his nose stoved in just for the heck of it.

Canteen brawls would encompass everybody present, but just as often, many sang on unconcerned, while much blood was being spilled and many bottles and glasses broken in frenzied pockets and furious corners.

It is only when chairs are airborne and windows lose their last shreds of respect that frantic canteen staff summon the duty officer who is expected to break up the several parties in full swing.

The only effective method of doing so was to stand at the door and scream . . . which was all the OOD ever did, for he had to keep an eye out for a host of projectiles that whizzed around and were surely aimed at his head. These included glasses, beer bottles, cans, ashtrays, seamen's knives and folding chairs. Occasional tables required a joint effort.

But order was grudgingly restored and the next morning he would be crow-hoarse, naturally, and glare at the recruits as though they had just been identified and confirmed as a new and virulent type of bacillus.

Paydays were also pay-off days . . . for Little England, faithful to tradition, had many desirable women who had grown up to carry on their services to the Services. The good ship *Rangalla* was serviced by a bevy of personable young women who would come to the perimeter at night, where sentries would help them over the barbed wire and lead them stealthily into the mess huts.

Some nights were good; others not so good, especially if only a few women could make it and had to accommodate thirty each. This, the women would admit, was no real chore, given an 11 p.m. start and 4 a.m. finish, but the boys found it all rather unappetizing. They queued, true, but with such impatience that not one could really give of his best. There simply had to be more women.

One pretty tart who said her name was Isobel, promised to bring more. 'Lot have in village, but some not young like us. Never mind if bring?'

'How old?'

'*Apoi*, not sooo old. Twenty-five, thirty about. That never mind?'

Carloboy, jerking over her on a bunk divested of sheets, was expansive. 'So bring and come. Even your mother, let her come. How to wait like this till the other buggers finish? Can you hear?'

Yes, they could hear. Everyone in line was so impatient. The crudest jibes were hurled at the performers on the bunk. It was hardly the atmosphere, Carloboy knew, for even the pleasure of a moment. The women knew this too. They suffered the recruits to come unto them and felt that any one taking more than the usual four to five minutes was getting more than money's worth.

'So finish quickly,' Isobel said, 'to go also have sentry changing before.'

This, too, was necessary. Usually the four to eight watch was manned by staffers. The girls had to be over the fence before four.

Energies were released in quick rotation, the queues, even if ragged and sometimes spiced heavily, orderly in the main. Cost per head was kept at an absolute minimum. It was supposed that there was a generous 'volume discount'.

Isobel produced more girls. Soon, fifteen women found *HMCyS Rangalla* a steady source of income, costlier per head, but that scarcely mattered. Soon, with the staff let into the act, they began to stay all night, were bundled in blankets and led to the bathrooms to wash and were even sneaked into the officers' toilets where lights could be turned on and the boys could see what they were getting and even take them on the cold tiled floor.

But it had to happen, sooner or later. Carloboy shook his head. 'Can't today,' he said ruefully, 'you ask the others and see. We're broke. Until pay day will have to wait.'

'But that never mind,' Isobel said, 'If want you do. Pay day giving can.'

Carloboy sniggered. 'That's a pukka thing. You heard,' he hissed to the others, 'Can fuck and give on pay day. What say?'

The boys were charmed. They hadn't reckoned on the genius of these girls. True, Shaw had called the English a nation of shopkeepers, but these illegitimate daughters of the British had their fathers beaten hollow. Thereafter the girls came in, each carrying a little pocket book. The fee, the name, was entered. Pay-off was on pay day. Nobody welshed because Missy, one of the women said, 'If paying won't, we again coming not. Here about hundred have. In Army camp how many have you know? Six hundred.'

Oh, the women were canny. They plied their trade fearlessly. They knew that the Armed Forces kept strict health controls on their men. They had nice, young, clean boys who just wanted to relieve themselves and weren't old enough to be vicious or perverted.

Missy, Isobel, Jane, Sudu, Nona . . . so many daughters of the night . . . and perhaps the zaniest of all the zany things in *Rangalla*: sex on the never-never!

10

History—The Ceylon Naval Volunteer Force

Before 1937 there was no specific Ceylon Navy. Even the country's laws did not provide for one. But the Ceylonese did serve under the Royal Navy during World War I and there were those who served on Colombo Port Commission tugs which the British pressed into service to sweep the approaches to Colombo harbour for mines.

The idea of the British possessions having their own navies was mooted in 1932 at the Imperial Defence Conference, where it was decided that each part of the British Empire must be responsible for its own seaward defences.

Be it dominion, colony or protectorate, each was to have its own naval force, assume its own naval responsibility as early as could be managed. This was the first shot across the bows.

Ceylon decided that, being an island, the seas needed to be guarded, ships or no ships; and that was how the 'Naval Volunteer Force Ordinance No. 1 of 1937' was passed. Now, the island had a Navy and 'the Navy' it was, through its many phases of growth—from the Ceylon Naval Volunteer Force (CNVF) to the Ceylon Royal Naval Volunteer Reserve (CRNVR) during Second World War, to the Royal Ceylon Navy (RCyN) of which Carloboy von

Bloss was a part, and, with republic status in 1972, the Sri Lankan Navy (SLN).

It has been a long, sixty-year road, and as this book relates, Carloboy walked just four years along it; but even as he heaved over Isobel in his *Rangalla* bunk, and marched, and saluted, and stripped down a Lancaster Carbine, and brawled with the best, his story too began with the commissioning of the first four naval officers in January 1938: Lieutenant F.B. Rigby-Smith (who, in civilian life, was in the Ceylon Wharfage Company); Lieutenant P.J.B. Oakley (who was Marine Superintendent, Peninsula & Orient Lines); Paymaster Lieutenant E.F.N. Gratiaen (who was to later become a Chief Justice of Ceylon); and Paymaster Lieutenant D.S. de Fonseka (later to be knighted, become Sir Susantha, and to serve as Ceylon's ambassador to Japan).

Four officers—two British, one Burgher, one Sinhalese. The British administration then appointed a Britisher to lead: Commander W.G. Beauchamp, and he was in charge of the infant force for the duration of the Second World War.

Now the ranks had to be swelled. Sixteen other officers were accepted, among them being two prominent Burghers, Hildon Sansoni and Arthur van Langenburg; and an intake of signalmen, gunners, Lascar seamen and stokers. It was time for the island to sit up and take notice.

On 30th January 1939, the Navy had its first ceremonial parade in front of the office of the Captain-in-charge, Ceylon—the senior Royal naval officer based there. This office was to later become the Naval Headquarters, but, in that year, it was the preserve of the Royal Navy, overlooking the sea at Galle Buck, and, as a shore establishment, commissioned *HMS Highflyer*.

Housing the new officers and sailors demanded a location by the port of Colombo. Kochchikade (often waggishly called Cock-eyed Kade) was the best available. It was to be the Navy's first stamping ground and there, much history still radiates. The CNVF headquarters which was built there, became the home of the Navy for many years. It cost Rs 28,000 to build (no more than US dollars 560 today, which shows how nice things were even in wartime Ceylon) and was sited just below the famous St Anthony's Church, by the landward perimeter of the harbour.

In time, the old buildings were replaced and a big illuminated sign rose over the new: CEYLON FOR GOOD TEA—reminding every passenger liner in port that here was the land of Lipton. None could know that below the sign, in the naval headquarters, tea was not the hottest of drinks. Rather, there was much NAAFI beer and whisky; and there were cigarettes at only one rupee a tin!

The NAAFI (Navy, Army & Air Force Institute) doled out the best and the cheapest even when Carloboy had butted in, and it would always be a matter of pride to his father, Sonnaboy, that his son could bring home Booths gin and Dewars and Johnny Walker at six rupees a bottle, Jamaica rum eight rupees and Wild Woodbine and Marcovitch gold tips at a rupee a tin. This, to Sonnaboy, was manna indeed!

With the war, the illuminated sign was dismantled. Black-outs were the order of the night and the sign would surely tell enemy aircrafts that an entire port lay, waiting for their attention. Pity was that the sign was never re-erected. The British had other problems, like the growing clamour for independence. Soon, they would have no claim to the tea anyway. They had stirred the pot for too long.

The Royal Navy had the task of bringing the CNVF to scratch. 'Weekend camps' were organized, with all personnel, mainly unmobilized volunteers, reporting on Friday afternoons to Galle Buck for training. It was a strange start, to be sure, almost a Mickey Mouse local Navy as many civilians uncharitably dubbed it, for uniforms were donned at weekends and the men marched and were inspected and taught drill and yelled at because their hair was too long. They learned to fix bayonets and do all those things Carloboy was now being made to do.

But mobilization had to come as Hitler became too threatening for words, and, on August 31, 1939 the CNVF became an unit of fully-fledged sailors, ready if needs be, to serve under the white ensign in any place, any time.

It was also necessary to move to the water. A new headquarters building was planned with its own jetty and a more seamanlike bearing. Thus, in 1941, was the new Kochchikade base by the sea commissioned. A brave move, to be sure, and the official ceremony on July 11, 1941 was carried out with much pomp by the Governor of Ceylon, Sir Andrew Caldecott.

The Commander-in Chief of the East Indies Station (C-in-CEI), Vice Admiral Ralph Leatham, was there, and so was Vice Admiral Geoffrey Arbuthnot. Two hundred distinguished guests were invited, among them being the Minister of Agriculture and Lands of the Ceylon State Council, D.S. Senanayake (later to become independent Ceylon's first Prime Minister). Another was the Ceylonese Minister of Health, George E. de Silva.

The sailors marched and presented arms and the ensign flew bravely and the ladies fanned themselves and looked at the port (a rear view, so to say), all a-bristle with derricks and masts and the chug-chug of tugs and the colliers making their own blazes of dust.

There was, and is, nothing really romantic about Kochchikade. To many, even the best of us, a harbour is most attractive when viewed from an incoming or outgoing vessel. The Kochchikade section always housed the colliers with their rust-red sides and grimy funnels. There was always the grinding, raucous sound of coal, tumbling down the black shoots and the ships, dirty beyond belief, would lie in the sun and assume a grim, utilitarian dignity.

The coal-grimed men on the barges were not impressed by the ceremony on shore. They slipped between the lines of ships, towing their loads of coal. Fussy tugs hooted and did their best to drown the governor's words.

Such a harbour it was, even then. Bibby boats, Brocklebankers, Glasgies, Glen Liners, motor launches dashing to and fro like shuttles through a loom.

Even as rifle butts hit the floor in a smart 'order arms', a Maldivian buggalow inched into its inner berth, its one big sail limp in the still air, its sides festooned with coils of rope, its hull glossy brown. None of these graceful crafts were ever built in the Maldives. It is said that in the distant past, Indian traders sailed to the Maldives, even built boats for the Maldivians.

The ceremony ended. Dutifully, the men marched away. For many years after, they continued to look on their place by the sea as their headquarters, and Sir Andrew said:

'If ever, as has been done in other parts of the Commonwealth, the men and ships of our local Navy should be placed at His Majesty's disposal by the Ceylon government for the duration of the war, you officers and men have, by proven service and efficiency, made certain that such an offer would be gratefully accepted.'

It was not to be. The offer was made two years later!

11

Of Christenings and Essence of Chicken and Firing on the Range

Naval training, as every recruit will tell, can be a most fearsome thing. The boys were drilled hard, worked hard, and, in that bracing hill station, developed the most amazing appetites. It made them very aware of a cardinal truth. The cooks had to be cultivated. They had to be, next to mothers and dogs, a man's best friend.

Tin plates in the hands of a ragged line of hungry sailors . . . some days were peaceable enough, fresh food, be it known, was in plenty. The stewards dished it out, and in the mess the stewards were important. They could give generously or not at all. It all depended on how they felt about the man who stood before them, tin plate held in great expectation.

Carloboy went through his first heaping portion in record time. He considered the beef to be particularly good and decided it would do his digestion no real harm to go for seconds.

Cook-steward Haramanis squinted. 'Again you're coming? Why, not enough you took?'

'Enough? With curry like yours? How about a little more rice?' He gave an agreeable smile. Keep the cook humoured. That was a golden rule.

Haramanis sniffed, 'If all come to take like you, galley staff will not have anything.'

'Go on! You buggers are eating all the time.'

Haramanis put two scoops of rice on the plate. 'There. Now go and eat.'

'What about the curries?'

'No more anything. Only rice.'

'Don't be silly. Plain rice how to eat? Put some curry also.'

'Haven't, haven't. You asked little more rice only. So I gave. So go and eat.'

'Haramanis, if you don't serve me in two seconds . . .'

'Hah! You're coming to threaten me!' Haramanis banged the ladle down, 'I'm going to report!'

'You bloody mangy little—Here! Take your bloody rice also and go!' It was so easy. The plate swung and with a ripe *thock!* Haramanis was plastered. He shrieked, turned to flee, and in that instant, the mess hall became a madhouse.

The other steward saw Yusuf advance, plate poised. He leaped the counter, dragging down the big aluminium pot of shredded cabbage. He could not make the door, for a tin mug of water took him below the right ear and he sat heavily, losing interest in all that subsequently happened.

Carloboy hurriedly helped himself to a dish, served himself and slipped out to the boardwalk. The things that were happening in the mess hall made eating impossible. He polished off his meal and watched interestedly as the Platoon Commander swept up, followed by a gibbering Haramanis who was shedding rice with every head-shake.

'Where's von Bloss! *Where's von Bloss!*'

Carloboy followed them inside. 'Here, sir.'

The man leaped, then swung round. 'You're under arrest!' he bellowed.

A mug whizzed by and he jumped nine inches east. '*Who threw that!*' He grabbed Nugawira by a shoulder. 'And you! *Where are you going with that?*'

Nugawira was toting a cauldron of curried beef.

'Where's the duty cook? *Who is in charge here?*'

Nobody paid the man any notice. They were all busy eating, second helpings . . . third helpings . . . Daft Fernando patted his stomach and beamed, 'That's why I like this Navy,' he said chattily, 'everytime enough to eat.'

The PC staggered under the unreality of the whole scene. 'Who is the duty cook?' he squawked.

Haramanis, at the door, was dusting rice out of the inside of his blue shirt.

'Don' know, sir,' said Roy Fernando cheerily, 'cook steward Haramanis was here, then he suddenly went.'

'Suddenly went!' the light popped on. 'Yes! *Because hit him with a rice plate!* Haramanis! *Come here, Haramanis!*'

'H-here sir.'

'What is the meaning of all this? You were serving meals? *Stand to attention when you're talking to an officer!*'

'Yes, yes sir.'

'What d'you mean yes yes sir?'

'I—yes sir.'

'Are you mad? You're a raving lunatic! Rice all over you! Bloody imbecile!'

'Yes—yes sir.'

'Von Bloss! Did you put rice on his head?'

'Yes sir.'

'Why? *Why? Why!*'

'He told to put, sir.'

'*What?*'

'Ask the others, sir. He said to put. I think you're right sir. He's mad. Real raving lunatic. An imbecile sir.'

The PC waved his hands helplessly, 'Thank God somebody agrees with me,' he said fervently.

'Don't know what he will do next,' Carloboy pressed home, 'If put poison in the food even . . .'

'*What!* My God, Haramanis! Go and bathe! Rice all over the place. Are you trying to kill people here! *Don't stand there like a bloody bishop with a crowbar in his arse! Get out! Get out!*'

(In the nineties Carloboy told his sons he would gladly give ten years of his life to be in Diyatalawa once again!)

And all the while, the process, painful as it was, was having its desired effect. They *were* beginning to think and act as sailors. Naval jargon fell easily from their lips and they came to understand the significance of the uniform they wore.. It was a world within a world, and to know it all was truly fascinating—from the humble reef knot to the procedure for mooring ship in heavy weather; from naval codes and call signs to star maps, fixed bearings and the basic trigonometry of navigation. Parade ground to classroom to rifle range. Route marches to ceremonial salutes; the mysteries of B-29 receivers and harbour intercom, boat and gunnery signals.

Yet, the recruits came into their own after each gruelling day on the parade ground and in the classrooms. It was mandatory that everyone be 'christened' and for the first two months, each was in turn set upon by the others that he may regard himself later as one who has been honourably initiated. It was a most earthy ceremony, actually, where the one to undergo the rites is stripped, laid flat on his back and christened. Resistance was futile and a total waste of effort, since the initiate was sat upon by about forty and thus totally immobilized.

The general order of procedure was as follows:

- All pubic hair shaved.
- A liberal smearing of boot polish on the denuded area.
- The penis caked with a mixture of anything spreadable. This may or may not include toothpaste, jam, shaving soap, Brasso, pipeclay, builder's putty, French polish, etc.
- A blob of anti-corrosive grey neatly put on the glans (solely for decorative purposes).
- Each testicle painted in red lead and anti-corrosive grey.
- A tube of toothpaste squeezed into the anus.
- Delicate haloes painted round navel and the nipple of each breast.
- Overall application of coconut oil with a final dusting over of talcum and cotton from a handy pillow.

- A final blessing. This would vary according to the available material at the moment and the promptings of the demons within. Todwell received the contents of a firebucket which held stagnant and pea-green water since the days of World War I. Carloboy received the contents of a big pot of dishwater from the galley. Winnie was pumped upon since the boys could not find anything suitable. Koelmeyer simply stood at the gasping Winnie's head. 'Close your eyes,' he said, 'I'm the bloody Pope,' and like a latter-day Gargantua, pissed tremendously, and Winnie glubbered and globbered and became quite turkey-ish.

The initiate was then released while everybody cheered and clapped and hooted and whistled street-Arab style. He was expected to make a rude gesture, which he did, and was then proclaimed 'one of the boys' and presented with a bar of soap and bottle of turpentine. Quite the kindest thing to do, actually, for Carloboy spent up to three days scrubbing away the evidence of his own christening!

But, as in any group, a few clung to their own views on many things. Ordinary Signalman Cowpea Perera thought long about advancement and quick promotion and how this could be effected simply by getting in good with the staff. Oh, Cowpea had his charms. In his village, he had been the curly-haired darling of a long line of village schoolmasters and a procession of village toughs who found him a ready receptacle for their vileness.

Pliant as the best of whores, Cowpea had endured every paedophile and come to enjoy every trick in the overt homosexual's book. It was gay abandon since he turned eight. He was also quite Peter Pan-ish, very much the earnest schoolboy, deer-eyed, soft-spoken and seemingly shy.

'Bugger is like a girl,' Carloboy said, and all agreed.

They were not to know that this bugger-like-a-girl was the cause of most of their troubles. Someone was snitching on them. Todwell sneaked ashore when on duty watch. No one could have known, but it *was* known. Bijja Fernando poured red lead into the petty officers' bath. There were no witnesses. The regulating petty officer vowed to leave no stone unturned . . . and the next day Fernando was hauled up, given twenty-one days number ten.

And yes, Cowpea would always be detailed to clean staff huts or the bandroom, which was a long way down the hill, past the married quarters. While the others toiled, digging, scraping, planting, repairing fences, painting, Cowpea would be buggered in the staff huts, or on the floor of the bandroom with clockwork regularity. What is more, Cowpea would tell them all . . . all the goings-on in the huts, what the recruits did or planned to do. He was a mine of information; a beautiful, clear-eyed spy who would assiduously suck Able Seaman Parippu Silva's cock, giving that worthy the greatest of pleasure.

Leading Seaman Jayasooriya was particularly impressed. He had, it was said with some reverence in certain quarters, a penis like a reaper's hook. Even the women of Bandarawela found reason to complain. But this recruit took him in without the bat of an eyelid. Jayasooriya found sex with Cowpea vastly pleasing. He liked the way Cowpea raised his legs, gripped him around the hips, lying the way a woman would. Why, the boy really enjoyed being fucked in the arse! Later, in the canteen, Jayasooriya would tell Petty Officer Karu, 'There, that's the bugger. Like a woman, men. Anytime you want, he's ready. What d'you say? Shall I detail him to the PO's mess tomorrow?'

PO Karu frowned. 'No, that won't do. Send him to the PO's heads. You're sure he's game?'

'Game? Must hang a To Let sign on his bum. He's game for anything.'

'By the way, was there a punch-up yesterday behind the heads?'

'Yesterday? No, didn't hear of anything like that.'

'Try to find out. Four days now and nobody has gone on the deck.'

'You ask Perera. He's the one who tells us everything.'

Thanks to Cowpea Perera, 'going on the deck' (which

was 'being punished') was pretty standard procedure. The boys decided that somewhere there was a loose wire that was fouling the circuitry. It was solemnly decreed that sneaks and tattle-tales must be punished for the sanity of all and the moral upliftment of the many. A most effective punishment was to close around a sleeping victim and, at a given signal, urinate. Six jets of urine directed at face, ears, neck and mouth—oh, especially the mouth if the sleeper was wont to keep it open—was sufficient to have the poor man gurgling in anguish, tumble to the bathroom in the chilly air and return shivering, to regard his sodden bunk dismally.

Another popular practice was to use the victim's boots (beautifully polished for morning divisions) as a latrine. Chaos and the shit would rise together in the morning. The unsuspecting man would plunge his foot into a boot that made squelching noises as the excreta squished out, clung to his socks and seeped out of the eyelets.

The case of Cowpea Perera called for sterner measures. It did not take long to find out the true state of things, and for once the boys were aghast. Why, this shy, quiet fellow who didn't like to join in any of the rough-and-tumble . . . He was . . . what could they call him? He was a bloody prostitute!

'And he's splitting on us while the staff are splitting his arse!' Todwell growled.

'That's why he's never with us at working party,' Sims said thoughtfully.

'Damn shame for all of us,' Carloboy said, 'and a signalman also. When we go back to Colombo you think they won't know? By now the news must have gone that there are some pukka arsebirds here.'

'So what are we going to do?'

'Catch the bugger tonight. Teach him a damned good lesson!'

'If he shouts and wakes the camp . . .'

'If the whole staff is screwing him you think they will believe us?' another objected.

'Can't be helped. He's a disgrace to all of us.'

'Shall we go and tell the CO?' Roy Fernando suggested.

'You're mad?'

'Then what shall we do?'

'He likes to give his arse, no? Tonight we'll give him something he won't forget. You still have those chicken capsules your mummy sent?'

Roy Fernando nodded, then his eyes opened wide, 'My God, don't tell me . . .'

Carloboy nodded grimly. 'You give me the capsules.'

Roy's mother had felt that her sailor son needed some pepping up. 'Whole day working with big boots,' she told her husband, 'Must be tired, no?'

Papa Fernando had snorted. 'What to tired? Must be dancing the devil there.'

'So never mind. Now at least he's doing something. Otherwise whole day on the road with the bicycle and getting complaints no end.'

She had sent her pride and joy a box of Brand's Essence of Chicken capsules. 'Good for you to take,' she had written.

Roy had given them a jaundiced eye. 'What a bloody thing to send,' he told the others, 'not enough the soup we're getting here? And I hate these things. Have to clip the end of the glass and pour out.'

The others had looked at the long cocktail-sausage-like capsules and decided that Roy could have them. He had pushed them moodily into his locker. With a chastened Haramanis doing the honours in the mess hall, who needed chicken capsules?

Carloboy had a demon in him. Everyone thought so and looked at him with some concern. At six-thirty that evening, Cowpea was seized, stripped and made to lie across his bunk. When Carloboy shoved the chicken capsule into his anus the boys all hooted gleefully.

'Now we will get chicken shit,' Sims carolled.

Cowpea made no protest. He had taken upright cylindrical objects of far greater girth. But when Carloboy straightened up, the capsule was no more.

'My God,' Winnie exclaimed, 'you left it inside? How to take out?'

'That's his business. Bloody sneak. Giving his arse to the staff and putting us all in trouble.' He seized Cowpea by the hair, raised the boy's head. 'Now go and tell your able seamen to put the hand and take it out!'

Cowpea struggled, was released. He tried to stand, then bent over, stumbled naked to the door. Tears filled his eyes, and his lips were white. He doubled over to pull up his trousers, straightened himself and gave a thin cry. The trousers clung to his knees as he fell. A thin curl of greenish liquid tinged with red touched the back of his thighs.

'He's bleeding,' Nugawira croaked, 'call the quartermaster!'

The boys panicked. Cowpea lay on the floor, essence of chicken oozing from his anus, and there was blood. Many ran for help. Roy Fernando, white-faced, said hoarsely, 'Capsule must have broken. Now we are all in the shit.'

Carloboy was unrepentant. 'Serves the bastard right.'

The OOD rushed Cowpea to the army medical reception station. 'What happened here?' he roared.

'Nothing, sir,' said Carloboy sullenly, 'he was rubbing something in his arse. Don't know what. Must have slipped and gone in, sir.'

'Godalmighty!' the officer gave a horrified squawk and ran out to telephone the MRS.

Carloboy said, 'That's our story, right?'

The others nodded dumbly.

'Will—will anything happen to him?' Sims asked faintly, 'if he dies or something . . .'

'Rubbish!'

'Shouldn't have used the glass capsule,' Sims said stoutly.

'So how to know it will break like that? Anyway, whatever he says, we must stick to our story. Otherwise we are all in trouble.'

They nodded soberly.

In the MRS, Cowpea went through the most excruciating torment. Slivers of glass had to be carefully extracted from his anal passage and the orderlies didn't like the smell of essence of chicken.

The medical officer was pleased. 'First time in the history of this dump, we took an X-ray of a bugger's arse,' he told CO Dharamdass who wanted every detail of the case and marvelled at the answers he received.

He told Sub-Lieutenant de Mel, 'Can't have this bugger in the service. You know what he keeps doing? Pushing anything he gets into his arse. Real basket case.'

In the MRS Cowpea cried and lay tight-lipped.

'How did it happen?' he was asked, 'did anyone catch you and put it in?'

'N-no sir.'

'Then you were pushing it in?'

No answer.

When he returned to *Rangalla* he was asked the same questions. He just looked exceedingly unhappy.

'Fucking pervert!' the CO stormed, 'pushing bottles up your backside. Must be getting a hell of a thrill! Collect your gear. You think we want your type in the Navy?'

Cowpea packed his kitbag. No one spoke to him and he wished to make no conversation. A ten-ton truck was leaving for Colombo. He was put into it. A leading seaman escorted him, carrying a sheaf of official papers, medical reports and a recommendation for immediate discharge, with the Commanding Officer's comments running to several pages.

Slowly, things returned to normal at *Rangalla*. The next week saw yet another discharge. Stoker Mechanic Felix was blood-tested positive for gonorrhoea. He spoke vaguely of a woman he had savoured in a small house below the Bandarawela railway station. The Navy did not want him either.

'If you had passed out and then got the clap we would have given you ten thousand units of penicillin and kept you,' Dharamdass said. 'But you're still a recruit. Remember that all of you!' he roared, 'as long as you are recruits you are nothing! We don't give a fuck for any of you! You become our responsibility only when you pass out. *Do you understand?'*

The boys said they did. They were just an 'intake'. They realized that the Navy could stomach them thus far and no farther. If they hoped for any future they would have to clear this first hurdle. They had to pass out to become sailors. They simply had to watch their steps. And it really wasn't so hard. The tree had shed its bad apples. Now, they all decided, was the time to meet that passing-out parade in fine fettle. They became, to everyone's relief, a well-knit body of recruits that, come hell or high water, stood together, ready to face anything.

The usual little things served to make the uneven tenor of their ways even more uneven. Things like firing on the range, which was always of a particularly hair-tearing quality. The butts would echo to the dull crumps of falling plaster. Sick Bay Attendant Siri and Ordinary Seaman Deen did their best to blast the protective bund to smithereens.

'Don't press the trigger. Squeeze it gently. Treat it like a woman!'

'I can't. I got no imagination.'

'Good God, von Bloss! What range have you set! Are you trying to kill your mother-in-law in Colombo?'

'Fire!'

'Hey, PO, my gun won't fire.'

'Let's see . . . don't muck about with it. For God's sake *stop waving it around!* Don't you know there's a bullet in the breech? Why, you bloody idiot, your safety catch is down . . . *wait till I get out of the way!'*

'Todwell, what are you doing, rubbing your cock into the ground?'

'Something bit me . . .' Todwell abandons his rifle to probe up his trouser leg. 'It's a bloody big ant!'

'Winnie, the target is in front of you. What are you waiting for?'

'I know, PO, but every time I take aim some bastard is pulling it down.'

'So why are you taking so long? You think the enemy is going to wait until you take aim? Fire, load, fire, load, keep that bolt moving! Christ! What a nut!'

'Koelmeyer! Three maggies. Can't you get on sight?'

'I'm trying, I'm trying.'

'Then try harder, you cock-eyed cunt!'

'Now this is the Lancaster Carbine. It's an automatic weapon, understand? See the perforated outer barrel? That's the chamber cooler. Fire in short bursts, do you hear?'

Taka-taka-taka-tak-tak-tak-taka-taka-tak-taka-tak-tak . . .

'Enough! Enough! Take your finger off the trigger! Bloody idiot! Let go!'

Udurawana jerks his hand away. The carbine teeters on its tripod.

'Short bursts, I said, no? Don't you understand anything? Ran through half the ammo belt!'

So did range mornings pass. By noon, the gunnery petty officer looked like a fairground Aunt Sally.

'Cease firing! *Cease firing!* My God, fall in three deep. Let's go before someone gets killed!'

12

History—The Ceylon Royal Naval Volunteer Reserve

When the government of Ceylon offered its naval volunteers to be a part of His Majesty's Navy, the offer, as Governor Sir Andrew Caldecott had predicted, was accepted. Britain needed all the men and resources of her colonies, and so, on October 1, 1943, the Ceylon Navy Volunteer Force was absorbed into the Royal Navy. It was now the CRNVR—the Ceylon Royal Naval Volunteer Reserve.

Kochchikade remained the headquarters for the duration of the war; and let it be said, it was a real Navy in every sense of the word. The men were afloat and performing magnificently in waters that were constantly churned by monsoon weather.

During the war, all Ceylon naval sea operations included the coast watch and patrol of the ports and approaches of Colombo and Trincomalee (where the British East Indies Fleet was in station). The men constituted a strong, well-knit seaward-defence force. Shore duties were minimal. They had the craft, and the sea was their home.

They would sweep the approaches to the ports, provide guard-ship duties even as far away as Diego Garcia and the Addu Attol, provide escort to unarmed merchantmen and were constantly out on search and rescue missions, or towing target floats for gunnery exercises and pushing out on patrols up to Barberyn Light and Hendala Light, checking marker buoys and light buoys and keeping a watching brief for any activity of a suspicious nature.

In Flagstaff Street, Colombo, the signals tower monitored the CRNVR operations on radar and with coded harbour intercom, and *HMS Highflyer* had its top communications men in the main signals office, on the tall bridge and in the wireless rooms below.

The CRNVR became the guardians of the shores. Besides the two HM tugs, *Samson* and *Goliath* (which, incidentally, still serve as tugs in the port of Colombo), there was *HMS Overdale Wyke, HMS Okapi, HMS Sernia, HMS Sambhur, HMS Hoxa, HMS Balta, HM Trawler Barnet, HM Tug C45, HM MFV 17, HM MFV 186* and *HM MFV 187*.

The latter, MFV's 186 and 187 were later despatched to Akyab in Burma where they performed magnificently in mine clearing in the Rangoon river.

Kochchikade became the special training ground for the signalmen/gunners who were considered the eyes and ears of the force and of special importance. Many educated young men were gathered in, mobilized to man the armament and communication systems. They became a vital part of the CRNVR and earned quick promotions. But the force also relied, just as heavily, on its Lascar seamen, seasoned old salts who worked on deck and kept the ships in fighting trim.

But oh, the signalmen/gunners had to perform on the parade ground too, and the parade ground at Kochchikade was small enough to make a column dizzy if it marched with the necessary right turns to stay in tight formation. Everyone longed for 'sea time', for to be drafted on board was to be free of the chores of the shore base, especially being drilled out of one's mind.

One of these signalmen/gunners was a young, fair-haired Burgher lad. He was Victor Hunter. He rose to become a naval commander and also serve as the Captain of the Navy many years later. He and Carloboy had to come together . . . as we will read of later.

HMS Overdale Wyke was promptly dubbed the 'overdue tyke'. And she was always OW to the men who liked her trim, deadly lines and the main armament—a 12-pounder—which was later mounted at Kochchikade at the parade ground. This gun replaced an older 12-pounder which had stood there for many years with its brass plate on which was inscribed the year, 1896.

Indeed, old OW was the first ship purchased by the Ceylon government from the Royal Navy. She was a converted trawler that had been fitted out by the Admiralty for minesweeping duties in the English Channel. She was not young, having been completed in 1924 at Selby by Cochrane & Sons Ltd. But she packed quite a wallop. Besides the 12-pounder, she was fitted with an Oerlikon (single mounting) and two 20 mm Lewis guns (twin mounting), anti-submarine equipment which included sixteen depth charges, two throwers and rails; a Marconi echometer and minesweeping equipment which was a single sweep orapesa.

It could make maximum speed at 8.6 knots with its steam reciprocating engines and could steam ten days at maximum without her boilers blowing.

She was small, trim and with plenty of bite. Overall she was 147 feet and at beam, 23 to 24 feet. Light, too, and this gave her the penchant to toss airily in a running sea.

The Royal Navy armed her and commissioned her in December 1940, and the Ceylon government bought her as is, offering to take delivery midway. So it was that an RN runner crew sailed OW to Port Said where Lieutenant P.J.B. Oakley of the Royal Navy Reserve awaited with a CRNVR crew of forty.

They sailed the overdue tyke proudly back to Ceylon, quite heedless of reports of enemy activity in the Indian Ocean.

Ceylon had her first fighting ship.

13

Of Royal Guards and Fancy Queens and Days of Soap and Glory

Diyatalawa's bracing weather made everything quite nip and tuck. The sort of coldroom atmosphere when even sagging matrons are assessed for whatever tattered potential remained.

All around were the mountains. The sea had to be imagined. A nice way, indeed, to begin life as a sailor.

It was believed by bow-legged naval types who strutted decks, that it takes about three months of torrid dams and blasts and what-the-fucks to make the average civilian into a slightly-below-par sailor. That's how it's done, it is said, in Portsmouth and Plymouth and other places of nautical suffering. Also, the Royal Ceylon Navy was modelled, and moved quite clodhopperly, on Royal Navy lines. This, too, was inevitable. There was no other way.

Days passed swiftly and everyone was gearing for the final passing-out parade. This was the threshold that had to be crossed. It was, to the recruit, the end-all of his training stint, the first pinnacle of achievement. It was, therefore, a dumbstruck intake that was told by CO Dharamdass that there would be no passing-out.

Carloboy gave a small hiss of disbelief. No passing-out? Had the Navy decided to dump them all into the nearest gash barge?

Dharamdass stared at them. His hands twitched, much like the attitude of a man who wished to strangle all who stood before him. 'No passing-out parade! Of all the lucky bastards, you are the batch that least deserves this! You are all to consider yourselves passed-out and ready to serve! You get that?'

Some nodded, some wagged heads wonderingly, some raised eyebrows while others clicked teeth and braced themselves for the worst. The Navy was doing them no favours. Something was up. Something, they knew, which was not going to fill their lives with sunshine and flowers.

'I have received a signal from Gemunu,' Dharamdass said, 'and it says that Her Majesty Queen Elizabeth the second is coming to Sri Lanka. Von Bloss! Stop chewing your lip! Did you hear what I just said?'

'Yes sir. The Queen is coming, sir.'

'The Queen of England, you horrible squirt! As a sailor you will always say Her Majesty the Queen, do you hear?'

'Yes sir.'

'From tomorrow, all of you will consider yourselves the Royal guard of honour!'

There it was. The sting in the tail. It plunged the camp into disarray. The signal had been quite breathless in content. Would it please the CO *Rangalla* to drill his recruits until they were, or he was, blue in the face so that the said recruits were rendered unmistakeably seamanlike and incredibly shipshape to be the Queen's Royal guard.

The more naïve considered this honour indeed, but it was later revealed that this was a matter of simple naval expediency. Recruits, the boys were told by a worldly-wise leading seaman, were in possession of new uniforms and were thus better equipped to uphold the prestige of the service before a visiting sovereign. QED.

All other routine was dumped. Life became an endless round of marching, marching, forming rank and presenting arms. They ached. They stiffened in all manner of places—places they didn't know they had—and Carloboy would fling his rifle down, flop on his bunk and scowl.

'Feel like sending the bloody Queen a letter,' he said, 'what, men, you think she knows what's happening here?'

'This is a hell of a thing,' Daft Fernando moaned, 'even make-and-mend cancelled.'

Make-and-mend was the customary Wednesday afternoon off for all ranks. Sailors were expected to use this weekly half-holiday to darn and sew and repair all items of kit. This was never done, of course. Wednesday afternoons saw everybody cut adrift. Bandarawela dreaded Wednesdays. Even the girls' schools closed early. Cancelling make-and-mend was a most unkind cut.

'If the Queen knows what's happening here . . . and all because she's coming . . . she'll—she'll . . . ' imagination could not encompass this.

'*Adai*, von Bloss, so what have we got to do? Will have to go to Colombo, no?'

'And march an' march there also. An' for what? Just to go to the jetty and present arms!'

'The jetty? You mean the harbour we have to go?'

'Otherwise? She will come by ship, no? Have a Royal yacht or something.'

'Yes, I know,' Nugawira nodded, 'called the *Britannia*. Sure to come to the new jetty they're making. That's why they're going to call it the Queen Elizabeth Pier.'

'Who?'

'How the fuck do I know? Government, must be. Who else?'

'Feel like sending a letter. Telling how we are marching, marching . . . and the polishing. How the inspection now? Bloody madness!'

Todwell chuckled. 'So when is she coming?'

'Who knows? Didn't even tell.'

'May give us medals.'

'Bullshit! Medals for what? Because we went and put a salute?'

Things got worse . . . or better, depending on the way the platoon commanders and the recruits looked at it. A guards instructor of the Royal Navy named Brady came to

Rangalla to assess potential and proceeded to blow several fuses. His broad Yorkshire accent made him quite unintelligible to the main body of those he had come to persecute.

This made for rather bizarre and most unreal moments when he waddled up to take command.

'Roy-yell grrth! Ain . . . heh!'

The boys stared at him nonplussed.

Brady turned to the Platoon Commander with the sort of concern one usually displays on receipt of a hurricane warning. 'Dahnt these mehn understand Henglish aht ahll?'

The PC was a very impatient man. Also, he didn't like this stuffy GI from Blighty at all. 'Oh, they know their stuff,' he assured airily, 'Let me handle them.' He then swung on the guard thunderously, 'Royal garrrd! Hough! Stand still! *Don't move a fucking eyelid! Slooooo'p arrrmz!* Head erect! *Simmons! Is your mother a bloody Kathak dancer?* Now the Queen will step on the saluting dais . . . Roooy'l garrrd! Royal saloooot . . . prezen arrrms! Slap those rifle slings smartly! I want to hear one sharp sound! My Jesus, Fernando, *I'll kick you all the way up Fox Hill!'*

GI Brady looked as though he had just been force-fed with the square root of minus x.

'Well, GI, that's the way to get things done around here.'

'Ayh . . . very good, sir. Only the quain meh not—ah—approve.'

'Don't give it a thought. She doesn't know these buggers.' He turned on the boys. 'Slooop armhz! Orderrrr arhms! Now lissen. The Queen will inspect you. She will walk past you accompanied by the Royal Guard Commander and Prince Philip and the Commanding Officer of the guard. You will stand like bloody statues! You won't twitch. Not a muscle. Not even if the bugger behind is feeling your arse! *Did you hear?* Now GI Brady will be the Queen and I am the Royal Guard Commander . . .' he led Brady to a corner of the parade ground, 'Stand still there! Here comes the Queen!'

This was too much. Someone muttered, 'Just look at them. Two bloody lunatics.'

The Platoon Commander waltzed up, left hand holding an imaginary sword. Behind him minced Queen Rosie O'Brady the First (and hopefully the Last). The Royal Guard tittered. Daft Fernando tried to suppress an insane giggle and went 'wooof!' and roars of laughter split the morning air.

The Platoon Commander lost his last shreds of dignity. 'Stop it!' he foamed, '*Stop laughing!*'

The boys hooted. They slapped each other on the back. They banged their rifle butts on the ground. They cackled the way midnight hags are wont to do. Winnie went into convulsions of a sort and had to be thumped vigorously. Sims pointed helplessly at Brady.

'Here comes the Queen!' he howled and the eruptions of mirth scared the crows on the yardarm.

'High port arms!' the PC screamed, executing a sort of Watusi, '*High port arms!* Run, you bastards, *run! Run!*'

They ran . . . round and round the parade ground for a long time. There was neither time nor space. Only the pounding of boots in the red dust. There wasn't a laugh left in any of them when they were finally brought to a dragging halt. Of GI Brady there was nary a sign. The PC stared at them frostily. 'Take five minutes. And muster back here. I've not finished with you yet!'

Something had to snap. The constant drilling was beginning to get on everyone's nerves.

'Join the Navy and see the world,' said Koelmeyer darkly. 'Huh!'

'Join the Navy and have a girl in every port,' Todwell snorted. 'What port?'

All they had were outlandish .303 rifles with warped stocks. All they did was march, march, carrying said rifles on their shoulders. Every day.

'What the hell is the use of this uniform anyway?' Sims wanted to know.

'Something,' said Carloboy, 'has to be done. Marching, marching, left turn, about turn, right turn . . .'

They agreed that, worst of all, they had to also listen to a litany of insults from the cretin who pranced behind them with a wild light in his eyes and a very red face.

'If we can get sick or something . . .'

Yes, the situation could be eased somewhat by reporting sick, but, as Aloy observed, a way of falling ill had to be discovered. And it was Aloy who hit on the idea of swallowing soap and washing it down with a couple of mugs of warm water. It worked, for soon he was a sort of going concern. He was removed to the Army MRS by shocked sick bay attendants.

This was too good to be true. Soap was swallowed at random and with scant respect to internal tracts, intestines or other such wriggly appurtenances that skulk in the average stomach. Daft Fernando did not throw away his shaving water. He drank it. Sims had to be dissuaded from ingesting washing powder.

'Why? It's like soap, no?'

'Better not,' Udurawana advised. 'Have chemicals in that. Just take bits of bar soap.'

By late morning they were all crowding the medical reception station of the Army hospital.

'Purging,' said an Army medical orderly to the staff sergeant, 'the whole bloody Navy is purging.'

'So why are they here,' growled the staff, 'there are no lavatories in their camp?'

The Captain, Ceylon Army Medical Corps, did not like them either. 'Sailors I don't like,' he said, *'and shitting sailors I can't stand!* You!' to Ordinary Seaman Deen, 'what did you eat this morning?'

Deen began to count off on his fingers. 'Half a loaf bread, two sausages, four eggs, four mugs tea, tomato sauce, three boiled potatoes, a packet of cream crackers, glass of orange juice and a mango, sir.'

'Jeeeesus! You have a bloody tub for a stomach? Who the fuck issues victuals in your mess?'

'I get two extra eggs,' Deen pointed out, 'because I am Muslim and I don't eat sausages, sir.'

'But you said you ate two sausages.'

'Yes, sir. They were beef sausages, so I ate.'

The Captain closed his eyes. 'No wonder you buggers are purging,' he breathed, 'I'll be in the loo for a week if I ate like that.' He turned to the staff with a grimace. 'I want to examine their stools,' he said. 'Four bloody eggs . . .' he looked at Deen in near wonder, 'cream crackers, sausages . . . Jeesus! Give them black coffee. No sugar, no milk, like bloody tar!' He stomped away, then turned at the door. 'There are only six lavatories here. I don't want a bloody stampede. And if any of you bastards soil this place, I'll—I'll run you out with a fucking bayonet!'

Each sufferer was given a dinky little ceramic bedpan and ordered to present samples of naval waste when the urge was next upon them. This they did docilely enough. Being in the MRS was relief enough. They thought of the others, marching in the sun, and smirked.

There were disadvantages, however. No food. The staff was quite emphatic. 'If you buggers eat lunch on top of all that breakfast we'll have to build new lavatories!'

Nobody questioned his judgement. They felt quite drained and, as is usual of the condition they had induced, there was some bodily dehydration. But the soap had done its worst and the rumbles in their bellies had dropped to hoarse whispers. Like a floor polisher being used in a far corner of a room.

It was two in the afternoon when the bomb walked in, stood among them and went off.

A very volatile captain stormed into the ward. He foamed. Yes, foamed, as though he had swallowed a bar of soap himself.

'Malingerers!' he howled, and stamped his feet. Both feet, very quickly. Like the mating dance of a prairie hen. A spellbinding performance, more so with the bedpan in his hand. What he next said was with such croaking fury that nobody could understand a word. Then, dropping the vaudeville, he advanced on them with a wild light in his eyes.

'Who is A-5550?' he hissed.

Carloboy sat up and gave him a look of piteous long-suffering. Even da Vinci could not have captured that expression.

'What did you eat this morning?'

'Bread and eggs, sir.'

A long intake of breath. 'I see . . . only bread and eggs?'

'Yes, sir.'

'Not soap?'

'Sir?'

'Soap! *Soap!* S-o-p-e—soap!'

'Oh, soap?'

'Whadd'youmean oh soap! Yes soap or no soap?' He fought for air, then burst out, *'did you eat soap?'*

'Soap, sir?'

'Will you *answer my question?* You—you—cunt of misery!'

'Yes, sir.'

'Well?'

'I didn't eat soap, sir.'

'So you didn't, eh? *Get out of that fucking bed!* Come here! Look at this!' pointing a finger into the bed pan, 'what is this?'

'Shit, sir.'

'I know that! And whose shit is it? *Yours!* And do you know what's in it? *Soap!* So you didn't eat soap—*but you shit soap!* You're a cute little bunch of bastards you are. Eat soap, start purging and come here to lie on my beds. *On my beds!* Out! *Out! All of you out!'*

They were all out of bed anyway. The big scheme had come unstuck. Worse still, they were still somewhat loose around the sphincters.

The Captain phoned the CO *Rangalla*. 'Send a truck for your lot. There's nothing wrong with them . . . yes . . . yes . . . they need extra drill, extra work, extra fatigue and an extra kick each in the backside. What's that? Oh no, I'm not going to kick them for you. Some of them are still going loose . . . okay, no sweat . . . only watch out for this lot. They're hell on wheels . . .'

He turned on the boys with a face that twisted repugnantly. 'Get dressed and get out. And don't ever come here again. Not even if you're dying. So help me God, I'll give the first one who comes here a thousand cc's of formalin. You know what will happen?'

They could have guessed. Carloboy frowned slightly. There was no need, he thought, to rub it in.

'He gets stiff. Like a bloody waxwork! A well-kept corpse! *That's what I'll do if I see any of you here again!* And you know how the formalin is given? *Injected up your arse!'* He swept out with bedpan-rattling force.

Todwell shrugged. They filed out sheepishly and stood in the sunshine, waiting for the truck.

'Bloody mad doctors they have here,' Carloboy said.

The motion was passed unanimously.

The reception at *Rangalla* was worse. Left nothing to be desired. After the cyclone had done its worst, leaving several popping eardrums in its wake, they settled to the decreed punishment.

'Hard labour,' Dharmadass carolled. 'That's the medical recommendation. Follow me. Left turn. Quick march.'

They were taken to the edge of a long, sloping ground. Yonder lay the married quarters. The CO rubbed his hands. 'Always wanted a road from here to there,' he told no one in particular. 'Go on. Get to the bosun's stores. Picks, shovels, spades, barrows. There is a pile of road metal at the front gate. Get it moved. Cut the road, lay the metal, use the heavy roller. I want a good road, do you understand? Warrant Officer Seraphin will supervise. Go on! Get moving! Picks and shovels first.'

WO Seraphin was not very enthusiastic. The boys laughed at him, called him Whispering Smith. Oh, he had what was generally accepted as a 'mouth almighty' but he also had his problems and looked on the recruits as a means to an end. The man had a lot on his plate, everyone knew, and to some extent, sympathized. But what does one do when the man stands dumbly by, accepts that his wife finds Petty Officer Rashid the better bedfellow? Seraphin had thought that he should woo his wife with all he could lavish on her. He showered her with gifts, which she thanked him prettily for, then hummed a popular tune of the times.

'Why are you singing that song?' Seraphin would ask.

'So what? I like it. Lovely, the words,' and she would sing:

'You were in my arms last night about this time . . . '

'Stop that!' Seraphin would shout, then grow tearful. 'Why are you torturing me like this? After all I'm doing for you and giving you. Next year I'll be sub-lieutenant also. We will have officer's quarters. Even now we can go to wardroom parties and all. Why are you doing this to me?' 'Oh shut up,' wife Dora would scream, 'just because you are a warrant officer you think you're big? What do you want? To salute you in the bed also?'

'If that Rashid comes here again—'

'So what will you do? He comes to see me, not you.'

'And what about the others? That Morell in Colombo. You think I don't know? And that Yeoman Ranawaka. I thought if come here you will behave . . .'

'Behave! What is so bad if I have some friends? You think you own me? What can you do? Borrowing money left and right. Even asking the recruits for money. Think I don't know?'

'Yes, asking,' Seraphin would snarl, 'borrowing for what? To buy for you things, that's what.'

'So who's asking? Why are you just bringing? Did I ask?'

'So why can't I buy anything for you? I'm your husband!'

Dora would sniff. 'Husband!' She would say it as though she were referring to the bubonic plague. 'Four years now I have put up. Can't do anything properly.'

'Oh, I can't?'

'You can't! Vain I married you. Can't even do the job properly.'

Seraphin would flop into a chair, a stricken, beaten

man. He knew that it was useless to argue. Those others in Colombo, this Rashid, they obviously knew how to keep Dora humming. He just could not.

'You were in my arms last night about this time . . .'

'Stop that! Stop singing that song!'

Poor Whispering Smith. The recruits paid him scant respect too. He had this irritating habit of sidling up to his quarry at working party. 'Eh, von Bloss, how 'you off fercash?' This was said sotto, usually through the teeth, making the words sound like the love–call of a cobra.

'What? Sir, what did you say?'

'Shhhhh . . . sooooftly. Don't wan'th'other to 'ear.'

Carloboy would lean towards him. 'Can't understand what you're saying, sir.'

'Shhhhh. Hummuch mon'y'yu got?'

'Money!'

Seraphin would nod vigorously, look around quickly. 'Erbout fifty iffu'have?'

'What?' (Loud and clear).

'Shhhhh!'

'How can I have fifty bucks?'

'You haven't?'

'No.'

'Then thirty even? Twenty?'

'I haven't, sir.'

The man straightens up, 'Get on with your work. Only asked to see what you will say. Come on, put some vim into it!'

'Yes sir.'

'No need to tell anyone about this, I think.'

'Yes sir.'

He would move away, seeking another quarry.

Todwell had sauntered up. 'I saw that bugger kuchu-kuchu-ing[1]. Came to ask money?'

Carloboy nodded. 'Pukka bloody officer. Last week took twenty from Wimal and another ten from Stembo. Came to ask fifty.'

'So you gave.'

'You're mad? Where have I got fifty?'

Todwell had grinned. '*When* have you got fifty?'

'Never, I think.'

The boys were not particularly enchanted. The road they were cutting was a downgrade and everybody kept getting in anybody's way while Seraphin got crosser and crosser, being unable to single out any of the miscreants for a little chat. Dollops of earth and clods flew in all directions and, because of the incline, the heavy roller acquired the knack of suddenly shooting off on its own while everybody scattered whooping like banshees round a Maypole.

Of real progress there was little, and the day did come when even the CO decided to cry quits. It was all Petty Officer Dayaratne's fault, actually. He had to go and kick Ordinary Seaman Jayasinghe. Nothing would have mattered if he did, but he missed by a mile (Jayasinghe being very nimble when it comes to evasive action), and sent the cookhouse dustbin into orbit. Unfortunately for the PO, the lid of the trash can, which had a most jagged edge, slid off and sliced into his leg. It took some time before he stopped hopping. He then hobbled to the sick bay, told Winnie to do something, anything, before he bled to death.

Winnie was eager to please. He laid the injured man on a bunk, pulled down the blood-soaked stocking, cleaned the wound and applied a pressure pad. He then reached blindly for a bottle from an array on a rack.

He was in his element. His first casualty; his first real action as a Navy SBA. He never checked . . . and emptied a bottle of Sloane's liniment over the raw gash.

PO Dayaratne shot out of bed as though he had been prodded with a hot poker. His eyes screwed up. His mouth fell apart. The yell of pure agony was heard, doubtless in Bandarawela. Winnie gasped, paled, dropped the bottle of Sloane's and took off.

The tortured PO leaped after him, still howling, seized a firebucket. It was the only weapon he chanced upon.

The civil engineers of *Rangalla* stopped not-building their road to watch open-mouthed, as Winnie, singing something from Verdi, raced down the slope. Hard behind came the PO. Somewhere along the way he had exchanged the firebucket for a fire axe. Seraphin blanched and trotted away. He know his duty. The regulating officer had to be brought abreast.

Carloboy put down his spade. At last, he thought, the climax of naval training was upon him. 'Look and learn,' he sang, 'This is how to commit murder in a seamanlike manner.' The boys yelled encouragement.

The fire axe turned in the sun, missed Winnie by half an inch and thunked on the heavy roller. Winnie accelerated, shot down the slope like a rocket. The PO shot past like two rockets. Then Yusuf let the roller join the parade. It rumbled after the PO like a tank with a stomach ulcer, caught him deftly behind the knees and pitched him forward. It then left the road in a smart navigational wheel and sank into a patch of soft, waterlogged grass. There it wallowed until enough men and rope were commissioned to haul it out. Two down, one to go.

They found Winnie having a nervous fit in a disused bathroom and all but carried him to the hut. PO Dayaratne was gently transported to the Army hospital where he clutched an orderly's hand and swore that when he was dead, if ever he was cut open, the name 'Winnie' would be found engraved on his heart!

Notes

(1) A delicious bit of localese to describe a low-key discussion.

14

The 'Overdue Tyke' and the End of the CRNVR

Truly could it be said that *HMS Overdale Wyke* was the Ceylon Navy's first historic ship. The next to be sailed into Colombo by an all-Ceylon crew was the Royal Canadian minesweeper, *HMCS Flying Fish*. She was a beauty, imposing with her forty-foot mast and a displacement of just 1,040 tons. Light. So light that when at sea only the strongest stomachs could stomach her. Also, she was on indefinite loan from the Royal Navy and remained so until a cyclone drove her inland from her anchorage at Talaimannar and broke her heart and her bottom.

Carloboy actually mourned her passing. Never had he enjoyed sealife more than on her pitching, bucking decks.

The government then purchased another minesweeper and called her *HMCyS Parakrama*. Vijaya was, according to tradition, the first Aryan king of Lanka. He came in from north India where his father was happy to see him go. He sailed in with 700 brigands and, with the help of a local witch, raised a kingdom, having put the locals to the sword. That was over five hundred years before Christ.

Gemunu was named after the southern hero-king Duttha Gamani (later softened to Dutugemunu). This man, in the first century BC, drove the Dravidians and Damilas (Tamils) out of the country and made of Lanka a single Sinhalese land.

Parakrama was another great Sinhala king who made of the country a veritable granary.

But *HMCyS Parakrama* came later. So did *HMCyS Vijaya*. What the CRNVR regarded with great affection and respect was the 'Overdue Tyke'. She had an executive commanding officer and two other officers (one the First Lieutenant and the other the engineering brass). There was also an engineer, three signalmen, three telegraphists, four special duty men, fourteen seamen, three cook-stewards and eleven stokers. Her main area of operations were the Colombo, Galle and Trincomalee harbour approaches which she swept diligently, and also provided escort and conducted patrol duties as well as serving as a guardship at Port T—the code name for Addu Attol, where a considerable part of the British East Indies Squadron was based.

Her day of glory came when on Indian Ocean patrol in 1945. The Italian Navy had been instructed to surrender to the Allies. Even as the *Overdale Wyke* steamed south, the ten-inch signals projector of an approaching warship began a flurry of dots and dashes. It was the Italian light cruiser *Eritri*.

The Italians had realized, long ago, that the Benito-Adolf relationship was getting their country nowhere. They were, they knew, on the wrong side and were suffering much for their choice. They welcomed the thought of surrender. They grew most excitable about the prospect, but then, the Italians by and large are a very excitable lot. When they are not getting all steamed up they sign Neapolitan love songs.

The Commandante of the *Eritria* was anxious to get the business over. He could have blown the *Overdale Wyke* out of the water. Instead he began a flurry of signals. He had his orders. He surrendered.

The Ceylonese boarding party was oh, so proud. They had captured a cruiser, fourteen big guns and all, without a shot. They accepted the *Eritria*'s surrender, spiked her guns, escorted her to Kochchikade. A perfect prize! It was, and still is, the most unique event in Sri Lanka's naval history.

The Italian crew were held in Diyatalawa and many died there. So you see, fruit seller Van Dort's story was creditable enough. The Royal Navy held their Italian p-o-w's in *Rangalla*. (It is not known, however, if these prisoners had the awful habit of swallowing pineapples.)

To this day, the *Overdale Wyke's* 12-pounder reminds the Navy of the gallant trawler turned minesweeper which the Royal Navy armed and put to sea to protect the coasts of Ceylon.

Beauchamp, the captain of the CRNVR, was a hippopotamus of a man. Commander W.G. Beauchamp was so broad of beam that the Navy shipwrights had to make a special desk and chair to accommodate his bulk. He persuaded the government to buy more anti-submarine craft and small minesweepers from Burma.

'The Irrawaddy Flotilla Company,' he said, 'they are working like little Burmese beavers. They have the ships we need.'

The government agreed and the Irrawaddy Company was pleased. They would deliver A/S and M/S craft. Built to the best Admiralty specifications: echo-sounding equipment, orapesa sweeps, the works. A silver mug was sent to the Navy, exquisite Burmese craftsmanship. A gift. The shipyard went to work but the vessels never came. All the Navy got was a silver mug. The Japanese invaded Burma, and Rangoon was never to be the same again!

To this day, in the Kochchikade wardroom, Commander Beauchamp's elephantine desk and chair remains. Also, the silver mug, and a fine assortment of Japanese Samurai swords taken from surrendering Japanese officers and from those who found their attempts at *hara-kiri* defeated. These invitations to ritual suicide were distributed to all Allied units.

As was typical of the British hold on Ceylon at the time, Paymaster Lieutenant Susantha de Fonseka was asked to turn in his sword, resign. De Fonseka was not only a naval officer. He was also a politician, and as a politician, he was accused of dishonouring the king's uniform.

As a Member of the State Council and Deputy Speaker, Susantha had gone directly to the House in uniform, directly from training camp in Kochchikade, having had no time to slip into civvies.

There, as a Lieutenant of the CRNVR, he had participated in a hot debate and made many scathing assaults on the poor price paid by Britain for Ceylon rubber. His constituency (Panadura on the west coast) was a rubber-growing one, and Susantha accused the British of bleeding the country.

The chief secretary, a Britisher, was suitably appalled. He reported to the governor that Susantha's conduct as an officer was most unbecoming. 'He was critical of His Majesty's government in Whitehall while in the king's uniform!' he yapped.

The governor was furious and called for Susantha's resignation (It is Simply Not Done, old boy!)

With the war over, it was time to make the Ceylon Navy unit self-sufficient. Admiral Lord Louis Mountbatten made, what could be deemed, a kiss-off inspection of the CRNVR, where he was full of praise for the men and their role in the defence of Ceylon. The war was over. Ceylon must ever be proud of her seamen and prouder yet of this fighting core of well-trained men. It was time to forget that this was a Royal Naval Reserve. This was His Majesty's Navy—a fighting force in its own right.

In a letter to Beauchamp, Mountbatten, as Supreme Allied Commander, South East Asia Command, wrote:

> '. . . I feel I must write you a personal note of congratulation . . . I was much struck by their smartness and bearing, and Rear Admiral Nicholson has given me a most encouraging report of their work. You must feel justly proud of your force . . .'

Soon after, Kochchikade witnessed the demobilization of the CRNVR and the departure of Commander Beauchamp.

Henceforth, the Royal Ceylon Navy would be led by a Ceylonese, Commander Royce de Mel.

Thus did the CRNVR die a most natural death. The Ceylon force was to be known henceforth as the Royal Navy with a nucleus of one hundred officers and men. This new force inherited the Royal Navy shore establishment in Colombo, *HMS Highflyer*, with its extensive complex of signals tower and bridge, sick bay, armoury, wireles cabins, seamens' huts and junior officers' messes, motor transport office, officers' quarters and wardroom.

'Highflyer' remained as a signals routing centre, a small office set beside the main signals office. The complex sprawled along Flagstaff Street, behind the King's House, the official residence of the governor. At Galle Buck, the Ceylon Navy also had the RN swimming pool which is in barnacle-crusted ruins today. The complex was re-christened 'Gemunu'. It was now a ship of the Royal Ceylon Navy, and so was *Rangalla*, which was the new name given to *HMS Uva*, and other naval coastal establishments in Karainagar and Talaimannar in the north. The Talaimannar base became *HMCyS Elara*. Also, the Navy took over the Ceylon west receiving station at Welisara.

In the years up to 1953, officer cadets were selected and sent to Dartmouth for training. Also, a Ceylon Navy contingent took part in the London Victory Parade.

This was the Royal Ceylon Navy that Carloboy joined in 1953, a Navy that came into being with the passing of the Navy Act No. 34 of 1950. The minesweeper *Vijaya* was already in its berth at Kochchikade when Carloboy signed up. It was sailed in from Grimsby under the command of Lieutenant Commander Rajan Kadirgamar.

Truly, a one-ship Navy. The *Vijaya* was all they had. In the north, all the Navy had were two small MPB's (motor patrol boats). They were the *Hansaya* (swan) and *Lihiniya* (seagull). Later two other MPB's, the *Diyakawa* (cormorant) and the *Korawakka* (teal) would join the flotilla, mostly on anti-illicit immigration duties. The only sizeable purchases in later years were the minesweeper *Parakrama* and the

HMCyS Kotiya (tiger) which was an SDB (seaward defence boat).

Small wonder, then, the boys found Navy life a chore. They were, what one would uncharitably term, 'harbour sailors'. People would time and again refer to them as the famous 'One-ship Navy'.

In 1953, Carloboy von Bloss found this situation most unsatisfactory. The *Vijaya* was the only saving grace. If only his cap bore the legend *'HMCyS Vijaya'* in gold letters on the black ribbon! How proudly would he wear it! To any he could then say he was on board a ship—not weeding or digging or scrubbing heads ashore!

But all said and done, the foundations had been well-laid. The Navy would not die. With republic status, it became the SLN (Sri Lanka Navy) and is a force to be reckoned with today. Carloboy wouldn't know . . . he upped and quit in 1957.

In 1958, being a glutton for punishment, he joined the Ceylon Army Signals Corps!

15

Of Bashed-in Doors and Royal Guard and Winking at the Queen

The final weeks of recruit training was upon the boys, the hours passing in a sort of desperate slow motion. The boys naturally became peculiarly restless and thoughts of the return to Colombo sparked a wave of indiscipline never before experienced.

Colombo. Carloboy thought of his old stomping ground with an eagerness that could hardly be contained. So attractive did the thought of the return become that he would sometimes stand on the parade ground, look up to the hills and follow the tiny line of the train that laboured up the track. There it went. The lifeline. The train that would take him back soon.

As the impatience grew, the boys became positively dangerous. A highlight of the final week was a riproaring shindig between the recruits of the Army and the Navy. There were enough black eyes, welts and bruises to distribute to their friends in Colombo as well. Bandarawela regarded the mayhem with horror. Earnest parishioners had even urged the priest to sing a special thanksgiving mass.

So it was that ninety fully-fledged sailors finally entrained for Colombo, ready to raise Cain on land or sea. It was said later that the CO and officers and staff of *Rangalla* had embraced each other and all but sobbed in relief, while Seraphin kept sniffing and saying, 'What about my door then? What about my front door?'

'Oh, fuck your bloody door!' The CO had blazed, 'what about Rashid? Still on crutches!'

It had been Yusuf's idea. The heavy roller, dragged out of the bog, had been kept at the bottom of the incline. Down the dip, and across the intersecting path, stood Seraphin's bungalow where, for the most part of each day, his singing, swinging wife, waited for the soft rap on the door. The boys were never tired of watching how Petty Officer Rashid, looking most nonchalant, with his cap pulled well over his eyes, would saunter to the door and tap.

The window curtain would move a fraction. Rashid would stand, glance around furtively. He would wait for the click of the lock, then quickly push at the door and slide in. Once inside he would give cause to the delectable Dora to sing her annoying song to her cuckold husband when he stumbled in later in the day.

'He's in again. That's the second time today,' Carloboy had observed.

'Every chance he gets,' Todwell had nodded.

Yusuf said that it wasn't fair. He eyed the roller for a while and a light dawned. 'Here,' he said, 'Help me pull this up the road a little.'

'For what?'

'Come and pull. We'll give that bugger the shock of his life.'

They twigged what the ordinary telegraphist intended and grinned widely. Chuckling, they helped drag the roller up the incline.

'Watch it,' Carloboy said, 'it must run straight.'

'All give a push when I say,' Yusuf puffed, 'otherwise it may just roll a little and stop.'

They positioned the roller with care, straining to hold it. 'God, it weighs a bloody ton,' Carloboy panted, 'will it go straight?'

Aloy made sure that every little stone was cleared. 'Like a bloody arrow,' he said.

'Now all together . . . push!'

The roller careened down the rude path, shot across the narrow road and with the malevolence of a Spanish bull, made straight for Seraphin's front door. It hit the thin dealwood with spectacular vim, smashed through, and there was a roar of blue fright and a puma-like screech which could have only been Dora not having an orgasm.

From the side of the house came the sound of splintering glass and the boys, even as they melted away, saw a figure hurtle out to fall heavily across a bed of barbetan daisies. It was Rashid, who seemed to have pressed an eject button, sailing out of the bedroom sans his pants. The sound of Dora having several fits of varying intensity was accompanied by deep groans from the naked Rashid. The man struggled to rise, then flopped down with agony writ all over his face in large wood type. 'My leg is broken,' he wailed, 'somebody help.'

It wasn't his leg. It was his ankle. The man was in an ecstasy of suffering.

'Vanish,' said Nugawira tersely.

'No, wait; can't leave him like that—'.

'But if we go to help—'

'You run and tell the quartermaster. We'll try to help the bugger. If anyone asks say we heard him crying out and went to see what.'

Rashid begged for his trousers. Dora had dragged on a housecoat and was yipping and yodelling at the roller that had come to rest in her hall and at the door which was no longer anything remotely like a door. Rashid was carried to the regulating office and laid out for inspection. He was not an attractive sight. Mud clung to his shrivelled penis which, in its circumcised state, was quite repulsive. The duty officer sent him to the sick bay where he was cleaned up and his swollen ankle prodded quite mercilessly. He was then made respectable and sent to hospital.

The duty officer shook his head. 'What that Seraphin's wife sees in him I'll never know,' he muttered.

When the ninety boys arrived in Colombo, they were in

much the same state of disorder and disarray as they had been when they stepped out at the Diyatalawa railway station two-and-a-half months ago. They were to be later told that their training had been clipped by two weeks, and all because of the Queen's visit.

At the gate of Gemunu they were mustered and looked over by a frosty leading seaman with pimples. 'From now on', he barked, 'Consider yourselves the Royal welcome service. After colours every morning you will fall in on the drill ground for parade. Number ten drill order. I don't have to warn you about your turnout. We have more imagination than the chaps at *Rangalla* and we use it better. You will now report to your sections. Signalmen and telegraphists to the main signals office; stokers to the motor transport office; electricians to the office next to the PO's mess; SBA's to the sick bay; cooks and stewards to the galley. Seamen stand fast! The rest . . . deees-miss!'

Carloboy, together with Nugawira, Yusuf and an assortment of Fernandos and Pereras, made his way to the main signals office. He introduced himself. So did the others.

A Yeoman, Barnett, gawked at the straggling bunch of sleepy-eyed recruits. 'Who the fuck are you? What d'you want? Go away, go away.'

'But we just came,' Carloboy said feebly.

Barnett closed his eyes. 'I know. Thank you so much. Nice of you to come. Pleased to meet you and all that. Do come again—in about two years. Patrick, we have a visitation of the pox!'

Carloboy gaped. If Navy Signals didn't know they were coming there had to be something very wrong with naval communications.

'We are from *Rangalla*,' said Daft.

'They are from *Rangalla*!' cried Leading Signalman Patrick, leaping from his chair.

'You mean you are O/Sigs?' the Yeoman asked.

'Yes, PO.'

'Not PO, man,' he said testily, 'not PO. What did they

teach you in *Rangalla*? There are no petty officers in Signals. The very idea! I'm an Yeoman of Signals . . . ' he leaned forward conspiratorially, 'PO's are of the common herd—seamen and stokers and even the telegraphists upstairs. You can call me Yeo. I like it. All of you are O/Sigs?'

'No, there are four O/Tels, Yeo.'

'Four? Who are the four? Shoo! Scat! Upstairs! Don't ever come in here unless the signal tower falls on you or something!'

The four scat. The wireless cabin was halfway up the winding staircase that led to the signals deck, bridge and masts.

'Well now,' said Yeoman Barnett, rubbing his hands together, 'how nice. A bunch of O/Sigs all our own. Haven't had little O/Sigs in here for a long time, eh? Patrick?'

Leading Signalman Patrick grinned.

Barnett looked them over. A pained expression crept into his eyes. 'But you look so bloody awful. What have you been doing? Jumping the railway engine with your clothes on? Ha, ha. We have our little jokes, eh? Patrick?'

Leading Signalman Patrick grinned.

'Have you seen your mess and got your bunks and lockers?'

'No, Yeo.'

'There you are. Can't have you in here looking like bloody louts, can we. Do you know,' his voice dropped to a whisper, 'even the Captain of the Navy walks these decks. Yes, and the chief of staff and officers here, officers there, officers-officers everywhere. I think they should get themselves organized, eh? Patrick?'

Leading Signalman Patrick grinned. Then he stopped grinning. 'Report to the signalmen's mess,' he snarled, 'Put away your kit, bathe, get the fleas out of your backsides, brush your bloody teeth, arrange your bunks, give your dirty linen to the camp laundry and report back in an hour! Get moving!'

They moved. When they looked back, Yeoman Barnett was trying to balance a pencil on his nose and Leading

Signalman Patrick was grinning. It was hard to tell who was the madder.

When they got back, the MSO was crowded. Yeoman Barnett was nowhere to be seen, but a goodly crowd of signalmen and leading signalmen welcomed them with cries of gladness. Buckets and mops were thrust into their hands. 'Scrub,' they were told, 'the staircase . . . you, you, upstairs—signals deck . . . arrange the flag locker . . . you—haul tight the halyards, get the projectors polished . . . you—go to the galley—bring tea . . .' They seemed to have come as a godsend. There was lots of work to be done, and henceforth they were the chosen slaves. Viva le Navy!

They were placed in the tender care of Yeoman Louis who was their signals instructor. That worthy kept them endlessly wagging their hands in semaphoric combinations and reading the Morse code on a blinker until their eyes burned. Then to the buzzer and the endless repetitions of did-daah—A; daah-did-did-did—B; daah-did-daah-did—C and on and on.

All this signals training went on after dinner. Three calls the Navy relished: 'Hands to breakfast,'; 'Hands to dinner'; and 'Hands to supper'. Each morning the recruits of *Rangalla* came together again, all ninety of them, under the wary eye of GI Brady who had that air of a man prepared to do and die for his Queen.

They marched. God, how they marched. They were even marched in the streets of Colombo in ceremonial number six uniforms. Leading Seaman Baldy trotted ahead of the column, beating a tattoo on a drum. They saluted the Queen *in absentia* so many times a day that the poor lady must surely have had queasy afternoons and incredibly dreamy nights. They practised street lining and were scattered all over the city roads where stray dogs sniffed their boots and raised eager hind legs. And they were each howled at no less than seventy-three times a day.

'Von Bloss! Your rifle is ten degrees out. Keep that fucking forearm parallel to the ground!'

'It's parallel, sir.'

'It's not! Don't argue!'

Carloboy shifted his forearm a fraction.

'Sims! Your web belt is a disgrace. And there's Brasso all over the bloody canvas!'

Sims keeps mum. Nothing helps when the Guard Commander is on the prod . . . Unless it was a big orang-utan strolling on the kerb singing 'Swanee'.

'Fernando! Fall out! *Fall out!* What is that thing on your head?'

'My cap, sir.'

It *is* his cap, but he doesn't tell the Guard Commander how it had flown off his head when he was on the flag deck of the signals tower and how it had been pancaked by a passing jeep on the road below.

'A cap? *You call that a cap! It's like a fucking urinal!* Are you going to stand on the quay with a cap like that? *Do you want to disgrace the Royal Guard?'*

As the days sped by, the business of disgrace became quite profound, vast in scope and application. They were, it seemed, reaching for that Ultimate State of Abjection.

'Do you want to disgrace the Navy . . . your country . . . your father and mother . . . the government . . . me?'

By the time the final full-dress rehearsal on the quay came around, they had smeared and sullied the good name and standing of everything within and beyond reach—the Captain of the Navy, the East Indies Fleet, the South East Asian Region, the Commonwealth of Nations . . .

Having displayed their firm intention to wallow in trenches of undrilled iniquity, they were by no means disposed to having the Queen think unkindly of them. Accordingly, they brought forth reserves of elbow grease in order to present, at the fateful hour, a brave show. Kits were brought to peak perfection. Prince Phillip, they were informed, would be in the uniform of an Admiral of the fleet. They were determined to show the man that they were as good a part of the fleet as any.

'She's quite a peach, isn't she?' Todwell said.

'Who?'

'The Queen.'

'Wha—oh . . . the Queen? Yes, men. Good-looker. Nice legs also, I think.'

'You know,' Carloboy mused, 'wonder what she will do if we put her a wink when she's inspecting us.'

Sims stared. 'Wha-aat? My God, they'll lock you up and throw the bloody key away.'

'Gorsh . . .' said Todwell with reverence.

'I say,' someone sang out, 'pukka idea.'

'So what's a wink?' another asked, 'Comes and goes—phut!—in a flash, no?'

The idea festered. 'So what'll she do? She's the Queen, no? She'll have to just queen it.'

Some gasped, other chuckled.

'Hey, von Bloss,' Nugawira carolled, 'what's the bet you won't do it?'

The conversation was getting serious, also quite out of depth. 'Who says I won't do it?' Carloboy demanded.

'Oh, you can. *Anybody* can. The thing is *will* you do it?' Todwell asked.

'And how will we know if you winked or not?' Bijja Fernando asked, 'as if we will be able to see.'

'And,' Sims chortled, 'what's the use of even winking if the Queen doesn't notice it?'

There were shouts of laughter.

'You've got to wait until she looks into your face and then put a wink,' Daft advised.

The idea took hold. 'What can she do? Whad'you think she will do? Can she complain to the Guard Commander that a sailor winked at her?' Carloboy argued.

'Serposin' she does?'

'Bullshit! She's the Queen.'

'So okay, maybe she'll ignore. But she can tell afterwards to somebody. Then what'll happen?'

'Who's she going to tell? Prince Phillip?'

'Oh balls,' said Carloboy (and he wasn't after canteen beer either), 'if she looks at me, I'll just close one eye . . . very slowly.'

The boys roared.

Greatly cheered by what would or could happen, they put the finishing touches to their kits and descended on the canteen to celebrate. Barely half an hour later, the bosun's pipe drowned the din of the canteen. 'Royal Guard will fall in outside the quartermaster's lobby. On the double!'

'Hell,' said Sims, 'is the Queen coming tonight?'

They slouched up to the small gateside cubicle with its gravelled walkway. There, they formed rank and watched as the duty officer swept up with an assortment of petty officers and leading seamen.

'All right! *Who's the bastard who's going to wink at the Queen?'*

So the cat was out and ranging free The boys were shocked. A Judas among them. Carloboy knew that the duty officer's eyes were scorching him. He decided to lie as firmly as he could.

'We were just having fun, sir . . . just thinking the Queen is a good-looker. I think there has been some misunderstanding . . .'

'Misunderstanding! *It'll be a bloody international misunderstanding!* What is it you have to say, von Bloss?'

'We were just having some harmless fun in the mess, sir . . . talking about the Queen—'

'And you said you will wink at her! *Did you or did you not?*

'Not actually winking, sir,' Carloboy lied firmly. 'Just said the Queen was very good-looking. If she was anybody else—'

'Then you will wink?' the duty officer pounced.

'Why, yes sir.'

'So that's the sort of bugger you are!'

'But sir, what's the harm in winking at a pretty girl?'

'*Shut up!* What's the harm . . . let me tell you something you—you—you lecher! When you are in the Queen's uniform you will not wink at girls! *Is that clear?* You will respect and honour the uniform you wear. *Is that clear?* Haramanis, what did von Bloss say?'

Haramanis had an axe to grind. He had never forgiven Carloboy for the hard time he had been given in the *Rangalla* refectory. Also, who could forget that plate of rice on his head? He cringed. He knew that all eyes—most hard, unforgiving eyes, were boring into him. 'He said—he said he was going to—going to wink, sir.'

'Wink? Wink? Wink at who? Out with it! Repeat what you told the quartermaster.'

'The Queen, sir,' (very faintly).

'Wassat?'

'The Queen, sir.'

The duty officer turned on Carloboy, 'So you were just having fun, eh?'

'He's lying, sir. He doesn't like me.'

'Oh, is that so? Well, I don't like you either. Do you want to cause a bloody international incident! You in this habit of winking at every bloody woman you see?'

'Yes—no, sir.'

The duty officer grimaced. 'I don't suppose you will actually have the balls to wink at the Queen . . . but I've heard a lot about you—*all of you!* You are the worst intake of recruits we ever had the misfortune to select. We are still getting reports from *Rangalla* and from the Army and Air Force camps as well. So!' very fiercely, 'You were a pain in the arse there but you're not going to be a pain in the arse here! *Is that clear?* This is a disciplined fighting force. Not a bloody home for vagrants or—or—' glaring at Carloboy, 'sex maniacs!'

He eyeballed them fiercely, hands clenching and unclenching *a la* the Boston Strangler. 'Von Bloss! I'll be watching you. *Like a bloody hawk!* If you bat an eyelid, move one fucking eyelash—so help me—bloody lunatics! Wink at the Queen! And that goes for all of you. Get out! *Get out!* Dismiss!'

The boys were very glad to. Haramani`s bolted to the galley, but not before Todwell elevated him a couple of feet with a swift boot directed unerringly at his backside. Carloboy raced after the weaselly cook but was foiled when the man leaped into the galley where a chief petty officer was checking the wardroom menu.

They returned to their beer somewhat dispiritedly.

The next morning they would be marched out to salute the Queen. Salute her. Not wink at her.

They all agreed that that was a great pity.

16

History—the Marshall Plan and the Japanese Aggressor

Eisenhower was very frustrated. 'Ships! Ships! All we need is ships!' he exclaimed.

On April Fools Day, 1942, the American Secretary of War and the Chief of Army Staff came up with a plan. They gave President Roosevelt a blueprint for the invasion of Northern France. An Anglo-American invasion. It was Eisenhower who authored the plan. He had been newly promoted and was in charge of US Army Plans and Operations staff.

The consensus was that the US should be on the defensive in the Pacific and be all-out offensive in the Atlantic. Two large oceans. All Eisenhower needed was the ships.

The plan was as good as any. The main idea was to keep Russia fighting, and all that was needed to achieve this was to turn the Germans west. Let the Russians think that Germany was backing away to tend its western front and the Russians would follow on with all the viciousness they could muster.

American ground and air forces would then meet the Germans head-on in Europe. Eisenhower was certain the European Axis could be destroyed. Then, the US could concentrate on the Pacific where Japan had become over-aggressive.

The crux of the matter was the moving of men. Eisenhower needed to move either two armoured divisions or three infantry divisions to Britain. That was all the force he could plan for, for that was all the ships he could muster. But, he insisted, up to 400,000 more troops and airmen needed to be moved to Europe in 1943. If only he had the ships, he said, he would have a one-million-strong force—up to thirty divisions—that would, with back-up air cover, storm into France, smash German coastal defences, and set up a Second Front in Europe.

But with Hitler causing initial havoc in Russia, Eisenhower knew he couldn't wait a year. Britain would have to power the first storm across the Channel, establish a foothold, a bridgehead in France and hold on to it until America could come in strength.

The Chief of Army Staff, George Marshall, agreed. He was convinced that northern France was the only place where a powerful offensive could be launched. He sent a memo to Roosevelt, stating that 'successful attack in this area will afford the maximum of support to the Russian front'. He also said that this was a priority. Japan would have to wait.

America had already deployed 132,000 troops, but the bulk of them had been sent to the Pacific to keep the Japanese in check. It was not an easy ocean to defend. Its range was staggering—from the Aleutians to New Guinea. Within this arc was Midway, the Hawaiian islands, the Fiji islands, New Caledonia and Australia.

The Americans simply had to hold the islands. They needed to concentrate on air power rather than sea power and the general idea was to make every island a stationary aircraft carrier. But they also needed heavy bombers and strong bodies of marines to hold the bases. Again, the need was for ships.

The US Chief of Naval Operations in the Pacific was a tough old salt. Admiral Earnest King. He had only one objective: avenge Pearl Harbour, drive the Japanese out of the Philippines and give Japan what-for. His plan was simple. Halt Japan; then hit her for six.

But getting the ships was the problem. German U-boats were taking a heavy toll of Allied shipping in the western Atlantic and the Caribbean. The US government was also faced with conflicting demands. For one, General MacArthur was peeved about his evacuation from Corregidor in the Philippines. He wanted an early counter-offensive. He also feared a Japanese advance on Australia.

Australia, too, was anxious, and moroever, the American public was clamouring for revenge. Pearl Harbour was foremost on everyone's mind. The Japanese had come, wrecked, and gone. What was the government doing?

Was it to be Germany and Europe first . . . or Japan?

Needless to say, King was most put out. Roosevelt endorsed Eisenhower's plan. Pressure would be put on Britain to join in an all-out campaign in Western Europe.

Roosevelt, in accepting 'Germany first', put Britain in a tight spot. Britain had tried to convince America that it was suicide to attempt a frontal attack on Germany. It was wiser to wait until Russian resistance had weakened Germany's military strength. The British also initially pooh-poohed the idea of a cross-Channel attack. There were, she said, not enough ships and landing craft.

America was not impressed. The plan (to be known as the Marshall plan) was the only plan she had. Roosevelt sent Chief of Army Staff George Marshall and his confidential emissary, Harry Hopkins, to London. They had to convince the British prime minister to fall in line. It was a do-or-die situation.

It was time, America thought, that Britain got her finger out.

17

Of Queen's Cups and Rowing Boats and Rolling out the Barrel

They marched out . . . band leading.

They lined up on the Queen Elizabeth Quay of the Colombo harbour, where the Royal yacht *Brittania* was tied up alongside.

They waited for the Queen of England.

They were inspected by GI Brady and the Captain of the Navy and assorted captains and commanders. They passed muster. The morning sun set their ceremonial bayonets ablaze and fired the buckles on their webbing. They looked good . . . and they knew it.

But there was a bit of a mish-mash. First out of the royal yacht, stepping out daintily in a dress of cool, apple green, was the Queen's lady-in-waiting. Perhaps she jumped the gun, but on sighting her, the shore battery jumped to the guns too. A 21-gun salute from the Galle Buck battery shook the air with great hollow thumps. Like a giant smacking his belly after eating his Wellington boots. *Bwackh! Bwackh! Bwackh!*

It was only after the Ceylon Armoured Corps had ceased firing that it was realized that an enthusiastic island had accorded the Queen's lady-in-waiting a Royal Salute, doubtless raising the good lady's self-esteem several notches.

Later, the Army maintained that the Navy had given the signal to fire and there was much recrimination with the exchange of lots of heavily-worded signals.

Her Majesty Queen Elizabeth II stepped onto the saluting dais in perfect peace and quiet, punctured maybe by the querulous hoots of an uncaring tugboat. Then came the tremolo of Lieutenant Commander Lawyer. It warbled, 'Royal Gaaarde . . . prezen—tarmz!' Prince Phillip saluted briskly. The Royal Standard clapped boisterously in the breeze. The band played 'God Save the Queen'. The guard stood, each as stiff as a stick of Brighton rock.

A pretty cursory inspection, actually. An officer strode ahead and turned to face Carloboy, glaring balefully at him as the Royal party approached. The Queen ignored them both. There was no reason why a reigning sovereign should look into any particular sailor's face, is there? Isabella of Spain did, we know, but that was Columbus, and she was one hungry woman.

Later, Carloboy told the others, 'So what the hell, men, the only sailor she looked at was Prince Phillip. And what did she do? Went and married the bugger!'

Formalities over, it was time for more fun and games. A special horse race would be held at the Colombo Turf Club course. It would be, naturally, the Queen's Cup. Her Majesty would be there . . . and so would the Navy, for over a million people swarmed in, each trying to get a glimpse of the Queen.

To this day, it is hoped, Petty Officer Ronnie Meedle has, among his souvenirs, photographs of the crowds, held in check by sheer Navy brawn. One photograph raised much comment. It showed Carloboy, Ordinary Seaman Vanlangenburg and Ordinary Telegraphist Yusuf grimly keeping back a press of thousands, their elbows locked together, feet dug firmly in and refusing to bend before the surging mass behind them. Perched on Carloboy's shoulders was a bejewelled, sari-clad lass of about twenty. She had climbed up there to get a grandstand view of the Queen. Carloboy, all said, grinned and bore her.

The developed photograph was taken to the petty officers' mess and then, being too good to be true, to the wardroom where it was examined by the very officer who had bawled out the guard on the eve of Her Majesty's arrival.

'Hah! I knew that bugger was a bloody cad! A woman on his shoulders and—and where are his bloody hands? What is he doing?'

Many imaginative theories were tossed around. Carloboy was summoned to the PO's mess.

'Ah, so it's you. Good. Saw this picture? Going to send it to the papers.'

'My god, PO, there was such a crush . . . .'

'Crush is right. Anything for a crush, no? Who gave you orders to carry girls on your back?'

'But I didn't know!'

'Balls! A woman climbs up your spine and you don't know? Tell that to the fucking marines!'

PO Meadle growled. 'I was there. Why couldn't she climb on my shoulders? You know this girl?'

'Never saw her before in my life.'

'OK, but what I want to know is where are your hands?'

'My hands?'

'Yes. Not to be seen in the snap.'

'But PO, we had to lock hands together behind our backs. Form a solid wall. That's what we had to do.'

'Oh yes—solid wall. And a solid piece of flesh on top of you. What did you lock your hands on? Her bum?'

There is no convincing a dirty-minded sailor. Carloboy shrugged, then asked, 'PO, can I have this photo?'

'What? Get out!'

When the Queen left, it was the Army's turn to see her off. The boys relaxed, slipped into their everyday routine, began to pursue their normal shipboard tasks. The main signals office was the centre for the routing of and distribution of signals. Between study hours, signalmen were detailed to take post here as messengers and gophers, clearing signals to every branch of the service. But there was the practical training too, which took the boys in number eight working blues to Kochchikade where they had to row large, cumbersome whalers in the port of Colombo, usually in the early hours of the morning.

This was much looked forward to and became particularly interesting when the big Peninsula & Orient passenger liners were in port. These vessels would ply the UK-Australia route and would steam in with hundreds of females lining the decks—tourists and passengers taking in the sights and sounds of the port.

The sailors would take in the sights too—always an eyeful—and it became customary to row up to the proud liners, ship oars, and spend the most of their time looking up. It was unanimously agreed that when considering a female's many charms, the worm's eye view was quite the best.

'Why the hell aren't you rowing?' the coxswain would demand.

'Shhh killick, just look up, will you.'

'Wha-oh-jeez! See that third girl from the left? Here, pull up a little closer.'

'How about the one next to that fat fellow with the straw hat?'

'Oh woooo!'

At the jetty, an exasperated petty officer would await their return. 'Where the devil have you been?'

'Rowing, PO. Rowing and looking.'

'Rowing and looking? What the hell sort of a thing is that? You're late!'

'But PO, how to row anywhere without looking?'

'Oh fuck off!'

Which, as we now know well enough, is standard Naval procedure.

It is also fortunate for the Sri Lanka Navy of today that Able Seaman Percy Nathali is no longer a force to be reckoned with. Just a few months before these words were written, the news came that Percy had turned, from a sailor's life to that of a farmer ashore. This would have been to Carloboy (if he were consulted on the subject) utterly, incongruously unthinkable! Percy, Carloboy realized, was the most obstreperous and redoubtable sailor any country could boast of: completely crazy and totally dismissive of discipline of any sort.

The new intake goggled. They had fancied themselves the new boys on the block, ready to take on any and everybody. They soon found that Gemunu had its own 'bad eggs'—men who had miraculously survived every heavy disciplinary hand. Of them, Percy, like that Abou something character, led all the rest.

The boys had a thirty-two bunk hut in which they were expected to maintain the naval code at all times. The hut figured largely in daily routine—beds to be arranged, floor scrubbed, the little veranda kept spotless, the drain running past it cleaned. The hut was not a refuge, really, for the adjoining hut, with its windows opening towards theirs, was the canteen, and there, as would be expected, sailors were permitted to be noisy and get noisier with each tankard of beer.

After a day's stint in the signals tower and the MSO, they would come in to flop on their bunks and consider their boots with a deep hatred. These had to be polished, as usual, and their gym shoes pipe-clayed for 5 a.m. physical training (universally loathed).

It was on such an evening, when they had come in with 'aaahs' of relief, that Percy popped in. He gave them a most affectionate smile. He carried a hand drill and a long length of rubber tubing.

Carloboy grinned. 'Hey Percy, what's that for?'

Percy bummed a cigarette and gave a small cackle. 'You know something? You guys are the most favoured in this whole shit'ole. You have a hut next to the canteen.'

'So?'

They knew that this unpredictable able seaman had not come in to discuss the location of their hut. Nathali, as the Captain of the Navy had once remarked, was a fiend incarnate. Seven years an able seaman, promoted to leading seaman in which exalted state he lasted a mere three weeks. His anchor had been torn off his sleeve for some particular devilry. He was a law unto himself.

He nodded solemnly at the boys. Like a parson who had just been shown the pearly gates. 'Yes, yes. Fine hut, fine hut. Really like the lie of it. Can you see—' he did the grand tour, 'your window, canteen window . . . other window, canteen window . . .' he walked down the line of beds, 'whose bunk is this?'

'Mine,' said Roy Fernando.

'Mmmm, wonderful. Nothing like a nice bunk. And beer. That's what makes everything worthwhile. I'm going to use this bed for a while, OK?'

'Use?' Roy stared blankly, 'Use how?' He studied the hand drill in Percy's hand nervously, 'you're going to bore holes in my bed?'

'Don't talk bilge. What do I want to do anything like that for? You want a hole in your bed, make one yourself. I'm going to—' he stretched luxuriously, '—lie down for a little.'

The boys stared. Bijja hissed, 'He's up to something.'

Then, with a dragging of work boots, Stoker Mechanic Ryan breezed in, made for the reclining Percy and asked, 'How? Everything OK?'

'Perfect,' Percy murmured, 'shoo these buggers out and shut the door.'

Ryan turned on the boys, thrusting forward his ham-like face, 'You heard? Fuck off!'

Theirs not to reason why. They went.

Carloboy said, 'Wait a bit, we'll take our plates and mugs. They'll pipe supper in an hour.'

'Yes, take, take and go.'

They stood outside, bewildered. Pushed out of their own hut. Something was afoot, but what? They went to the canteen, sat, kept an eye on their hut through the open windows. An assortment of seamen, many of them Percy's cronies, were inside. It was beginning to look like the gathering of a witches' coven.

'What the hell is going on?' Sims asked.

Carloboy shrugged.

The evening mellowed. They had supper, then drifted back. The door was firmly shut. So were the windows. No sound save an indistinct snoring.

Nugawira put an ear to the door. 'Snoring. Sure I'm sure. Come and listen.'

'Gone to sleep in our hut!' Roy said bitterly, 'Like bloody pirates they have taken our hut!'

Carloboy pondered. 'But why should they? There's something up, I'm sure. Let's kick the bloody door in.'

They found that the Navy in Colombo made doors too stout for the most concerted assault. Perhaps another heavy roller . . .

Then Daft raised a drippy boot, 'Ai, what's this?' He pointed to a stream of frothy liquid which was seeping from under the door. It became a thin stream that coursed around their feet to the drain.

'Piss!' said Yusuf, 'It's piss!'

The liquid was certainly of the right colour.

'Piss? Jeeeesus, they're pumping all over the floor?'

They banged lustily on the door. Yusuf crept around to the space between huts to thump on the windows. The hullabaloo brought the duty officer on the double.

'What's going on here?'

The boys shook their heads, did not trouble to give him the customary salute. 'We can't get into our hut, sir. The door's locked on the inside.'

'Who's inside?'

'Don't know sir.'

'What's all this stuff? My God, what's this? *Have you bastards been pumping all over the place!'*

'Sir, it's coming from under the door, sir.'

'What the devil—' the duty officer banged on the door, 'This is the OOD,' he boomed, *'Open this door at once!'*

No answer.

'One of you fetch a shipwright. Tell him to bring something to force the door.'

'Yessir,' Nugawira trotted off.

The amber liquid kept flowing.

It took shipwright Silva twenty minutes to remove the heavy lock and lo! when the door swung open there was a sight to freeze the toughest duty officer. Six sailors . . . fast asleep. From the slats of the window over Percy's head a length of rubber tubing emerged, and from Percy's end of this tube poured the liquid that had been mistaken for urine. The floor was awash with it. Beer! The hut reeked of beer. Three bunks were soaked in beer. Percy and his cronies lay, comatose, each wearing the hint of a seraphic smile. They were blotto on beer—gallons of it, while gallons more piped out in a steady stream.

The boys gaped, then together with the duty officer, crowded round Roy's bed and the snoring Percy. Silva examined the rubber tube and gave a wide grin.

'Ah sir, very cute these fallows, just see what have been doing.'

The duty officer saw, and strange things must have danced a gavotte before his eyes. He seized Percy by the hair, jerked him up. The able seaman merely sank back in a stupor.

Silva pushed open the window, dived out and hooted for the leading seaman who officiated in the canteen. 'Oi! you fine fallow, no? Free beer all giving to this side. See how much beer have left in your barrel.'

The leading seaman was dumbstruck. He poked his head out of the window, saw the rubber tube stuck into his large 176-gallon cask and choked. Then he howled, 'Take that bloody thing out!'

'Can't, can't,' Silva howled back, 'If take out pipe, will all come from the hole. Mus' get a bung to block.'

The duty officer told the boys, 'Carry these buggers out one by one. Put them in the corridor. Get the QM here, and call an SBA.'

They hauled the six beer-laden men out. Next door, the canteen was in ferment. Their hut smelled like a brewery. Beer-sodden beds were stripped and the stores opened to issue new mattresses and linen. Percy and his cronies slept on . . .

Even the First Lieutenant couldn't summon the imagination to decree fitting punishment. 'There's only one thing I'd like to do,' he glowered, 'shoot you and dance on your graves!'

Percy was drafted to Talaimannar, to *HMCyS Elara,* a shore base in the north of the island where he was expected to prevent, as best as he could, the illicit immigration of south Indians to the island.

Peace reigned in Gemunu. Only the leading seaman who administered the canteen remained jumpy. He had, he said, 152 gallons of beer in his barrel. Now he had only 24. And there were other of Nathali's stripe in the camp. He implored the First Lieutenant to get rid of Percy's cronies as well.

The First Lieutenant wobbled. '*What!* I sent Nathali to Elara. Alone he's a national disaster. Use your head, killick. What do you think will happen in a place like that if the others are there with him?'

Did we say peace? Scratch that. Okay, comparative peace, anyway. We'll settle for that!

18

History—Target Ceylon . . . Japan's Westward Advance

America was unable to appreciate, at the start, how the British Chiefs of Staff were dismally considering the threat to their Indian Ocean and Middle East communications after the Pearl Harbour disaster. Also, America's battle fleet had been hit for six.

The Japanese, led by the Army of Yamashita had pushed the last American survivors out of the Philippines, and Japan now held the Dutch and British East Indies, Singapore, Malaya and the Sumatra Straits.

There was no doubt about it. Everything pointed to a westward advance. The Japanese would strike across the Bay of Bengal and seize Ceylon. The scenario was disturbing. Once Ceylon fell, the next move would be to cut the Persian Gulf oil supplies and then link up with Italy and Germany through the MiddleEast.

The Royal Navy was desperately short of capital ships. Britain needed adequate naval power closer home should Ceylon fall, but the Admiralty had sent five battleships and three aircraft carriers to the Indian Ocean. This had left the Royal Navy very sparse in the Atlantic and the Mediterranean.

In March 1942 Admiral Sir James Somerville, who was in command of Britain's Force H in the Mediterranean, was sent to Colombo. H was to take overall command of the five battleships and aircraft carriers and have strategy consultations with Sir Geoffrey Layton who was in charge of the Ceylon station.

The Chiefs of Imperial General Staff were very satisfied with Sir Geoffrey. He had been made Flag Officer Commanding, Ceylon, and later Supreme Commander of all the British forces in the island. Admiral Layton was an 'action man'. He improvised the island's defences and even requisitioned private properties to constructed airfields and emergency landing strips. And he saved the RAF a packet.

Two squadrons of Hurricanes were on their way to Java, but Layton ordered their diversion to Colombo. He said it was a gut feeling—and he was right, Japan had seized Java and holding the Java sea unchallenged. The Hurricanes would surely have fallen into enemy hands had they continued to fly east.

Somerville did not like the situation at all. His Eastern Fleet was not what he would have wished for. Four of his five battleships were old, slow, fat ladies, short of breath. They were unconverted veterans of the First World War and highly vulnerable.

But the reports were not so good either. Japan was closing in and were now in the occupation of the Andaman Islands, only six hundred miles from the Indian and Ceylon coasts. Intelligence was confident that the Japanese would launch a carrier-borne attack on Colombo.

Somerville decided to counter any such offensive. He moved his ships out of Colombo and patrolled the seas around Addu Atoll, the coral island lagoon 600 miles south-south-west of Ceylon's east coast.

He was in no position to take on the Japanese at the Andamans. The safety of his small fleet was his first concern. Any loss would cripple him, for there would be no reinforcements for a long, long time.

Britain, too, was stretched very thin. There wasn't a

single capital ship to guard the eastern Mediterranean, and, in the North Atlantic, the big German battle cruiser, the *Tirpitz* was becoming a dire threat.

Somerville's first obligation was to prevent, with every ounce of his being, any hazard to the supply lines to the Middle East, India and Ceylon. To do so, he had to keep his fleet afloat and intact. He could take no risks.

Germany, too, was aware of the implications. On 13th February, 1942, Chief of the German Navy, Grand-Admiral Raeder sent a communication to Hitler. Raeder constantly pressed Hitler to joint Italy in attacking Britain's Middle East bases and seize the Persian oilfields. His thinking (extracted from the 'War Files') was as follows:

'Once Japanese battleships, anti-aircraft carriers, submarines and the Japanese naval air force are based on Ceylon, the British will be forced to resort to heavily-escorted convoys if they desire to maintain communication with India and the Near East . . . The Suez and Basra positions are the western pillars of the British position in the Indian Ocean. Should these positions collapse under the weight of concerted Axis pressure, the consequences for the British Empire would be disastrous.'

In London no one was as worried as Field Marshal Sir Alan Brooke. It was certainly a gloomy run-up to Easter 1942. North Africa had to be cleared; the Mediterranean opened. Britain was fighting hard to patch holes. Cairo was not safe; Persia was threatened; India's eastern flank was growing increasingly vulnerable. Even Australia and New Zealand were open to attack. Communications through the Indian Ocean could be severed at any moment.

Suddenly, Ceylon became immensely important. The Allies also realized that Hitler was relying on Japan to do a lot of dirty work for him. Japan could take Ceylon. It would give Hitler the edge he needed to storm down south Russia, seize Persia and the precious oilfields.

It seemed that there was this one point in World War II history: that the fate of the world depended on whether Ceylon would fall or not!

19

Of Dust-ups and Signal Watch and Wall Crawlers at Night

One hears of 'terrible twins'. A term applied to two members of the human race who join hands to dislocate all around them. Like Adolf and Benito, for example . . .

In 'Gemunu' they were Ryan and Hughes. Stoker Mechanic Ryan, to give him his due, and Able Seaman Hughes.

Both were tall, beefy, very European-blooded Burghers with fair hair, pale eyes and a predisposition for beer, more beer and brawls . . . in that order. They would burst out all over at the slightest provocation. Indeed, they sort of manufactured their own provocations, whereupon the base went into a state of emergency and the duty officer would discreetly retire to the wardroom, having posted a runner to keep him abreast of developments.

The runner, an ordinary seaman with a hyped-up imagination, would enjoy the bringing of good news from Aix to Ghent. He would trot to the wardroom in Flagstaff Street:

'Sir, canteen door smashed, sir.'

A low groan.

Later in the evening the news would improve in dramatic quality. 'Sir, duty PO is in the sick bay, sir.'

Another groan. Then: 'What's wrong with him?'

'Whole head bleeding, sir. Hughes hit him with the quartermaster's kettle.'

'Where—where's the QM?'

'He's running on the beach, sir. Went Mount Lavinia side. Don't know where.'

Half an hour later: 'Sir, all laundry room windows gone, sir. Ryan's hands all bleeding. SBA Wijesekera telling his veins are cut.'

A most theatrical groan, 'Can't they take him to the sick bay?'

'How to take sir? Like a mad bull jumping and breaking everything.'

This was Ryan's problem. When tanked up and on the prod, the sight of glass was one of those 'provocations'. Window panes pained him. They had no right looking so transparently smug. Every time the beer took hold, every window pane in the camp fell to his flailing fists. The sick bay staff were tired of binding his cut wrists and lacerated fingers and knuckles, for no sooner was one patch-up done and the window glasses replaced when *wham!* more broken glass and more sutures.

But Carloboy owed many thanks to Ryan. If it were not for this glass-hating, beer-loving sailor, he may have been in what was surely the biggest jam of his naval career. Maybe there were bigger jams. You be the judge as you read on . . . but they were jams with honour. The particular jam we will proceed to recount was a most unpleasant one; but it all came right in the end, settled with that particular forthrightness Ryan was famous for.

It was the morning when the Royal Canadian Navy sailed into Colombo. Two anti-submarine frigates, grey and grim, nosed into harbour. They were on a 'show the flag' cruise and Colombo was one port of call on their run to Gibraltar.

The warships were berthed slap in midstream, in plain view of the signals tower. Two wickedly-lined, sleek, grey ghosts among the gaily-funnelled, rusty-sided freighters. The duty signalman of one of the ships was eager to get information. He flashed to the duty signalman on watch: 'Where do we find the girls' and Daft took the message to Lieutenant Wickrema who had several seizures.

HMCyS Gemunu had a ringside seat to a Canadian caper when four very wavering Canadian sailors, squeezed into a single rickshaw and each waving a bottle of Booths gin (White Satin, mind) whooped down the camp road, waving cheerily to officers and men of the Royal Ceylon Navy and singing a bawdy French song full-throatedly.

The rickshaw wallah, determined to earn his daily bread, hung determinedly to the shafts. The wonder was that he could not only draw his spirited load but also keep his feet on the ground.

The men of the Gemunu crowded the gates, whooping and cheering. This, they agreed, was shore leave with a vengeance. The rickshaw creaked to a stop and one of the Canadians rose precariously, bowed. 'Alors,' he croaked and waved an expressive hand. Then he saw Lieutenant Basil. He gave a straggling salute, squinted and grinned from ear to ear.

Lieutenant Basil, his eyes twinkling, returned the salute crisply. Then he yelled the men to attention. 'Off caps!' he roared.

As a man, caps were cleared.

'Give our visitors a send-off! One!'

Caps soared in the air with accompanying shouts of jollity.

'Two!—Three!—On caps! Dismiss!'

The Canadians were in ecstasies. They hurled their caps over the wall. A bottle of Booths sailed over the gate, was smartly caught by Telegraphist Jansze who thanked heaven fervently for great mercies.

As the men trailed away, Lieutenant Basil told the quartermaster, 'Kick that rickshawman's bum and tell him to get that lot to the port. Once won't do. Kick him twice.'

That evening Yeoman Barnett told Carloboy that the time had come to prove himself a very alert and full-fledged sailor.

'Von Bloss,' he said, 'I'm disappointed. You see before you a distressed and disillusioned man.'

Carloboy could never fathom this Yeoman. He always talked crazy. One never knew what he was leading up to.

'Von Bloss, old son, you have dashed my hopes, blighted my dreams, poked a rude finger in my arse'ole, made my nightmares come true. Patrick, just look at him.'

Leading Signalman Patrick grinned. 'Horrible he is, Yeo.'

'Ah, Patrick, you are indeed a crutch. A shoulder to lean on. Horrible you say? Hmmmm . . . now that you mention it—of course he is! And, Patrick, he calls himself a signalman.'

'Ah,' said Patrick. The exclamation carried untold nuances.

Yeoman Barnett dreamily inspected his nails, traced a forefinger over a tattoo on his forearm, closed his eyes, opened them, closed one eye, squinted down his nose and scratched his crotch busily.

Carloboy decided to pitch the ball into his court. 'Is anything the matter, Yeo?'

'Everything, old man, everything. The whole world—' sweeping an arm, 'is on the outside looking in. Matter and form is the essence of all, is it not?'

Carloboy blinked. 'Oh, I thought it was something else. The way you're scratching—'

'At last! At last! A man, Patrick! Did you hear? A man! Even as we are mutually agreed that he is a horrible little shaver, a thing of indiscipline, an affront to the species, a black misery, he thinks not of his own inadequacies. He seeks no line of defence with which he may shroud the deficiencies of his baser self. What does he think, Patrick? What does he think? Why is this nice Yeoman scratching his balls!'

He grabbed Carloboy by the shoulders, spun him around to face Patrick. 'I see redemption,' he intoned, 'yes, redemption for this thief upon the cross. While the world slings mud he thinks selflessly about the itching balls of others!'

He strode to the door and, with a patriachal gesture, exclaimed, 'This day, Signalman von Bloss, shalt thou be in Paradise. No more shalt thou carry tea up and down the stairs and be a messenger of the gods with two-and-a-half and three stripes. Tonight, from midnight to two hours before the dawn will you be the eyes of the Royal Ceylon Navy. Patrick will elaborate. I go—I go to consult an oracle about a pimple on my mount of Venus. We will meet at Philippi . . . '

And he went, only to turn, poke his head through the door and say, 'And Von Bloss, I find your concern for my private parts most touching—*and personally bloody insulting!*'

Patrick grinned.

Carloboy frowned. 'What the hell was all that about?'

''xactly what he said. We have to keep a visual watch on those Canadian warships. Yeoman Louis said it was a good idea to give the junior sigs a duty shift. Tonight. Four hours each. You will be on from twelve to four. Right?'

Right it was, and Carloboy climbed the stairs at ten to midnight, relieving Roy Fernando who said that the only thing interesting was the building to the south. The Canadian ships just wallowed in their stream berths. 'Not a bloody peep out of them. But check the building behind. Here, take the binocs. There, the bedroom window. Buggers are having a pukka time.'

True enough. A man and woman were celebrating the *Kamasutra*. Carloboy grinned, turned to remark on a particular posture which was immensely interesting and found himself alone. Roy, yawning tremendously, was tottering down the stairs.

Shrugging, Carloboy swung the binoculars around. The sea, the rocks of Galle Buck, the port, the two warships wrapped in sleep. There were deck and bridge lights and a watch kept, obviously. He shrugged again, placed the long, brass-cased telescope on the signals projector and swivelled the lantern. He was disappointed. The projector could not be tilted sufficiently to take in that bedroom. He moved around the tower platform, high over the sleeping camp.

The wind from the sea was cold and he wondered what sort of damn-fool Canadian would wish to transmit signals to the Ceylon Navy at that hour, unless it was some horny warrant officer who sought directions to the closest cathouse. He gave a small exclamation of impatience. The couple in the bedroom had decamped. Perhaps to the shower. All he saw was a very rumpled bed.

In the port, the stout sons of the maple leaf were very much asleep. The whole Navy is asleep, he thought disgustedly. He went inside, settled down to wait out the hours. There were too many of them. Every minute, he grumbled to himself, was a bloody hour.

Feeling cramped, he rose, walked stiffly to the shallow wall of the platform, peered down at the buildings below. A movement caught his eye. Staring intently, he discerned a figure steal into a sort of quadrangle. It was carrying what looked like a wide box.

Wondering hugely, he tripped downstairs to the wireless cabin where Nugawira slept over the morse key.

'Oy! Nugawira! Get up!'

Gentle snore.

He placed a mouth to the O/Tel's ear. *'Mayday! Mayday!'*

Nugawira kicked out. 'Where? Where?'

'Hah! Just as I thought. Sleeping on duty. Come on, quickly! I want to show you something. Hurry up, before the bugger goes.'

'What—what bugger? What are you doing here?'

'Come *on!* Hurry up!'

They ran downstairs, made for the stores section. Carloboy had a pretty good idea where that quadrangle was. They were in time to bump into a stores assistant who was dragging two boxes along the corridor.

'What the hell is happening here?' Carloboy demanded.

'Shh. Don't make such a big noise,' the fellow said, 'you'll wake the sentry below.'

'Whadd'you mean wake up the sentry. Is the bugger sleeping?'

The stores assistant who was Kariya, gave a nervous titter. 'He was sleeping when I came. Everyone sleeps at this time.'

'Not us,' said Nugawira piously . . .

'And not you, I see,' said Carloboy, 'what are these boxes? What's in them?'

'Nothing, nothing, you're von Bloss, no? Who's your friend?'

'Nugawira. Telegraphist. And what are *you* doing here this time of night? I think we should tell the MSO to call the duty officer.'

Kariya heaved. 'What for? I'm just doing some work I forgot to do earlier. You fellows can help me, actually. If I don't get these boxes out I'll be in trouble tomorrow. Nothing much in them. Old stuff.'

Nugawira pushed his head forward. 'Damn funny, I think. Boxes have nothing, you're doing nothing. Only carrying nothing in the middle of the bloody night and now we must help you?'

'There's old stuff in them,' the S/A said, 'condemned stuff. Last week the stores officer told me to get rid of it and I didn't.'

'So?'

'So tomorrow the base stores officer is having an inspection. If this stuff is found I'm in trouble. I suddenly remembered and came to take them.'

Carloboy hadn't the foggiest about naval stores procedure, but he had his doubts. 'So why couldn't you move the stuff earlier? Waiting till the middle of the night. . .'

'I told you, I suddenly remembered. They're always saying take this out, junk that. Nobody bothers. Who's to know there'll be a bloody BSO inspection?'

'We-el—'

'So where are you taking this anyway?' Nugawira asked.

'The QM's office. Or I'll dump it in the sick bay. Anywhere. They cannot be here tomorrow when the inspection begins.'

Something wasn't right. Carloboy frowned. Something he had seen from the tower. The S/A had moved out of the shadow of the wall. A wall that overlooked the street. It joined the stores and led to no door. That's it! Door! 'You mean—you mean you have the keys to the stores?'

'Yes—I mean—that is . . .'

'You mean you're a bloody liar! I saw you with a box over there. Near that wall. What were you doing there? The door is back here.'

'What do you mean? Who asked you to come here interfering like this? This is a stores matter. And what's your duty post? I'll report you!'

Almost casually Carloboy put out a hand. It smacked flat into Kariya's chest, pushing him away most scornfully. 'So you're going to report. Then no harm if I knock your bloody teeth out? You can make a good report then.'

Nugawira sat on a box. 'Yes. That's the thing. You go and report. You took these boxes from the stores. The BSO gave you the key?'

Carloboy tore aside the leather strap around one of the boxes. Burberrys and seamen's jerseys. Thick, blue Royal Navy issue, only doled out to men on overseas cruises when its winter. Also, only issued to senior hands and officers when in Diyatalawa.

'This stuff is condemned? Who's the damn fool who will condemn this? All brand new. So what's your story now?'

The S/A swallowed hard. 'OK, OK I'll tell you. You think these are the only boxes in there? There are hundreds of them. Stacked to the roof. Ever since I joined, they have been there. Eight years. Full of bloody dust and cobwebs. This is old Royal Navy stuff. No use to us at all. Hundreds of boxes. You think rats won't eat them?'

'So you thought you'll help yourself?'

'No, men. You think I'll just do a mad thing like this?'

'Mad thing is right!' Nugawira snorted.

The S/A sagged. 'I have some problems,' he muttered. Next month I am going to get married also. I need some money quickly. Then I thought of this winter wear all lying here. For what does the bloody Navy want winter wear? Is there a winter here? And what ship will we have to go overseas? I got a buyer for this stuff. From Nuwara Eliya. Everyone wears warm clothes there. I'll tell you what? When I sell these I'll give you a thousand rupees. . . .'

'What? You think you're going to take this away? And another thing, how did you get into the stores?'

Kariya pointed to the wall.

Nugawira rose, went to the ledge and peered out. He gasped. 'On this ledge? You went on this ledge?'

'Yes.'

'And you carried the boxes along this? Boy, you must be really mad. One slip and you're finished.'

The ledge was just a foot wide, overhanging the road about twenty feet below. Immediately below was a nasty, spiked, iron fence. The S/A had inched along to smash a window and enter the stores. And he had then carried out the boxes, one by one, along that same perilous ledge.

Carloboy stared at the ledge, at the boxes in disbelief.

'Von Bloss,' the man was saying, 'I'm not a rogue. Honest. I was—I'm really in a mess. Desperate.'

Carloboy was unhappy. Eight years service. The man could make leading stores assistant in another year. Maybe he was in a hole. 'I'll tell you what,' he said, 'put the boxes back and get out and we'll forget about all this. What do you say? Sorry. That's all I can do. Otherwise, I'll have to report you. You want to do number one and be kicked out?' (Number one punishment was a jail term.)

Kariya tensed. He knew he had no choice. 'All right,' he said eventually, 'but I'll have to carry them back again.'

'So? You carried them out.'

'Can you help me? We have to do it quickly. Don't know when the duty officer will come on rounds.'

Carloboy and Nugawira looked at each other. Supposing one of the Canadian warships had tried to make contact visually or on radio telephone . . . or, perish the thought, supposing that screwball Barnett came to check on the night watch. . .

'The quicker we put these back and push this bugger out of here the better,' Nugawira said.

'OK. Come on then. Are these heavy?'

'No, about ten or twelve pounds,' Kariya muttered.

The boxes were strapped down with leather bands. They did up the box they had opened as best as they could. 'Right then, let's carry them back. Don't slip or anything for God's sake. And don't look down.'

Inch by inch, with every step as dicey as the one that lay ahead, they took the boxes back. It was, Carloboy swore, the slowest eighteen feet he had ever walked. Nugawira was pale when they finally stepped into the quadrangle. Carloboy wiped the perspiration off his forehead. Kariya melted away. They dated upstairs, intent on coffee.

'He took off too bloody fast for my liking,' Carloboy said. 'Risking our lives like that. I wanted to kick his arse.'

'So never mind. The stuff is there, no? Only thing is the window is broken.'

'I think we must keep an eye on the bugger.'

'He was shit scared,' Nugawira opined.

'Yes, but it was a bit too easy, the way he gave in. We should have reported—but . . .'

They watched the water begin to bubble on the small hotplate. 'Hurry up and make the coffee. My God, it's past three.'

The Canadian warships had been on their best behaviour. Sims came, yawning most obscenely, at five minutes to the hour. He was mystified when Carloboy told him to keep an eye on the quadrangle below the wall.

The days passed without event. The Canadian warships sailed away and visual signals watch was discontinued. The S/A too was not to be seen, nor did they seek him. In a week, the feeling of misgiving Carloboy had had, disappeared.

It was a full month later, on a bright and well-polished morning when even the Captain of the Navy had come to naval headquarters without having given his batman the customary wigging, that the bubble burst. Carloboy and Sims were in the main signals office. Nugawira and Bijja in the W/T office. The Fernandos were in the signals tower. Yusuf, having been rather obstreperous in the earlier hours of the day (it was said that he had invited Leading Seaman Ranawana to suck his cock, anytime, any day) was scrubbing the wooden staircase with wirebrush and soft soap. It had begun as a day that beamed 'all's well'. It is on such days that explosions and other such nasty things usually occur.

Barnett toddled in. 'Oh, this Navy. Such swabs and cut-throats and yo-ho-hoing in every place,' he warbled, 'avast, you of the shining morning faces. Lubbers all, I say! The Olympus of the gods seethes. Skulduggery and piracy. Have you not, you in your sarcophagi, heard of the crushing events of the day?'

Leading Signalman Alfie cocked an eyebrow.

'Aha! I thought as much. The signals branch. The eyes and ears of the Navy, knows naught. Have you not observed how Corey keeps dashing in and out of his office this morning?'

'Lieutenant Commander Corey, sir?'

'To give him his due, yes. Such a fretful flurry of a man.'

'But what has happened, Yeo?' Carloboy asked exasperatedly.

'What indeed! Lend ears, me hearties, for I have fearsome news to tell. Today, the aforementioned Corey, the SOB—which is stores officer base and not what your sullied minds would instantly suggest—went to the stores. And there he found a broken window, and his little heart leaped. So he stood and looked and looked and stood and then he ordered a stores check and is now most upset. Two boxes of officers' overcoats have decamped. Gone. AWOL. And they seem to have smashed the windows in order to effect a getaway. By now, knowing these boxes, they have crossed the border and are riding away into the sunset. And our SOB is rushing here, rushing there. Such a to-do.'

'Excuse me, Yeo,' Carloboy said. His voice was tight. 'I have to go to the W/T office.' He raced upstairs, his brain two steps ahead. That S/A must have taken the boxes after all. How? When? He collared Nugawira and brought him up to date.

Nugawira paled. 'It's that S/A all right,' he breathed. 'He must have come back on another night.'

'I don't think so. There must have been a car or something waiting that night to take the boxes away. He must have come back after we went off watch. Damn! I told Sims to keep an eye on that wall.'

'So, what now?'

'Let's get hold of Sims. And then, the best thing is to tell Barnett the whole story.'

'That mad bugger?'

'I know, but all that mad talk is just a pose. If we want a good man on our side, I think Barnett is the best.'

Nugawira shrugged. 'Half the bloody time I can't even understand him. You can?'

They cornered Sims who listened open-mouthed. When they went to Barnett, he listened with a silence they found unbelievable. When they had told the tale he glared at them with much distaste. 'Infants! That's what you are. Infants! When you see a man in a place he is not supposed to be, you report him. That's the Navy way. What's the duty officer for? I know, he's usually screwing somebody in the wardroom, but your duty is to call him, give him time to button his trousers and come. That's accepted procedure. And, infants, you left your posts. A vile thing to do at the best of times.'

'Yes, Yeo, but what are we going to do?'

'Wait here. And try to do nothing. I will have words with the SOO.'

He was back in ten minutes, crooking a finger. 'Come along, vile ones. You will tell the SOO what you told me. Look him in the eye and tell all.'

The staff officer operations gave a crooked grin. 'All you buggers are in it. The very night there was wireless and signals watch. Station bugger keeps watch from the top. Wireless cabin bugger and stores bugger take the boxes. You mean to tell me one man can go on that ledge and smash windows and carry boxes and all?'

Barnett frowned. 'I think these two are telling the truth, sir.'

'Truth! Who wants the truth! I want the buggers who did this.'

Carloboy felt that things were getting out of hand. 'But, sir—'

'Quiet! If you did not steal, you aided and abetted. You know what that means?' He thumped the bell on his desk. A petty officer came in. 'March these two to the lobby. Tell the regulating office that they are to be detained.'

S/A Kariya was placed under close arrest and the police came on the scene. Statements were recorded. Kariya, held in the guards office, was grilled, and finally admitted to the theft. He gave the names of dealers in Diyatalawa and Bandarawela who had bought the overcoats. He said that Carloboy and Nugawira were his accomplices. He spread a neat story, a most convincing one. Carloboy and Nugawira had recently returned from Diyatalawa, hadn't they? It was they who told him how merchants in those parts wished to buy warm clothes and paid well for Navy overcoats. Yes, he went to Diyatalawa and met the dealers. They had outlets in Bandarawela as well. But it was Carloboy and Nugawira who had done the spadework. He arranged to supply the stuff. All he had to do was take the boxes to a contact in Front Street, opposite the Colombo Fort Railway Station.

The police arrested the contact. The boxes were traced and the goods recovered. The Diyatalawa police took two men into custody and sent them under escort to Colombo. They identified Kariya as the naval rating who had made the supply. But they also said that two other ratings were involved. This, it was later learnt, was said on Kariya's insistence. The police had cheerfully put all the bad eggs in one basket, leaving them together in the police guard room to discuss their predicament. It was simple. Kariya told them how and why the scheme had come unstuck.

'Two other fellows saw me,' he said hoarsely, 'promised to keep quiet and then went and told.'

'So who are these fellows?' one of the dealers had asked.

Kariya described Carloboy and Nugawira as best as he could. 'One is a big Burgher fellow. Big nose and shoulders. You'll know him if you see him. Name's von Bloss. You remember that and tell the name to the police.'

'So never mind that. What does he look like?'

Kariya took pains describing Carloboy. 'Other fellow is darker. Small chap. Very short. Round face. But if you describe the Burgher fellow he'll also get pulled in. He's the fellow who went and told everything.'

The SOO was not impressed. He spent a cozy time with the police crimes officer and said he didn't trust Kariya at all, at all. 'What we should have is an identification parade.'

'For why?'

'Because you guys put the suspects together. Bad show that. Now see their statements. They say two other ratings are in it. One says that one of these other men actually contacted him in Diyatalawa.'

'So must be true, no?'

'I don't believe one word. How can recruits shipped direct to Diyatalawa know that there are boxes of overcoats here?'

The Inspector shook his head. 'So then what?'

'Simple, my dear fellow. The two men who told us about the theft cannot be accomplices. Best thing is to have an identification parade. Let's see if these dealers can identify the two men.'

'But they even gave us their names.'

The SOO snorted. 'When? After you put them in the same cell with the accused? Aha, so the S/A could have told them the names.'

Barnett broke the news. 'Now listen, you two. The men who bought the stuff have said that you and the S/A are in it. We are convinced—and let that be a straw to cling to—that they have been put up to implicate you. This have they done. Gave your names too. Most co-operative they were. So it has been decided. If they know you, let them point you out. There! The acid test. What say you? Stand before your accusers. Like—now who the devil was that? Sir Galahad? No . . . . my strength is as the strength of ten because my heart is pure . . . something like that anyway. But comfort yourselves. Nobody here doubts you. Even the SOO is now convinced that you have been scuppered because you gave the show away.'

'But yes, suppose they identify us . . .'

'Then you are in deep shit. I shall stand to attention and watch you slowly sink out of sight.'

This was no comfort at all. Carloboy stared dumbly. 'But that Kariya could have told them what we look like.'

'Of course he did. You are fair and big built, and you,' turning to Nugawira, 'are the shortest bugger in the Navy. Very easy to identify. You know,' he mused, 'Nugawira is a dead duck. All they have to do is look for a midget. Very dicey business this is, to be sure.'

Carloboy nodded sadly.

'So never mind. As long as you know you haven't a prayer. Now, having put the fear of God into you, I will consult with the First Lieutenant. I will see that the order of the identification parade is well arranged. Fret not, you simple ones, those bastards are going to make a whopping big mistake.' He tapped the side of his forehead. 'You will see what brains can do.'

Carloboy was as fine-strung as a carload of polecats when the quartermaster hailed for an assorted group of sailors to assemble outside the canteen. He listened. Nugawira, himself, many others. As the names reeled off he began to understand what Barnett had done.

'Ratings will fall in a single rank as follows,' the quartermaster chirped, 'Able Seaman Hughes, Able Seaman Mendis, Cook-steward Haramanis, SBA Wijey, Leading Signalman Alfie, REM Aloy, Signalman von Bloss, Stoker

Mechanic Silva, Shipwright Silva, SBA Winnie, Telegraphist Nugawira, Stoker Mechanic Ryan, Leading Telegraphist Gibbs, Signalman Sims, Leading Seaman Samath.'

Fifteen men. But what an order! Extreme left was Hughes, fair, tall, brawny as a Dutch closet. Mendis was Hughes' darker twin; Haramanis, an inch taller than Carloboy was hunched, thin and oldish, while SBA Wijey was even thinner and gangling. Alfie, tall as Wijey, was fair; while Aloy and Carloboy were of equal height. Carloboy was quite beefy while Aloy, a shade darker, was more gracefully moulded. Stoker Silva, next to Carloboy, was short. He was of the same colour and build as Nugawira and Carloboy was startled. 'Good lord', he thought, 'where has Barnett dug this stoker from?' He was just as short as Nugawira. Ryan, Gibbs and Sims were all fair-complexioned. Gibbs was portly and had a bit of a tummy. Sims was lean and Ryan was as big as Hughes with muscles the medical world had yet to learn of. At the other end, Samath was very much in the same cast as Aloy.

Lieutenant Commander Darley then called the line to attention. 'Signalman von Bloss, Telegraphist Nugawira, fall out. The rest close rank.'

Here was another mystery.

Darley said, 'Go to the PO's mess. In the hall are two police officers. Report to them that we are ready to hold the identification parade. They have a man with them. You will bring the police officers and the man to the canteen.'

Barnet rubbed his hands. 'Ah!' he said, 'Go, my children. Off you go. To the fiery furnace. Beard the lion in its den.' He sounded quite prophetic.

A man sat in the PO's mess. He was in the custody of two police officers. He wore a soft blue coat and a sarong. Most personable. He also reeked of money, from his demure handkerchief in his coat pocket to his soft-grained leather sandals. He paid Carloboy and Nugawira scant heed when they entered the mess, requested the officers to follow them.

In the canteen, the man's eyes flicked along the line-up. Barnett said to the police officers, 'This parade has been called so that positive identification can be made of two men who sold or negotiated to sell naval property to this man.'

'That is correct.'

'And are we to assume that this man knows, has spoken to and seen the two men and can now make positive identification?'

'Yes. This man has given us the names also. Von Bloss and Nugawira. They were with the other man when terms of sale were discussed.'

'Good.' Barnett rubbed his hands. 'We are glad to know that we can now weed out two more undesirables. Since your man has seen and spoken with von Bloss and Nugawira he should have no difficulty picking them out.' He paused, gave a benign smile. 'As you know, we have our little ceremonial in all such things. Two ratings will walk with the gentleman as he proceeds to pick out the culprits.' He told Carloboy and Nugawira, 'You two, accompany this gentleman.'

Carloboy stared dazedly. Later, he swore, he could have died. Could have died laughing. They paced alongside as the man walked. He pointed to no one.

'Well?' said Darley.

'I know the men,' came the uncertain mutter.

'That won't do. This is an identification parade. You must point them out.'

Carloboy and Nugawira stood impassively at the end of the line.

'When you come to the men you may inform the sailors who are with you,' came Darley's sharp bark.

Thus prodded, the man went to the 'von Bloss' and the 'Nugawira' he had decided on on his first tour. He jabbed a finger at Ryan.

The rest was mayhem of a rare order. Like Guy Fawkes night and Vesuvius and several synchronized bowel movements and what happened in Iran each time the Ayatollah mumbled through his beard. Quite unimaginable and wholly devastating.

20

History—Easter Sunday, April 5, 1942

What happened in the skies over Ceylon on Easter Sunday, 1942, proved to be one of the turning points of the war. The day before had progressed routinely enough. A lone Catalina, patrolling south-west to south-east, spotted a fleet of four fast Japanese battleships and five aircraft carriers approaching Colombo. The fleet was supported by a large force of cruisers and destroyers.

The pilot sent a warning to Colombo and flew dangerously close to the armada. He was shot down, but even as his flying boat spun, a ball of smoke and flame, he had succeeded in raising the alarm. That was Saturday, April 4. He had barely the time to bail out, plunging into the sea just as his plane smacked the water with a dull crump of exploding tanks.

Sir Geoffrey Layton, flag-officer commanding the Ceylon station, acted with speed and decision. He ordered the immediate emptying of the port of Colombo, rushing merchant vessels to sea and sending the warships out where they would have a fighting chance. Many merchantmen were ordered to steam north, lie off in shelter. Layton then ordered the battle-readiness of thirty-six Hurricanes. The Japanese could not be certain about the island's state of readiness. They must have hoped for another Pearl Harbour. Certainly, they did not expect a fight.

It was shortly before eight on the morning of Easter Sunday when fifty Japanese bombers, escorted by an equal number of Zero fighters, swooped in from the south.

In Colombo, at the church of St Michael's, the Revd Hardy, an affable Englishman, was conducting the Easter service. The collection had begun and all over, worshippers were digging into purses and pockets. The Revd Hardy was pleased. As was the practice, the Easter Sunday collection in the Anglican Church went to the vicar. Then the air raid sirens went off.

A verger rushed to the vicar. 'It's a real air raid,' he said hoarsely, 'the Japanese are bombing Colombo.'

Father Hardy ignored him. The collection could not be interrupted, Japanese or no. Worshippers paled, fidgeted nervously. They gave, numbed, not caring how much. All they wanted was for the exercise to end, for the vicar to tell them what they feared.

No sooner was the collection over, Father Hardy cleared his throat. In a loud voice he announced that Colombo was under attack. 'I want you all to lie on the floor,' he said.

Everyone did, but the vicar never lived down the incident. The collection, to him, had been more important than any bomb the Japanese cared to drop. Why had the Japanese to be so, so inconvenient!

The Colombo military airport bristled. Every plane there was, even those that could hardly stay in the air, let alone manoeuvre in a dog fight, took off to meet the enemy. And it was all owed to the pilot of that lone Catalina, Squadron Leader L.J. Birchall, who had radioed warning.

Birchall, later decorated with the Distinguished Flying Cross and given the OBE, had been on a routine reconaissance. Even as his plane was shot down, he bailed out, only to be seized by the Japanese. Questioned, he insisted that he had had no opportunity to report his sighting. Thanks to Birchall, Colombo did not become another Pearl Harbour.

The Japanese raid lasted twenty minutes. They did not like head-on collisions. They had sought to flatten an island which they supposed was both ill-equipped and ill-prepared, and were rudely awakened to the fact that this island could bare its teeth with effect.

The Japanese had had less trouble with India initially, when they assured Subhas Chandra Bose the freedom of India from British rule if he helped them win the war there. They regarded Bose as their Fifth Columnist and, as we know, Bose, as the head of the Provisional Government of India, declared war on Britain and the United States in July 1943. Yet, over sixty thousand Indian troops were held in Japanese P-O-W camps. The relationship there was anything but sweet.

And Japan had to take Ceylon. The island had much to contribute to the Allied war effort. Rubber trees were double tapped. Ceylon's entire tea production went on contract to the Board of Trade in London. Ceylon was also a vital stepping-stone to the Middle East.

In the fighting that followed, twenty-five Japanese bombers were shot down and the defenders lost as many planes. Harbour and dock installations were damaged, and at sea, two British cruisers and a destroyer were sunk by low-bombing aircraft. Yet, a British Squadron Leader, C.J.T. Charles Gardiner, said in summing up, 'God was with us; otherwise we could not have possibly got away.'

There was much elation in Colombo and London. The attackers returned to the carriers, mission unaccomplished.

They had not done the island any real damage. One of their pilots had actually dropped a bomb on the lunatic asylum! The air defences of Ceylon remained unbroken and the fleet by and large safe at sea. The Japanese decided to steam north-east, leave Ceylon's waters. Obviously, to them, Ceylon was in a high state of preparedness—or so they thought.

London attributed the success to the foresight shown by the chiefs of staff and the presence of mind of the two admirals in charge of the island and the Eastern Fleet. The air defences of Ceylon were the key to the Indian Ocean. The Japanese had failed to force the lock. For the first time since the start of the Japanese onslaught, a major assault had been repulsed.

Luck (or was it God?) played a great part indeed. Admiral Somerville, watering in Addu Atoll, received the news of the raid, decided to hunt down the retiring Japanese fleet. There was no one to tell him that he was outnumbered two to one. Somerville was possessed by the thought that the danger to the Indian Ocean and Britain's communications with India and the Middle East remained . . . as long as the Japanese continued to rove the sea unchallenged. He had little carrier strength, even less gunpower as he steamed vengefully on, intent on meeting, giving the Japs what-for.

Luck, did I say? Yes, luck indeed, that Somerville was ordered to pick up survivors of the sunk British cruisers. The Japanese admiral Nagumo, steamed north-east, into the Bay of Bengal, thinking to wait, bear down on any British force that dared come against him. The two did not meet.

Had Nagumo met Somerville he would have gained an important victory—a victory that would have given Japan control of the Indian Ocean, isolated the Middle East and even brought down the government of Winston Churchill.

Somerville was ordered to withdraw his battleships to the African coast. Nagumo turned his anger on Ceylon's north-east coast. He despatched his bombers to hit Trincomalee.

21

Of Armchair Voyages and Dust-ups and Morse-coding in Talaimannar

Ryan's ham-like fist shot out; a piston of a fist and it moved blurringly. Light-blue coat sailed back, buckled jarringly against the ping-pong table, permitted himself a small, broken groan, and collapsed.

It took three men, Barnett and the two police officers, to keep Ryan under control.

'Bleeding bastard!' he howled, 'pointing his finger at me. Let go! I'll pull his balls off!'

Darley fled, doubled up, hooting like crazy. He sat in the regulating office and laughed so much that the regulating petty officer summoned an SBA.

Barnett was the hero of the hour. When the contents of a firebucket had been liberally sprinkled on light-blue coat and the Surgeon Lieutenant confirmed that the vicious heart punch would have no permanent effect, everybody clapped Ryan on the back and congratulated Barnett, while the officers of the law scratched their heads and asked what of the other accused waiting his turn in the PO's mess.

'Take him—take both and go. You want him to get a hammering also? Both buggers are lying. I told you they have been put up to this.'

The officer's nodded. They were full of praise for this 'Navy method' and when light-blue coat was told that von Bloss and Nugawira had been with him all the while he made a sort of bleat, the sound a goat would make on being sodomized by an Arab, and lay back. Everything in his world was falling to pieces and his diaphragm seemed to be in the clutches of a mad foundryman.

The S/A met a warrant charge, went to jail for a spell and was discharged from service. Light-blue coat and his partner also went in for eighteen months. Ryan swore that he only tapped him and what the hell was wrong with the pansy anyway? Von Bloss and Nugawira emerged from the cloud with sighs of relief.

Nugawira said, 'One thing I like to know . . . who was the fellow going to pick as me?'

That, regrettably, would remain a mystery.

The passing months found them firmly anchored on land. This, to their chagrin, was most disheartening.

'What the hell is the use of this uniform if we don't go to sea?' Sims would growl.

As an opinion of some merit, this was wholeheartedly endorsed.

Taking a bus home would tangle them in sometimes quite unreal situations.

'Hello, sailor boy,' someone would say, 'been to England? Tell me, is Bedford in the north or south? This fellow says south.'

Or, 'Been abroad?'

Or, 'Ever been to Singapore? Banda Street? Sha! The brothels . . .'

One of the boys was a regular romancer. He was well up on his geography too, and was most convincing about the places he never visited.

'England? Grand old place, men,' he would say quite nonchalantly.

His fellow traveller would perk up.

'I'm lucky to have really done the round. Actually this is the first time I've been ashore for any real length of time . . .'

His listener would give a gusty sigh. 'Lucky for you. I have to think twice even to go to Kandy.'

'Ah, but it's no picnic I can tell you. Lot of hard work.' And the look on his face is so smug. He revels in the scene he paints. 'Not like working on the big passenger liners. A warship is different. But it's a real chance to go to all sorts of places. What's your name? I'm sure I've seen you somewhere before. You live in Wellawatte?'

The man ignores this. He asks, 'And what about the Trucial Coast?'

'Trucial Coast? Oh you mean Aden and places? All over I went. Basra, Bahrain, Oman, Yemen. All very rich. They're digging for oil now. You must see Aden. Big town is Crater . . .'

'And how about Africa?'

'Kilindi, Nairobi, Zanzibar, right down to Jo'burg. That's what we say for Johannesburg. Why, I'm sure I have seen you somewhere before.'

'Oh, I must get off. Can you ring the bell—thank you . . .' and leaning a little closer, the man hissed, 'see me in the PO's mess tomorrow. Come right in and ask for Chief Petty Officer Jansen, right?'

'I went home in a bloody panic,' he told the boys the next day while they hooted and drummed their heels on their lockers.

'So what happened, you bloody idiot?'

Oh, quite a lot had happened. The poor chap had been brought before a gathering of chief petty officers and petty officers, formally introduced to one and all as Sindbad the Sailor and made to relate the story of his many voyages. It had been a gruelling morning. He had then been given a drink of water and booted out.

Carloboy too had his shore-going mishaps. Two seedy characters, very much under the influence and stiffening the air around them, regarded him with alcohol-laden contempt.

'These buggers in their blurry youniforms. You know?' one asked the other.

'Yesh—hic—yesh.'

They stared at Carloboy who looked away stonily. His father, old Sonnaboy had always maintained that drunks must have some leeway. 'They don't know what the hell they're doing,' the old man had said, 'Just let them be.'

Carloboy had thought this good advice.

'Only blurry ha—harbour shailors. Ask to see if went outshide the breakwater. Only—only big show.'

'Helluffer—hic—helluva Navy.'

The rest of the passengers listened avidly. A nice young thing began to giggle and Carloboy saw red. He gripped one of the drunks by the back of the neck and made a general announcement that he had no wish to bandy words with reptiles, but if, however, said reptiles wished to bandy fists outside the bus, he would be most happy to oblige.

The other man hauled himself up and swung a fist. Carloboy used his free hand to plaster the man in the face, breaking the bridge of his nose. Blood spurted, spraying the white front of his singlet. The bus erupted as the stricken man slumped back, bloodying the seat and the front of his trousers.

Carloboy went berserk. He dragged the other up, hauled him to the rear of the bus while ladies gave little shrieks and men rose, then edged nervously back to their seats. The bus stopped and a frantic conductor leaped off as Carloboy dragged his victim out. Inside, others were hustling Bleeding Nose out. Satisfied that both his tormentors were sprawled on the kerb, Carloboy leaped in as the bus roared off. He took a seat feeling slightly foolish. It was no fun being the object of attention all the way home. Also, his uniform was a sorry, blood-spattered mess. His sister Marie saw him enter and had hysterics. He grinned and dumped his singlet in a bucket at the well.

'What happened?' Sonnaboy asked.

'Hit a bugger. Only one shot I gave him. Don't know where all the blood came from.'

His mother glared, bit her lip. 'Can't even come quietly home,' she muttered. 'Going to fight. Like the father.'

Sonnaboy poured himself a drink. 'Like a small peg? There, the bottle is on the dinner wagon.'

'No. I'm going to bathe. Must wash the singlet also.' He cut a lime in half in the kitchen. It would remove the blood stains.

Barnett was his usual lunatic self the next day. 'Parting,' he told them, 'is such sweet sorrow.'

'He's off again,' said Bijja.

'I heard you,' Barnett carolled. 'No, my sons, I'm not off. *You* are. Ah, I see the puzzlement on each ugly pan. You, von Bloss, Daft, Sims, you are to be complete signalmen. Complete, did you hear? Wait—' he raised a hand as Carloboy made to speak. Actually, Carloboy wished to make protest, for every time Barnett said anything, supposedly for the good of all, there had to be a catch. 'Tell me, von Bloss, tell me truly, what is your receiving speed on the buzzer?'

'That's a telegraphist's business, Yeo. We are signalmen.'

'Oho! Hearken to the dimwit. In his ignorance does he open his mouth and all over the land is heard the sound of a fart. A signalman, let it be known, is a signalman when he is a complete signalman. Or, some say, a complete idiot. That is a matter of no small debate, I assure you. You, my sons, must know everything about everything. How much of a signalman are you? Let me give you the big picture—semaphore, mirrors, Aldis, Very's lights, flares, flags, yardarm hoists, codes and ciphers, aircraft signals, local harbour signals, tide signals, boat signals, X and Z codes, radiotelegraphy, radiotelephone, light buoys, identification, ball hoists by day, bearing signals, distress procedures . . . hah! I see that your eyes have now retreated a yard behind your ears!'

They stared at him speechlessly.

'You three, forget the visual signals you think you know all about. A telegraphist is a telegraphist, but a signalman is also a telegraphist. Today is the tenth, isn't it? Yes, the tenth of September. You will be good, efficient telegraphists by the fifteenth, for on that fateful day, me hearties, you depart for Talaimannar—'

'Wha-aat!'

'Talaimannar. Small place. Palmyra palms. Good toddy, I believe.'

'But Yeo—'

'Your drafts have come. There, in the wilderness you will bloom like the roses you are. Or is it cactus flowers. Hard to tell just looking at you, but I shudder at the thought of closer scrutiny.'

Drafted to Talaimannar! Carloboy could only gape. The other end of the country? Hot, dry, white sand, not a girl in sight. And Morse Code!

'The goats, I'm told, are most attractive,' Barnett murmured.

They gave him a withering look. He beamed, then trotted off.

'Who is CO "Elara"?' asked Sims. 'Elara' was the name of the naval shore base at Talaimannar.

'Lieutenant Gunasakes.'

'That's not so bad. And who else is there?'

Carloboy chuckled. 'Nathali! Nathali is there.'

'Mus' be a real mad crowd. All the rotters get pushed out to "Elara".'

Carloboy scowled. 'Thank you very much. I suppose we are jut ripe for the place.'

Sims grinned. 'Could be fun. And if there is a crazy mob there, join them, I say.'

'I don't like it at all,' Daft moaned.

'Oh shut up! How long will we be stuck there?'

'Who knows? Like the other side of the moon, that place. Might be forever. Once you go there, everyone forgets you.'

Todwell was most solicitous. 'So cheer up, I'll keep your ends up here. Now, If you will give me your girl friends' names and addresses . . .'

A well-aimed pillow shut him up.

22

History—Trincomalee

Undoubtedly, Trincomalee is one of the most magnificent natural harbours in the world. It flourished as a seaport in 1598 BC and it is marked on Ptolemy's ancient map of Lanka, where it is called Gokanna. It was also Gonagamaka to the ancient Sinhalese.

The wrecks are there too. Shipwrecks of all periods—from an unknown Portuguese warship to hulks of World War II. The inner and outer harbours are dotted with several small and mostly uninhabited islands and the many coves and bays are of singularly charming aspect.

The British found Trincomalee simply splendid. Long before Hitler, they had come to Ceylon, ousted the Dutch. The Dutch had come in much earlier to oust the Portuguese.

The Portuguese built a fort in Trincomalee in 1623 (first known as Fort Trikenemalle). They built it of hard stone from an old pagoda. The King of Lanka, too, had begun to build a fort on the Ostenburg hill which is within today's naval dockyard. When the French and British came threateningly ever nearer, the King abandoned the fort he was building and retired to the central hills. The Dutch took it over, made use of it to fight off the invading British.

Built on the Ostenburg ridge, this small fort is practically unknown today. It is hidden under heavy undergrowth. The Dutch concentrated on Fort Trincomalee which they had wrested from the Portuguese in 1640. They gave it yet another name: Pagoda Hill.

In 1671, the French arrived in Trincomalee. They had plans to grab the town, to expand their territory, command the Eastern world. They made small headway. When the British landed troops in Back Bay and made a surprise assault on Fort Trincomalee, the Dutch fled to Ostenburg. Three days later, Admiral Edward Hughes called for Dutch surrender.

The British were pleased. They now held Fort Trincomalee, a marvellous promontory very like a peninsula. On each side were sandy and rocky bays. Why, they could command the entire east from here. They renamed it Fort Frederick, after Frederick Augustus, Duke of York and Albany, second son of King George III.

The British took Fort Ostenburg after a short, fierce skirmish. It was a good hole-up place. The Dutch had underground quarters for their officers and a part of it was a residence for commanding officers of garrisons.

By 1800, Fort Ostenburg was armed with fifty British guns. At the onset of World War II, the British Admiralty used the Fort as a wireless station. The many outer buildings which the British constructed are now the married quarters of sailors of the Sri Lanka Navy.

Japanese Admiral Nagumo was determined to send Ceylon a message. The raid on Colombo had not been to his liking, but there was Trincomalee, seat of British naval power. He could not simply steam away.

The people of Trincomalee never thought that they would be attacked. News of the Colombo raid had come in, but that was Colombo, hundreds of miles away, another coast. Most of the population had found employment under the British Admiralty and the War Department. The farmers, the producers, were happy. There was a ready market for their produce—vegetables, rice, poultry, fish.

It was around 6.30 a.m. on April 9, 1942 that the Japanese bombers came. Nagumo had special targets. He wanted the destruction of the oil storage tanks at China Bay and the dockyard. He also wanted to sink as many ships as he could. Trincomalee, he knew, was a military and naval base of great importance to the British.

The bombs rained down. They fell on Fort Frederick, the Air Force base at the naval dockyard, China Bay, and the oil fuel depot. The loss of life was most severe, especially as thousands of civilians were already at work.

In China Bay, the Tata Company of India was erecting hangars for the RAF. Men were working on the roofs. The bombs, slim torpedo-shaped and gleaming silver in the sunlight, took a heavy toll.

'I saw planes in groups of six, come over the base,' a survivor later told the press. 'There were so many men working on the hangar roofs, fixing and painting the cross beams. When the bombs fell I saw them being tossed like dry leaves in the wind. I crawled under a concrete cylinder. When the raid was over I saw dead bodies everywhere. Many were just masses of burnt and smoking flesh. I couldn't stay there. I took my bicycle. I had to carry it over the dead. Then I pedalled away as fast as I could. I was crying and thanking God that I was alive.'

Administration failed miserably. Everywhere in the dockyard was turmoil and death. Again, it was the civilians who perished. The Commandant of the Essential Services Labour Corps (ESLC), who was also a Captain, Ceylon Light Infantry, confirmed that many civilians had died and there was none to attend to the dead. The bodies lay there for up to five days. Eventually, the ESLC removed the corpses for burning to a place called Alles Gardens, north of Trincomalee. This is where the war cemetery now is.

All Japanese attempts to destroy the oil tanks in China Bay failed. The bombs just did not find their mark. Nagumo ordered a kamikaze attack. It was the first such suicide mission witnessed in Ceylon. Two airmen and a gunner screamed out of the sky, their fighter diving viciously. They hit one of the tanks with a roar of metal and flame and the splintering of wings and undercarriage. One tank, three lives. Later, parts of the Japanese fighter were gathered together around the burnt tank and enclosed within an iron fence. The skull of one of the Japanese airmen was also found and added to the grim souvenir. Some years later, the skull disappeared, removed, possibly by some unknown souvenir collector.

In the harbour a cargo ship burned fiercely and many warships also destroyed, but the Royal Navy set to work with a will. The remains of the stricken vessels were salvaged, the parts used to build a jetty inside the dockyard. Everyone said that the Japanese took more lives, caused more havoc in Trincomalee, but peculiarly, very few mark Nagumo's raid there. Maybe it was the Easter Sunday raid, a day so significant to the large British Christian community in Colombo, that caught the eye of the historians. The raid on Trincomalee was all but forgotten. True, many more died there. Also, Ceylon saw its first kamikaze attack . . . but in Colombo, the church bells pealed after the raid and that is held long in memory.

In London, the Chiefs of Staff Committee was in two minds. The air action over Ceylon had been repulsed. Twenty-seven Japanese planes had been downed. But the Japanese fleet was still in the Indian Ocean and, as far as they knew, their Eastern Fleet was retiring westward. There was no sign of transports and they did not like the situation very much. They knew that they were very weak in the Indian Ocean.

Attempts were made to get the Americans to make a counter-move towards Japan, draw the Japanese away, but the First Sea Lord had not been very convincing. On 7 April the COS made frantic calls for air support from Wavell[1] but as Viscount Portal, Marshall of the RAF said, there was little chance of this.

Yes, the empire was in a precarious position. How could it keep going through 1942? Yet, they had pulled it off in Dunkirk. It was a time to believe firmly in miracles.

Notes

(1) C-in-C India, Field Marshall Sir A.P. (Earl) Wavell had a long and distinguished career. From C-in-C Middle East to Supreme Commander in South-east Asia, he was recalled to India and became Viceroy. He was also proposed as Governor-General, Australia.

23

Of Toddy Trips and Goat Hunts and Five Thousand Bottles of Beer

Carloboy found that the Navy could be most accommodating. He actually got two days leave in preparation for draft. He took the opportunity to give Colombo the careful once-over. The Swan's girls had to be met and Yvette, who had set him on fire ever since her birthday party. Although in her billowy birthday dress, he was gratified to find, as he fondled her urgently beneath the banana trees in her rear garden, that she had not worn her knickers. And, above all, there was Barbara whom he loved (or so he believed) to distraction. Barbara Heinz was a little beauty. Everything about her was so, so adorable, from the way her lips made those delicious O's of surprise, to hazel eyes framed with long lashes and the dimple at her pert chin. Her brown hair was a puff-ball of small, springy curls and she could not think of anyone but Carloboy whose Navy singlet stretched tight across his chest, its sleeve-ends biting into his biceps. Barbara loved uniforms. Her uncle, a major in the Army, was her idol. Now, a devil-may-care sailor occupied her every thought.

Carloboy sighed. Leave all this, he thought ruefully. But even his fondest goodbyes were touched with that glamour the Navy somehow injected into even the lowliest deckhand's life.

Anti-illicit immigration duties. A nice phrase. An important-sounding one, hinting at drama and derring-do at sea. His family, his friends, most of all his many girl-friends, were impressed. Barbara said, with eyes that glistened, 'Be careful—if anything happens to you—' and left her fears unsaid.

Carloboy held her hand gently. 'What can happen to me?' At least he had the confidence that he above all, was immortal. What could happen? Indeed, so much had happened in his nineteen years . . . and here he was, the past in limbo, the present to be lived to the hilt, the future a matter of the least concern.

And he made his next diary entry: 'September 15, 1954. Drafted to *HMCyS Elara* at Talaimannar for anti-illicit immigration duties.' It was the beginning of high jinks.

Dry. Dusty. Dead. That was his first impression of the good ship *Elara*, which lay alongside the quarters of the Inspector of Police of the area who had a pretty niece with a nice Spanish name, Carmencita, and dark eyes that watched the Navy's every move.

Up a red road, leading to left from the camp was the toddy tavern, where the foaming, intoxicating sap of the palmyra spathe was served in cleaned coconut half-shells, or in tight-woven little panniers of young palmyra fronds. This was the drink of the *hoi polloi* of whose numbers the sailors of *HMCyS Elara* were a major quantum.

Able Seaman Percy Nathali, for one, claimed bosom friendship with the tavern keeper. He drank on the never-never, the account squared every pay day. Morning physical training was little more than a brisk trot to the tavern where after much libation the men would walk back rubbing their bellies and belching fearsomely, their innards awash with the milky fluid.

Elara tended to ramble. Its decks of white, burning sand; its bridgework consisting of a dilapidated building that served as canteen, mess hall, regulating office, victualling stores and armoury. Rats galore there were and they held nightly parliamentary sessions in the victualling stores.

The men bedded under canvas and there was, for naval effect, a mast and yardarm, a white naval ensign that had seen better days, a couple of jeeps and a five-ton truck and a radio that could only raise Luxembourg at two in the morning.

The ops room was situated a mile away, at the home end of the long Talaimannar pier. To this ops room, a converted railway compartment that commanded a view of the sea, the pier, the railway station and the palmyra jungle, the signalmen were posted daily. Inside this box, which was quickly dubbed the 'coffin', were transmitters and stacks of batteries and nary a flag in sight. Yeoman Barnett was so right. Signalman von Bloss was now a telegraphist, whether he liked it or not. Colombo, *Gemunu*, had to be raised every hour. The old tuning signal and preamble became to him as second nature, *4SJ, 4SJ, 4SJ DE 4QRS, 4QRS, 4QRS QRU QRS K.* Which, decoded, was *Gemunu, Gemunu this is Elara, Elara, Elara, do you hear me, what is my signal strength, over.*

In Ceylon's long and chequered history, Gemunu was a great warrior king and Elara an Indian who popped in one day and usurped the throne. History tells us how Gemunu got his act together, marched on the capital, told Elara to come out and fight, slew the usurper and regained the throne. All this happened in the times before Christ.

To this hourly preamble, *Gemunu* should have, by right, replied: *Elara, Elara, Elara, this is Gemunu, Gemunu, Gemunu, I hear you all right. To hell with your signal strength! I'm coming over on my war elephant and you're going to see stars, my lad!*

Nothing as sensational as this would ever happen, of course. *Gemunu* would reply: *4QRS, 4QRS, 4QRS, DE 4SJ, 4SJ, 4SJ, QRU7, QRS8, K.* And signals would be exchanged, mostly weather reports and sitreps on day-to-day anti-illicit immigration measures and countermeasures. A weary, weary job which Carloboy found most uninspiring. 'It's the same damn thing every day,' he would grouse, 'what the hell does Colombo want to know about the weather here for?

Sea slight to moderate, weather fine, swell slight. So what else can you expect in this damn place?'

But in camp . . . ah, what a crew that was! Leading Seaman Poopala was a bearded terror with a face very like those terrible depictions of Ogmios of Celtic mythology. He would gather his beard into little tufts, tying each with a coloured ribbon, each time he reached the high-water mark after copious draughts of beer and toddy. Indeed, to be tanked to the gills was an occupation all on *Elara* took most seriously.

There were telegraphists a plenty, for *Elara* not only had the sailors to seize *kallathonis* (illicit immigrants) off-shore, but was a vital shore base, providing a link between the Army, the police posts of the area and Colombo in the on-going war on illicit immigration. South Indians kept sneaking in across the Palk Strait. They would come in by the boatload, women, children, even their dogs, while some hardy souls would make the crossing alone. One man who was found on a small islet had sat astride the trunk of a banana tree. All he carried was a bicycle chain and a little bundle of his meagre belongings strapped to his back. When the banana trunk could no longer stay afloat, he found himself close to one of the many tiny islands that dusted the sea off the northern peninsula. He crawled ashore, ate leaves and tender thistles. When he was taken off by a Navy patrol, he was half dead of thirst. At the internment camp, he said the bicycle chain was his only weapon. Many *kallathonis* carried such weapons, to beat off the Navy men who had to seize them at sea. Not on shore, mind, for once ashore arrest and deportation involved the usual lengthy legal procedure.

It was Leading Stoker Mechanic Ronnie Maddo who turned the men's attention to the great goat scourge. Stray goats—droves of them—menaced the camp. The sailors of *Elara* did not seem to mind. The goats were a part of the whole, unreal scene. But the animals developed peculiar tastes. They had this fondness for caps, and it all came to a head one day at colour guard. A peculiar turnout.

Regulating Petty Officer Thomas was appalled when he rohed up for inspection.

'Van Heer, von Bloss, Maddo, Johns, where are your caps?'

'Wearing them, PO.'

'What! What are those things? Those are not caps!'

'That's all we have, PO.'

Each was wearing the cap-band and ribbon. Nathali had chortled loud and long. 'Hee, hee, stick in a few feathers and you can join a Red Indian lodge.'

'To hell with you,' Maddo had growled, 'you think this is funny? The goats have eaten them.'

'Fall out!'

Shades of Diyatalawa. They fell out.

Commanding Officer Gunasakes eyed them bleakly after the morning salute. 'If you know that the goats eat your caps, why don't you keep them out of reach of the animals?'

Maddo wasn't convinced. 'Sir, it's not what we must do. It's the goats. We must stop them boarding the ship.'

Gunasakes closed his eyes. Horrible visions rose. A proud warship out on the briny, the captain on the bridge. A goat at the helm. On deck, goats skipped smartly. Every time the captain screamed an order the goats would raise their heads and answer in chorus 'hei-heh-heh-heh-hei'. He smiled glassily. 'I agree, Maddo, but in this damn no man's land there are decidedly more goats than humans. And, as I see it, the goats will eat anything.'

'Also,' Carloboy reminded, 'humans eat mutton, sir.'

'I know,' the CO said, a tinge of regret in his voice, 'but who am I to endorse any nasty thoughts you may have; especially—' he looked at Carloboy intently, '—since I will have no idea what you intend to do.'

Carloboy nodded. 'Yes, sir.' He also made a mental note to take his seaman's knife to the throat of the very next goat that came his way. The CO was a real corker. He had agreed that mutton would be most welcome as long as he was spared the gory details.

'Sir,' said Van Heer, 'we should organize an anti-goat squad.'

Again the faint smile. 'We should, Van Heer, we really should. But let it be on the lines of repel boarders. I do recall how well boarders were repelled in the old pirate days.'

'Oh yes sir,' said Johns enthusiastically, 'decks used to be slippery with blood.'

'That was in the Caribbean, Johns. But then I believe resistance was offered. Here too there could be resistance. Angry goats have this trick of lowering their heads, taking a line on any handy backside, and charging. Yes, you will have to repel in the traditional manner, but—hum—I trust your methods will not be too—too repelling.'

The CO would go far, Carloboy thought, and he was right, for Gunasakes did rise, right to the top. He became, years later, Captain of the Navy!

It was Percy Nathali who fired the first salvo in the anti-goat uprising. He had reason, having discovered that the jersey he had hung on the line had been reduced to two forlorn sleeves and nothing else. A sedate nanny, her dugs like a cluster of footballs, with scraps of his jersey still in her mouth, was making for Daft Fernando's kitbag.

With a whoop that sent Able Seaman Van Dross bolting through the rear flap of the tent, Percy leaped upon the goat, executed a sort of armlock and hauled the bleating creature into the canteen where many lolled, quaffing their evening tankards.

'Behold your enemy!' he roared, 'a stout matron, boys. Look at her doodads. Bursting with the milk of goatly kindness. Van Heer, grab her head and keep her occupied.'

Van Heer blinked. 'What? How the hell do I keep her occupied?'

'So do something! Sing a bloody song. Show her your cock. Can't you use your brains?'

Fetching an enamel jug, Percy squatted. 'Milk-o!' he sang.

The animal unleashed a hind leg. It got Poopala on the shin and his yell rattled the windows. 'Grooh!' he howled, 'I'll kill the fucking bastard!'

'Milk her first,' Percy said, 'give her a chance. Once I get these things going she'll stand still.'

'So get going, get going! What are you fiddling with her knobs for? Where's that bloody axe?'

An interesting combination . . . warm goat's milk, straight from the tap . . . and beer.

Ronnie Maddo launched his own hostilities. He had gone to the heads, and the heads in *Elara* was a squared-off area fenced in with palm-leaf thatch and sectioned to afford each man a squatting plate upon which he could balance himself and make night soil. He could also look up at the sky, contemplate on the mysteries of the universe, or whatever else sailors are wont to think upon at such undignified moments.

Maddo, it appeared, had positioned himself and was gazing down, regarding his penis morosely. What the hell was the use of the big, fat thing that hung so uselessly with no opportunity to rise up and be useful? Then, a goat had poked its head through the thatch and looked at him.

This, to Maddo was a gross invasion of privacy. Leaping up, he gave a blood-curdling yell. *'Repel Boarders!'* and rushed out, quite forgetting to clean his backside and put on his trousers. His naked fury, literally, was a rallying call. Rushing to the tent, he seized a hatchet and with a huge whoop led the others who streamed out behind him.

The goats of many colours, cruising about the camp, sensed trouble. They tossed their heads, bunched together and eyed the men apprehensively. Poopala launched himself at a wicked-horned creature that sidestepped neatly, bleated indignantly into the fallen seaman's ear and danced nimbly away. Van Heer pelted behind a rangy fellow that loped off, snub tail erect, completely unmindful of the call to 'Halt!'

Johns succeeded in grabbing at a hindleg. He hung on. The goat was brought to its knees, but glutton to the last, it twisted over in its struggle and fixed its teeth on the front of John's singlet and began chewing.

The camp was shambles. The goats fled, through tents, over bunks, through fences. One stayed long enough to take Daft's stockings. Eventually, all the men had was John's catch, held down firmly by half a dozen men.

'So what do we do now?' Van Heer panted.

'Kill the bugger!'

'Who?'

That was the big question. Eventually the animal was dragged behind the galley and Carloboy selected the keenest knife there was. He did, everyone said, a nice job. The next day it was unanimously agreed that the mutton was excellent, and cooked to a turn.

Fishing at Talaimannar was an equally rewarding occupation, especially when it was known that Nathali was a dab hand at drying fish. The men would leave camp at night, walk the silent road to the pier with rods and offal from the galley for bait. They would park themselves at the end of the pier where the waves below would look like silver-edged bolsters, rolling to shore. Magnificent fishing. The two-and three-pounders they caught were taken to camp, filletted in the approved manner, garlicked and vinegared, liberally sprinkled with salt and thereafter dried in the scorching sun.

Yes, things were pretty lax on the *Elara*. Much time was spent on the whalers, on coastal patrols. The long boats fitted with outboard motors would take them two miles to sea where the swells moved like switchbacks. Or they would cast around in jeeps, making hectic runs to Mannar and Thoddavelli and other such outlandish places. It was a ritualistic part of such excursions to bring in a goat. Skinning and disembowelling became Carloboy's duty. He was acclaimed a most proficient butcher and the CO would sometimes say, 'You, Crusoe, come here.'

'Crusoe, sir?'

'Haven't you read the book?'

'*Robinson Crusoe*, sir? Yes sir.'

'Good. He liked goats, you recall. Even made clothes of the skins,' and he would go away grinning.

'Hey, mutton man, what did the CO say?' Poopala would sing out.

'You call me mutton man again and the next bugger I skin will be you.'

It was mandatory, customary, whatever, to send the next door inspector of police a choice cut of haunch. This made everyone happy, and especially Van Heer who liked going over to chat up the dark-eyed Carmencita. Nobody—and certainly not the police—would initiate any sort of inquiry into the alarming depletion of the goat population. Naturally, the animals had owners but who or what they were was anybody's guess.

Well-fed on cost-free mutton, the victualling store naturally turned a handsome profit. So did the canteen, and Carloboy, who presided over its affairs, said, 'We have over a thousand rupees profit, sir.' It was the day when he was checking accounts with the regulating petty officer.

The CO shook his head. 'My God, let me see . . . it's all beer! Do you realize that we have to drink about five thousand bottles of beer to show a thousand-rupee profit? Impossible. Check the figures again. And the stocks.'

RPO Thomas said he had checked.

'Impossible. Thomas, are you telling me that this camp has consumed five thousand bottles of beer in three months? It's—it's incredible!'

Thomas chewed a lip. 'We-ell sir, there are twenty men. Ninety days, five thousand bottles. Why, that's not much, sir. Each man drinks three bottles per day. More than five thousand.'

'Yes, yes, that may all look good on paper, but five thousand . . . my God, if Colombo hears about this. We can't show this profit, do you hear? The sole objective of this base appears to be to drink beer. Don't the men do anything else?'

'Why sir, they do all that is detailed.'

'Humph! Then they don't do enough. Five thousand bottles! I don't believe it. Von Bloss, we must break up this profit. I don't want calculations. Any way you look at it it must be a bloody world record.'

'We could throw a party, sir.'

'Party? Party, you say! To drink more beer? Everyone will be crawling around with their bladders full and in the morning this camp will be standing in a pool of piss!'

'But sir, it's a good idea,' Thomas said, 'We pay for the beer. Welfare expense. And that's the end of the profit. Outpost regulations allow welfare parties to boost morale, sir.'

Gunasakes melted. Yes, even in this nowhere place, morale was important. 'Hum, you have a point there, RPO.'

'Sir, we can throw a good party,' Carloboy urged, 'get some chickens and a goat or two. That's no problem and no cost either. And we can invite the police and customs men . . .'

The CO snorted. 'No sense doing things by halves, eh Crusoe? Here, use the bloody thousand rupees and have your party. I'm taking the train to Colombo. I'll come back in a week when it's all over!'

24

History—The Receding of the Japanese Menace

The Japanese did not have it easy over Trincomalee. Admiral Sir Geoffrey Layton ordered the remaining Hurricanes and six Fulmer fighters from the fleet air arm to repulse the raiders and defend, at all cost, the naval base. This they did with a vengeance, inflicting so much damage that three of Admiral Nagumo's carriers were forced to return to Japan to refit.

This was not really registered to its real effect in London, where Churchill was trying to get Anglo-American unity to work in an ordered way. The Americans were all for attack. The American people, that is. Their forces in the Philippines were in bad shape and German U-Boats were sending many of their ships to the bottom. They wanted revenge. They wanted the war to end.

England wanted to save India from the Japanese. America's General Marshall wanted the invasion of Europe. On April 14, 1942, the chiefs of staff pressed for American assistance in the Indian Ocean. Eventually, some agreement was reached. Churchill accepted America's intent to treat Germany as the main enemy, but he also got America to acknowledge the importance of safeguarding India. If the Japanese advance in the Indian Ocean was not stopped, it would be disastrous. Indeed, many things could happen. The Middle East could be cut leaving India at Japan's mercy; Turkey could be hemmed in and oil supplies in the Caucasus threatened. Both Persian and Iraqi oil could be lost to the Allies. Yes, the picture was not a nice one. America decided to give air support in India and the Indian Ocean.

It was the best anyone could do, especially with General Marshall disagreeing with the American Naval Chief of Staff, E. King, who kept insisting on more US land forces to capture bases in the Pacific; and MacArthur in Australia making like demands in order to launch an anti-Japanese offensive.

One could sympathize with the see-saw manner of the many chiefs of staff pow-wows. The Japanese forces in the Indian Ocean had sunk two cruisers and one aircraft carrier on April 7 and 8. Japan had to be contained. By the time Somerville's battleships had swept away to the African coast, Burma had fallen and over half a million refugees were fleeing to the Indian border.

Panic swept India. Many fled the eastern cities. There was stark fear in Calcutta where much British shipping was holed up. Wavell was bitter. He questioned the need to send two hundred heavy bombers to attack a single town in Germany while all he had were twenty light bombers to meet a Japanese onslaught that had already claimed three warships and much merchant shipping. Australia was also jittery and demanded an increase in troops and aircraft. This was the bedevilment of the Allies—how to keep the balance.

It was in this atmosphere of Allied fluster and flurry that Admiral Nagumo turned back. A reprieve, certainly, for the centre of gravity swung back to the Pacific. The British were relieved. They felt that Japan, after overrunning Burma, would turn on China and thereon operate in the Pacific, moving east, no longer to concentrate on India or Australia.

Come to think of it, it was the gutsy Ceylon reaction to Nagumo that turned the tide. The Japanese fleet turned back and the waves of panic on the subcontinent spent themselves. Even MacArthur wrote to Wavell on May 8 , 1942, opining that Japan's soundest course would be to move south, securing her hold over New Guinea and other island groups, then extend her presence in the Pacific before attempting any large operation against India[1].

Yes, the tide had turned. Japan lost its advantage and would never recover it. The Americans were ready to scream in. The Pacific would become a cauldron and the most dramatic battles would soon be fought.

Notes

(1) Ref. *United States Army in World War II: Strategic Planning for Coalition Warfare*, US War Department Official History, 1953.

25

Of Parties and Roast Chicken and Raising a Headman's Hackles

Initially, there was little enthusiasm.

'Party!' Daft snorted, 'What party without girls?'

This was a snag. The only female would be Carmencita and that, too, if she came. Chances were she wouldn't, because even the most broadminded of police inspectors could hardly be expected to bring his niece into a camp where the men would soon descend into various depths of alcoholic stupor.

Carloboy had the one persuasion. 'Free drinks. All you want to drink. We'll invite the Army and the customs and get some arrack—and—and crabs and chicken . . . and no CO!'

That made everybody interested. 'No CO? You mean we don't have to sit around like bloody Englishmen and say "cheers"?'

'Zactly'. We can do what we like and have a pukka time.'

Everybody cheered up. Percy Nathali said, 'We'll go to Mannar and buy what we need.'

'You? Why?'

'Why, to buy chickens and crabs. I know the villages here. You want to buy chickens in the market? You're mad?'

Carloboy sighed. 'OK, lets' go.'

They took the jeep and hurtled off in a cloud of dust, purring back three hours later with two dead goats, a sack containing thirty pullets that had been practically commandeered from the tiny village of Erukkalampidi, and a large string bag which held a hundred crabs. As crabs, they were whoppers. The jeep was bloodied with the fresh-killed goats, smelt of crab and chicken shit. Percy leaped out, spat, and yelled to the cooks.

Amazingly, he had been most helpful. Having wrested the chickens away from nonplussed villagers, and the crabs from the Mannar lagoon fishermen for a song, he had then said, bluntly, 'You owe me money.'

Carloboy stared.

'Two goats. Eighty pounds of mutton. Two bucks a pound. That's a hundred and sixty bucks.'

'But I killed those damn goats. We didn't pay for them.'

'That may be, but the whole idea is that we buy mutton. Then what about the chickens? Four bucks each we paid. What was the asking price? Eight bucks. So you owe me four bucks per chicken. Let's see . . . that is—'

'Not a bloody cent! So that's why you came, to take money off me?'

He had grinned. 'Nice try anyway, no? But you can buy a drink at least; and what about the arrack?'

That was in order. They downed a pint each at the Mannar tavern and carried twenty bottles to the jeep. Percy set two bottles aside. 'They're for me.'

Carloboy shrugged. 'Now I suppose you'll be crawling all over the mess, high as a bloody kite.'

'Tell me of anything better,' he said solemnly, 'but this arrack is medicinal. It's good for colds and stomach pains and fever and catarrh . . .'

'Balls!'

'If you say so, must be good for the balls also. How about a few bucks to pay the toddy tavern?'

'You still owe money there?'

'What else? What's the use of money if you can't owe

it? You give me thirty and I'll square the account. Then I can start again in a big way.'

Carloboy had shaken his head dazedly. There seemed to be no earthly cure for this sailor, except, perhaps, the arrack, which he insisted was an universal pánacea. They had called at the toddy tavern and were welcomed to stay. Percy paid his bill and the man had beamed and pressed two *pattays* on them. After the arrack, the toddy made them belch gloriously and the hot sun made the road almost disappear before their eyes. But they made it to base anyway.

In the afternoon, Carloboy was rudely disturbed by Cook-steward Jinasena who announced that all the chickens were dead.

'Dead?'

'Shitting, shitting and died. All gone,' Jinasena said sepulchrally.

Percy did not turn a hair. 'So? We can buy some more. Have money, no?'

'You and your bargains,' Carloboy stormed, 'They unloaded sick fowls on us. *I'll* buy the fowls this time.'

'OK. You go then, I'll bury this lot.'

Carloboy glared at him suspiciously. It was not like Percy to volunteer to do anything. But the man looked the picture of innocence. When a new batch of chickens were brought in, there was no sign of Percy.

'He said he will bury the dead fowls?' Poopala asked, 'what to bury. He put all in a bag and took and went.'

Carloboy refused to think of Nathali's strange ways. Trust the man to find an easy way out. He must have simply tossed the chickens into the thorn scrub. He set about getting the party organized. The RPO had been on the blower and was pleased that there would be many thirsty guests. Army men from the Thoddavelli camp, a few customs officers, Inspector Paul from next door (sans his niece) and an assortment of police sergeants who had a post at the jetty.

Everybody pitched in, and the cooks had many willing helpers. By six that evening, *Elara* smelt divine—roasting chicken, curried crab, barbecued goat, beer to overflowing and pale-amber arrack to work up a storm. The party was a hit from the word 'go'.

John was ecstatically excellent in a floor show with Poopala. They sang their own renditions of selected nursery songs. There stood Poopala, his beard bedecked with coloured ribbon, his fly wide open and his eyes searching for some distant meadow.

'Little boy Blue, come blow on my horn,' he cried, and Johns pranced up with a bicycle pump and puffed diligently through his open fly.

Amid howls of encouragement, they obliged with several encores and received a standing ovation for 'I love little pussy' where Johns stripped, tucked his penis between his legs and stood, for all the world, like a very hirsute maiden while Poopala stroked his bush and crooned, 'I love little pussy, her coat is so warm . . .'

Songs were robustly sung, and the liquor flowed. And the songs! The Royal Navy had taught the boys well. What ship would ever sail without the songs! Songs that would always live, wherever there was a deck and the lower deck men to sing them.

The old shanty about the North Atlantic Squadron made the moon blush and, at the fence, where Carmencita crouched, and to where the men of *Elara* took turns to dally, the words were a fitting accompaniment to what went on in the inspector's garden.

For forty days and forty nights
We sailed the broad Atlantic,
And never to pass a piece of cunt,
It drove us nearly frantic.

That was the first verse, to which the sailors roared the chorus to the consternation of every *kallathoni* creeping by.

Away, away with fife and drum,
Here we come, full of rum,

Looking for women who'll peddle their bum,
On the North Atlantic Squadron.

The rest of the verses made the moon dive for cover and the cloud that obliged was applauded by the men who went to the fence. Ah, this Carmenicita could take it. A regular trouper, she certainly was!

The cook she ran around the deck,
The captain he pursued her:
He caught her on the afterdeck,
The dirty bastard screwed her—

The cabin, boy, the cabin boy,
The dirty little nipper,
He filled his bum with bubble gum
And vulcanized the skipper—

The captain loved the cabin boy
He loved him like a brother,
And every night between the sheets,
They cornholed one another.

The second mate did masturbate,
No cock was higher, wider,
They cut it off upon a rock
For pissing in the cider.

We're off, we're off to Montreal
To fuck the women, fuck them all,
And pickle their cunts in alcohol
On the North Atlantic Squadron.

There was a whore from Montreal,
She spread her legs from wall to wall,
But all she got was sweet fuck-all
From the North Atlantic Squadron.

There was a whore from Singapore
Hung upside-down inside a door,
And she was left split, worn and sore
By the North Atlantic Squadron.

The boys were at their best. Full-throated, full-bloated, and making most disciplined disappearances to the fence. Nobody really noticed the way a man would rise, leave the circle. If RPO Thomas did, he made no comment. Frequent visits to the heads were to be expected. Carmencita must have spent many nights dreaming of one such as this. Her uncle, quite slurred of speech and dripping crab juice on his lap, could hardly be alerted to the fact that his niece was now under her fourteenth man. He had more pressing things to do—like listening in glee to the rousing song about the harlot of Jerusalem.

Carloboy sauntered away when the others were telling the Army about the seduction of Mary Jane of Drury Lane—a ballad that was always belted out, whatever the occasion.

Once there was a servant girl
Whose name was Mary Jane,
Her mistress, she was good to her
And kept her free from blame.
She knew she was a country girl
Just lately from the farm
And so she did her bloody best
To keep the girl from harm.

Carloboy pushed down the barbed wire, wriggled through. Carmencita sat on a path of cemented floor that extended from the kitchen drain. She smiled when he squatted beside her. 'They're singing real dirty songs, no?' she said.

It was the first time he had heard her voice. 'There are others waiting,' he said, 'so we must hurry.'

'I know, but you can wait a little? Or you want to do now?'

He pushed her back, placed his hand on her vagina. 'It's all wet. How many came so far?'

'I don't know. Thirteen, fourteen, I think.'

'And they all put inside?'

'Yes.'

'And you allowed? If you get a baby or something . . .'

'You don't worry about that . . . ' she caught his penis as he slipped down his trousers. 'Mmmm it's big. Come on top.'

Carloboy straddled her. He was quite drunk, he knew, and nothing else seemed to matter. He entered her with ease and plunged back and forth while she clasped his buttocks and pressed against him, nuzzling at his ear, his neck, the side of his face. The cement hurt his knees but he was too caught up in the frenzy of the moment to mind the discomfort. And he would not come. The liquor held him in a vice. Hard and demanding for release he thrust in, deeper, as deep as he could go. He heard the slap of his flesh against her abdomen and then her quick gasps as she climaxed, tightened her knees against him and caught at his lips with her teeth as he rode on until suddenly, he was panting and all the stars in the northern sky above seemed to explode. He burrowed into her, streamed into her. Months of continence had made him a sexual engine. He felt the semen pumping into her, the head of his penis throbbing, ejaculating, firing into her full-barrelled.

He kissed her. 'How do you feel?'

She lay back, her mouth slightly open, her breath hissing softly. 'Only with you it came. I thought you will never stop.'

When he withdrew, she reached for her skirt, mopped at her crotch with it, then stretched out her legs slowly. 'Any more are coming?' she whispered.

'You want more? You must be tired.'

She made no reply.

'I'll go and tell you can't wait outside any more.'

She shook her head. 'They'll be angry. Might think you told me to go away. Never mind. Let them come.'

'But they will be really drunk by now. If they make a bloody noise or something . . .'

She took his hand. 'Come inside. They're all singing.'

Carloboy hesitated. The words of the Mary Jane chorus came loud and clear:

Singing bell bottom trousers
And coat of navy blue,
Let him climb the rigging
Like his daddy used to do.

'Inside? You mean inside the house?'

'Yes. In my bed. It's easier, no?'

The Forty-second Army Corps
Came in to paint the town,
A band of bawdy bastards
And rapists of renown,
They busted every maidenhead
And staggered out again,
But they never made the servant girl
Who lived in Drury Lane.

Carloboy followed the girl indoors. He was hard as he watched her, naked from the waist down, carrying her damp skirt in her hand.

'Uncle won't come now, no?' she said.

'I don't think so.'

'Good,' and she lay athwart her bed in the little side room and Carloboy unbuttoned her blouse, squeezed her small breasts. He stood over her, between her knees as she touched him, her fingers tightening on his cock.

'You want the light?' she asked, 'the switch is there.'

He shook his head. He caught her legs, raised them until her knees touched her shoulders. Her vagina glistened as the moon peeped in. He entered her, half crouching, simply gliding in, and he knew that this time he would be very quick. Through the barred window with its half blind, came the saga of Mary Jane:

> Next there came the Fusiliers
> And a band of Welsh Hussars,
> They piled into the brothels
> They packed into the bars;
> The maidens and the matrons
> Were seduced with might and main,
> But they never made the servant girl
> Whose name was Mary Jane.
>
> Early one morning a sailor came to tea,
> And that was the start of all her misery,
> At sea without a woman
> For forty months or more,
> There wasn't any need to ask
> What he was looking for.

'I was sent here by my parents,' Carmencita said when they lay together. 'They don't want me. Some boys did it to me in Colombo and I was only fourteen. I got pregnant. My father wanted to kill me. In the hospital they took out the baby and my father said to sterilize me.'

'So that means you cannot get any more babies?'

'Yes. They did something. Turned the womb, they said. They wanted to put me in a home, but my uncle said to send me here.'

'Your uncle is married?'

'Yes, but he won't bring his family here. Children are in school in Colombo.'

'Then he's alone . . . I thought his wife was here.'

'He's alone.'

'He's fucking you, no?'

'How do you know?'

'Why else will he bring you here? He's fucking you, no?'

'Yes.'

'So you don't care?'

'What do I care? Let anybody do anything. I'll never get married. I can't even have children. What do you want me to do?'

He asked for a candle
To light his way to bed,
He asked for a pillow
To rest his weary head,
Then using very gentle words
As if he meant no harm,
He asked the maid to come to bed
Just to keep him warm.

She lifted up the covers
Just a moment there to lie,
But he got his cock inside her
Before she could bat an eye;
And though he'd got her maidenhead
She showed no great alarm,
And all she said to him was
'I hope you're keeping warm.'

'I must go now,' said Carloboy, 'you want to rest or what?'

'If my uncle is busy then tell anyone else who wants to come. But you must come again. Even in the daytime never mind because whole day my uncle is at the post. He only comes in the evening.'

Early in the morning
When the sailor had his grind,
He gave to her a ten bob note
To pacify his mind;
Saying, 'If you have a daughter,
Bounce her on your knee,
And if you have a son, dear,

Send the bastard out to sea.'

Now all you servant girls
This warning take from me,
Don't ever let a sailor
Get an inch above the knee;
She trusted one, the ninny,
In his naval uniform
Now all she wants to do, my boys,
Is keep the Navy warm!

'You took your bloody time,' Van Heer growled, 'I'm off. How was she?'

'Good,' Carloboy nodded. He reached for the beer.

And then came Able Seaman Nathali, strutting in to join the frolics, a beatific smile on his face. He walked with the slow, deliberate care of a man who was pickled to the eyeballs. He seemed to be oozing toddy, and he carried a large tin dish piled high with whole roast chicken. He entered the circle of revellers unsteadily and stood there as if waiting for someone, preferably the Queen, to pin a medal on him.

'Hey! Percy's brought roast chicken,' Sims said, 'you're going to eat all that?'

'Dishish mine,' Percy said.

Carloboy stared. The man had to be crazy. Those were the chickens he said he would bury. 'You can't eat that! Those fowls died, no? Sick birds. You want to get some poisoning or something?'

Percy cackled and sat down with a thump, the stack of done-to-a-turn birds spilling out to the sand. He closed one eye and regarded Carloboy solemnly. 'They're OK. Already—alraydyate two.'

'Bloody mad bugger! Those birds purged an' died!'

'Sho? Showatt?' Percy waggled a finger. 'Sholedem to the tavern. Thash what I did—dood—did . . . pluckemmed an' sholedem to tavern. Good ole Percy no? Goo' ole tav'n alsho. Gave some rossefowl to bring. Where's the beer?' He took a bottle and swigged deeply. 'Blurry good eating,' he said happily, tearing a drumstick off a bird. 'Purgean die. Ho, ho,' he waved the drumstick as though he was conducting an orchestra, 'purgean' die. Dasher good one.' He guzzled more beer and rubbed at the froth on his upper lip. 'So why did the buggers purgean'die? Arsk me 'n'I'll tell.' Another cackle.

He was drunk as two lords —with some information he wished to impart. It suddenly dawned on Carloboy that Percy had had a hand in the untimely death of those thirty birds. 'You damn shit! What did you do?'

'Do? Do to who?'

'You did something to those chickens.'

He began to laugh. It was contagious. Soon, everybody was laughing which wasn't a pretty sight at two in the morning. A board meeting of hyenas. Percy lay in the sand, pedalled his legs and howled.

When the spasm passed, he pointed a shaking finger at Carloboy. 'Canvas needle,' he crowed, 'pokeder canvas needle. Straight up the arse'ole!'

Even the upright RPO Thomas almost fell off his bench. The night erupted. Maddo sobbed helplessly on Van Dross' shoulder. This called for a celebration. If the drinking was in foxtrot, it now had to quickstep. Gradually, the men of *Elora* slipped into oblivion. Across the fence, Carmencita had had her last encounter of the naval kind. That last man had been too woozy to make any sort of mark. He had mumbled and mumbled and jerked himself silly against her stomach and then gone to sleep. It had been quite an effort to raise him, lead him to the barbed wire and push him through. She then went to bed and did not stir even when her uncle blundered in, pulled the sheet off her and fell upon her heavily. He could not perform either. He just lay on her, dead to the dawn that was but a short time coming.

Carloboy tottered to a tree, surveyed the wreckage blearily. Poopala lay on the galley steps, a customs officer's cap on his head. The Army was comatose. Navy caps and Army berets lay in a happy jumble.

Thomas swayed into the regulating office, trying to grin through a yawn. 'Look at those buggers. They've exchanged uniforms. And who is that naked bugger? An Army sergeant? Have to sort them out in the morning.'

Carloboy slid to the roots of the tree. His head dropped. He knew no more.

A week later, when stomachs had been blotted and wrung dry and the CO was told of the wonderful time he had missed, the village headman came calling. It was Poopala who caused the stir because he never liked this headman who he considered was nothing but a major pain in the gluteus. The headman had like feelings, not particularly for Poopala but for all sailors. For one thing, these sailors were methodically working through the goats in the village! There could be no other explanation, but his appeals to the police had fallen on deaf ears.

His rage had known no bounds when he came upon Poopala dragging the carcass of a kid into camp one day. Poopala had seen the animal, whooped 'dinner!' and seized it. It was the work of a moment to lop off the creature's head and drag it across the road. That he left a broad trail did not matter at all.

The irate headman confronted Poopala with a barrage of Tamil. His jaw dropped when he was treated to a salvo of equally furious Tamil into which more nasty words had been added than the headman had ever dreamed of. Poopala exhorted him to do all manner of things, things that would have tried the soul of the world's greatest contortionist. He was also urged to go home, fuck his mother, his wife, his daughter and his goats—in that order. The headman fled, mouthing terrible curses and returned with a shotgun.

The first shot sailed over Poopala's head and broke the regulating office window. RPO Thomas dived under the table and proceeded to have a fit—quietly.

'Repel boarders!' Maddo yelled, and the men stormed out, charged the headman who dropped his gun, turned to flee. He was grabbed and lost his sarong in the mêlée. He was then frogmarched into the mess, a picture of gasping

Tamil nakedness which was not a pretty sight, any road.

Gunasakes rushed in to sort out matters and Poopala was sent on immediate draft to Colombo. He was displeased.

'But sir—'

'But nothing! You were a menace in Colombo. You were sent here. You have become a super-menace. Go back to *Gemunu* and be an ordinary menace!'

Before taking the mail train to Colombo, he got roaring drunk and engaged in a giant barefist battle with Nathali. One peach of a blow blew Percy off his feet, spreadeagling him across the carrom board which split down the middle—naturally.

They sobbed and hugged each other on the railway platform.

26

History—Pacific Operations and the Problem of Ships

When American Army bombers appeared out of the blue over Tokyo on April 18, 1942, it made the Japanese realize that they didn't have it all their own way. The Americans bombed Tokyo while, from the California coast, US carriers and cruisers began to move towards the Coral Sea. The Japanese had threatened Port Moresby and the approaches to Australia and this had to be stopped at all costs.

By the beginning of May, the American fleet was in the waters south of the Solomons. They could pinpoint the Japanese on radar and had no wish to get too close. After Pearl Harbour, many damaged battleships were still in Californian dockyards.

It was a strange battle to be sure. Neither fleet ever saw the other, but they could still hit out at each other with their torpedoes and launch their aircraft from their carriers. Even as the contending ships' big guns remained silent, heavy losses were inflicted by each side on the other and Japan had to abort her advance on Australia. For the Americans, that was victory enough.

Still, while this vast game of hide and seek was being played over vast stretches of air and water, Corregidor fell—the last American outpost in the Philippines.

Wavell kept worrying about India. On May 1, the chiefs of staff met to discuss his protest that land, sea and air forces for the defence of India were not being despatched quickly enough. The trouble, as everyone knew, was ships. Both Britain and America were facing a disastrous shortage of ocean transport. Also, the distances of sea over which troops and aircraft had to be carried were vast. America lacked escort vessels and the ability to organize convoys.

This was something the Allies had no instant answer to. German U-boats and Japanese submarines were sending thousands of tons of shipping to the bottom. In May and June, 1942, over a million tons of shipping was sunk by U-boats. By the end of the half year, the figure was more than four million tons.

Also, there was the loss of tankers—prime targets for enemy submarines. Oil was vital, and when in the first quarter of 1942 more than 600,000 tanker tons were sink in the Atlantic, the mood of the Allies was one of desperation. On June 19th, US General Marshall told Admiral King that the losses in the Atlantic and the Caribbean was a threat to the entire US war effort.

The US had launched an immense shipbuilding programme at the beginning of the year, but the loss and damage to Allied vessels stubbornly exceeded replacements. Supplies of war—supplies to help Russia as well—were piling up in British and American ports. Even ships that were loaded couldn't set out for lack of convoys. The situation was hopelessly grave. The commitments were heavy, the means to carry them out, skeletal.

But with grit and gum-chewing, iron-jawed determination, the Americans poured into the central Pacific. Ceylon had held out ably enough. India was slowly but surely being reinforced by troops and aircraft; and the Japanese had retreated from the Indian Ocean. The Americans knew that it was now the Pacific or nothing. Battle time was upon them. They were confident. Thirteen fleet carriers and fifteen escort carriers were being readied in US dockyards. They were looking forward to air supremacy in the Pacific.

This was how, in the first week of June, the dramatic news came in. A US carrier fleet, outnumbered and with no battleship support, had trounced the Japanese at Midway. Four Japanese fleet carriers had been sunk and the supporting battleships and transports had turned back.

Japan lost a lot. She lost, above all, the chance to expand further. Her days of air supremacy were over.

27

Of Soaking Mail and Drowning Jeeps and the Mutton Line to Railway Town

One thing held much terror for Telegraphist Danny. Sharks. He hated sea patrols in small boats which, he believed, aroused the curiosity of sharks. It was said that as a little boy he used to watch his father being beaten up by irate Afghan moneylenders. His father would rush, panting, indoors screaming for the barricades to go up and gasp, 'Bloody sharks! They want my blood. Damn sharks, everyone of them!'

When he learnt that there were such things as sharks in the sea, he had considered the foolhardiness of ever joining the Navy, but things were not as bad as he imagined. One warship and that was all. Mostly, he was ashore and that, as far as he was concerned, was where a sailor should be. *Elara* put paid to this feeling of security. *Elara* expected of every man to do his duty, and one of these duties was to make up a whaler crew on sea patrol. He would, on such occasions, grab a central position on a crossplank, shunning the gunwales as though they were poxed.

Came the day when the Navy's only ship, *HMCyS Vijaya* anchored in the Palk Strait while on coastal patrol. The *Vijaya* had been commissioned to sweep the Strait, show some muscle, because of an alarming rise in the influx of illegal immigrants. Also, the customs johnnies bleated, smuggling to and from south India was rampant.

The mail for the men of the *Vijaya* was directed to *Elara* . . . and Danny was one of the boat crew sent through the Pamban Channel to deliver letters to the *Vijaya*.

'So now we are postmen,' he moaned. 'Why must I go? What about Nathali?'

'Because Nathali is mad, that's why. And because Lieutenant Commander Lawyer hates the sight of him.' This Lawyer was the *Vijaya*'s skipper.

They strung up a sail in a stiff breeze and bowled out merrily enough. Danny sat, biting his lower lip. Very strange he looked as he tried to scan all the water around him from horizon to bow wave all at once. Two furlongs out, and then he tensed. There were fish. Big fish. And they were surely coming towards the boat.

Porpoise are gentle, playful fish. Also, they like to perform and bow to the applause of mackerels. Like schoolgirls at an eurythmics display. They enjoy finny life to the full. Danny froze, his eyes popped and, suddenly finding voice, screamed, 'Shark!'

Carloboy chuckled. 'Don't be a silly bugger. Those are porpoise.'

Danny paid no heed. Anything as sleek and as grey as those fish were, had to be shark. Or close relatives, at best. He began to clamber towards Van Heer. 'They're coming. They saw us. Let me go!'

'Go? Go where? You want to climb the fucking mast?'

Porpoise, let it be said, are friendly fish. The fisherman's friend. They like humans, and a boat, to them, means company. They came around, arching gracefully out of the water, flipping spray and diving under the boat. Sheer elemental glee. The crew had no time to admire this aquatic display. They were trying, in as restrained a manner as possible, to pin Danny down and hold the boat in trim. One or the other should have been done.

'Ow! Hold him. Bloody bastard kicked my shin!'

'Twist his arms behind him!'

'Here, hit him with this oar.'

'*Shark! Shark! Help!*'

'Shut up, you bloody lunatic!'

'Let me go! They're trying to—grooh!—jump into—oof!—the boat!'

The whaler rocked violently. Carloboy wrenched down the sail. 'Here, tie the bugger up in this.'

'*Help!*'

'Will—you—shut—up! Throw you into the sea! That's what I'll do. Let the sharks eat you!'

Danny broke free, jack-knifed, swung out wildly. The whaler, being a most self-respectable craft, keeled over.

The first to break surface was Danny who continued to waggle his arms and yell until Van Heer clipped him severely over the ear.

'Shut up! Do you hear! Shut your fucking mouth! Help to turn the boat—and where's the bloody mail?'

Danny dog-paddled into the circle of men. Electrician's mate Panditha was straining against the whaler, trying to right it. 'I hope a bloody shark comes now,' he said nastily, 'I won't lift a finger. I'll watch and clap while it eats you.'

'Yes,' said Van Heer, 'finger by finger, toe by toe, guts by the yard.'

Danny worked frenziedly to put the boat on keel. Van Heer swam after the mail that was bobbing away in the general direction of India. The porpoise were delighted. These humans had actually jumped in to play with them!

When the whaler was on its way again with is salty crew and soggy letters, Danny crouched in the bows, looking most woebegone. The men of the *Vijaya* would have much to say, he knew. Ink had run on most of the letters and they all were of the consistency of overboiled macaroni.

The men of the *Vijaya* said very little. They were dumbstruck.

'What is this?' First Lieutenant Walid asked.

'Mail, sir.'

'Mail? You call this mail?'

'It fell in the sea, sir.'

'*Get off my ship! Now!* You—what's your name?'

'Von Bloss, sir.'

'And what the fuck are you?'

'Signalman, sir.'

'Right. QM, hail Telegraphist Roberts. Get out, all of you. I don't want to see any of you near this ship again, do you hear? Ah, Roberts, signal to CO *Elara.* Interrogative is your mail waterlogged. Ours is. Interrogative why do your carriers swim with our mail when boat is provided. Concerned at procedure adopted. Appreciate reply. Yes. Wait a bit. Add, and up yours too. Got that? Good. Get on the buzzer.'

Getting bogged down with the mail was one thing, but there were other instances of 'rank naval irresponsibility' (a phrase Gunasakes liked very much) that made life so glorious for the unrepentant men. There were, to district-wide detriment, excursions to Mannar. When as many as sixteen nautical fiends climb aboard a jeep and scorch the road with accelerator touching gravel, anything could happen—and it usually did.

Enroute they would wash down the dust with foaming toddy, and in Mannar the Army and the Navy would meet and drink furiously and scrap in the grand manner. Nathali was ever the hero. He once confounded even the hard-drinking fishermen of the coast by downing a pint of arrack and eight bottles of toddy, then weaving uncertainly to the gate of the customs officer's house to cock an eye at that man's exceptionally pretty daughter. The girl in question, would make her own history in that sleepy hollow, but that, the chronicler begs, must come later.

Occasionally *Elara* would receive word from the police post that a landing of illicit immigrants was expected. The given ETA, the police would grin, was at dead of night. The police got a big kick out of keeping the Navy awake.

This meant beach patrols and the most demonaic of *Elara's* crew were selected. They would stalk the beach, armed with the crudest weapons imaginable.

A light at sea would determine the possible landing place. The men spread themselves across the sand, waiting for the boat to come in. Carloboy preferred to stay in the water. He hated the sand which seemed to erupt with hermit crabs no sooner someone sat on it. Sometimes the boat they waited for was just an innocent *vallam*—a fishing craft.

'Here it comes! Go, go! Go!'

The men would streak out, take to the water with murderous yells and the poor fishermen would scream in fright at the bunch of barebodied men brandishing knives and clubs. The fishermen did the only thing they could think of—they threw out the largest of their catch, believing that the fish would appease these pirates.

On a particular night, it was a 24-pound bonito. It knocked Sims silly, spreading him in the surf. Streams of Tamil coupled with the rawest invectives ripped and roared as sailors and fishermen established diplomatic relations.

Sometimes, however, the landing was thought too far away to walk. 'What? Near Punguditivu? That's miles away!'

'All right,' Thomas would groan, 'so take the jeep.'

It was a soggy-looking night. The moon was the colour of Spanish rice and the sea like tar. Only one rippling band, where the moon looked down on herself rather despondently, told of the slow swell and the rheumy efforts of the waters. Even the sands were black and specks of phosphorous winked on the crests of the low, lazy waves that wavered and fell to go *zizz* along the shore.

At the wheel,Ionditha found it particularly exhilarating to go to sea. Rather than bowl along the firm, high sand upshore, he kept ripping back and forth in short diagonal sweeps, into the waves and out, raising long splashes of water and ho-ho-ing like the devil.

'For goodness,' wailed Daft, 'oh, for gracious!' He always ran out of words when alarmed.

'Don't slow down. Keep your foot down,' Johns shouted.

'For why?'

'Bloody idiot. If you reduce speed, we'll get stuck. This sand is like bread pudding!'

•

'Ho, ho, not to worry. Four-wheel drive, no?'

The next moment, a large, bothersome wave suddenly rose up out of a hidden shelf and slapped the jeep broad-on. Panditha was startled and the hoots of alarm from the others gave him no comfort. A big wave meant a depression.

'Turn for the beach,' Nathali yelled.

They swerved for the high sand mounds but another wave rose up, swamped them. Wheels spun furiously. Soft sand became mud. Bread pudding became rice pudding. Abandon ship!

Leaping out, many found themselves in a deep trough, the water closing over their heads. Spluttering and cursing, they hauled themselves ashore. Daft stepped out of the jeep with some dignity. He thought he had a foot of water beneath him. He disappeared with a yell and emerged, blowing angrily.

'Bloody six feet!' he croaked, 'big-big hole.' He waddled out. Another wave scattered them higher up the beach.

They sat and regarded the jeep which was low in the water. The sandstone ledge was crumbling to accommodate it.

'Now what the fuck do we do?'

'It is drowning,' said Daft. 'Going into the hole.'

'Pull it out. That's what we have to do.'

'How?'

A group of fisherfolk from the coastal huts trotted up. They held a convention. Johns perked up. 'These are the buggers we want. They'll pull anything.'

After a lot of half-baked Tamil, they made the chattering spectators understand. Yes, the Navy needed them. Johns explained, 'They spend their lives pulling nets. Jeep will be nothing for them.' He got the fishermen together and gesticulated wildly. They nodded and raced away.

It was an eerie sight. Thirty black-bodied men, three stout ropes, an apology for a moon, an India ink sea and only the muted hiss of a breaking wave. It took almost one puffing, panting, wheezing hour. The jeep came with much reluctance. It was very wet and very annoyed. Every effort to start it was met with stubborn refusal.

They hauled the vehicle to the road and left it there, then trudged wearily to camp. Upcoast, a boatload of *kallathonis* landed, found the coast clear and thought themselves very fortunate.

On the black waters bobbed a white thing. Daft Fernando's cap was on its maiden voyage, on its way to India.

The CO decided to keep his men otherwise occupied. 'It's a waste of time and effort,' he complained, 'they go, they do something completely unseamanlike, and they come. The local fisherfolk are complaining. The village headman is a bundle of nerves. Is there anything we can do to make this place shipshape?'

RPO Thomas clucked sympathetically. 'Sir, maybe we could organize joint patrols.'

'With the Army? Not on your nelly!'

Another cluck. 'At least we have a good signals post, sir.'

Gunsakes sighed. 'Yes, there is that . . . but there is far too much of this and-a-good-time-was-had-by-all business. This place is the trouble. Brings out the worst in everybody. By the by, I wished to ask you something. The men go night fishing, don't they?'

'Yes sir. I don't object. Keeps them out of mischief.'

'Out of mischief! Don't make me laugh! What about Signalman von Bloss? He and Sims. Fine pair Colombo sent us. Crackers and ginger snaps. For three evenings now I have seen them go to the pier. Carrying a sack.'

'A sack, sir?'

'A sack. You must know what a sack is? Do you know what's going on?'

Thomas was mystified. Gunasakes gave an exasperated snort. 'There are more things in heaven and on earth, eh?' he intoned, 'check it out and report, will you?'

'Aye aye, sir.'

Carloboy needed an assistant. Somehow, the thought had never struck him earlier. Too wrapped up in the devilry of all that *Elara* stood for, and in heaping quantities, he had lost sight of a very obvious fact: the railway. Here he was, the son of a railway engine driver, and the trains that were brought each evening to the Talaimannar pier to take in passengers from the ferry boat from Danushkodi, south India, were driven by railwaymen of Anuradhapura.

Anuradhapura! How could he have ever forgotten Anuradhapura. He had spent the best years of a roistering boyhood there, fallen in love there, kissed his first girl there. He had ridden ponies and fought and roamed the jungles and fished in the big reservoirs. Delirious days. And one late evening, when going to the pier he heard a shout.

'Oy! Von Bloss! Hey, you're von Bloss' son, no? Where's your bloody father?'

It was driver Werkmeister, grinning through his beard, the legs of his khaki shorts a span below his knees. Carloboy stopped, stared. Everything in that time-ago world rushed into his head. He went to the engine. 'Daddy's in Colombo. Dehiwela.'

'Heard he's put in his retirement papers.'

Carloboy shrugged.

'So you're here, eh? Why did you join the Navy? Wait'll I tell Doreen. She'll have a fit. Edema and Vanderwall are in Mount Mary. Others are still around. Ferdy came back. His son also joined the Railway. My God, why don't you come and see us? You have leave, no?'

The thought made Carloboy dizzy. Railway town. He had always had such a special love for the place. How could he have forgotten?

'Hey,' Werkmeister was saying, 'can you organize some crabs to take back next time? I'm working up again on Friday.'

More food for thought. 'That's a nuisance. Have to box them and bring from Mannar. But if you like I can get you mutton. Any amount. Free.'

'Really?'

Carloboy nodded. 'I'll bring to the pier on Friday.' He became expansive. 'You tell the others also. I'll bring mutton every night. Cut, cleaned, everything.'

'Fine. Saram is working tomorrow. You can bring?'

'No sweat.'

And so did the goats begin to disappear at a dizzying rate. The men had to range into the palmyra scrub to find them, but there was the satisfaction in knowing that thanks to their endeavours, railway town Anuradhapura, was well-fed.

RPO Thomas paled. 'A mutton line! You have started a mutton line? My great godfather! So this is what you're lugging out every evening. What am I going to tell the CO?'

'What to tell,' Carloboy growled, 'This is none of his business.'

'You shut up. Anything you do in this camp is his business.'

'Madness to give free,' Nathali chimed in, 'at least one rupee a pound must charge. Sha! Good business this is.'

'You shut up,' Carloboy snapped, 'these drivers are my friends. You want to go to Anuradhapura, they'll take you on the engine. No tickets.'

'So who wants to go to Anuradhapura?'

Carloboy ignored him. 'So tell the CO we are taking dried fish. He knows we are drying fish here.'

'For what?'

'What?'

'For what are you taking so much dried fish? That's what he will ask.'

'Tell him for my friends.'

'Hmmm,' Gunasakes said, 'His friends, you say? In the railway . . . yes, I know von Bloss is from a railway family. But every night . . . that's a lot of dried fish, even for the railway. Hmm . . . well, no harm in that, I suppose.'

'No sir,' said Thomas fervently, but was jarred when at the door he heard the CO say, 'Most unusual. Dried fish with legs. Must be a species of these parts.'

Thomas fled.

28

History—Midway

The Americans called it their 'unsinkable aircraft carrier'. This was Midway Atoll, 1100 miles north-west of Honolulu.

Japanese Fleet Admiral Yamamoto had reason to believe that he could take Midway. The Americans, he knew, were in trouble. They had lost their carrier, *Lexington* in the Coral Sea and this was a loss the Americans could ill afford.

Yamamoto was determined that within a month, Midway would be his. It was time to move his pieces across the Pacific chessboard. It would be checkmate with a vengeance when he took Midway.

But the Americans had to be kept guessing and Yamamoto decided on a fake attack, closer to the American mainland. He despatched a naval force towards the Aleutians, kept a bigger force to home in on Midway. He thought that this would confuse the Americans. They would take the Aleutians threat seriously. They would surely divide their forces. And, at least, there would be hesitation—the sort of hesitation that would prove fatal.

He did not reckon on US Admiral Chester Nimitz who, as Commander Pacific, understood much about Japanese naval tactics. Nimitz knew that there was a Japanese force heading for the Aleutians, but it seemed too obvious to him. Japan wanted him to know.

Nimitz did not divide his forces. Also, he had not enough ships to divide. He considered the Aleutians a most unsavoury target. The islands were mostly always shrouded in fog and the weather over them was always vile. Surely the Japanese knew that. What sort of effective air operation could they carry out? No. The real target was Midway, and Nimitz readied his defences and found them very lean indeed.

All he had were two big aircraft carriers, the *Enterprise* and the *Hornet*. The *Saratoga* had been gashed terribly by Japanese torpedoes and lay in Pearl Harbour under extensive repair. The *Yorktown*, too, was a sorry sight. When it limped into Pearl Harbour on May 27, workmen and sailors lining the shore could not believe it stayed afloat. The hull was speared by shrapnel, the superstructure in a state of near collapse.

A fire had swept the great carrier, burning and blackening its paintwork and the flight deck was cratered. There were gaping holes everywhere.

Nimitz had to have carriers. He was told that even at breakneck speed, repairs on the *Yorktown* would take ninety days. He demanded that the carrier be made ready for action in three. The US Navy needed a miracle, and Nimitz was determined that the miracle be performed.

It is said that over 1400 workmen swarmed the stricken carrier. Within 48 hours it left dock to anchor off Ford Island. Air crews were picked at random, men who had never worked together before. Even the captain, Vice Admiral William Halsey was in hospital. A replacement, Rear Admiral Raymond Spruance, was rushed in. New, untried men in a battered ship, hastily patched.

On May 30, 1942, the *Yorktown* was ready to sail. With her escort, she nosed towards the battle zone. She was Task Force 16.

Also heading for Midway was Task Force 17, the *Enterprise* and the *Hornet* under Rear Admiral Frank Fletcher. He was to rendezvous with the *Yorktown* on June 2, about 300 miles from Midway.

There's nothing more beautiful than a Pacific atoll. Green-water lagoons, reef embraces, sugar beaches and incredibly blue seas. Long before the war, the China Clippers landed on Midway on their way to the Far East. On June 2, it was aswarm with seabees and US marines and anti-aircraft guns in their sandbagged nests. Nimitz ordered all the fighters to be fully fuelled. He had guessed right. A Catalina pilot had spotted the Japanese task force under Nagumo approaching Midway.

Chuichi Nagumo was the great Japanese naval hope. True, he had turned tail in the Indian Ocean, but that was a 'tactical withdrawal'. It was Admiral Nagumo who commanded the force that belted Pearl Harbour. He was now headed for Midway with four carriers, and on approach, launched his planes—fighters, dive bombers, torpedo planes carrying heavy bombs. One hundred and eight in all.

All the men of Midway could scramble were 26 fighters. They flew out, thirty miles to westward, saw the V-formation of approaching enemy planes and climbed to 17,000 feet. Then levelling off, they dived. It was a desperate attack plan. Some of the old F4F Wild Cats simply ploughed through the Japanese formation and could not recover from the steep bank. The Japanese Zeros were the better machines. These Mitsubishi OO's were called Zekes by the Americans. They were faster and turned tighter.

Nagumo was pleased. Only nine US fighters survived, returned to base, and of these, seven were in very bad shape.

While this battle arrowed in the sky, Nagumo sent his raiders in. They screeched over the two main Midway islands, tearing the installations to pieces. Yet, as the Japanese strike leader observed, the airstrips were still operational. Nagumo was not worrying. He had softened the Midway defences. Now he would take over. He would land his troops on the atoll under the blistering guns of his big ships, and he had the giant battleship *Yamota*—the largest battleship in the world, a 68,000 ton behemoth. What could withstand the power of its big guns?

The Americans turned desperately on the source of their torment. Ten US fighters made for Nagumo's carrier force, Avengers and B26 bombers. They could not know of the firepower they would meet. Of the six Avengers, five were downed in a solid curtain of shrapnel. Two bombers simply tumbled out of the sky. The others spun away for home. Not a single hit was scored.

Again, sixteen planes went after the Japanese carrier *Hirya*, and again, half their numbers were shot down. Army B-17 Flying Fortresses from Midway maintained a height of 20,000 feet. They returned unharmed but accomplished nothing. It was a grim picture.

On June 4, Midway was in bad shape. Most of its aircraft had been destroyed and the islands were a smoking ruin. It was then that Nagumo considered the strike leader's report. It began to bother him. As long as the runways were operational, he could not risk an invasion. A second air attack was necessary. But he also had to be sure that there was no US naval force in the vicinity. He was sure that Yamamoto's ploy had confused the Americans. Nevertheless, he sent out four float planes to search the seas. He ordered the search planes to be aloft by 4.30 a.m. and was not told that the last of the planes had been launched at five. For Nagumo, this would be a fatal thirty minutes.

With the spotters out, Nagumo waited. He armed his fighters for a second strike on Midway, but he waited. Two-and-a-half hours. No sightings. Another fifteen minutes. Still no report of an US fleet. He was sure now that there was no risk. Another fifteen minutes. His attack force was ready for launch . . . and then came the news from one of the float planes—a report that should have come in half an hour earlier if that plane had been in the air at 4.30 a.m. as he had ordered. The US fleet had been sighted.

Nagumo called for clarification. Another fifteen minutes, and he yet had no real description of the enemy. He was rattled. Were there carriers? He could get no definite answer. He dithered. Should he attack Midway or go after the US fleet?

On the *Yorktown*, Spruance found himself closest to the Japanese. He thought he had pinpointed the position of the Japanese force, but again, there was an error—an error of about forty miles. Spruance knew that the combat radius of his planes was 175 miles. To launch now was to send his fighters to operate at the limit of their range. Many would never return.

But he disliked waiting, even if waiting meant that he would be closer to the enemy. He signalled Fletcher. The order was to go!

One hundred and fifty-two planes took off from the *Yorktown, Enterprise* and *Hornet*. The forty-mile error was tragic. Torpedo planes of the *Enterprise* never saw the Japanese. Some turned back, low on fuel, others limped on to Midway. The fighters, drained of fuel, were less lucky. They crashlanded into the sea.

From the *Hornet*, Torpedo Squadron 8 swung away when they came to the point where the Japanese were supposed to be. Streaming out on this altered course they sighted the Japanese at 9.20 a.m. just eight miles away. Even as they primed for attack, Japanese Zeros shot up and tore into them out of the sun. Below was the thunder of anti-aircraft guns.

Torpedo Squadron 8 hadn't a prayer. With fuel tanks near empty, they dived into the enemy fire. Fifteen planes. Thirty men. Only one man survived to grab a seat cushion that floated in the water, cut away his parachute and watch as the Japanese steamed majestically past him. Not a scratch on any of them. His whole squadron had perished, and not one had been able to even touch the enemy's paintwork!

Came the torpedo squadron of the *Enterprise*. Fourteen planes. Ten were shot down. Then the planes of the *Yorktown*. Twelve planes. Ten shot down. But Nagumo knew he was in trouble. His Zero fighters, zooming down from high altitudes, had to climb again to stay manoeuvrable. Their attack pattern demanded this. The waves of US planes did not give them the chance to regain altitude, and many simply tore into the sea. Suddenly, Nagumo had no fighter cover . . . and there, swooping out the blue, were the slower dive bombers of the *Enterprise* and *Yorktown*. They had the Japanese in their sights, and there were no fighters to harry them.

Down through the anti-aircraft fire they came. The Hell Divers, and it took less than a minute to release their bombs and pull out, arching upwards. It took less than a minute to change the whole shape of the Pacific war.

The Japanese carriers were ablaze; holed flight decks, elevators twisted, deck plates stoved upwards. Everywhere on the decks planes burned, aviation fuel burst into starry furnaces and torpedoes exploded. The *Akagi* began to sink, the *Kaga* and the *Soryu* were wrapped in columns of oily smoke.

Nagumo transferred his flag to the light cruiser *Nagara*. He spoke incoherently, a shattered man. He could no longer effectively command.

Another Japanese Admiral, Hiroaki Abe, saw that the carrier *Hirya* was still operational. He ordered an air strike. The Japanese bombers winged vengefully away, found the *Yorktown*, its decks cluttered with fighters being refuelled. Many of the Japanese bombers were shot down but six got through and their bombs found the heart of the big carrier. Even as the men abandoned ship, a Japanese submarine closed in and with deadly spite, split the dying vessel. The submarine next torpedoed the destroyer *Hammann* that had rushed to the *Yorktown's* aid.

Night fell. Nagumo steadied himself, considered his options. All his carriers were destroyed. He had no air power. But he could still engage and destroy the American fleet. He had big, hard-hitting battleships and cruisers. Under cover of darkness, he sailed east. He would come upon the Americans and destroy them.

But Spruance anticipated the Japanese move. He did not know how much strike power the Japanese had, but he decided to take avoiding action. At all costs, there must be no night battle.

Dawn came. The Japanese knew they were defeated. They had been unable to engage the enemy fleet. And now, Nagumo had to run, for with daylight, the American bombers would return. He ordered the retreat westward. Operation Midway was ended.

For the imperial Japanese fleet, it was an imperial Japanese cock-up!

29

Of Priests on the Prod and Sentimental Journeys and the Test of the True Signalman

As would be expected, Sundays came and went with their usual hot monotony. No one, for example, thought of church, although the regulating office did have provision for a church parade. This was usually quite an imposing thing, where men who sought the benefits of communing with God (who only deigned to see them on the first day of each week) would spruce themselves and wear clean number tens and form rank before being led to the holy place. There, they would sit and ogle the women and wish that the bloody priest would shut up and get on with whatever he had to do.

The outing was welcomed in Diyatalawa or in Colombo, for it gave them much to do with their hands especially when on their knees and confident that the pretty things next to them had found the answer to their prayers.

Elara was another kettle of fish. Indeed, 'fish' seemed to be the operative word, for the priest who circuited the district conducting services and baptizing babies hither and yon, received his coin in fish. So powerful was his hold on the poor blighters who constituted his flock that the first catch of each day went to the priest. His was a fishy business indeed. He dealt in fish. He organized the sale of fish. He could even give *his* fish cheaper than those who gave him fish.

None of the men of *Elara* were interested in a church that had its foundations on mackerel and bonito. Furthermore, there were no other attractions. The only thing that looked good in long skirts was the priest himself, and he, naturally, did not count.

In Mannar, quite a different situation had begun to develop. It was the rainy season and still, under a cloud-laden sky, people tended to sit and gasp. The palmyra fronds crackle and the humidity becomes unbearable. The closeness of the atmosphere makes the goats nervous and even the wind does nothing to help.

There, the old parish priest had a junior who would whirr along on his motorcycle to far-flung places where there were palm-thatch churches. He would say a Mass here, a Mass there for the faithful. He was a tall young man with a dashing goatee, smoke-blue eyes and hands which were lean and thin-veined.

He was an Italian, a missionary who had been sent to serve from his monastery below the Dolomite hills. And, being a virile, handsome man, he had considered the customs officer's daughter (the girl Percy Nathali had raised eyebrows at) and found her far from wanting.

The men of *Elara* when on their rounds, usually rooting out places where they could imbibe, would sometimes encounter this priest. He would be on his motorcycle, cassock tucked over his knees. Behind him sat the girl, her hands clutching at his hips as he thrummed swiftly by.

The men would whoop and wonder where this strange couple were going. As evil-minded as they were, they never thought of the extreme possibility—that the priest and his pillion rider had more things than holy water to keep them together.

Then, Nathali fell ill.

'It's the heat,' Thomas said, 'and he's got a skin rash. I told the bugger not to eat so much dried fish.'

As a sick man, Nathali was hopeless. He developed a crackling fever and began to pour iced beer on his head.

Gunasakes sniffed and said, 'Take him to Mannar hospital. He'll die of pneumonia and I don't want to log that.'

'Sir, is it malaria, sir?'

'How the devil do I know? Ward him. At least we'll have some peace around this place.'

Stirring things were happening in the hospital. Hundreds of angry people at the gates and a decidedly anti-Church atmosphere.

'What the hell?' Panditha asked.

Inside, Roman Catholic nursing sisters checked out Percy and wheeled him to a ward.

They were tight-lipped and quite pale, and refused to tell Carloboy about what was going on.

In the men's ward an old priest was seated, glaring at the Italian who lay in traction. The man had apparently broken a leg and injured his spine. The story, in all its blushing beauty was all around, sizzling from bed to bed, ward to ward and had reached epic proportions in the female ward where Customs officer Ganam's daughter lay, her head swathed in bandages while her furious father had been sedated after expressing a desire to tear the Italian priest limb from limb.

Carloboy saw Nathali to a bed. The man had, a doctor said, either malaria with some curious side effects or had some strange malady with a malarial flavour. He had to be tested and observed and neither task would be one to enthuse over. It could also be liver, but that would depend, the doctor said, on how much liver the man actually had.

Percy sat and leered at the matron. 'Call this a bloody hospital?' he complained, 'Nuns! Who wants nuns? Where are the bloody nurses?'

'Shut up,' Carloboy hissed, 'You heard the doctor? Even he is not sure what is wrong with you. All red and yellow and like a damn bonfire. First they must bring the fever down.'

'Never mind that. What's all the row about that priest?'

Carloboy grinned. 'Pukka priest. Have been taking the girl all over Mannar on his mo'bike. Her father did not know a thing. Mother is in fits now. Sitting at home in the kitchen and hammering her head on the grindstone.'

Percy was never too ill to be interested in such complicated human situations. 'Don't know why I joined the Navy,' he protested, 'should have been a priest. Any woman will come. Nobody will suspect, no?'

'Lie down.'

'So what's all the bloody fuss? What happened? These sheets are stiff! Dettol smell. These buggers want to make me sick?'

'You're already sick. Shut up and lie down.'

'So what happened?'

'Went on the motorbike and crashed somewhere. What else? He is injured, she is injured, whole story came out. You remember we saw them once?'

'Yes, yes . . . sha! must have been taking and screwing her in the bushes. One thing, any girl you take on a motorbike and go, easy to fuck.'

It was never easy to understand Percy's line of thought.

'How is that?'

'Why, men, bumping and going behind. Cunt is getting well rubbed, no? Must be well-oiled by the time she gets down. Must buy a motorbike.'

They took Percy away to Pathology. Carloboy and Panditha roamed the ward. Decent enough for this neck of the woods and the nuns ruled with an iron hand and starch in their eyes. A lot of stuff seemed to swirl around the priest who was visited by a Bishop and all manner of clerics who had come from Jaffna to tell him how hopelessly human he was and therefore, a priestly misfit. At least, he should not have been found out. Quite unpardonable. And what about the good people of the parish? Most reprehensible. Most ungodly. Most un-Mannar-ly.

The Italian priest stared at his accusers with contempt. Yes, he would return to Italy. The women there liked to have their bottoms pinched. He didn't want to be a priest. It cramped his style. His blasted cassock had got entangled in the wheel. How can any red-blooded man get about in a cassock that waits to trip him up?

Percy spent a week in hospital to the grief of everyone there. It was, they diagnosed, a condition brought about by liquor, fried food of a most doubtful nature, more liquor, the intolerable consumption of dried fish not wholly cured, more liquor and still more liquor. He had sailed close to an allergic shock, and it was fortunate that he had the constitution of a mountain gorilla and cast-iron intestines.

The Italian priest was hobbling around his bed on a crutch. One leg was still in a cast and he had shaved and looked most cocky.

'So you're going back,' Carloboy said.

'Going I am,' he chirped, 'you are Navy man, yes? You like eet here?'

Carloboy shrugged. 'The girl has gone. I hear her father sent her to Hatton or somewhere.'

His blue eyes clouded, then he gave a short bark. 'So they come they go poof. Let me say to you, Navy man, you theenk I want to be prist? Look a'me. Well you look a' me, so! What see you, what-a you theenk?'

'So why did you become a priest then?'

'Ah, long story iz mine. Long, long. When I was, how you say, leetle, my mama poot me in San Theodoro. An' for why? You can say for me why?'

'So you tell me.'

'My mama ver' week she iss. My papa he die and here I am, not stillborn I was.' He shook his head. 'Dead iss my papa. Dead and gone and never I saw heem. Only grave to go and rid the name of my papa on stone put there. Sorry me, no?' He paused and cupped his chin in his hand. 'Poor pipple we are. Ver' poor. When I seven my mama say you go to monastery. There you be and become prist. I ask-a why. I not wanteeng to be prist. But go she say I mak-a da vow she say. So I go and there I leeve an' home I do not go. An' the friars they say they mek me prist and I cannot say anytheeng anymore.'

'So you became a priest?'

'Yes, yes. But the girls, ah molto bello. They come to the chapel and to baptize the bambinos and I am thinkeeng, how you say, hot hot, and when they come to Communion, mama mia . . . ' he seemed to drift into a reverie and Carloboy studied him curiously. He thought of a long time ago when he too had wanted to be a priest. That was oh, light years ago, and it all came tumbling back. Here, he thought, but for the wisdom of my father, sit I, broken leg and all!

'Anyways I weel go. But I telling you Navy man, before I go I weel do something. I weel do to tell this bishop what I theenk . . .' he leaned forward and his blue eyes took on a new light. 'Yes. Befo' I go I weel take my cassock, yes? My cassock will I take an' hang eet! Yes. Hang eet! Torlest tree in Mannar I weel hang eet. Then go I weel. Ah, the girls een my village. You come I show you.' His hands moved in demonstration. 'Beeg, beeg bubbs. Bubbs, no?'

'Boobs,' said Carloboy.

'Right. Bubbs. An' legs. Ah, long, round, and. . . fuck-a them all I can. Beeg problem this cassock. Many many girls how you say, shy? Yes, shy. Theenking prist not theenkin to fuck them. Now I fuck them. Ev'ry one I fuck. Might and main, no? Yes. Might and main I fuck. But cassock I hang. Torlest tree in Mannar. Torlest tree, what you theenk?'

Carloboy grinned. This was a prist—priest—he liked very much. 'Good,' he said, 'hang your cassock and go. Fuck them silly. Best thing after benediction.'

The man grasped his hand. 'Man you are before my own heart!'

'After,' Carloboy said and gave him an encouraging pat. He wished he could be in Mannar to see the end of the saga. A cassock dangling from the tallest tree in Mannar would give the locals much to talk about. Why, they might even make the tree a shrine!

In camp, he went before a requestman's parade.

'Signalman von Bloss requests permission to grow a beard, sir,' Thomas said.

Gunasakes squinted. 'Why?'

Carloboy didn't know either, but the Navy *did* give a man a special allowance if he wore a beard. Something to do with naval tradition. Yes, that was the word. Tradition.

'It's Navy tradition, sir.'

'Humph. That'll be the day. You want the thirty rupee allowance, is that it?'

'Yes, sir.'

'Request granted. Another scruffy bugger on board. Full beard, do you hear? No shaping it to your liking.'

'Yes, sir.'

Railway town received him with mixed feelings. The embryonic beard had a mind of its own. It liked growing out in a number of directions at once. Driver Vanderputt's daughter adored it while Heather de Jong wrinkled her pretty nose. Carloboy had leaped off the engine at the Anuradhapura station and drawn a deep breath. He wanted to laugh, to cry, to choke, to run along those steamy roads. It was a homecoming of sorts. Eventually, having drunk his fill, he crossed into railway town, walked its old familiar avenues, saw the old iron rail fences, the gaudy curtains in the windows, the potted coleus on the verandas, the gardens with the big banyan trees and rain trees, the hedges of Madras thorn and heard the tinkle of a piano.

A piano . . . and yes, there sat a tall, long-fingered girl at Werkmeister's piano. She was playing 'Mona Lisa' and playing it badly.

'Your bass chords are wrong,' he said.

She turned, startled large grey eyes on him. 'I don't know the notes. I'm just picking it up by ear.' She studied him. 'Who are you?'

Her mother bustled out. 'Carloboy? My goodness, child, just look at you! So small you were when you were here. Went to see your old house? Tamil guard is there now.'

'Mummy, who is this?' the daughter asked.

'Why, von Bloss, child. You remember them . . . when uncle Meerwald was here. But how can you remember, you were a baby, no? Come, come, you must be tired. Come to the kitchen. Marie, see and take your books from the settee. Your father will come and shout.'

Railway town made much of Carloboy. They all came to say the mutton was top-hole and the young ones congregated to hear him play. It had been so long, but once at the piano, he belted out all they asked for and the evening became a regular party with booze a-plenty.

Carloboy was happy. This, he thought, for the sixtieth time, was home. He played on and on and Sandra Vanderputt stood beside him, watching his fingers fly on the keys and kept asking him if he would like another sandwich . . . or a cutlet . . . or if she could ask her father to pour another drink.

Oh, there was leave. Stacked up, actually, because nobody on *Elara* had anywhere to go. Weekends in Anuradhapura became a marvellous part of existence and Sandra drew him like a magnet. He knew that, given time, he would have her, and that when that time came, sooner or later, she would be very willing.

But someone up there, someone doubtless concerned for Sandra's virginity, blew a whistle. The Navy must have heard, and the Navy intervened. Carloboy was aghast. He had come to *Elara*, hating the very thought of the banishment. Now, all he wanted was to stay. He knew that the next time he visited Anuradhapura, there would be no more holding back. Railway town, too, was aware of the 'romance' and was all for it. Sandra was a sailor's girl. She had ripened at first, then accepted it in good humour. Other railway town daughters envied her. There was something magical about the uniform.

Brenda Von Haght was a stickler for detail. 'My, men, it doesn't tickle when he kisses you?'

Sandra would giggle redly, 'His beard? I like it.'

Drafted! All signalmen had to return to Colombo. The news left Carloboy speechless.

Eventually, 'When?' he asked.

'Tomorrow.'

'What! Tomorrow?'

'Yes. A replacement arrives tonight. Evening train, so you lot pack off tomorrow night.'

Only last week, Sandra and he had sat on the bund of the Nuwara Wewa, the city reservoir, and she had obligingly spread her legs while his squirming finger had dug in under her knickers and he had made her wet and urgent for more.

'So suddenly? What is all the bloody hurry?'

She had come, panting heavily and pressed her legs together, trapping his hand while he kissed her breathlessly and did not know what he could do with his own rigid member.

'Qualifying exams for all you buggers.'

'Exams? That's a hell of a thing. What exams?'

She must have known he had to have relief. Her fingers unzipped his trousers and probed his underpants. It was the work of a moment to take out his penis, watch it throb in her hand. She began to push with her finger, back and forth.

'I told you, qualifying exams. What are you looking as if a duck has fucked you? Colombo, men. Colombo! And if you pass the exam, pay increment also.'

He had come in her hand and she ran down to the water to wash away the semen and run back to kiss him and cuddle close and let the breeze blow her brown hair across his face. They made plans for the next week. 'Your mummy goes to Mass on Sunday morning, no?'

'Um—yes.'

'So you stay at home. I'll come in the morning when she's gone. Your daddy said he's working Colombo on Saturday, so he won't come back till Sunday night.'

'Only about two hours we will have. That's if she stays to chat. She'll be earlier if she comes straight home.'

'That's OK. We have time.'

She had kissed him urgently. 'You'll be careful, no?'

'Don't worry. When it is coming, I'll take out.'

Yes, like Onan, he would spill his seed on the floor. It would still be good, he had thought.

'I wish I got drafted,' Thomas said, 'this place is getting me down.'

Carloboy left him, slightly dazed. What was he to tell Sandra? He had to write. Explain. What would she think? That afternoon he walked behind the heads, tossed a handful of sand at Carmencita's window. It was no trouble creeping through the fence, and he rode her furiously. With her, at least, there was no need for *coitus interruptus*. She said she was sorry he was leaving.

'Balls,' he said, 'you have enough to screw you here. And new fellows are coming. What do you care? Navy the whole day, your uncle in the night . . .'

'You're angry,' she said simply, 'why are you so angry?'

'Because I'm going, that's why.'

The girl misunderstood and held him close. 'So don't be angry. When you get leave, you take a train and come. I'll be here.'

Carloboy lay on her, his head against her forehead. But he was a true child of Nature.

Here was a bird in the hand. He began to move, then increased rhythm stabbingly. She raised her hips to meet his every thrust.

When he boarded the train, he took a left-hand seat. He didn't want to see railway town from the carriage window. As the train neared Colombo, he went to the washroom and with much effort, scraped away at his beard. The dingy washbasin and the small trickle of water did not help much, but he managed to shave. Let the Navy say anything, he swore.

Barnett, who studied them with a frown when they presented themselves at the main signals office, finally declared that somewhere, somehow, the Navy had missed the bus. 'You were sent to *Elara* as conscientious signalmen,' he said sadly. 'You come back to us black, disrespectful, caps like FL's, shoes like old tubes of toothpaste . . . look upon them, Patrick. Extraordinary Signalmen. Now why didn't the Navy think of that designation? They were quite an obliging, ordinary bunch of half-arses before they left. Look at them now. Hah!'

Patrick grinned.

Carloboy thought of his diary entry. All it said, baldly, was: *3rd March, 1955. Drafted to HMCyS Gemunu*. It said nothing about this welcome back.

Patrick stopped grinning. 'You buggers have a talent for looking like the bottoms of trash cans!'

'Extraordinary Signalmen,' Barnett murmured.

'There's nothing extraordinary about them, Yeo. They're just plain cussed. One year in *Elara* and they're wild. Wild! Well, let me tell you something. This is a nice MSO. A nice, neat office. You remember this place, don't you? We like to look nice here. We are in the NHQ and there are a lot of big brass here. Now if you will look at me what do you see?'

They looked.

'Spotless uniform, starched, ironed, trousers neatly creased, stockings four fingers below the knee, shoes shining. Not an Irish pennant in sight. You see my cap? A dusting of Goya Black Rose on the rim. It keeps my hair from getting greasy. Smell my arse . . . I spray it with lavender . . .'

'Oh Patrick,' said the Yeoman dreamily, 'You never told me.'

'Now look at our Yeo. Immaculate, I tell you. Immaculate.'

'I'm the immaculate contraception,' Barnett murmured.

'So what have you to say for yourselves?'

'I'll tell you killick,' Carloboy said, 'we have been travelling all night and only got here half an hour ago. We got third class travel warrants. You ever travelled third class in the Talaimannar mail? It's the bloody black hole of Calcutta. Tamil women, poultry, *kallathonis*, black cigars, people smelling of gingili oil. We haven't slept a wink. Babies howled the whole night. One woman had a stomach like a dhoby's bundle. There were children sleeping in the latrine and on the luggage racks. Then a truck picks us up at the station. A dirty truck. And wet. No canvas top and the MTO must have left it out in the rain. So we come here and the quartermaster yells, report to the MSO. We haven't slept, haven't bathed, we are tired as fuck-all and there's no bloody lavender in our arseholes!'

'Hear, hear,' said Barnett, 'why, the man is a silver-tongued orator, Patrick. He presents his case in a most seamanlike manner. So we now know why they look like overcooked corpses, don't we?'

Patrick curled a lip.

'Von Bloss, stop breathing fire and waxing worth. We have misjudged you, but then this is what awaits the best of men. Look what they did Jesus Christ. And Abraham Lincoln. Let us now proceed to put you wise. You are tired. You don't like Colombo. You don't like us. Good. You wish you were back in *Elara* eating goats . . . aha! we know all about the fun and games, me hearties. But be assured, you were summoned back for the good of your souls. Here, too, will you find mutton, dear chaps, and it will be even dressed as lamb. Pay no heed to Patrick. I doubt he sprays him bum with lavender. The aroma of hydrogen sulphide is what I usually get when he is downwind. From tomorrow, my chocolate drops, you are going to school.'

He wagged a finger when they made to speak. 'Yes, school. Eventually, you will be tested and if any of you fail the qualifying exam, I will do terrible things to him. Very terrible, I assure you. You will study. You will learn the ANSB[1] by heart. And you will get the X and Q codes implanted in your brains. You will do R/T[2] with me as well as flaghoists. Yeoman Louis will take you in navigation, boat signals, harbour signals, the bloody works. Patrick will conduct semaphore and Aldis. Alfie will take recognition signals, procedure and MSO routine. Ranawana will take W/T and V/S[3] and after three months you will sit a test—'

'You mean we have to learn all that in three months?' Daft paled.

'I could give you the whole syllabus, but then you might soil this place in fright and Patrick will be very annoyed.'

Patrick grinned.

Barnett waved a hand in benediction. 'Today, take a breather. Go to your huts, clean up, masturbate, get organized, sleep. Don't screw the cat. I chanced upon a particularly fine-looking tabby in your hut this morning. Cultivate it. You could train it to pounce on your cocks at zero five hours each day which will be more effective than our traditional wakey-wakey, eh? Patrick?'

Patrick grinned. 'OK,' he said, 'so get going. Von Bloss, you can bring us a can of tea before you turn in.' It was his way of reminding Carloboy that he didn't like being talked back to. Carloboy ignored him, turned to the door.

'Von Bloss!'

Carloboy strode out with the others. Barnett soothed the indignant Patrick. 'There, there . . . poor fellow must be a little hard of hearing. I think it's all that goat he's been eating. I must ask my doctor's wife about this.'

What Patrick told the Yeoman he could do with the doctor's wife was never known, but it must have been something most seamanlike and in the best of naval tradition.

Intense training. Deep, dogged, determined and utterly damnable. Daft took it to mind, heart and subconscious with the soreness of a martyr being chewed by a lion with bad teeth. He began to mutter in his sleep and then would struggle up, fling off his sheet and yell, 'Corpen two zero!' and open wild eyes to find himself wheeling a man-o'-war in a tight 20-degree arc with one hand and hoisting an imaginary signal with the other. These nightly performances got on everybody's nerves.

'What's he saying?' asked Todwell crossly.

'Stuff his mouth with soap,' Sims suggested.

'Shh. Lissen . . .'

The mumbling became more distinct. 'The way is off my ship—you may feel your way past me—the way is off my ship . . . you may—'

A hard pillow cut off the litany.

'That's flag Peter at sea!' Daft yelled, leaping up, wide awake.

'We know, you silly bugger. Now go to sleep!'

But half an hour later the man would crank up again. 'Oscar in harbour—I am carrying mail . . . Oscar in harbour—I am carrying mail . . . Oscar in harbour—I am carrying maaa-yoorrgh! grooh! glub!'

Sims was using the hosepipe.

To their everlasting credit, they were all given a congratulatory 'Yoicks! Tally-ho' by Barnett who said he was chuffed. 'Oh, I'm so pleased. Today as a special treat I will show you a 90 millimetre film of my wife taking a bath. She does very nice things with soap.'

Daft had fared very well indeed. Examination over, Yeoman Louis gave him an encouraging pat. 'Well done, Daft, I can see you put a lot into this.'

Daft looked at him weakly, gaped and tottered away.

'What's the matter with him? He's sick or something?'

Carloboy grinned. 'Must be overstudy, Yeo.'

'Dearie me. I hope he's all right.'

Yes, Daft was all right. They were all all right. They had breezed through and scored top marks. Carloboy bought Daft a beer. The man gulped, made big eyes and gulped again.

'I'll tell you something,' he said, 'You ask me anything—any fucking thing about signals now . . . I don't remember a thing. Not a thing!'

'So never mind. You got through.'

'Yes, I got through. Let's get some more beer.'

They did.

Notes

(1) The Allied Naval Signals Book
(2) Radio Telephony
(3) Wireless Telegraphy and Visual Signals

30

History—Japan's Dream of Empire

It all began with the Sino-Japanese war of 1894-95. Japan began to develop an appetite for conquest. She started with Korea and Taiwan, and these made her greedy. She was determined to match the West in prestige . . . and might. It was no accident, then, that she began her ravage of a continent and an ocean—from Burma to the Aleutians, from the coastal waters of Australia to Manchuria.

But Japan did something else. She loosened the western yoke on many restive Asian countries. For hundreds of years, most of Asia had lived under foreign rule. It was the Pacific war that toppled this old colonial order and this may explain why, to this day, there is a certain Asian ambivalence over the Allied victory in Asia.

True, the Asians of the time came to have little sympathy for the Japanese. Historians have recorded these feelings, mostly of dread and revulsion. Under Japanese occupation people were accused of the flimsiest things . . . and executed. Even to meet a Japanese in the street was fraught with danger. A citizen could be slapped, kicked, made to bow and take the near careless buffets of men who looked upon the vanquished as cattle.

The cruelty of the Japanese conqueror was terrible. Cruelty that made it very necessary to convene those war crimes tribunals when it was all over.

But Asia had its dilemmas. The Japanese at first offered many Asians an end to colonialism. In Indonesia, for example, the people wished to get rid of the Dutch. Indians were demanding that the British quit. Vietnam wanted the French to get out. Then were those Asians who supported the Japanese 'collaborators'. There were those who actually betrayed nationalistic guerrilla and resistance movements to the Japanese, and there were those who simply worked for the occupied governments. Why, even pro-independence leaders worked for the Japanese.

Aung San of Burma did so. So did Manuel Roxas of the Philippines; and Sukarno planned his country's independence with the help of a Japanese-trained Army.

The Japanese found it cosy to their expansionist ideals to declare an Asia for Asians. They cultivated Subhas Chandra Bose, when he quit India's Congress Party because the party paid scant heed to his call for revolution against the British. Japan also built up Aremio Ricarte as their key man in the Philippines. And Burmese leader Ba Maw actually reviewed Bose's Indian National Army in the company of Japanese Prime Minister Hideki.

But the Japanese also began to show the extent of their arrogance. By 1945 Asia was glad to have the Americans back. There was immense relief at the Allied victory, but they were also not going to undergo another Allied occupation. They were not going to be pawns in a game where one empire builder exacts revenge on another.

It had been a time of much trial for Asia. From 1937 to 1945—a period of occupation, destruction, disaster and death. On July 7, 1937, Japanese soldiers had approached the Chinese border town of Wampang. They said they had lost one of their men and wanted to enter the town. The Chinese refused to open the gates. That was the famous Marco Polo Bridge incident and it triggered the eight-year war between China and Japan. Millions died.

On March 7, 1942, Japanese soldiers entered the home of the Dutch mayor of Batavia. They marched the mayor and the colony's resident to jail. They had entered Batavia after their victory over the Dutch in West Java.

The Indonesians never suspected a thing. The Japanese, they were sure, should help them build their own, independent nation. Hadn't the Japanese swarmed in with Indonesian flags on their armoured cars and battle wagons? They shattered the statue of Batavia's. Dutch founder, Jan Pieterszoon Coen. The Dutch-named Van Heutsz Boulevard was given a Japanese name: Jalan Imamura. The Dutch Tamarind Street (Tamarindelaan) was renamed Jalan Nusantara. Batavia became Jakarta.

And the Japanese made their purpose painfully clear. No one could fly the Indonesian flag. The Indonesian anthem could no longer be sung. Local culture was all but wiped out. Even the clocks were set to Japanese mainland time and the people were compelled to learn Japanese.

In Korea, the degradation had begun much earlier and World War II was just another chapter. As far back as 1910, when the Japanese had marched into Korea, Korean Prime Minister Yi Wan Yong signed the annexation treaty that made Korea a Japanese colony. Then the unremitting exploitation began. Korean farmers grew their rice to fill Japanese bellies. By 1937, Koreans were forced to take Japanese names, write in Japanese characters and speak only Japanese in their homes. We are now aware how, in World War II, Korean girls were shipped to the front lines to serve as 'comfort women' for Japanese soldiers. Up to 139,000 women were forced to serve as prostitutes.

Burmese nationalists actually turned to Japan for help in their anti-colonial struggle. Several were taken up by Japan's self-serving slogan: 'Asia for Asians.' Aung San and Ne Win actually went to Japan for military training, then slipped into Bangkok.

When the Japanese swept into Burma, they destroyed everything. The Allies were forced to retreat to the Indian border. But the Burmese soon realized that they had a Japanese controlled puppet government. Aung San realized how he had been hoodwinked. In March 1945, he took his men over to the Allied side.

The Japanese landed in Malaya in 1941 with 5,300 men. That was off Kota Bahru, but earlier rumours of war had made the Malayans gear themselves to defend their homeland. The British had the Indian Dogra Regiment posted at Kota Bahru. The battle was fierce, and despite the heroic stand taken by the Indian soldiers, the Japanese 18th Division won through. At the same time, other Japanese divisions entered the towns of Jitra and Kroh.

The British had to flee Penang on December 14. The Indian and Eurasian regiments began to withdraw. The order was to retreat to Singapore, but when the troops reached Malacca they found that their British leaders had disappeared. Soldiers without leaders. Many just stripped off their uniforms, discharged themselves and went back to the villages as civilians. But the Japanese were everywhere. In Negri Sembilan. In Kuala Lumpur. They searched every village, every house, stole all they could, took every bicycle they found. And, sickeningly enough, there were hooded informants who accompanied the Japanese, pointing out British sympathizers.

Singapore had reason to be confident. The British had assured them that all would be well. The British actually regarded Singapore their Eastern Gibraltar. But the Japanese came: a swift attack down the Malay peninsula, led by General Yamashita Tomoyuki, the Tiger of Malaya.

The bombs rained down, lorry loads of the dead were carried away and the British had to admit defeat even though their forces outnumbered the Japanese three to one.

The Japanese had plans for Singapore. They renamed it Syonam, the light of the South. Oh, they were so proud, so sure of themselves. Even the Germans had told Tokyo that it would take up to nine months to take Singapore, and they would need five divisions. They achieved in two months. A race to Johore Bahru, a massive aerial pounding, and victory!

Singapore would be the capital of Japan's Greater East Asia Co-Prosperity Sphere . . . and the first thing was to establish a rule of fear. Thousands were executed, suspected of resistance. Heads of those killed were placed atop poles for public display. They stripped the people of everything, executed those who had nothing to give. And even when the British came back in 1945, the people were not going to forget. No more foreign rule. They could no longer rely on foreign rule. The British had given them a false sense of security; the Japanese had murdered thousands of their people.

Hong Kong had almost two million people when Japan attacked that colony on December 8, 1941. Thousands starved. British prisoners-of-war were brought into Stanley Prison. The tortures, the privations, the gruesome executions have not been forgotten. People even turned cannibal and hawkers sold the meat of corpses, claiming that it was dog meat. By 1945, there were only 600,000 people in Hong Kong. Many had been forcibly taken away to China. The horror haunted the colony for a long, long time.

In the Philippines, a 30,000 strong peasant movement was organized against the Japanese. The Filipinos fought alongside their American colonizers but to no avail. With the fall of Bataan, the country's fate was sealed. And even the recapture by the Americans became a living hell for many. More than 10,000 were killed, caught in the joint pincer of American bombardment and Japanese savagery. There was no hesitation, at the end of it all, to look on Manila as the worst victim of devastation in the Pacific.

This was how the dream of empire rose . . . and died. This was the empire that would raise the Greater East Asia Co-Prosperity Sphere; that would grow fat on the lands of the Pacific and the Indian Ocean. This was the empire that would rule the East and be the giant of the hemisphere, in position to command the world's most populous regions and the natural resources of many nations.

It must have been galling to know that they were kicked back, defeated on their own turf; more galling still to realize that German-spawned scientific technology, the technology of her own ally, would be put to work in America in order to bring about her humiliating, scorching defeat.

31

Of Sundry Eruptions, the Language Dilemma and Other Fish to Fry

Colombo. Back, Carloboy thought, to the rancidity of this other Big Apple where, with every bite, one had to spit out a maggot. For one thing, home was as bad as ever, in a state of mild chaos that, his mother insisted, was all his fault.

'My fault? What did I do? I was in Talaimannar. If the bloody roof comes down here its my fault? If—'

'You're the one who sent all the crab and dried fish.'

'And you're the one who brought a mangy baby into the house. Bloody scabies! All the buggers are scratching.'

It was an outbreak of the old, old enmity. Mother and son glared at each other and saw nothing but hatred in each other's eyes.

For some, strange, unexplained reason, Sonnaboy von Bloss had gone with his wife to a convent and orphanage. In those times it used to be very much in order for the good people of the city to go to these institutions fòr a child who was to be a servant. True, one picks up a girl child of very tender age, but that child is easily moulded. At six she will begin to sweep the house, help carry out the wash, fetch and carry, help tidy the rooms. At eight she will carry water, sweep the garden, put the firewood out to dry, destone the rice and learn to cook. At ten there will be far too much to do and far too many kicks and slaps to make her do it. The little unfortunate will wash bundles of dirty linen, scrub floors, scour lavatories, weed the garden, cook, bathe the dog and pick up after the children. At thirteen she will steal food and go to the co-operative store and carry home the shopping bags and slit firewood and take out the garbage. She will also develop breasts which would be squeezed by the sons of the family. She will also attract the attention of the man at the oilman stores who would use his greasy fingers to stroke her and give her fifty cents to buy toffees. At fifteen, child and virgin no longer, she will scrub the pots and blow the kitchen fire and work, work, work until at the end of each day she will be too exhausted to protest when the elder son pushes her legs apart and enters her.

That was the pattern. Why, then, did his parents bring home an acid-faced baby—a boy—and with spreading patches of inflamed skin all over its body?

Carloboy had only one explanation. They had to be mad. The baby had infantile scabies. So he had sent home a couple of boxes of crabs and a box of dried fish. His father liked crabs. Dried fish cost the earth in Colombo. And the damn scabies was catching. He was appalled. The whole family scratched and scratched and had begun to look like polka-dotted albinos. Violet gentian, liberally applied, made his sisters look more awful than they already were. The baby, caked in fuller's earth and some oily muck that must have been a soothing jelly, howled and howled and resembled a palpitating snail.

'So bad to eat crabs and salted fish when there is a skin disease,' his mother snarled, 'that's what I'm tellin'.'

'Then why did you eat? Could have given the neighbours. And how was I to know? Did anybody write? Even one line? No. That nobody will think to do.'

He slammed out of doors. 'Sit and scratch! Damn good for you. Not enough you have, went to bring some other bugger's bastard!'

He went around the house, hauled his bicycle from the rear veranda. The rear tyre was flat, the front brake cable hung, snapped off over the brake shoe. Fuming, he wheeled it away, strode across the plank bridge over the canal, then to the bicycle repair shop at the top of Vihara Lane. His father had gone to the railway head office at Maradana. The old man had decided to call it a day. Werkmeister had been right. Engine Driver Class I Sonnaboy von Bloss had put in his papers for retirement.

Carloboy had heard the rumblings even in Anuradhapura. A new official language policy. Every government employee would have to take a qualifying exam in Sinhala—the national language. Suddenly, a politician who had a mouthful of a name that smacked of the Jew and the Briton, had begun to wallow in the myth of Sinhalese superiority. In 1956, he would force the switch to 'Sinhala Only' as the sole official language of the country, replacing English and not paying much heed to the Tamil language either.

Carloboy had listened to the way the drivers of Anuradhapura, at many different levels of alcoholic influence, had debated the issue.

True, there was the basic mass urge for social equality. It seemed that the English-speaking minority called the shots. But this politician himself was a product of Oxford, a brilliant product, let it be known, and he should have known better.

Even as these words are written (and this is 1996), the Sinhala Only experiment of the fifties has proved disastrous. The people were made to ignore English at considerable cost and disadvantage to themselves. And to this day, the plums of office in every sector still go to those who have a knowledge of English, just as it was in the colonial past. Those who accepted Sinhala Only, basked in the dream of 'our country, our language', and spurned English are today a disadvantaged people.

'It's all bloody politics, what else?' guard Harry Ball had said: 'Trying to get the vote. All the villagers will vote for him, no? Going to give them a place in the sun, he's saying.'

'I say, you don't know, men, what he said in 1943,' said driver Beven. 'Trouble is you fellows must study the way things are going.'

'So you're the bloody know-all, no,' said Ball. He tells the others, 'Pukka bugger this is. Before buying arrack, he's going to buy the *Reader's Digest*!'

This makes Beven a most interesting Burgher to be sure. 'No! Truly?'

Beven soldiers on. 'In 1943 Jayewardene[1] wanted to declare Sinhala as the only official language. That's the bugger who started all this. He wanted Sinhala to be made the language of instruction in all the schools. It must be compulsory for all public exams and English must be thrown out.'

'Bloody bastard! He was mad or what?'

'Cute bugger. Said the Sinhala language needed protection. All politics, what else?'

'One thing, nobody's going to make my children study in Sinhala!'

'Hear, hear. Pour another drink, men.'

Yes, the rumblings were very much in evidence. Carloboy went to Pereira Lane, shouted up old friends, then pulled in at Eardley's. There was as ever a welcome at Eardley's. Here he had lived when he left home in the time before he joined the Navy. Here he would bathe, change, write a letter to Sandra, play cards, and, in the evening, go to Vaverset Lane and then to see his grandmother at St Lawrence's Road. Barbara would not be expecting him. He looked forward to seeing her with the greatest of pleasure.

Suddenly, he was sure it was good to be back. Why, Wellawatte was a blossom-time of girls who stopped, stared and giggled. Who was he, they must have wondered. A new boy on the block? And who were those ravishing creatures who claimed to be his cousins of a sort? Kingsley da Brea was his mother's cousin actually, and the meanest-tempered man in all Dehiwela. Carloboy's friend, Malcolm

Abayakoon had cautioned him. 'Don't mess around there, men. You're dicing with death. The old bugger is a killer.'

And that he was. Liquor made him go berserk. He took out his feelings of unstoppable rage on the citizenry—policemen, bakers, vendors, latrine coolies, young toughs who had the temerity to look at his daughters . . . and when there was a lack of object matter, his one and only son who was also named Kingsley and was more the family knave of hearts.

Sonnaboy told his son, 'Go to your uncle Kinno's house. You know where? That's right. Say none of us can come with this damn scabies. His son died yesterday. He sent a message. Funeral is tomorrow. Just pay your respects and come.'

Dead? A nice boy like that? Tall, bronzed, wide-eyed and full of fun. 'But how?'

'I don't know. Cerebral malaria, they say. But there is some unnecessary talk. Don't go to hang about. Ipseems the father gave the boy a good thrashing. Had marks all over him.'

'Uncle Kinno must have hammered. Who else?'

'Never mind all that. Just go and pay your respects and come.'

Maybe Kingsley de Brea killed his son. The talk around the untimely death was dark and accusing. It was true. The father had thrashed the boy terribly, but it was the sister, Shirley, who took Carloboy aside and whispered, 'Don't tell I told. You won't tell anybody?'

'Tell what?'

'Shhh. After Daddy beat Kingsley he—he dragged him to the canal and threw him in.'

Carloboy stared.

'Some men jumped in and pulled him out and carried him home. Then he got like delirious and mummy took and went to the hospital. He died in the hospital.' Her eyes filled with tears. 'Now we are afraid. See the way daddy is crying now . . . but if he starts drinking don't know what he'll do.'

Carloboy stormed away and faced the quivering man. 'Why are you crying,' he demanded coldly, 'when he was alive all you did was hammer him. Now what for crying after killing him!'

People gasped. The mother, Iris, hung on Carloboy, implored him to leave. She was a young, shapely woman, many years younger than her drunkard husband. 'You came here to start something?' her voice was high, unnatural. 'This is a funeral house! My son is dead!'

Carloboy shook her hands off him and looked around. Who were these people? He had never had much truck with them. The daughters, white-faced, trembled. There was Fairy. Yes, her father had actually called his eldest girl Fairy. And Joan, and Shirley. And Shirley, at fifteen, was the star of the show. So exquisite in this tumble-down house by the canal. Without a word, he strode out.

Shirley came to where his bicycle was. 'You're mad?' she breathed, 'now the hearse will also come. Are you coming to the cemetery?'

'No. I'm going home.'

'I'll come with you if I can,' she said huskily.

'So come. I'll take you on the bar.'

'My God, Mummy will have a fit. But I go to the Polytechnic. You can come there and meet me.'

'Right,' and he rode away and told his father, 'If he came out, I would have hammered him.'

Beryl, listening tight-lipped, went to the bedroom. 'Hammer him,' she muttered crossly, 'that's all they know to do. Hammer everybody.'

Sonnaboy bubbled with plans. 'Commuted pension I'll get. Pukka, no? Thirty years service. Provident fund, association money. They'll commute it and give me a lump sum. More than fifty thousand. And still I'll get pension every month. And if I want to go back and work, can always apply to work in Maradana. Guards inspector's office or some other place. I had a long chat with Wadood. He's the secretary of the Locomotive Enginemen's Union. Straightaway I became a member. The LEU can take up my case anytime I want to go back and work.'

Beryl listened and her lip trembled. Her husband retired. At home. Life seemed to drag out before her like a long, long tongue, dry and sat upon by myriads of flies.

Carloboy discovered, to his regret, that many of his friends were leaving the country or were engrossed in plans to leave. They were not, they declared, going to have Sinhala thrust down their throats. The government, led by Sir John Kotelawala, stood for 'parity of status' for Sinhalese and Tamil as the official languages of the country. The Burghers were all at sea. A commission appointed to report on the language issue had actually advocated a single official language. The chairman of the commission, Sir Arthur Wijewardene, who had been a Chief Justice of the Supreme Court, had noted:

> The replacement of English by *Swabasha* (one's own language) would have been very much easier if, instead of two *Swabasha* languages as official languages, one had been accepted . . .

This put the Tamil's back up.

The Burghers found this all too unreal. What about their mother tongue, English? Suddenly, it seemed that the island considered it necessary that English be displaced. Even in 1943, J.R. Jayewardene, for motives best known to himself, was determined to ditch English. He wanted the business of the state council to be conducted in Sinhala. He called for the translation of all important books of other languages into Sinhalese. He asked for the appointment of a commission to report on all that was necessary to effect the transition from English to Sinhalese.

Oh, there was much flowery rhetoric. This chronicle will be doing readers a disservice if the outpourings of the architects of future chaos are not recorded. Listen, then, to the impassioned motion of J.R. Jayewardene in 1943.

'It is argued that . . . if we displace English and make Sinhalese and Tamil the official languages, we will be shutting out a large world of literature and culture from our people. They little understand that the world of literature is already a closed book to ninety per cent of our people . . . In the field of literature, of science, of culture, we have been entirely barren of achievement.

'It was not so when the native language was the language of government. I think history records that wise men both from the East and the West came to the shores of Lanka to read the books that were preserved in the sanctuaries of the Buddhist Sangha (priesthood). If one reads the travels of Huen Tsang, Marco Polo and Fa Hien, and the lives of great Western philosophers such as Doctor Paul Dhalke and Rhys Davies and others, we would find the contribution that this country made to world literature when we had our own language as the official language . . .

'But (today) the official language is English, and that is why this country is always in danger of being governed by a small coterie who go through . . . English schools, whereas the vast majority who go through Sinhalese and Tamil schools must always be in the position of hewers of wood and drawers of water . . .

'The great fear I had was that Sinhalese, being a language spoken by only three million people in the whole world[2] would suffer or be entirely lost in time to come, if Tamil is also placed on an equal footing with it in this country. The influence of Tamil literature, a language used in India by over 40 million, and the influence of films and Tamil culture in this country, I thought, might be detrimental to the future of the Sinhalese language; but if it is the desire of the Tamils that Tamil also should be given an equal status with Sinhalese, I do not think we should bar it from attaining that position.

'Language, Sir, is one of the most important characteristics of nationality . . . it is because of our language that the Sinhalese race has existed for 2,400 years and I think that . . . on the eve of freedom as a free country, we should prepare for a national official language . . . English should be deposed from its position as the official language of the country and Sinhalese and Tamil . . . should be made the official language of Lanka.'

No wonder the Burghers were upset. Everywhere there was much debate on the employment of the Sinhalese and

Tamil languages. Queerly enough, many of these debates were conducted in English! Let the Sinhalese scream at the Tamils in Sinhala, and let the Tamils cut loose in Tamil and let the Burgher sit back and wonder at this new Babel scenario.

The Sinhalese backwoodsmen were naturally delighted. They had no truck with English anyway. The pressure grew and grew and the demand was heard everywhere: Sinhala Only! We are the majority. Our language. Our country. Sinhala Only!

Parity? How can you condone parity with a 70:30 ratio? Is that parity? Die hard nationalism was rising everywhere.

Carloboy shrugged. People in Colombo didn't seem to know the first thing about living each day to a satisfactory finish. He had vast fields to conquer and a lot of territory to operate in. But sometimes, as we will now learn, his interests were very close to home indeed.

It was most interesting to take note of the tall, fair, Sinhalese girl who lived in the house beside their side fence. The stretch of side yard looked into the rear garden of her house across an untidy fence. He had no thoughts of her whatsoever when he took his bicycle to this fence one hot morning. The MSO had been agog with the news of the upcoming Joint Naval Exercises, Trincomalee. Several ships of the Commonwealth navies would participate. Ceylon would figure with her only ship, that was certain. And, as always, a strong contingent of signalmen would be needed.

He squatted to clean his bike and the dash of water made him raise his eyes. The girl was seated at a large tub which her mother kept filing with water. Her black hair glistened down her slim shoulders. She wore a cloth that was tucked in around the top of her breasts, and used a small pannier to pour water on herself. And she was looking directly at him.

He kept rubbing at the fork of his bike, his eyes on her. The mother fussed around and then handed her a cake of soap. While she soaped her arms, her shoulders, the mother stood behind, rubbing at her back, scrubbing down her spine and kneading the back of her neck.

The girl kept her eyes on him, then ran her hands over the cleft of her breasts. As he watched, she loosened the knot of her cloth, dipped her hand inside, began to soap her body. Perhaps it was the cloth. It clung wetly to her. He could see the movement of her hand. He sat transfixed. She looked around as though to make sure she would not be noticed, then dropped the cloth to her hips. She did not move; just sat there, her breasts shining, a pale statue, willing him to look at her.

Carloboy made a slight motion with his hand. The girl's head turned, then she began to soap herself, pushing up against her breasts, fanning her hand to her navel. Suddenly, she jerked up the cloth. Her mother was close by, then came to stand before her. He saw her rise, then stoop to soap her legs.

Carloboy swore softly. The mother had cut off his line of sight. He felt himself stirring and he hunched down to his knees, waited.

This time she stood, tall, long-limbed while the mother poured water on her. She was rubbing at her crotch within the cloth. One leg gleamed up to mid thigh where the cloth overlapped, then parted. Suddenly she was alone. The mother left, returned with a towel. She put the towel into her daughter's hands and went indoors.

He was sure she smiled. She slung the towel about her shoulders and in one quick movement undid the cloth. She stood, naked and beautiful, long shapely thighs, slim calves, small waisted and young-breasted. Then, with a sudden shyness, she whipped the towel around her, let the cloth fall to the ground and retreated into the veranda, then indoors.

Carloboy rose and felt a tremble of excitement in his knees. He would keep an eye out for her. Getting over the fence would be no trouble but that garden was too large, too open to walk into without exciting comment. But there was a rude sort of out-building that held firewood and dry coconut fronds. From his room window, he kept watch. There were servants, he noted. An old woman and a young girl. The mother was always fussing around in the rooms that were an extension to the veranda. A kitchen, probably.

And yes, she was around too, looking towards the fence. It was the work of an instant to wave a hand, show her where he was, point to the outhouse and indicate that she should go there. She made no sign that she understood, but a little later he heard the crackle of dry fronds. She was there.

With his heart beating fast, he slipped out, squirmed through the fence, keeping the outhouse as a screen to his approach. Then he whipped in, caught her, embraced her, pressing against the old, mossy brick. They did not speak. He raised her dress. She wore no underwear. He pressed his cock against her. No, he could not take her that way. The floor was dirty and a litter of old wood. Swiftly he turned her around, pressed down on her shoulders, making her bend, her buttocks arched towards him. He entered her from behind, clasping her around the stomach, heaving into her. Then she spoke. '*Ikmaning*,' she said in Sinhala, 'quickly!'

And quick it was, working like a dog over a bitch, and he came and clumsily withdrew, the semen daubing her backside. She turned, smoothed down her dress and smiled. He held her, kissed her face. 'You go,' he said, 'I'll wait and go when no one is looking.'

She nodded and walked out, casually enough, her bare feet kicking at a patch of lily grass. He waited a while, found no one about and darted out.

Todwell said the next day, 'I'm off watch today. How about you? Let's go to Mutwal in the evening. I have some friends. We can put a good booze. Have some nice girls also. Only thing can't get them alone. House is always full of people.'

Carloboy shook his head. 'No, men. I have things to do at home.'

Yes, he had other fish to fry.

Notes

(1) J.R. Jayewardene, a young politician in the Ceylon State Council of the time. He eventually became the first Executive President of Sri Lanka.

(2) Today's Lankan population is 18.3 million which makes the number of Sinhalese language speakers (including those who are not Sinhalese) about 16.4 million.

32

History—Finding a Winning Strategy and Bickerings in the Ranks

The trouble was the Allies had too much on their plates. If it was Germany alone, they would have got together with fewer pyrotechnics. Japan was the wild card they had to also trump, while those in Europe found Hitler the greater menace . . . naturally.

On May 21, 1942, US Admiral King gave an extensive exposition of the operations in the Pacific which he intended to conduct in 1943 and '44. He insisted that it was necessary to sever all Japanese lines of communication. He said the US would concentrate on Rabaul and Truk, and then the Marianas, the latter being the key to the situation, because the islands were located on the Japanese lines of communication.

This was all good stuff, but Churchill had his own stubborn plans for India. He wished the C-in-C India to be purely in command of India and not muck about with any operations outside India. Also, there was the need to appoint a Supreme Commander who would co-ordinate British and US operations in that theatre.

Many felt that Churchill was being just plain pig-headed. After all, the operations in Burma and Assam were also connected with the immediate defence of India. Also, the Allies were now working for the liberation of Burma, the support of China and a Japanese defeat.

The base *had* to be India . . . so India needed its own C-in-C. Churchill did not think Wavell was the man for the job. He looked on Wavell's long silences and quiet manner as an indication of a lack of drive. He wanted Wavell out of Burma. He then began to think of moving Wavell to India.

In truth, the one factor guaranteed to upset at any time, was Churchill. He changed his mind so often that nobody could be sure of what the global strategy for winning the war really was. At one time, Churchill was determined to win the war by bombing. Everything must be sacrificed in order to bomb the enemy into the dust. Then he called for patient self-sacrifice. The nations of the continent must be prepared to bleed themselves dry, just as the Russians were bleeding and sacrificing tremendously to drive Hitler back. Then again, he would demand that all effort must be directed towards the Mediterranean—against the Balkans and Italy. Then he would switch to Norway. He wanted to 'roll up the map in the opposite direction'—pull the ground from under Hitler's feet. Then he would demand that all these plans be put into simultaneous operation. The huge shortage of shipping didn't seem to faze him at all.

It took a long time to pound out a global statement on strategy to win the war, but finally it was accepted by all—even Churchill—and despite the many individual views the chiefs of staff held.

US Admiral King was certain that the war could be won by action in the Pacific. To him, the other fronts did not count.

US General Marshall wanted the Allies to mount a cross-Channel operation with up to thirty divisions. He was not interested in what was happening on the Russian front. He simply wanted to clear Europe his way and win the war.

Viscount Portal, Marshall of the Royal Air Force, kept demanding that England gather together the largest air force possible. Only then will there be victory, he said.

Admiral Dudley Pound, Admiral of the Fleet, RN, was all for a huge anti-U-boat war. As long as the German U-boat menace existed, there could be no Allied victory.

Field Marshall Sir Alan Brooke was certain that operations should be first concentrated in the Mediterranean. Once German forces were dispersed there, the Allies could go to Russia's help and bring about a situation where cross-Channel attacks were possible.

Yet, they hammered out a strategy, and then Churchill, who had agreed to it all, who had passed it and had even congratulated his team, tossed it all out. He hated altercations. He wished to repudiate practically half of it, alter all the Mediterranean divisions.

This made the Americans look on the British with dark suspicion. Eventually, a compromise emerged, but Admiral King simply shrugged and set his jaw. Whatever the plan, he would continue to demand and get his ships and the landing craft he needed in the Pacific. He was not satisfied that the Allies', first objective should be the defeat of the Axis in Europe. He was not satisfied with the assurance that after this was achieved, the US and Great Britain would concentrate their entire forces against Japan. He had a war to wage. He had, he considered, an unremitting war to wage. He would extend pressure against Japan until he had reduced her military power and forced her unconditional surrender.

And he got his way. By the beginning of 1944, despite the fact that Hitler was planning massive countermeasures against the Allies, America was allocating even more men, planes and assault craft to the Pacific. She seemed to pay scant heed to the agreement that Germany should be attacked first. There were thirteen American divisions in the Pacific, only ten in the UK and Mediterranean.

King made his claims heard, the US alone was responsible for the Pacific war. He teamed up with his military colleague and rival, General MacArthur. Together, they played a game of leapfrog from island to island. They would take some Japanese possessions, isolate others. Their first target was the Solomons—a chain of islands stretching north-west to south-east, between five and eleven degrees south latitude. Guadalcanal was the largest and southernmost of these islands, lying east of New Guinea, north-east of Australia.

King and MacArthur were very confident. Indeed, MacArthur had always been considered a superb strategist, and there is little doubt that his south-west Pacific campaign was a masterpiece.

The only hitch was that the US operations in the Pacific were planned exclusively by the Navy department. There was little or no reference to the war department and as a result, the allocation of resources, as between the Pacific and Europe, was a sort of hit-and-miss affair.

Lieutenant-General Sir Ian Jacob, in his *Diaries* called it a game of grab. The Navy grabbed the ships they needed, the Army grabbed whatever it could. The Navy controlled the landing craft and that caused problems for the Army. Also, the Navy always tried to go it alone, only bringing in the Army when it was sometimes too late. This was to happen at Guadalcanal. The Marines who were thrown ashore found no follow-up, no maintenance support, no transport. It was only then that the Navy called the Army in. It was very nearly too late.

33

Of Seatime and Target Tows and Frying Flying Fish

They were, Patrick said, a favoured lot. The gods had smiled. The news had made the MSO jubilant. They were to go to sea.

'Are you good sailors?' Barnett asked.

Carloboy never liked such questions, and Barnett had a repertoire all his own.

'If I left my wife in your care, would you fuck her?'

'Why Yeo, as if I would.'

'What? You're telling me my wife is not good enough for you?'

This left the poor signalman stuttering. A good sailor, to Barnett, could be anything—from a rum-swigging hornpipe dancer to the man who made the biggest noise in a brothel.

'Yeo?'

'Didn't you hear me? Are you a good sailor?'

'Good in what way, Yeo?' Nothing like lobbing the ball back into his court.

'Just look at you, my son. Kitted, booted, capped, lop-sided. So you're a sailor, aren't you?'

'Yes Yeo.'

'Sez you! Look upon the waters and weep! There, where the waves roll, the swells swell . . . hmm, I always wondered why they were called swells . . . yes, the swelling and the rolling and the crests and the troughs. Ah, my spirit rises. Do you know what I see . . . an endless field of masturbating mermaids. Such frenzy . . . and have you been out there, there, where the mermaids are sperm maids?'

'No, Yeo.'

'Thought so!' he snapped, 'and you call yourself a sailor. Ye gods and little fishes! I am surrounded by fakes. They dress like sailors, they swear like sailors, they bugger the mess boys like sailors, but sailors they are not. Not! Do you understand von Bloss? You are a sham!'

Carloboy sighed. 'If you say so, Yeo.'

'Oh, I do, I do. But I will make of this base clay a metal of some merit. Mark well my words, signalman. A-roving you will go. You and the others who are but a clutch of lubberly land crabs. Boats will be provided. Such is the generosity of the Navy. Tomorrow, at dawn, you will go to sea.'

Carloboy stared. 'For—for what?'

Barnett waved airily. 'Oh, it is all arranged. The Army needs some battery practice. God knows they need it. Can't aim for toffee. They have these big guns at the Rock House battery. So they want some target practice.'

'So why must we go anywhere?'

'Listen, dense one, and then will enlightenment come. It may take time because of the thickness of your skull but it should soak through. Three boats. Leading seamen will navigate so you will not be called upon to take the wheel. But two signalmen will man each boat . . . and, pay heed, you will tow a target float. Eighty yard lines should suffice. Even the Army can't miss by eighty yards.'

This was getting stickier and stickier. 'And if they do?'

'Then they may hit your boat. A pardonable mistake of course. Don't you know that nobody's perfect?'

'This is crazy! Those buggers will shoot us out of the water!'

Barnett wagged a finger. 'Naughty, naughty. I deplore this negative attitude. Very unlike you. And what if they do? You can swim, can't you? Here. This is the list, the crew of each boat. And the MTO will ferry you to Kochchikade. Take heart, oh you of little faith. I shall watch your progress with my spyglass from the tower. Doesn't that comfort you?'

'Comfort my arse! And I'm with Daft. Who is this Leading Seaman Sonnadara?'

'Good man, I am told. Rammed a pilot boat last week but said he had no choice. The port commission is very upset. Very crowded, the harbour, that's the trouble. Our leading seamen don't take kindly to navigating in crowded harbours. The open sea, my lad. That's what we want. That's where you will go.'

Carloboy quivered. 'Bugger will ram the pilot station or something and we will all drown even before we go to sea.'

'Nonsense. How can anyone drown near the pilot station? Ah, yes . . . a berthing overseer did. Fell off the pier and never came up. Very strange. The man preferred to stay under. There's really no accounting for tastes, is there? Divers found him a week later. Caught in some struts he was, and they had to pry him loose. Such a to-do there was—'

'If you're trying to scare me—'

'Scare you, my poppet? Me? The soul of kindliness? Even my wife says there's no one more kindly, more—'

'Oh, fuck your wife,' Carloboy muttered.

'But of course I will. Nice of you to remind me. But pray let me continue. You are a trial to talk to, von Bloss. Now, when they laid this berthing overseer on the pilot station jetty he was a most peculiar sight. His stomach was stretched to bursting point. Like a Mickey Mouse balloon. And then there was this big pop, and the balloon burst. Now what do you think of that?'

Carloboy wrinkled his nose.

'It caused a panic. A bursting berthing overseer. Most unexpected. Drowned, yes. Dead, yes. But to explode? Went with a bloody bang, he did. Belted the boat crews with bit of his insides and peppered the pier with his intestines.' He shook his head. 'I tell you, von Bloss, some people behave very strangely when they are dead. I hope you will not be like that if the Army gets you tomorrow.'

Sonnadara grumbled all the way to Kochchikade. So did the other seamen who were to coxswain the launches that would tow the target floats.

'Three targets,' he snarled, 'now the buggers won't know what to shoot.' At the jetty he glared at the towlines. 'That's eighty yards? Looks more like forty to me more like forty to me.'

'Eighty, killick. Good grassline.'

'So why couldn't you make it hundred, you idiot? Just look at the sea. Big waves, no? If had an extra twenty we can keep some slack, no? Where are the bloody floats? My God, flat bottoms! Von Bloss, here, take this rope to that float. Secure at the nose, and check the target pulleys. Are there oars? See if there are oarlocks. Damn fools think we are going to pull floats through this harbour. No room to pull a coffin. Yes, yes, you stay on the float. After we secure at the North Pier you can come aboard.'

The others were executing similar procedure. Daft stood by sheepishly until Sonnadara said, 'At the North Pier you will pass the grassline to the float, raise canvas, secure guy ropes and check that all lines are running free. You know your running hitches, no?'

Daft opened his mouth. What was this horrible man talking about? How does a hitch run? He gulped and nodded.

The flat bottoms had no oarlocks. Carloboy scratched his head. At the Rock House battery, the Army scratched theirs. Where was the Navy?

'How do I row this thing to the pier?' Carloboy asked.

Sonnadara came over, also scratched his head.

'Now we'll have to commence towing from here.'

Sonnadara glared. That he hated this assignment fiercely was very evident. He was already on mulct of pay for damaging a pilot boat. He regarded the float with loathing. Then he brightened. 'There, at the stern. There's an oarlock. Bloody fools we are. These barges have to be sculled. Go and get long oars.'

The bosun at the Kochchikade stores scratched his head. 'Sculling oars? Wait, I'll see if have. All nonsense this is. Just tie the floats and take and go, will you?'

Carloboy gritted his teeth. 'You think this is a bloody picnic? I don't know how to scull a boat.'

'Simple, men,' said the bosun, brightening up, 'just poke the oar in and wag it side to side. You'll get the hang of it. Ah, here have some. Help me move this junk.'

Carloboy looked at the long oars with distaste. 'Better if had some long poles,' he said, 'could have just pushed the bloody floats.'

'Poling in this harbour? You'll be stuck in ten feet of bottom silt.'

Ships in port did not know whether to laugh or to cry as the strange procession meandered by. Carloboy's shoulders certainly wept buckets. The morning sun roasted the back of his neck. He simply couldn't make the float behave. It went in every direction but the one it was supposed to take. It crept between mooring ropes, nudged mooring buoys, scraped against anchor chains and banged its sides against gangways and wallowed alarmingly in the bow waves of hooting launches. Carloboy sweated. Suddenly, this harbour seemed to be a vast unending repository of the grimiest ships in the world and he was on a crooked course that was definitely going nowhere.

At the end of the North Pier, Sonnadara fumed. So did the other seamen.

'Where's that bloody von Bloss? Can you see if he's coming?'

Daft shook his head.

On other floats, Sims and Perera laboured just as much. Sims tried to follow Carloboy, found that the effort made him dizzy and simply sculled recklessly on, ignoring direction. He bumped into all manner of things: shipsides, marker buoys, got entangled in a cat's cradle of ropes and was almost run into by a snorting ash barge upon which grimy men sat and said rude things to him.

But they made it, and Perera pleaded sick and Carloboy flopped on the pier and asked whether this was anybody's idea of fun. Sims looked at his hands, studied his forearms and the sides of his upper arms. 'My muscles have got muscles,' he said.

A berthing master waddled up. 'No boats allowed here. What is all this?'

The men looked at each other, then in one voice yelled, 'Fuck off!'

The berthing master was gone before the breeze drowned the sound.

Beyond, the white caps tousled the sea. The target canvasses were raised on their makeshift masts. Each canvas had been liberally smeared with Black Japan. Big, black inverted triangles, twenty feet tall, the grasslines were secured.

Sonnadara was unhappy. 'You think there's eighty feet here to pay out?' he asked Able Seaman Mendosa.

Mendosa, who was also 'Cupper' Mendosa and the most noted and colourful homosexual in the service, nodded. 'Pay out to full and let the bloody things go anywhere.'

Able Seaman Foenander shouted from the helm of his boat, 'So come go! It's rough out there. Keep the floats at thirty feet until we pass the breakwater.'

When the first running sea hit them, they bucked in a mass of spray and jolted over the crests. The grassline sang. Sonnadara *was* a fine seaman. He pushed out alongside the big troughs, nosed through the whitecaps, and Carloboy suddenly felt that the world would never stand still again. He had imagined that this would be the same millpond he had known in Talaimannar. Oh no! And why was it that the sky and the sea kept switching places? The small launch rolled, dipped, burst through the rollers and rose sickeningly to poise like some proud horse until someone shot its legs away. There was a numbing sensation in his ears; and what was all the salt doing in his mouth? He spat, then leaned over the side to spit and spit again.

Sonnadara howled, 'What the hell is wrong? We are getting close to range area!'

Daft folded up. He flopped on the heaving deck, holding his stomach. He was pea-green and glaze-eyed.

Carloboy couldn't care less. He was consigning his breakfast to the waves. He didn't hear the sound of the guns from the Mutwal battery or see the fountains of whatever as shells fell around the floats. He was spilling his stomach and his throat burned and his face was the colour of khaki. Would this never end? He tried to beg Sonnadara to turn back. Blearily he looked around. Nothing but an enormous basin of leaping water . . . or was it a leaping boat . . . he vomited, again and again.

When the boats turned, he was stretched on deck, eyes closed, retching to the pulse of the launch and heedless of all around him. His face was bloodless and then, with a groan, he brought out a large dollop of white mucus that looked like some bullet-ridden mushroom. It was his stomach, he thought. He had thrown up his stomach. There was a greenish spittle on his chin.

Sonnadara cursed mightily, stepped over his crew to slip the float line. 'To hell with it,' he shouted.

The line whined as it shot outwards and the float curtseyed its thanks and allowed the waves to sweep it shorewards. The other boats also freed their floats. The Army had proved once again that it was a waste of time to shoot at targets. It would have been better (and more entertaining) if the Navy had fired the targets at them!

'Your first time, no?' Sonnadara said, 'So good. Got all the bile out. Go and eat something. You'll see, you'll be OK now.'

'If I keep getting seasick like this—' Carloboy croaked.

'Nonsense. Barnett sent you, no? That bugger! But he did you a favour. Must be sending you for JET exercises. On the *Vijaya*. That's why he sent signalmen for this. You wait and see, you won't get seasick again.'

Talk of fiery (or watery) baptism. Sonnadara said he had got so sick his first time out that he had split the lining of his throat. 'Even now I can't drink hot tea. It burns inside. You think this JET will be a picnic? Bay of Bengal. Terrible sea. Run all the way up to Singapore lighthouse sometimes. And war exercises, *putha*[1], no seasickness allowed. You think you can fall down and die like today?'

It was a very sober bunch of signalmen who reported back to the MSO. Barnett eyed them appreciatively. 'Very good, my lads. You come back well laundered. Dry cleaned, I should say. Do you not feel all goodness and light within you? All your sins have been taken away. The evil of your dirty tum-tums. Mucky things, these guts that coil within us. Like the serpent of Eden, I warrant. You know, dear hearts, it was such a wrench, sending you out this way. Hurt me more than it hurts you, I assure you. Daft, what do you think of the sea?'

Daft scowled.

'Do I see bitterness? A life of pitch and toss, eh? You, Sims?'

'Don't rub it in Yeo,' Carloboy muttered. 'We were sick as dogs.'

'Strange, these expressions. Patrick, have you ever been sick as a dog?'

'No Yeo. Three dogs, I think.'

'Curioser and curioser. But now, me hearties, you are ready. Right as rain. That's another one I can't fathom. Is rain always right?' He rummaged at his desk. 'Here you are. That which you have panted after like the hart seeking the stream. Here, read and raise thanks to the Lord.'

Carloboy frowned. What sort of a bombshell would this be?

'Draft orders, poppets. Six signalmen, six telegraphists. Let me see . . . Leading Signalman Alfie, Signalmen von Bloss, Daft Fernando, Sims, Perera, Saw Silva and Leading Sparks Gibs and Telegraphists Bijja and Yusuf, Nugawira and Roberts. Now isn't that nice? The eyes and ears of the service. Trincomalee awaits, and you go on board in three days. Do I hear wild cheers?'

They gaped. Drafted on board the *Vijaya*. Something they had so earnestly prayed for.

'Yeoman of signals will be Louis. PO Tel will be Weerasinghe. Signals officer—let me see—yes, Lieutenant Wicks. Watch out for him. He smiles. Always watch it when an officer smiles.'

Sims asked, 'Do we get pre-draft leave?'

'Go away you horrible man! The nerve! Leave! Is that all you think of? Of course you get leave. A hideous naval mistake but there's nothing we can do about it. But better, it is thought, to fuck your fill and go to sea than go on board and bugger the shipwright. Oh, and speaking about buggering, watch your afterworks. Able Seaman Mendis is also drafted. Compulsory draft. He had apparently been very active in camp. Can't have our sentries sodomized at night in Flagstaff Street. Shocking things go on in the small hours, I tell you.'

Barbara Heinz squealed when Carloboy ran his hand up her skirt. And she couldn't give her mother a satisfactory answer either. Just crimsoned and lowered her eyes. Mrs Heinz was upset. She told Carloboy not to darken her doorstep again. He swaggered home, then made a quick sally to the outhouse in the neighbouring garden.

Strange girl, he thought, as he positioned her against the wall. She had few words, never wore anything under her dress, and never touched him. Perhaps she was too shy. This time he massaged her clitoris as he worked gently in and out. Suddenly she gave a gasp and he felt a tightening at the pit of her stomach. She grasped his hand, thrust it hard against her. Her eyes were shining when he turned her around to face him.

'What?' he whispered.

She made no reply. Only clung to him tightly, then broke away to peer through the crack in the wall. Without a word, she slipped out.

The customary diary entry was made: *August 1, 1955. Drafted on board HMCyS Vijaya.* Yes, he was going to sea.

At first glance, the *Vijaya* looked pretty imposing. Small, true, but then, she was just a minesweeper. Painted a wicked grey with her pennant numbers large and black on her sides, she toted a big four-inch gun for'ard, four Bofors and depth charge racks. Mushroom ventilators sprouted all over her upper deck, and her bridge was airy and quite spacious although her signals office was an armour-plated doll's house. She displaced only 1,040 tons and broke the hearts of a like number of seamen in her first years of commission at *HMCS Flying Fish* of the Algerine class of Canadian minesweepers.

All the gear that advertised her peculiar sea duty was stacked aft of the quarterdeck—immense coils of grassline, sweeps and paravanes and other paraphernalia. Her boat deck was cluttered with the engine room hatch from which the most lurid oaths and curses wafted ever upwards. This hatch was smack in the middle of the deck. There was also the officers' galley hatch, well protected with a thick mesh and lying to one side of the smokestack.

This deck swept up to the fo'c'sle, the breakwater and the welter of anchor chains and lead cables as well as the cylindrical hoisting gear.

Between decks, she was a fine example of naval architecture. The wireless cabin was roomy albeit gloomy, the wardroom and officers' mess designed to hold as much liquor as considered necessary, the galley like a smaller version of Dante's inferno and the mess for the miscellaneous types (electricians, signalmen, cooks, supply assistants, telegraphists, shipwrights) the cruddiest of all, being situated ahead of the foregun above and in the bows. It took the biggest beating of all each time the ship put to sea.

'Just think,' said Aloysius, tapping the bulkhead, 'the bows. Like a damn arrowhead, the shape of this place. And outside this plate, nothing but sea.'

Koelmeyer shuddered. It was not a pleasant thought.

As sailing date approached, the complement began to bulge. The norm᠎al ship's crew was 90. Now it was 120, which was considered essential for JET. There would be many detailed exercises in navigation, anti-aircraft and anti-submarine manoeuvres. Suddenly, as Louis told his charges, the ANSB would come alive.

'Von Bloss,' he said, 'you remember the manoeuvres for Operation Cabbage One?'

That was a typical anti-sub hunt. There would be a convoy of destroyers and anti-submarine cruisers, screening aircraft carriers or tankers. But an enemy submarine creeps through, blasts the leading escortee. Signals are vital as the escort vessels wheel and begin their line hunts. The submarine hasn't a prayer unless the captain blows all tubes and sinks to lie doggo at the bottom.

'Everything depends on the right signal, the correct flaghoist,' Louis said, 'don't forget, ships maintain radio silence at war. You will now see how important your exam was. Here, all you have learnt is brought to life.'

Daft gave his gods a beseeching look.

Sleeping in the mess was rarely done. Some took to the mess tables below, but many preferred the boat deck or curled up under the big gun. In harbour, everyone spread canvas on the fo'c'sle but at sea, making the customary ten knots and often a sluggish eight, it was only the man who was prepared to sleep through anything who defied the sea and kipped on deck.

It was a shock to see Nathali's impudent face. That worthy seemed to dog Carloboy wherever he went. He came on board with little yelps of agony. Seasoned old reprobate that he was, he knew that life on board, and particularly on the *Vijaya* was no picnic. From *Elara* to the *Vijaya* must have seemed to him like a descent from paradise to limbo.

'Percy, what the hell did you do? They chased you out?'

'Story of my bloody life? All I did was kill the rats in the victualling store.'

'So that's OK. The rats are eating everything there.'

It seemed that Percy and Maddo had decided to spend a night in the victualling store. The rats came down the light flex, then leaped to the floor.

'From the roof, down the light wire. That's the way they come. You should have seen them. Families coming down. Uncles, aunties, grandchildren. Like a fucking circus. We took sticks. If the light is on they won't come, so we lit a kerosene lamp and kept it near the door. Had to lock the bloody door, otherwise they will run out that way.'

'So what happened?'

'Nothing. We killed about thirty buggers. Only that Maddo forgot to take out the bulb and the shade. First clout he smashed both. But that's never mind. Plenty of bulbs in the stores. But some rats must have been watching from the roof. Everytime they come down they get whacked. One thing, smart buggers, these rats. They started to come halfway down, then jumped. Then we had to chase them and clout them. Then about two-three jumped on Maddo . . .'

It must have been, for the rats, a sort of kamikaze affair. We, who are about to die, will bite your ears. Maddo had gone crazy. A flying stick had broken the kerosene lamp. They had both tried to push at the door although it opened inward. The kerosene caught fire and then the bags of rice and flour and lentils had begun to burn.

'My God, you set the place on fire?'

'Not me. That bloody Maddo! He ran to the heads. Any trouble, he goes to the heads. One small lamp. Should have seen the mess. And all the firebuckets full of sand. Who wants sand, men? Not enough the bloody sand in *Elara*? Mountains of sand.'

Percy shook his head. He had lost all faith in naval efficiency. 'By the time they put out the fire, half the victualling stores roof also came down.'

Carloboy chuckled. 'So they sent you here. And Maddo?'

'I think he's being sent to Karainagar. Damn good for him. There are leopards there.'

Karainagar was another naval outpost in the north. There, the sea was bordered by heavy jungle and life was a bed of cactus. And yes, there were leopards. These creatures thanked their gods for the sailors provided until the sub-lieutenant armed his men. The leopards were displeased. Legitimate meals were not supposed to shoot at them. The Captain of the Navy was most displeased. He found, on a tour of inspection, a hut full of leopard skins. He thought earnestly about closing the base.

They upped anchor on the morning of August 6. Percy took to sleeping on deck in a big way. The *Vijaya* swept out of port. Everybody was on their toes.

'Stations for leaving harbour!'

'Close all X and Y doors and shipside scuttles!'

The engineroom indicators clanged. Mooring crews clambered up the ropes and the tiny gangway was raised, secured. On the bridge stood Lieutenant-Commander Shan, who was broad-faced, hawk-nosed and with a dusting of grey in his hair. This was his first sea-going command but Yeoman Louis cautioned his men, 'Don't you forget it. The captain knows his stuff. Trained in Dartmouth. Got his gold sword for navigation. A fine seaman he is.'

They hugged the coast and the *Vijaya* bobbed and bounced, like the customs officer's daughter on the back of the priest's motorcycle.

It was when they were at the headland of the Great and Little Basses lights and steaming past Hambantota, that the ship was rent by a flurry of curses. Percy, sleeping on deck, had been hit in the face by a flying fish.

There's something undignified about being slapped on the kisser with a wet fish. It's a sort of ultimate insult. Nathali grabbed the offender that was squirming into his sheet and marched to the mess where a sleeping cook was rudely awakened and coaxed to the galley. The fish was cleaned, fried and devoured at three o'clock in the morning. Thereafter, he took to sleeping below and the whole mess would reek of beer until wakey wakey.

Notes

(1) Sinhalese—son

34

Guadalcanal and Iron Bay Sound

The Marines were making their landing. Landing craft, leaving their ships far behind; heavy steel helmets, criss-crossed bandoliers of ammunition, light trench mortars in their arms, guns . . . they each carried up to forty pounds of equipment.

Major General Alexander A. Vandegrift was their divisional commander. He was worried. What opposition would there be on the island? And where was the Japanese fleet?

At sea, Vice Admiral Richmond Kelly Turner was just as worried. But he was also certain that the Japanese fleet could not react immediately. What was important was to get the men ashore, quickly.

As the landing craft ground into the shale, the men leaped out. They crouched, arms at the ready as they waded out of the waist-deep water. There was no opposition. If there were Japanese on the island, they were not on the beach. The Marines began to advance inland.

August 7, 1942. The Marines had landed in Guadalcanal.

It was agreed that this would be, primarily, a land battle. It was the first move in the King-MacArthur island-hopping campaign. But to the north-west, Japanese Vice Admiral Unichi Mikawa knew of the American move. He readied all ships close enough to Guadalcanal. To him, there was only one thought. The Americans were landing troops to destroy the Japanese airfield that was there. And, for this landing, the Americans had sent ships—and ships were what Mikawa wanted. The Marines would destroy the airfield, then pull out. So the US ships would be waiting for recovery. This, to Mikawa, was a golden opportunity. He must destroy the US Navy vessels before they got away. He ordered the cruiser *Aoba* to close in, also the heavy cruiser *Kako*, and other vessels.

The Marines moved inland. In the bay north of Guadalcanal, near Savo Island, American and Australian cruisers patrolled anxiously. They had received submarine reports of Japanese fleet movements. So did the heavy cruisers *Quincey, Astoria* and *Vincennes*. They were alert, but did not believe that anything could happen suddenly.

Night fell. All was quiet. The Japanese closed in, ships darkened, slipping like sea snakes through the water. Suddenly, the *Quincey* was held in a blaze of light, the searchlights of the *Aoba*. There was no escape. A close-range salvo took her even as she began to swing her guns. She just rolled over, mortally hit. The *Astoria* and the *Vincennes* followed and the Australian cruiser *Canberra* took the full venom of torpedoes even as the Japanese ships executed high speed turns to leave the bay. Four proud ships. That stretch of water came to be known as Iron Bottom Sound.

On Guadalcanal, the Marines blanched. They heard the thunder of the cruiser's six- and eight-inch guns, the hard claps of the destroyer's five-inch burst.

Mikawa was happy. His raiders steamed northward along the slot, and no US planes followed. He had destroyed the US naval force. His ships headed for New Ireland, their Northern Solomons base. He didn't reckon on US submarine S-44 which was hovering around the New Ireland harbour of Kavieng.

The S-44 was at periscope depth when its skipper, Lieutenant Commander Moore saw and could scarcely believe his eyes. Japanese ships! Four cruisers, a screen of destroyers. He selected the biggest cruiser, the *Kako,* and closed in. Four torpedoes, and fired from as close a range as 700 yards, could not miss. The *Kako* sank, its boilers exploding as the water closed over them.

The Marines in Guadalcanal looked at each other helplessly, then soldiered on. They slept in the forest and walked on the next day until they broke through to the airfield. They had no naval protection. The Japanese knew this too. They began to run soldiers and supplies in. A large force of the 17th Army was despatched with orders to drive the Marines into the sea.

The first land battle took place on the night of August 20. It was a disaster for the Japanese. Their Commander shot himself when he realized how badly his detachments had fared. More than a thousand of his men died. The Marines lost 35.

Again, Japan poured reinforcements in. This time, on September 12, it was the famous Battle of Bloody Ridge. The Marines held on grimly. A very bloody pattern had been established and the hapless Marines knew that without help, they would soon be whittled down, killed to a man.

The Americans began to pour in ships and planes to prevent the Japanese rushing troops to the island. It was on November 11 that a huge US fighting force was sent out. A large convoy carried them, among the ironclads being the cruiser *Atlanta* and the destroyers *Monssen, Cushing, Laffey* and *Juneau.* A bitter action followed and many of these vessels were sunk. Then came the battleships *Washington* and *South Dakota.* They ploughed in, 16-inch guns blazing. The Japanese fled, many of their cruisers smashed.

On Guadalcanal, the Marines fought on. They had fanned out all over the island. The Japanese, with no help coming in, began to pull out. Some got away in transports sent to fetch them. Many died. It was six months before the last of the Japanese left.

February 7, 1943. A lot of mistakes had been made, but finally, Guadalcanal was in US hands.

35

Of a Wardroom Rear Action and Canteen Carouses and the Hula Girl of Jail Road

The old Navy joke used to be the one about the young cabin boy who was the darling of his ship. When the captain was not labouring over him, other officers were, and being a very obliging fellow, he did not object to the attentions paid him by the lower deck. His fame spread, and when the Navy found him too hard to countenance they drafted him to another vessel where the skipper was a fierce Methodist and who tolerated no hanky-panky.

The cabin boy found this rather off-putting. He knew he was looked upon with much longing, but the men kept themselves to themselves. Came the day when they put to port in Singapore and liberty was allowed. The captain addressed them on the quarterdeck. He warned them of the horrible fate that awaited those who sought the pleasures of the flesh. He promised to do very nasty things to them if they were reported in any of the red light areas. He also advised them that he had alerted the military police of the Singapore shore base, *HMS Terror*. And terror is what he promised those who offended him. Also, he reminded them, he was easily offended.

The liberty boats shoved away and among the libertymen was the cabin boy who was seeing Singapore for the first time.

As was customary, the first boat to bring the men back left the ship at eight. A few returned. They apologized for keeping the boat waiting, but they had been busy.

'Ho! Busy, were you?' said the duty officer, 'twenty minutes late!'

'We went to Mount Patrick, sir.'

The nine o'clock boat was also late. Again the plea was that the men had gone to Mount Patrick. A count was taken. The cabin boy was missing. He returned promptly on the 10 o'clock boat, whistling cheerfully, and was bawled out by the duty officer.

'Don't tell me you also went to Mount Patrick!'

'No sir. I'm Patrick!'

Food for thought indeed!

Able Seaman Mendis was not the only deviate the *Vijaya* held. There were many others, both of a passive and active bent and this, in the Navy, was accepted on the principle that a sailor is entitled to make for any port in a storm. The chronicler makes no comment. When there is little, practically no sight of the opposite sex, men will turn to those who can give them relief. This was considered reasonable enough and all on board were placed in the category of consenting adults should they care to consent.

The first news of such carrying-on was conveyed to the captain who told the master-at-arms that he was not the custodian of a sailor's morals.

'But sir, if we allow this sort of thing to go unchecked . . .'

'I know, but they were in the shipwright's store and doing whatever it is in private. What made you go barging in?'

'It's that Jambong, sir. I saw Mendis give him a wink and then both went aft.'

'And you followed?'

'Yes sir. I waited outside a little . . . then I pushed the door. They were—'

'Tell me, who was buggering who?'

'Mendis, sir. He was landing Jambong. You know Jambong, sir? Fair Malay boy, curly hair, very nice-looking . . .'

'I see. You noticed that, did you?'

'Sir?'

'I don't think you should worry yourself, chief.'

'But sir—'

'I'll talk to Jambong.'

'But I'm putting Mendis on a charge, sir.'

'Only Mendis? But there were two men involved.'

'But Mendis was doing it sir. Jambong was the victim.'

'And did he say he was?'

'N-no sir.'

'Then forget it. There are some things we have to learn to live with.'

'But sir—'

'Forget it, chief. Be like Nelson. You know of Nelson, don't you?'

'Nelson who, sir?'

'You may go, chief.'

The engine room officer who was with the captain and was grinning at this exchange, said, 'He wanted to put Mendis on a charge . . . you know the whole story, sir?'

'I can guess.'

'The master-at-arms tried it on Jambong. The boy refused. Engine room hands were talking about it the other day.'

'I thought so. Not a nice man. Shall we draft him ashore?'

'Well . . . he is a good chief. We'll need him for JET.'

'I suppose so.'

Sub-Lieutenant Hugo was yet another port in a storm. He didn't look for 'victims'. All he wanted was to cultivate a strapping young sailor who could give him the satisfaction he craved. He waddled around ship and decided on Sims, who was startled at the blunt proposition.

'Come with me to the wardroom.'

Sims went.

'Close the door. Now . . . how do you like my arse?' Hugo did have a very pronounced backside.

Sims stared at the man in disbelief. 'Sir, what—what?'

'Oh come, men, as if you don't do these things. Here,' dropping his trousers and leaning over a table, 'you fuck my arse, then you can go.'

The sight of that smooth brown bum roused Sims. It certainly was a welcome sight. Just like the cook woman's at home.

'So hurry up, before somebody comes.'

Sims took out his penis. 'My God, I'm screwing an officer,' he thought, and closed in.

Seemingly, Hugo enjoyed it very much. Sims heard him grunt, 'harder, harder, push it in, men,' and all the while his hand was busy, masturbating furiously. Sims spent himself.

'Don't take it out. Wait like that till I come.'

Glued to the officer, Sims stood, breathing heavily as the man jerked, then ejaculated. 'Aah, that's good. Now take out. There, use the washbasin. You come again, right? I'll see you are let off all deck duties. Here, take this.'

Sims took the one hundred rupees. Why not? Payment for services rendered. He left the wardroom slightly dazed; but he felt fine. Really fine. That was a relief he had badly needed. He was quite cheerful in the mess.

'What's the matter?' Carloboy asked, 'You're looking very pleased.'

'Oh, just thinking of something.'

'Bet it's some cunt,' Electricians Mate Koelmeyer said.

Sims nodded. 'Yes, a nice big hole.' The man had found a new dimension—one he had never thought he could be in. This there's-a-first-time-for-everything business was quite satisfactory.

Which, as has been said, is what the Navy can do to the best of men.

No, there was no seasickness. The old mal-de-mer that the men thought would seize them, convulse their bowels, scorch their insides, could get no grip on them. Carloboy and company, acknowledged how right Barnett had been. A small boat performs ever so badly in a running sea. That gunnery target exercise had done its damndest to beat the stuffing out of them.

The *Vijaya* was small, and it slithered, weaved, ducked and bobbed terribly, but it was a stout ship and larger by far than an oily boat. She rose and fell in the water with dignity. In short, it was 'plain sailing' as far as they were concerned, although there were times, especially in the incredibly rough seas off the Basses, when there would be some threatening belches and a wooziness that came and went although it did not push their stomach contents up the tube.

And then they were pushing against the currents to Foul Point, steaming bravely into Trincomalee. The harbour was a splendid sight. Littering it were the warships of the Indian, Pakistan and British navies. Every one bigger than the *Vijaya,* true, but the Pakistani destroyers *Tariq* and *Taimur* seemed but a handsbreadth longer and no more.

Alongside the NHQ jetty was a long cigar—a submarine—and the lights began to flash from the two-funnelled cruiser, *HMS Superb*. They were ordered to tie up at the oiling jetty. The *Superb* was the flagship of the Fleet Commander. She had a skipper who liked to have fun, and the man had to be taken off in disgrace as JET progressed. That will be dealt with at the appropriate time. What was of signal importance was that the men of the *Vijaya* could go ashore.

It was a goodly lot who did: Stoker Mechanics Arnie and Dyan, Telegraphists Nugawira and Yusuf, leading seamen and able seamen in heaping quantities and signalmen forming their own boisterous brigade. Those in the know said that there was only one place to go—the fleet canteen situated close to the Admiralty House pier. Indians, Pakistanis and Brits had the same thought. Here, then, was a naval gathering of the clans.

The fleet canteen was as large as a cathedral, and it sprawled in much the same way its occupants would sprawl after copious draughts of beer and brandy. Carloboy favoured arrack and Ribena which he found a wonderful combination, very like wine that had the wallop of a soft-headed mallet.

The barkeep raised an eyebrow. A little man with a moustache two size too large for his face. He slapped down the bottle of black currant juice and the pint of arrack. 'This is a new one on me,' he said doubtfully, 'what does it do?'

'Nothing much,' Carloboy grinned, 'But you'll see.'

'I can wait,' he grinned back. 'I've been behind this bar two years. Thought I'd seen everything.'

Men of all hues. Red-nosed Brits, quite superior because they had been brought up to believe Britannia ruled the waves. They did not rule the fleet canteen however, being hopelessly outnumbered by hordes of thirsty Indians and Pakistanis who drank with much ceremony and told amazing stories of their lives to all who would care to listen.

Carloboy looked around, and there, against a wall between two bracket lamps was a piano. A piano! Who would have believed it? A beefy British marine was punishing it with one finger and seemed quite put out that it gave him no harmonious response.

Carloboy took a long draught of arrack and Ribena, smacked his lips and told his companions, 'Let's make this place jump. C'mon, grab that table near the piano. Let's get the Indians jumping.'

They swarmed around the piano. The marine was sure he had found the lost chord. 'Out of tune it is,' he squinted, 'dandy do oi play me muvver's peeyano.'

Carloboy clapped him on the shoulder. 'I'll make it talk. Here, get that top lid open. Must be all choked up inside,' and he sat and suddenly there was a crash of chords, a crazy bass and the Indians swayed to their feet as *Dil Deké Dekho*—a rollicking film number of the times burst out.

It was a riot. The men of the *Vijaya* who had never known of the talents each other possessed (save, of course the necessary and obvious ones such as skirt-chasing, hard drinking and other pursuits of the flesh) became too jolly for words. Shouts sped across the hall like bullets. The Royal Navy wanted 'Genevive' and the old parody 'Ethelred the Unready'. Many converged to plonk glasses around. 'Avadrink!' they roared, 'play Luv's ole shweet shong!'

'Waddabout God shave th' queen?'

'Shave her your bloody self!'

'What you are drinking? Achcha! Rum a little you will have?'

A hulking sergeant of marines seized Nugawira. 'Walts! Walts!' he bellowed. 'You walts with me, right!'

This was a sight to paralyse the most stout-hearted. Six foot four and five foot four. Nugawira was grabbed, lifted off his feet and swirled around while Carloboy grinned and belted out 'Cockles and Mussels' which dragged on and on because each time he tried to stop, a little Brit stoker with a piercing voice would wail, 'soshe weelder wheel barooooo . . .' and everybody shouted the chorus again and again.

There was too much booze. Everyone wanted the pianist to wet his whistle and the hall boomed to:

Rooll me oooover—in the clooover
Roll me over, lay me down an' do it again

Arnie held the floor with a brilliant rendition of 'Sweet Violets' and Nugawira, quite dazed after his mad caper, swallowed gin, upchucked and had to be rubbed on the back and given more gin. Soon, there was too much liquor for the good of any damp soul. Yusuf solved the problem by tipping assorted drinks into the piano until he was hauled away and sat upon. Simply not done, he was told sternly. And at last, staggering out, one eye closed because he was seeing double, Carloboy was gripped by a man who said, 'Pukka time, men, pukka!'

'Who—who'r'you?'

Able Seaman Binkie grinned. 'This is Arthur. Goodole Arthur. How are you?'

'Who's Arthur?'

'My fren' Arthur.'

Arthur wrung Carloboy's hand. Old man, white-haired, wiry and lean. 'You mus' come home. Jail road. Nex' time you are out come home. Binkie knows where. Come with him.'

'What for?'

'My home, men. 'aver piano. You come an' play.'

Binkie said, 'We'll come. Don'worry.'

Arthur beamed. 'Anytime you like. Girls will be pleased.'

Carloboy was too drunk to mind that last remark. He saluted the quarterdeck as best as he could and ignored the QM's glare. All he wanted to do was to lie down. Why the devil was the ship turning in circles?

But their ox-like constitutions and an ability to consume enormous breakfasts had them all up and about the next morning. There was much work to do.

Exercises at sea followed an ordained course. The combined fleet would steam out and play merry hell in the open sea, anywhere between the Andamans and Singapore light, or the Andamans and the Nicobars, or, if there was little Admiralty enthusiasm, around Foul Point and the deep water outside China Bay. As a signalman, Carloboy began to relive the days of his training, hands blistered by hoisting and hauling down flag signals, eyes red by straining to read Morse flashed from tiny yardarm blinkers, his brain buzzing with the many cryptographic systems since each message had to be in one of the many signal codes.

It was war—mock warfare, with the fleet split into two forces and ordered to fight each other. The *Vijaya* was pushed to her utmost, fourteen knots, that made her mast shudder alarmingly with the pulse of her engines and the stokers were dying slow deaths in the heat of the boiler rooms.

But the off days in port did come and then there was the deck routine which largely depended on the master-at-arm's bile. If he woke after a wet dream, the men would be chipping decks all day or painting the sides. The *Vijaya* seemed to hang together, held by the succeeding layers of paint. Such feverish painting seemed to be absurd. OK in Trincomalee, they agreed, but a pathetic dissipation of energy in Colombo where the ship occupied a berth surrounded by a bunch of black-hearted colliers. Well, there was not much a sailor could do. It was the old business of complying and, for universal peace of mind, not complaining.

And then Binkie said, 'Let's go to Plinkett's.'

'Who?'

'Plinkett, men. You remember we met him outside the fleet canteen that night . . .'

Carloboy shrugged. He would not remember even if he had been introduced to a Hotentot singing 'Ave Maria'.

'Jail Road. 'Member he told to come and play the piano?'

'At his home?'

'What else? Must see his daughters. I'm putting a cap to the elder one. Have a younger one also. Come go.'

Carloboy hesitated. 'But I want to go to the railway station. Friend of mine is there. My father's friend. Driver Jacks. Must go and see him.'

Binkie looked sad. 'I thought if you come and play and the old bugger starts drinking, can make him drunk.'

'Why?'

'What men, if make him drunk, can get the daughter, no?'

A powerful argument indeed. Carloboy wavered. 'But what about the mother?'

'No mother. Only old man and the daughters.'

Arthur Lascalles Plinkett. An Anglo-Indian who had served in an Indian regiment, then settled in Ceylon after his wife had passed on. He had two daughters, and being ex-Royal Army and off-white, held sway in Jail Road.

Daughter Annette was a mess favourite at the dockyard naval camp. She liked sitting on petty officers' laps when she was not dancing the hula-hula, and would go to that secluded bit of beach near the oiling jetty where the men of the Navy would form a queue to savour her charms. Annette had shared her father's bed since she grew up. Plinkett knew that sooner or later some uniformed moron would want to marry her. He had turned to his younger daughter Abela who filled the breach exceedingly well.

The 'uniformed moron' was Binkie, of course, who was determined to marry the perambulating Annette and show her the error of her ways. Plinkett knew how much the oiling jetty contributed to the lubrication of his daughter, but Binkie, who always maintained that he had been well brought-up, did not know as much about his lady-love as her father did. Indeed, all he had to do was say, politely, 'If you will excuse me, Arthur, I'm taking Annette to bed.'

Plinkett would have waved him a benediction and merely said, 'Have another drink first. It helps.'

Carloboy agreed with Binkie, 'So you get the old boy drunk. You screw the daughter. What do I do?'

'The other girl is there, no?'

Again, a very good point. Can't argue with that. They went.

Plinkett took his time. He had much to say about the days when he was the regimental boxing champion. Why, he was light-heavyweight champion of India! He gave them a stirring demonstration of ringcraft, sprawling over a divan and reducing a chair to matchwood, and he wanted to sing, which was a mistake because he sounded like a violin with a broken nose.

But Annette went indoors at his bidding and emerged with a flower in her straw hair and an abbreviated bodice and a skirt of trailing ribbons and Plinkett roared his approval. 'Play something Hawaiian,' he bawled and piped 'Aloha Oye, Aloha Oye' and Annette danced and bounced her hips and shook her hips and shook her bum at Binkie and swept her long hair from shoulder to shoulder. Binkie sat pop-eyed.

It took time to drag Arthur Lascalles to bed. He lay, mouth open, grunting with a patch of spittle on his pillow. Binkie was pulling away at Annette's ribbons as though she was a Christmas present.

Abela led Carloboy to the tiny parlour. 'Play one more song,' she said softly, 'and can you show me the notes?'

With her hip pressed against his side, Abela touched the keys as he told her to. He felt her warm against him as he said, 'A,G,G,G,F,E,D,C,E,E.'

She played the notes, sang softly to each, 'I love you, for sen-ti-men-tal reasons . . .'

His hand was up her skirt, his fingers under the edge of her knickers. She moved her legs slightly apart. She kept playing the line of music over and over again as he reached higher, pulled at the waist elastic, brought the panties to her knees. She bent, kissed the side of his forehead and squirmed, dropping the scrap of cloth to her ankles. It was the work of a moment to draw her to the faded settee. She was nineteen, she said, and no, she was not a virgin. He mounted her awkwardly, but settled himself when he was in her. Small, tight, and very satisfying indeed. He lay on her, waiting till he was hard again and she clutched at his shoulders as she climaxed and tried to draw her legs together. All the while, Annette kept humming, humming. Carloboy recognized the tune. It was the Hawaiian Wedding Song. He smiled.

'You sister hums Hawaiian songs even when someone is fucking her?'

'No,' Abela giggled, 'she must be dancing.'

'Dancing? Then what is Binkie doing?'

She giggled again, 'Must be watching. When she's in this mood, she only wants to dance.'

Binkie brooded. 'Won't allow, men. You and your bloody piano. Only doing the hula.'

Carloboy was in a generous mood. 'So you go and screw Abela. Only hurry up. We'll miss the last boat.'

Plinkett snorted in his sleep.

'You'll come and play again?' Annette asked. It was a bargaining chip. With the prospect of another Hawaiian evening, Annette swept Binkie to bed and, as he said later, it must have been the fastest fuck in history. God knows, he had been tensing for it all evening and it was all over before he knew he had begun. He was still wagging his head sadly when they stepped into the boat.

A week later, in Dehiwela, Sonnaboy von Bloss read his son's letter and roared. 'Bugger has been going to Plinkett's.'

Beryl was nonplussed.

'Plinkett's, men, in Trincomalee. You remember that bugger I hammered on the platform? My God, he shat, shat and ran!'

Beryl sighed. How was she expected to remember any one person her husband had beaten up? The line seemed endless. But she nodded. 'Yes,' she said faintly.

'Put him one in the stomach. He farted. Then I gave him a kick and he shat in his trousers. Did the bloody bolt, shit coming down his legs.'

Beryl shuddered. She hated these memories, most of all.

'Must write and tell Carloboy.'

Carloboy sat on a ventilator, reading his father's letter. He laughed, then tossed the broken envelope into the sea. He began to whistle 'Lovely Hula Hands'.

36

The British Military Occupation of Ceylon

There were several internal defence schemes in Ceylon since the First World War. This undoubtedly contributed to the island's state of readiness. The British, to this day, will maintain that the military occupation of Ceylon was very necessary, although it was also thought that all it did was bring into the country a large amount of money.

What worried the British administration of the time was that after hostilities were over, it would be hard to get people to return to their old ways. They would want the same war-time wages and benefits and the same financial status they enjoyed in wartime. Many gloomily said that there would be social chaos.

It would be interesting at this juncture, to leave the Americans in the Pacific, the Europeans in the Atlantic and the Mediterranean, and step back in time to a day in 1872 when a British tea planter in Ceylon, Colonel Gordon-Reeves, sent notices to the British planting community. He said he wished to form a volunteer corps of mounted infantry. He pointed out that all planters had one or two horses and, if the response was good, they would all be sworn in in Kandy, the hill capital of the island.

The response was good. Sixty-two men enlisted and the military bungalows in Brownrigg Street, Kandy, were the venue of the swearing-in ceremony. Gordon-Reeves assumed command as a major and he had sixty-one troopers under him. They were accepted as a mounted company of the Ceylon Light Infantry and later became a separate unit of the Ceylon Defence Force.

In 1897, men of this mounted infantry went to the diamond jubilee celebrations of Queen Victoria and in 1899, they went to South Africa when the Boer War broke out.

That was an interesting campaign. Governor Sir West Ridgeway obtained for the men the necessary equipment from India, and the force was assembled in Colombo on January 24, 1900, preparatory to departure. Horses, too, were provided from Bombay.

The *Times of Ceylon* of January 31, 1900 carried a glowing account of the farewell banquet which was followed by a torchlight tattoo:

> Never before in the history of Ceylon has such an unique and inspiring a spectacle been witnessed as that which marked last night's send-off banquet to the Ceylon contingent at the Galle Face Hotel. The enthusiasm was unparalleled and the scene will long be remembered by those who were privileged to witness it. Great were the preparations, and it is only those who undertook the arduous duties of committee-men who knew the anxiety and care which those preparations involved. As early as half past seven the hotel presented a scene of animation which is not easily described. The hall, verandas, passages and the staircase were thronged with a huge mass of people, which were augmented shortly after by the members of the contingent who formed up inside the hotel near the main entrance, ready for the reception of HE the Governor and staff. His Excellency drove up at 8 p.m. with Sir E. Noel Walker, Captain Currie, ADC, and Captain Toogood, and a move was at once made

> to the banquet hall. There was no difficulty in seating the diners, a large body of stewards being at hand ready to indicate the location of the seats at their respective tables. Upon entering the hall, admiration of the decorations was expressed.
>
> The music was much enjoyed, and whenever a popular air was played the company heartily joined in. The balconies overlooking the dining hall were crowded with ladies, who watched the proceedings with great interest.
>
> His Lordship the Bishop of Colombo said grace in a few appropriate words, and about 10 p.m. the toast list was proceeded with.
>
> The Governor proposed the Queen, and the Bishop proposed the Governor's health, and before the Governor replied he asked the company to 'light up'.

The contingent sailed for Cape Town on the *Umkuzi*, a battered old ship.

Shortly after, a Ceylon Planters Rifle Corps was formed on May 5, 1900, commanded by Captain Farquharson, R N. He was made a Colonel and was possibly the only known Captain of the Navy who became a Colonel in a volunteer regiment.

Many Boer prisoners were sent to Ceylon. They were kept in a P-O-W camp in Diyatalawa and many died there. Their remains still lie in the big war cemetery there. When the war was over, these prisoners were sent back. They were each asked to take an oath of allegiance to the British. All did, except one stubborn old man named Inglebek (Englebrecht). He became a thorn in the official side until the British government in Ceylon made him a game warden of the animal sanctuary of Yala in the south-east.

So it was that Lord Kitchener sent the Ceylon Government a letter from Simla on July 28, 1903. It was very much to the point:

> The Ceylon contingent did very good work in South Africa. I only wish we had more of them.
>
> Kitchener, General
> Simla, 28.7.03

This then is how Diyatalawa became a service training centre. Soon after the Boers left, the camp became a training camp.

Indeed Ceylon saw some of the finest British regiments. There were the Gordon Highlanders, the Warwickshire Regiment, the Royal North Lancs. The Highland Light Infantry and the Gloucester Regiment were stationed in the island during the Boer War because of the large number of Boer prisoners sent for internment. After that came the West Kents from South Africa and the Worcester Regiment. Thereafter, Ceylon saw the 98th Infantry and the Punjabis from India.

It would be interesting to reproduce another *Times of Ceylon* report in part, on the farewell speech made by Governor Sir West Ridgeway where he made much importance of Diyatalawa:

> I specially hope you will attend the camp of exercise at Diyatalawa as numerously as you can. Government has gone to a great expense and trouble in equipping Diyatalawa, and it is an ideal training ground . . . A week or a fortnight at Diyatalawa is worth months anywhere else. The climate is so exhilarating, the country so adapted for manoeuvring that the instruction you receive is as pleasant as it is useful . . .

Shortly after Diyatalawa was made into a training centre, a house was built for the Admiral of the East Indies Fleet on a hill overlooking the Navy camp.

In 1911 came the coronation of King George V. A small force of officers and NCO's sailed for England where they received coronation medals. The King had come to Ceylon in 1901 when he was Duke of York. So did the Prince of Wales and the Duke of Connaught who, in 1907, unveiled the South African War Memorial in Kandy.

Again, a Ceylon contingent attended the coronation of King Edward VII and, in 1909, General French came as Inspector-General of the British forces to inspect all Ceylon troops.

Then came World War I and Ceylon did not really figure. Many men did apply to go to the front but had to be content with doing town-guard duties and keeping local units on their toes. However, an overseas contingent of the Ceylon Planters Rifle Corps, composed of eight officers and 221 other ranks did embark on the *SS Worcestershire*. They fought well, and eventually the tally rose to 800. Of this number, 80 were killed and 90 wounded.

During World War II, the Ceylon Light Infantry, which was Ceylon's oldest volunteer regiment, increased in size to four battalions. Also, there arose the Ceylon Artillery Volunteers that proved to be a very useful gunnery defence unit.

Ceylon was, therefore, both militarily and navally, very certain of herself. Also, there was much royal house interest in the island—an interest that brought the Duke of Gloucester twice to her shores; once in 1934 and again during World War II, where he inspected the troops at the Royal Botanical Gardens at Peradeniya in Kandy.

The year 1941 was crucial. It saw the arrival of more British troops. First came the Leicester Regiment under Colonel Phillips. This regiment was composed of the King's Own, the Queen's Own and the Leicesters, all in one division.

Then came the 7th Artillery, the East African Regiment and, of course, there was the Indian Regiment. Many others came and went—the 51st Royal Artillery, the Lanarkshire Yeomanry, the Border Regiment. Many of these troops were sent on to Burma or India. And then came the headquarters personnel of the South-east Asia Command to converge on Kandy.

All the huts in Kandy and Peradeniya were not good enough for the big brass. The British power machine would base itself in the central capital and make of it a good, strong, quite permanent home.

37

Of Command Changes and Bara Khana and a Faceful of Bucket for a Bumptious Blighter

It all started with very simple exercise—shifting berth. It was then that the men of the *Vijaya* realized that something was very wrong indeed. All they had to do was slip moorings, refuel at the oiling jetty and get back to berth.

Problem was that the skipper was at a command confab at Admiralty House and had other things on his mind. He was to soon leave for England—a career move with a stint of higher naval training that would give him acting Commander ranking and make him a top brass.

But that morning a flag hoist had been made to inform the Flagstaff that the *Vijaya* could not live on beer alone. At the oiling jetty was *HMS Comus*, under the command of a very excitable Scot. Then came the orders from the shore bridge. The signalman there rattled it off on the lamp at breakneck speed, and in the morning light, it was a long hard-to-read blur because the sender never really released the shutter handle which would cut the light after each letter.

'What's that?' Daft moaned, 'Chinese?' He moaned a lot these days.

First Lieutenant Tilaka was chuffed. Why, he was in command. He took the signal from Carloboy and looked important. 'So we are to tie up alongside the *Comus*. Send this message to NHQ. To Lieutenant Commander Shan. *Vijaya*. Slipping moorings . . . it's eight now . . . say nine hundred hours. Number One. Got that?' He then hurried to the bridge, piped for the engineering officer, shouted down the voice tube for Lieutenant Ratna, yelled for the signals crew and generally put everybody's back up.

Sub-Lieutenant Hugo ran up the bridge gangway, saluting smartly. He then slipped down to the wheelhouse while Tilaka glared over the metallic glass and made all manner of gestures to the bow crew.

'Let go aft!' He screamed, almost blowing away Yeoman Louis's ear.

Louis bellowed the command to the boat deck.

'Slow astern port.'

Held by her bow lines, the *Vijaya* swung in a crude arc until her way was on her, and as the lines slipped, she began to go astern until it seemed she would run blind into the *INS Godavari*.

'Stop engines! Stop engines! Slow ahead starboard! There, that way!'

The man was excited. He nearly shouted 'Whoa!' And suddenly, with propellers churning slowly, the *Vijaya* moved towards the jetty where the men of the *Comus* were dragging the big fuel pipes across deck and putting out the fenders.

It is always a manoeuvre that needs to be executed to a nicety. Tilaka had a lot of textbook knowledge. Approach bows on, reverse engines with a hard to port or starboard, churn up a lot of water and swing the stern, all the while keeping an eye on the drifting bows. The thrust to port or starboard will make the bows swing and the engine room commands must be timed precisely. The man on the bridge must know the way his ship swings and how much sweep room his bows need. Unfortunately Tilaka didn't.

'Stop engines! Hard astern! *Stop engines!* Stop, I tell you Why won't it stop? Stop!'

The *Vijaya* had no use for such idiotic orders. She was a determined young lady who, given the slightest provocation, raised her skirts and said 'Follow me!' The port engines blew, and her stern swung, but it was too late. On the *Comus* captain Merry held up imploring hands.

'Back! Back, oi say!' And with an oath, he scrambled down the ladder, screamed to the deckhands to stand clear.

Fuelling crews gaped, then dropping the large pipes, leaped away just as the *Vijaya's* bows struck with a screech, tearing at the side of the *Comus*, raising a shower of paint chips, sparks, and a commotion that was unbelievable. Guard rails twisted and as it was said later, it was fortunate that the boat davits had been swung inwards.

Captain Merry's eyes bulged. Shaking his fists, he danced in rage. 'Take any fookin' thing,' he howled, 'but leave me bloody lifeboats!'

Tilaka collapsed. Signals buzzed around him, over the disaster area like hornets, and from NHQ Lieutenant-Commander Shan wanted to know what. 'What the fuck?' he asked and it was Louis who finally got on the projector to inform him that the *Vijaya* was now alongside but the side it was along was more like his great-aunt's backside. Merry sent out a long, sweary, damage report but apparently this was not too serious. Only fooking irritating. Only fooking irresponsible. Only fooking umbrageous. He then threw his dictionary into the sea. There weren't any words he could find to express his feelings.

Shan took a fast jeep to the oiling jetty, walked across the *Comus* and stood at the snapped guard rails and the tangle of broken brackets. The *Vijaya* had shaved a large swathe of paint off the sides and there was denting of the plate. He stepped across with an oath, raced to the bridge.

'See me in my cabin, Number One,' he said, 'now!'

When Shan cleared lower decks three days later to tell the men of his departure, he also announced that Lieutenant Tilak was to assume duties elsewhere. 'It is not usual that a Commanding Officer leaves his vessel in the middle of JET but circumstances demand it.' He gave the men a 'make and mend', in other words, a day off, and left that evening when many of his crew were ashore. Tilaka went too, and not in the best of spirits.

It was only the duty watch that saw the arrival of Lieutenant Commander Victor and Lieutenant Walid. Victor sprang up the gangway, shrugged off his coat and eyed the quartermaster.

'Don't you pipe the captain on board?' he asked frostily.

'Sir!'

'Forget it!'

The officers went to the wardroom, rang for the steward.

'Whisky,' Victor said, 'and a tin of Gallaghers. Have you any Glenfiddich?'

'No sir.'

'Get some from the NAAFI tomorrow.'

'Yes sir.'

Carloboy heard it all on his return. He was in a state of deep contentment. He had spent a very satisfactory and satisfying evening with Abela and looked forward to a whopping supper. 'New captain? Who?'

'Victor,' the QM said. 'Burgher bugger. Like you.'

'What's he like?'

The QM shrugged. 'Don' know. We'll see tomorrow.'

Lieutenant-Commander Donald Victor was a blue-eyed, rugged seaman who looked every inch his two and a half gold stripes. He was as restless as a parcel of polecats when in harbour. He would stand at the bridge rail, twirling a forelock of his hair with his finger and scowl at the sea slopping lazily around the anchor chain. But those eyes would light up with blue fire when putting to sea. Action at last . . . and he would break into a boyish grin that endeared him to all the men.

The month sped on and they began to spend more time at sea, conducting bigger and more complicated manoeuvres. Even re-fuelling was done on the run with the *Vijaya* heaving to alongside tender vessels, shooting lines across and heaving in the heavy fuel pipes.

Suddenly, it was a matter of challenge. Ceylon's only ship needed to do its best before the rest of the fleet. Everyone seemed to look on the *Vijaya* with a patronizing air. Since she was not capable of high speeds, she had to always leave harbour first and, after exercises, chug in last. During manoeuvres in column, she always trailed at the end of the line. But sometimes ships were ordered to reverse order of column, and all those trim destroyers and frigates would be forced to cut revolutions until the *Vijaya* took her place at the head of the line.

This would always be a big moment for the crew, and they would pass the other vessels at 500-yard distance, beating pots and pans and metal cauldrons wrested from the galley and cheer madly. Many would also turn their back on the deck crews of the other vessels and drop their trousers. This being a much-favoured practice, the Indian, Pakistani and Royal navies soon became very familiar with the shape, colour and general aspect of the backsides of Ceylon!

On high-speed manoeuvres, however, sleek destroyers would cut behind the *Vijaya*'s stern at 25 knots, and the quartermaster would race for the boat deck as the bow wave swamped the quarterdeck.

But the *Vijaya* could ask for no better skipper. It was a delight to trail in after a gruelling day and receive a congratulatory signal from NHQ. Victor, all agreed, was tough, and fair, and an exceptional seaman. And he knew what the men needed. When he cleared lower decks on his first morning of command, he stood on the pom-pom platform, looked down at the company on the boat deck and said: 'I am Lieutenant-Commander Victor. And this is your new Jimmy, Lieutenant Walid. I expect the best. No more, no less. Supplier officer, splice the mainbrace!'

Caps flew in the air as the men cheered themselves hoarse. By the time the shouting died, the stewards were ready with the rum. There was a rush to the messes for tin mugs, for a Navy noggin is no mean measure.

It is not often that the call goes out to splice the mainbrace. The mainbrace is the main yardarm-wire brace that is of stout grassline. Should the brace snap, or the sea air weather it to a point where strands begin to rust, it is necessary to splice a new length of grassline that would replace the weakened area. And this is no kindergarten task. In the days of the old wooden ships, the mainbrace was rope as thick as a kangaroo's thigh. Splicing that would take many hours. With fist-thick grassline it would take hours too, and longer if the vessel was at sea. Reward for such arduous work was a noggin of rum to the crew.

Oh, tradition was everything. The Navy must have been told what a noggin was, but who would bother to measure out a noggin of rum? The men grinned as the rum was liberally sloshed into their mugs. Nathali contrived to hold out his mug for seconds, which he received. Jamaica Red Heart, no less, and gulped down at eight in the morning, it did wonders for morale.

Victor was listening in on the B-28 receiver on the bridge. It was the captain of the *INS Ganga* who seemed to be celebrating something or another.

'Yes, this is Captain Victor. How can I help you, captain?'

'Ah yes. Captain Victor? Why, what is the matter with captain Shan?'

'I'm in command now, captain. Shan had to leave to—'

'My gracious! Such a nice man he was. Why, why? What happened?'

'Nothing. Nothing at all. He is due in Dartmouth.'

'Aaah. For a minute I was thinking . . . But that is now never mind. Captain, I want to invite you. Now we are half-way over. Two weeks to go home. On *Ganga* for this JET I always give a half-way party. Good for the men.'

'A grand idea, captain.'

'Grand? Yes, yes, so I am thinking also. This is third JET for me. So boats also I will send. From here I see you have one painter at the jib and one launch. Not enough. Not enough.'

'You mean a party for all?'

'Yes, yes. 'Allo, 'allo? Suddenly having interference. Ah, yes, OK now. Lunch party for all and send all the men you can. We are having all mess tables on boat deck under canvas. Can't otherwise with crows. Captain, you having these crows on the yardarm? Having many here.'

Victor grinned. 'Lunch it is, captain. But duty watch will remain.'

'Yes, yes. But when you come you can say how many you keep back and we will send them food also. You like samosa, captain? Good with whisky. And bara khana for all. Best basmati. My cooks make fine chawal; and keema and mutton korma. So you will come. At what time I can send the boats?'

Victor gazed out to sea. He didn't like the sound of those dishes. Bet there's a lot of oil and curd. He knew that the Indians take much milk curd. Oh, what the hell, samosa and whisky sounded good. 'Any time convenient to you, captain. I will have the men assembled. Number ten dress is OK?'

'Fine, fine. Even UK eights never mind. Send all you can. My launch will come for you and your officers at eleven. That is OK?'

'That is OK. Thank you. Will a case of malt whisky help?'

'Malt whisky? What you have got?'

'Glenfiddich. Same Grants distillery.'

'Ah, excellent. Excellent. Scotland's best, no?'

'Nothing better.'

'OK captain, I will be waiting.'

The *Ganga* was a big ship. Her sister ship the *Godavari* was also in port, and the men of the *Vijaya* found many of their fleet canteen boozing buddies from both vessels lining the afterdeck to give them a vociferous welcome.

Captain Chowdhary had been right. Trestle tables (from where the hell had they found trestle tables?) stood in row upon row on the boat deck. The breeze oo-ed between the canvas that stretched over it. Carloboy found the messes sparse but everything else very orderly and very spick. Brasses glittered. Even the funnel flue shone with its new lick of black paint.

There was beer—a bottle each per man—and a meal they would not forget for a long time. The rice was garnished with peas, cloves, cinnamon and caraway seeds. There was chicken with curd and potatoes, a korma with sweet peppers, tomatoes and onions, a curry of prawn and potato and another of mushroom and egg, pappadams, bowls of dahi or milk curd, mint chutney and lime and lemon pickle, and banana halva. They found it all so different, so satisfying. They simply ate, and ate, and ate.

Maybe it was not Nathali's idea of a party. He kept murmuring about 'one bottle of beer and that's all?' But when the boats took them back at four he was unaccountably merry. So were a group of Indian stokers who had invited Nathali to the engine room where they had produced mugs and two bottles of French Polish.

'French polish!' Nathali had hooted, 'you fellows are crazy?'

'Shoo! Only label is French Polish. This is good rum.'

And good it was, and Nathali's day had brightened considerably.

It was not such a pleased bunch of signalmen who were told to take the duty boat to *HMS Superb* the next morning. There, Yeoman Louis told them, they would listen to a lecture on Asdics—anti-submarine signals and manoeuvres—and be treated to a demonstration of the latest echo-sounding apparatus. 'As you know, we estimate the range and distance of an enemy submarine by reading the time it takes for an echo to bounce back off its hull.'

'We know, we know,' said Yusuf grumpily, 'but Yeo, what for going to that big ship? I don't like it. Can't understand anything those white buggers are saying.'

'Then listen better, and look bright!' Louis snapped, 'don't just sit there like a bloody aborogine who does not know what a commode is!'

'I know what a commode is,' Yusuf said, 'a commode has four stripes.'

'Will someone tell me what the fuck he's talking about?'

'A commode, Yeo. Why, you told us in Colombo that the captain of the Navy is a commode.'

'A commodore, you idiot!'

Yusuf blinked. He didn't see much of a difference. The rest of the men whooped.

They would be taken like a bunch of nursery kids on a sunday school outing, to the flagship of the Commander-in-Chief, East Indies, where they would be suitably impressed at its size, its two funnels, its big guns and its complement of 560 men. The bridge would be as big as a church and the flagdecks to port and starboard big enough to throw a rowdy party. They would actually visit a charthouse and the telegraphists were expected to take stock of what a good sea-going wireless cabin was really like. The Vice-Admiral's flag would be at the top gallant, and they should try, above all, to look intelligent. They would be treated to elevenses and they should eat with dignity and not the way they reached for the korma on the *Ganga*.

'So what you're saying is that these guys are better than us,' Carloboy demanded.

'I'm not saying anything like that,' Louis said crossly, 'all I'm saying is make a good impression. Don't let the *Vijaya* down.'

'Oh that? Don't you worry, Yeo.'

But Carloboy did make an impression. With a bucket. He had to return a much chastened man.

The lecture on anti-submarine signals was interesting enough and the tour of the big cruiser something that made them think of their own ship with some misgiving. And then, they were led to the long afterdeck where a bunch of Goanese deckhands grinned and told them to park themselves and brought out a large pail of tea and a heaped plate of sandwiches.

So this was British hospitality. Carloboy fumed. Sent to the stern to sit on the deck and take tea with the Lascars. Not that he minded. Indeed, they didn't mind at all. Not Yusuf and not Daft either. What riled Carloboy was the way a Brit chief petty officer strode the deck, sniffing superciliously.

Carloboy had just given Sims a mug of tea when the CPO strode up, looked at them nastily.

'What are you bleeding black buggers doing? What's in the bucket? Tea!' He spat the last word as if it was Epsom salts. 'Drinking on deck! Haven't you black bastards bin told to go below? You!' He shouted at a Goanese cook, 'Who asked you to bring this tea here?'

The men of the *Vijaya* gaped.

'Who are you calling a black bastard?' Carloboy asked.

The CPO glared. Then, with a hefty kick he sent the pail of tea skittering. 'Tea on deck!' he bawled, 'who told you to have a tea party here? Fucking black bastards!'

Whump! It was the work of an instant. There was no time to take the situation to higher authority. The bucket, slopping tea, clattered at Carloboy's feet. He seized it, swung it, and then slammed it full in the bloodshot CPO's face. The man croaked and went down, a large gash opening out across his nose and one cheek. Blood streamed from his mouth as well. On the quarterdeck a duty officer squawked and the turmoil grew as men rushed to carry the stricken chief to the sick bay and surround the 'black bastards'. A master-at-arms stood, rifle at the ready. They were marched to the boat deck, placed under guard until a fussy warrant officer marched up, told the men of the *Vijaya* to follow him. Below the bridge, they were lined up outside the Captain's cabin.

'And he called you a black bastard?'

'Yes sir.'

'Who slung the bucket at CPO Baird?'

'I did sir,' Carloboy said.

'Hmm. What are you, sailor?'

'Signalman, sir.'

'Yes, but what are you? Are you a Ceylonese?'

'Yes sir.'

'But you are not black.'

'No sir.'

The Captain was told of the invitation to visit, the lecture by communications, the break for tea.

'But why were they told to take tea with the Lascars? Who gave such an order? Dammit man, if we invited these men here they are our guests. Summon the men who were taking tea!' Turning to Carloboy, 'You don't like to be called black, eh?'

'I'm not black, sir.'

'Yes, I can see that. Any fool can see that.'

'And we are not bastards, sir.'

'True, true, too much of this rushing to conclusions. But you cannot come on my ship and hit my non-commissioned officers with buckets. What does the Navy teach you, signalman?'

'I'm sorry sir.'

'I dare say you are. So you say. Ah, cook Ranji. Yes. Don't fidget, man. Tell us what happened.'

Cook Ranji swallowed. 'We drinking tea, sir. Leading Signalman Guffey he said have some fallows from Ceylon to give tea. Said will send them to where we are and to give some tea.'

'Guffey, eh? Get Guffey here. And then?'

'So we give tea sir. We give sandwiches also. The CPO Baird come and telling me cannot take tea in the stern.'

'Yes?'

'But always we take tea there sir.'

'Why?'

'Sir?'

'Why don't you take tea in the mess?'

'Sir, we are natif peoples sir. Others don't like too much when we are eating-drinking with them.'

'I see. Are you aware of this, Nuttall?'

Warrant Officer Nuttall gave a faint 'No sir'.

'Very well. So what did Chief Baird do?'

'He come up and shout and then he kick the tea sir.'

'And what did you do?'

'N-nothing sir. What to do. I am only Lascar sir. That's what everybody saying. Nothing I can do.'

'And this man hit Baird with the bucket?'

'Y-yes sir.'

'Very well, you may go. Nuttall, arrange a boat to take our visitors back. Ah, Guffey, was it your decision to have these men take tea with the Goanese?'

'I was told to give them tea, sir.'

'Yes, yes, I know that. So you sent them aft?'

'The Goanese were having tea, sir.'

'And what about you? Where did you have tea?'

'In the mess, sir.'

'I see . . . well, signalman—what's your name?'

'Von Bloss sir.'

'Von whatever. You will be detained. The rest of you may go. Guffey, you will take Signalman von Bloss to the wireless cabin and keep him there. Give him tea. I must know of Baird's condition.'

'Sir, the sick bay says he is all right. Only that he has lost a tooth. He has been patched up. He wants to press a charge, sir.'

'Of course he wants to, and he may. Guffey, you may go. Both of you. Remain in the wireless cabin at my orders, do you understand?'

'Aye aye, sir.'

Baird was asked if he had a good eyesight. He didn't understand.

'You seem to have some difficulty, chief. You don't know black from white. And also, who is your father?'

'Sir?'

'You heard me, chief. Who is your father? Is he a merchant, or a tram conductor, or a chief magistrate or what?'

'I—I don't very well know, sir.'

'What? Are you telling me you don't know your father?'

'No-no sir.'

'Then you don't know much, do you? Ever heard of the pots that called the kettles black?'

'N-no sir.'

'Nuttall, place this man on a charge. Captain's defaulter. Nine hundred hours tomorrow!'

On the *Vijaya* Yeoman Louis blanched. 'What?' He screamed, 'He did what? My God! Now there'll be a huge inquiry and—and—I told you fellows to behave, no?'

Sims scowled. 'Calling us black bastards. We didn't go to get insulted.'

'Must have said to the Goanese. Did he look at you and say it?'

'No, Yeo, but—'

'But what? This is too much. Too much! One of you keep bridge watch. Go and relieve Gibbs. signal is sure to come. God knows what the Captain will do.'

On the *Superb* Carloboy was asked, 'Who's your signals officer?'

'Lieutenant Wicks, sir.'

'Well, Signalman von Bloss, you may go. You will take my greetings to Lieutenant Wicks. Wait outside till I write him. It is to be given to him personally, you got that?'

'Yes sir.'

The coxswain on the boat taking him to the *Vijaya* grinned. 'Broke Baird's tooth, did you? Say, you're the piano man! Next time you come ashore I'll buy you a drink.'

Lieutenant Wicks was puzzled. A most cryptic letter. 'Above all,' Captain Clarke had written, 'don't call him a black bastard. He should be kept away from buckets.'

'What is all this?'

'I don't know, sir. Told me to give it to you.'

'What the devil have you been doing?'

'Me? Nothing sir.'

38

History—End of the Honeymoon

With the coming of the South East Asia Command to Ceylon, great big NAAFI buildings were erected. Also cinemas and concrete tennis courts and reinforced concrete roads. There were armies of local workers, many of whom did not work for the wages they received, and local contractors made big bucks. The labourers were paid wages they had never ever dreamed of receiving.

Army trucks went around, collecting estate labourers to work in the camps. This caused havoc on the plantations. Both tea and rubber were considered essential crops and both were hit by alarming labour shortages.

As contract rates for work and wages began to rise dramatically, bribery and corruption was rampant. Coconut thatch for roofing and timber for building rose drastically in price. Cement could only be obtained on permit and soon the whole island seemed to be operating on a permit system.

The war was costing the British government an expenditure of fourteen or fifteen million pounds a day, and in Ceylon, the military seemed determined to spend as much of it as it could. It had 15,000 people on the register, paying wages to all even if only 8,000 worked, while thousands of others held jobs about which they were totally ignorant.

Also, the Wrens moved in, as well as the WAAF's and the Americans who had their own signalling company. The RAF had a 'C' camp in the hills and the Air Officer Commanding, Air Commodore Chiton, also had his bungalow 'up-country' which was called Air Cottage. Naval Headquarters was at Upper Chatham Street, Colombo.

As far back as 1917, during the World War I, Ceylon was divided into three military areas—Colombo, Southern and Northern. Colombo was commanded by the Officer Commanding Troops; the Southern division by the Ceylon Mounted Rifles; and the Northern sector by the Ceylon Planters Rifle Corps.

By 1940, all the district planters associations formed internal security schemes in their districts. But, as everyone knew, there was an appalling waste of money. In fact, for the first ten years up to 1941, the Government of Ceylon was almost bankrupt with the excess of expenditure, about rupees fifty million, caused mainly by all kinds of appointments and emoluments.

It was the military occupation that increased the revenue. During the war years the civil defence commissioner had millions to spend and play with. Above all, no accounts were allowed to be published. Many, especially in the state council of the time, were emphatic that a great deal of money had been wasted. They were at a loss to understand how the expenditure of the civil defence commissioner had any real influence on the war.

And yes, there was the opposition. An opposition that voiced itself in the most vituperative manner and which spoke volumes for the mood of the Ceylonese members of the state council.

One minister: 'Ceylon is a small country and the people have not the force to establish their rights. The mighty British have played ducks and drakes with them.'

Another minister: 'There is no getting away from the truth that only a bloody revolution as happened in France years ago can find a solution of these economic ills.'

Some of the remarks of the state council bear repetition:

• 'There will soon be a parting of the ways, not between Sinhalese and Tamils, but between the people of Ceylon and the Britishers.'

• 'When the bombing took place, what happened? First, the non-Ceylonese disappeared; the exploiter, who was exploiting Ceylonese labour went 3000 miles away, and we could not get at him.'

• 'Gratitude is a word unknown in history of imperialism. The European is now safe, and England is now safe with a litter of broken promises and pledges.'

• 'If all the Europeans were to leave Ceylon tomorrow, I shall be very happy, provided they take away the Tamils they have brought from India with them, and do not leave them here.'

• 'The English are not fighting the countries like Ceylon and India.'

• 'Churchill and England are fighting for freedom of the world? This is not so. Churchill and England are merely fighting for the freedom of England and English people.'

• 'For 116 years of British rule, the people of this country were reduced to a condition of destitution and the government coffers were left in a condition of financial distress.'

• 'The freedom of Ceylon would come with the liquidation of the British empire.'

• 'A very curious order was given to all English people to get out. It would have been a very good thing if everybody had left the island and left us in peace.'

• 'Ceylon wants a hundred per cent severance from the British yoke.'

• 'We must fight now if we want complete independence.'

• 'The British empire is one of the greatest barriers to the progress of the world.'

• 'We do not want the British language spoken at all in this country and the earlier it goes the better.'

• 'The outside power is not interested in the true welfare of the people but is only anxious to preserve its prestige and the interests of the outside capital that is invested in this country. The Britisher is here to protect his tea and rubber for export or to sell his goods from England. All he wants is that the people should be kept above subsistence level to work his estates and buy his goods.'

• 'This is an administration that is doing all that is possible to facilitate the amassing of wealth by foreigners.'

• 'The stumbling block to progress of the Sinhalese nation is the menace of foreigners.'

It seemed that the honeymoon (if there was one) was over. What was galling, during the period of the war, was that Ceylonese had to die in Trincomalee solely because of the British presence there. Worse still, the small east coast town of Batticaloa, which was in no way ready for anything like Japanese bombing raid, was also targetted. Why? Because British ships, racing downcoast from Trincomalee to avoid being attacked in the harbour, were also chased and bombed by Japanese Stikas off Batticaloa. That's when the British aircraft carrier *HMS Hermes* went down.

The question was, why had Ceylon to bear the brunt of a war she had no part in? It was easy to whip up anti-British feelings in the island. Whatever Ceylon had gained from the military occupation, indeed the whole British occupation, was being buried under an avalanche of nationalistic fervour.

Freedom was what Ceylon looked for. World War II had shown the island that this freedom was worth fighting for!

39

Of Darken Ship and Night Strikes and a Cobra in the Heads

Night watch is a dreary thing, especially when in port. Signalman von Bloss leaned against the binnacle, his eyes straying ever so often to the diamond arrangement of lights that was the NHQ yardarm. All around the *Vijaya* the fleet lay at anchor. Some creaked, some made little gaspy noises, some glubbed in the water. Carloboy knew that on every bridge there would be a signalman, blearily looking around and counting the minutes just the way he did. Eight to twelve. He would rouse Daft at midnight. And Daft had his orders too. Wake Sims at 4 a.m. and also the duty officer. The duty officer was Sub-Lieutenant Hugo. Now why the devil had Hugo to be roused at four?

Sims had grunted. 'Now the bugger will come to the bridge to talk,' he said.

Oh, there would be a lot more than talk, he knew. Sims kept his secret well. He had come to enjoy buggering the Sub-Lieutenant who had, he thought, a made-to-measure anus. He had wondered many a time whether Hugo was being served by others of the crew. There was a tall, rangy electrician named de Haan who was said to have the longest cock on board. On board, mind, for in all the Ceylon Navy nobody could match Able Seaman Warrick who had what was affectionately called a 'kidney wiper'. It hung, it was said, when unconfined, to a close eight inches over his knee, and that too when in flaccid condition. When at red alert and rarin' to go, it was reputed to be thirteen inches long, and that, as scores of women in Dehiwela, and Wattala and Ragama and wherever Warrick went, said, was an impalement of the most extreme sort.

Carloboy suddenly jerked up. Yes, there on the NHQ yardarm a tiny orange light had started to blink.

FFFF it said, and again FFFF. He searched his mind. What the devil was the code? His hand went to the small Aldis lamp, then checked. FFFF—Do Not Answer. And he had nearly done so!

The call was repeated several times until the NHQ signalman felt certain that every ship in port had taken note, that every watchman knew that there was a message to follow. He paused and sent BT, the break before the message: Dash, dot, dot, dot, dash. Then the message: Crash Darken Ship.

Immediately Carloboy was on the buzzer and shouting down the voice tube. 'Crash Darken Ship, sir. Admiralty order.' He alerted the duty electrician. The exercise, for that it was, went like clockwork. The *Vijaya* lost itself in a caul of black. Not a light showed. Every scuttle dropped its deadlight. All around, other ships also seemed to disappear. No, one blazed its lights and seemed to glitter more than ever in the blackness all around.

Carloboy chuckled. 'Bloody mutt must be sleeping. He's going to catch it.'

As the Admiralty had said, this was JET. This was war. This demanded an alertness that made all the difference between kill and be killed.

Then, in the black well that was the boatdeck, strange forms emerged. One sidled to the bridge gangway. 'You're up?' a voice asked.

'Yes. Who's that?'

'Never mind. How long is this darken ship business?'

'Don't know. Who are you?'

'You just stay where you are. Master-at-arms will come now to see if anyone is smoking on deck.'

'So?'

'So don't smoke.'

'I can't,' Carloboy said, 'I'm on duty.'

'Just telling, that's all,' and the figure melted away. There were other figures. Carloboy could not make out who they were or why they chose to creep along the boatdeck. He was sure one was very like Stoker Arnie but he wasn't certain. Then suddenly, the night was split by a cry of deep agony. That someone fell, he was certain.

'Serves the buggers right,' he muttered, 'must have fallen in the dark.' He shouted, 'Who's there? Is everything all right?'

No answer. Only a low gibber and the sound of scuffling, then another painful groan.

Carloboy hesitated. He could not leave post. He buzzed the duty officer. No reply. Apparently Hugo was out of his bed too. He shouted, hoping the QM would hear him, but there was no response. He looked towards the squat ghost that was the NHQ. Not a blink out of it. Then the B-29 gave a squawk. Why didn't he think of that? All he had to do was use it as an internal telephone. He turned the needle to the harbour intercom wavelength and called the *Vijaya*.

Bijja's voice came loud and clear. 'This is M390 over.'

Procedure was dumped. 'Bijja. That you? Can you come to the bridge?'

'Who—who—what? Who is this?'

'Von Bloss, men. On the bridge. Hurry up!'

'Can't. I'm on duty.'

'Then stick your head out and yell for somebody.'

'You're mad? Wardroom is nextdoor.'

'So yell! I think someone is hurt up here. Can't see a bloody thing. Get some help! Over. Out. Hurry up!'

Bijja did raise the alarm. He nipped out, banged on the wardroom door, had a frightened duty steward run out, then ran to Lieutenant Walid. Soon, a group of seamen led by the First Lieutenant made their way topside where they found the body. With much cursing, they carried it below where the sick bay light burned dimly. The NHQ yardarm blinked. 'Negative Crash Darken Ship'. Well, that was a relief. Deck lights came on and the QM spread the news on the hailer.

In the sick bay, the master-at-arms lay, two puffy blue welts across his stomach and a swelling at the diaphragm where the blood had collected and was turning black. His breathing was thin, agonized. A rib was obviously broken. He was examined, then swathed in a blanket and carried carefully topside where a boat was called alongside to speed him ashore. He had been beaten with something very hard.

'Like a length of pipe?' Walid hazarded.

'Yes, or—or a belaying pin. Something used as a club.'

'Brutal assault. I don't like it. We have a lot of this darken ship business. Where was the duty officer?'

Hugo said he had been on lower deck inspection when the order to crash darken had come. And no, he hadn't heard or seen anything.

Carloboy sat with Daft after midnight. They sipped coffee and ruminated.

'I don't like it,' he said, 'Some buggers were waiting in the dark to hammer the chief. They must have known he will come. You know, Mendis hates the bugger.'

'Anyway, you didn't see anything, no?'

'No, but one bugger spoke to me. But still, I'm not sure who he was. He said the chief will come and told me not to smoke.'

And the next night the signal was repeated. This time, at eleven. Evidently, the Admiralty was dissatisfied. One ship had blissfully ignored signals and that one ship was given a most recriminatory message at dawn. This time, it was Alfie who sat on the inner ledge of the bridge score, read the light, called for immediate darkening of the decks. Again, there was a victim. It was the Malay seaman Jambong. He was not beaten. He was held and painted. Broad daubs of Black Japan across his baby face. He howled and waved his arms and rushed to the quarterdeck steps where he broke into a stream of Javanese. The QM grabbed him, hauled him below, where he bubbled furiously while the chippie worked on him with turps and rubbed him raw with sacking.

When at war and out for blood, a ship is not expected to show lights at night. Night exercises gave more opportunities for the new breed of Rembrandts and others who liked to prowl in the dark. With sunset the ship doused all lights and steamed on, a grey ghost.

These nights in the Bay of Bengal were very black indeed. Clouds always put the moon in purdah and even the stars seemed to have downed tools. There was little Captain Victor could do. Someone had to know what was going on, he reasoned, but he would shrug and regard his officers balefully.

'You mean to say you have no idea what started all this?'

'I have personally secured all stores areas,' said Lieutenant Wicks.

'But they're painting each other every bleeding night? Mess inspection. There must be paint and brushes hidden somewhere.'

'I was thinking, we should post sentries at the gangways, sir.'

'And in the morning what will we have? Painted sentries?'

'Paint and brushes can be well hidden in the engine room . . .'

'What? In my engine room?' This from an indignant engineering officer.

'Gentlemen, let me get this straight. You may inform the men or do I have to clear decks to do it? All hands will be locked in their messes. Duty watch will sleep on the afterdeck until their turns come. Any man seen about the ship who has no reason to be about will be placed on a charge. Is that clear?'

There were some objections. Men go to the heads. Especially when they are swollen with beer.

'And now there are no more assaults, sir. Only this painting business.'

Hugo murmured that perhaps the men would eventually work things out between themselves.

Victor grunted. 'The one thing I do know is that I have a set of brush-happy miscreants on this ship. And it's among the seamen and stokers. And you noticed something else? The chiefs and PO's are keeping their heads down.'

'That's true, sir.'

Yes, the tongue-lashings, the overbearing attitudes of some of the chiefs and petty officers had dropped to zero. After all, it is no fun to bump into a vague form who carries a pot of Black Japan and a brush in either hand. Such men seemed to have a radar system of their own. They would stalk their quarries and when within range, paint them with broad stripes of black and vanish below in a trice.

It was the engineering officer who said he had a theory. He had given the affair some thought and took his views to Victor the next day.

Victor listened, sent for Jambong. 'You bloody little weasel!' he roared, 'don't you dare deny anything! My God, you're the cause of all this! How many are using your arse for a sock? *Come on!* I want names. All those you are dropping your pants for! All those you refuse. *All the names!* And then, by God, *I'm going to bump you out of the force, do you hear?'*

Sheet-faced, stuttering, the story was told. Jambong had complained loud and long about the way the master-at-arms was harassing him. Always trying to take him to the after steering compartment. No, Jambong didn't like the master-at-arms. He was a dirty man. One day he had pressed him against the bulkhead and kissed him. Yes, others did it to him but he liked them. They did it nicely. They were good men and they protected him . . .

'Who are they? *I want names!'*

Eventually the sordid story was known. Those who could not bugger Jambong had seized him one night, daubed him with paint. Reprisals followed.

Victor drummed his fingers on the table. 'Place this

man under close arrest. He will be sent under guard to *Gemunu* tomorrow!'

When Jambong was led away to the bridge, Victor asked the engineering officer, 'Tell me, what made you twig this?'

The man told the skipper of the complaint made to Captain Shan by the master-at-arms.

'I see. Send the chief to *Gemunu* too. Can't have a company of fuck-arses on my ship. Who was the other man? Mendis?'

'Yes, but he was sent here because *Gemunu* wanted to get rid of him.'

Sub-Lieutenant Hugo came in. He learned of events and cocked an eyebrow. 'These men who were screwing Jambong, sir. I think I can bring them to heel.'

'Very well. Give them hell, Hugo.'

'Oh, I will, sir. You'll have no more trouble from that lot.'

Hugo was true to his word. All artistic endeavours stopped. Hugo reported that he had made them realize the error of their ways. He was very pleased with himself.

While Hugo kept order, (he actually had the culprits stand in line in a sort of get-thee-behind-me-Satan formation), Joint Exercise Trincomalee took the *Vijaya* for long rides where the Bay of Bengal was in its most resentful mood. Dirty weather made everybody snappish and guy lines had to be strung as walking the decks became nigh impossible. The waves seemed to rise out of nowhere and the bows would nosedive into them, taking in tons of water that swept down the fo'c'sle to hiss through the boat deck. Hatches had to be tight shut, clamped down with the big rivet wheels, but the water dripped in annoyingly.

Astern, in the stokers and seamen's mess, the intake of water remained an abiding mystery. How it got in was the subject of much debate. Plates were examined, bulkheads tapped, hatches relined with hard rubber, but all to no avail. Arnie left his shoes on the floor (after duty officer's inspection, of course) and woke up the next morning to find them afloat, in a foot of water. It scared him. He tumbled out of his hammock, stood shin deep and yelled, 'Get up! We're sinking!'

But they weren't. Pumps inhaled the water, and in port the mess was as dry as it should be. The seamen took to sleeping on the galley tables. 'You can drown in your sleep there,' Arnie said sepulchrally.

Finally the Captain ordered a compartment-by-compartment examination, from galley to heads, to electricians stores, shipwright stores to seamen's mess and the after steering. The water had to come from somewhere. Decidedly, it was not coming through the sides.

The two places where water was in constant use were the galley and the heads. The galley was cleared, the tanks examined, all pipes tapped and found functional. And then, the shipwright whizzed down the deck and fell, panting, at the sick bay door. 'Cobra!' he yelled, 'Cobra in the shithouse!'

There were others who were engaged in their lawful occupation in the heads. Koelmeyer always went there to masturbate. When the shipwright saw a pipe move, he rubbed his eyes, stared, and saw that it was a large snake. He yelled. The pipe began coiling upwards. This was too much. Also, his yell brought Koelmeyer out, cock in hand. Stoker Wickrema, who was discharging cargo heard the cry 'Snake!' and leaped off his seat. There was a rush out of the heads while others rushed to it. Very hard to manoeuvre when a narrow gangway is suddenly filled with earnest souls going in opposite directions. And yes, it *was* a cobra, and it was in an unpleasant mood. It had coiled around a cistern and eyed the men meanly. Then, on the premise that discretion was the better part of being hit on the head with a boat-hook, it slithered warily down and oozed through a flush hole.

'Where'd it go? Where'd it go?' the shipwright hollered.

And the mystery of the water in the seamen's mess was solved. The heads flush flues had remained open when at sea. Water kept washing in, followed the slope of the deck and collected in the mess.

The skipper was annoyed. Duty officer inspection had been too lax.

Leading Seaman Welli, a fine boxer, ran to the armoury, then to the boatdeck from where he saw the cobra earnestly making the crossing, twisting its way through the water with ease. He blew the snake's head off with a single .303 bullet. He was a superb marksman.

40

History—The Taking of Iwo Jima

Even the Americans looked on Iwo Jima as a lousy piece of real estate. But the island was important. The Americans needed a way-base between the Marianas and Tokyo.

Early 1945. America's island-hopping campaign had brought Japan close to defeat, her Pacific empire chipped away. Now, from the Marianas, big US B-29 bombers struck at the Japanese mainland. But each bombing run required a round trip of 3000 miles. A long and perilous flight. Also, the Super Fortress bombers had to fly without fighter cover. No fighter had the operational range to make the trip.

Going it alone, the bomber crews knew that if they were shot down, they hadn't a prayer. There was no friendly place where they could ditch their planes. There was no friendly naval presence to pick them out of the water.

Another island, close to Tokyo, had to be taken. The US looked at the Bonin Islands. Among this volcanic cluster was Iwo Jima, occupied by the Japanese and a miserable looking place of volcanic rock ledges and black sand. An extinct volcanic peak rose at one end of the four-and-a-half by two-and-a-half-mile island—Mount Suribachi—and the Japanese had two airfields there as well as the usual shore defences. They had big gun emplacements on the slopes of the mountain, and there was the problem of the beach: black sand, ash and cinders and a terraced shore that ran into the water in long, ten-foot-high steps that would make landing difficult. A real lousy piece of real estate indeed.

But it had to be Iwo Jima, and the Americans readied the 3rd, 4th, and 5th Marine divisions to lead the assault on February 19, 1945.

On Iwo Jima, Lieutenant Kuribiyashi in charge of the Japanese garrison, knew of the American intention. It was no secret. The Japanese knew that the Americans needed to base themselves closer to Tokyo.

Kuribiyashi stuck to a plan of defence that had little bravado. He ordered his men to dig in as deep as they could. Nothing must be exposed to the softening of US air strikes and the bombardment of ships. The Japanese were to remain doggo until the US Marines were on the beach. Then they will fight . . . and fight on to a finish. It was all Kuribiyashi could do. He and his men had to ride out the first storm of air and sea bombardment.

February 16. The Americans began the softening-up process. A savage air-sea bombardment. They could determine nothing of an enemy presence on the beaches or inland. Were the Japanese so well entrenched that this first attack did nothing, did not even touch them . . . or had they been badly flattened, overwhelmed that the landing would be as easy as pie? And what of the beaches? The Americans knew of the ugly, vicious Japanese beach defences. Bamboo spikes just below the low-tide line; steel and concrete tank traps; tangles of barbed wire below the surface; oil drums that could be opened and ignited by an electrical impulse from ashore; dynamite wrapped in waterproofing material.

On February 17, underwater demolition experts were sent out on tiny LCPR's to chart the bottom, check the beaches and destroy obstacles. LCI gunboats also headed for the beach. On Iwo Jima the Japanese watched with concern. The LCI's were assault craft. They could be full of Marines. The gun crews on the slopes of Mount Suribachi grew nervous. They forgot their orders to lie low. Training the big guns, they opened fire with deadly effect.

Many of the US gunboats were destroyed in that first salvo, and the US battleships immediately laid a smoke-screen over the area while the destroyers began to blaze away at the muzzle blasts that opened like yellow mouths on the mountain. For the Japanese, the retaliation was disastrous. Many of their big guns were knocked out, cannon muzzles dangling uselessly on the slopes.

The Americans were more or less satisfied. They had planned their landing on the eastern beach from where it would be a quick advance to the airfields. This flank was dominated by the mountain. They now knew how much firepower the Japanese had casemated around the slopes.

Also, the demolition experts reported no obstacles to landing other than the volcanic terrain that would be a problem for amtracs. The only worry was that there seemed to be much Japanese firepower around the mountain. Well, there was no help to it. The landing had to be made.

The Pacific islands still talk of that pre-landing bombardment of February 19. It was the heaviest of World War II. The island became invisible in the clouds of volcanic dust that rose hundreds of feet in the air with each explosion. As the Marines landed, the ships' batteries increased range, streamed their shells inland. Over the terraces, the Marines moved inward. They had met with no resistance. They were all out of the water now, ready to fight.

This was what General Kuribiyashi was waiting for: the time when the Marines would be most vulnerable. The first unit was already gathering to storm inland. It was the 1st Battalion, 27th Regiment, 5th Marines. Kuribiyashi gave the order to fire.

Mortar and machine-gun fire sliced in. The platoons were tossed apart, men died, but none stopped to count. They had to get off the beach. Beach Red Two, they called it, on Iwo Jima's east coast. They had to get to Airfield No.1 and then to the other side of the island.

Even as night fell, the Marines were digging in at the end of the beach, pinned down by Japanese fire. The ships fired star shells to light up the grim scene, give their men the chance to pick off the Japanese machine-gun nests.

The morning of February 20 saw the Marines on the beach in full force. Now they would fight every inch of the way. A fight to the finish. The Japanese also knew that they would never leave Iwo Jima. They would simply have to kill every American they could.

The big problem for the Americans was Mount Suribachi. As they moved inland, they found that the Japanese had dug in around the slopes and held an excellent advantage. Somehow, it was necessary to take that peak. Above all, they had to fly the US flag from that summit, show the ships' spotters that the peak was taken.

The fighting was frenzied as they climbed, died, rolled grotesquely downslope in their death struggles. But they climbed, ever up. The Japanese had occupied every hole, every fissure of that extinct volcano. It took two days for the Marines to blast them out. Finally, on February 23, a band of young Marines reached the top. They were led by Lieutenant Harold G. Schrier. In the crater, they found a length of pipe. They had a small US flag. They lashed it to the pipe, raised it. Down slope, the Marines who were mopping up decided that the flag was too small. A larger Stars and Stripes was taken from a landing craft—56 by 96 inches. When it was raised, a photographer who was with the landing party took what was perhaps the greatest war photograph of the time. So heroic, so statuesque was the attitude, the pose of the men, planting that second flag on Iwo Jima, that statues were later made from that astounding photograph. These statues have always been symbols of victory to the American people.

But the fight was not over. The Japanese kept up their defence. They fought from trenches, from caves, from holes in the ground. Long, bitter, unrelenting. It was on March 26 that organized Japanese resistance ended, but for months thereafter diehard stragglers continued to emerge from caves and holes in the mountainside and continued to fight till they died.

There were, before February 19, 22,000 Japanese on Iwo Jima. The Americans could eventually take no more than a thousand prisoners.

The Marines lost 6,000 men. Over 18,000 were wounded. But Iwo Jima was theirs. When, on March 4, the first B-29 bomber landed at Airfield No. 1, they all knew that they were now within range to knock Japan for six!

41

Of Not Quite Going Home and Fouled Propellers and a Corpse to Watch Over

Suddenly, it was all over. Binkie walked the deck looking quite devastated. He was going to marry Annette. The man was stupefied that it had all panned out so simply. Old Plinkett had merely nodded. 'After JET, you take leave and come back. Can get married here.'

Carloboy pitied his friend. Annette had had more sailors than there were fleas on the proverbial dog. He thought he would appeal to the man's sailor-sense. 'So how many times have you fucked her?'

'Oh, three-four times,' said Binkie airily.

'Then why do you want to go and marry her?'

Binkie was nonplussed. Didn't Carloboy understand that three-four times was a mere nothing? He just couldn't get enough of the girl who didn't seem to mind if he mounted her five times a day.

'So you're going to marry her? And then what?'

'As if you don't know,' Binkie grinned, 'fuck, fuck, fuck, and no damn hula music.'

Carloboy sighed. He firmly upheld that there was no sense buying a cow when milk was cheap. 'So it's all set, then?'

'All set. Old man said can't afford a big wedding and all. Who wants all that? Anything I don't mind. Once I take her to Hendala where I live . . .' he paused to consider the delicious possibilities, 'whole day she won't need clothes. What for wearing anything when I'm at home?'

They were to sail back September 10. The C-in-CEI decided to call it a day. The *Vijaya* was highly commended and the fleet canteen exploded in more ways than one. Nugawira created a sensation, more so since he was such a little fellow and liked, as far as possible, to keep out of trouble. The fleet canteen was very much alive—the usual festivity but, being the last evening ashore for many of the crews, this spirit was multiplied to the power of eight. And liquor, one has to admit, does bring out the worst in some.

Nugawira found the attention of a big British Marine most trying. The man's face was draped in an oversized ginger moustache and he had the complexion of a well-slapped rump of pig. He kept leaning forward and leering.

Nugawira frowned. 'What the hell do you want?' he asked.

'Small Ceylon boy. I like you.'

Nugawira rose, came to the piano. Quite the biggest of the boys was Yusuf, but he knew that Yusuf never mixed in. The Royal Marine followed, put a big hand on Nugawira's shoulder. 'I said, I like you.'

Carloboy stopped playing, swung round. 'Hey you! Leave him alone!'

A few in the vicinity smelt trouble. Nugawira struck at the man's hand. 'Take your bloody hand away!'

Carloboy rose, pushed his stool away. The Marine towered, an ox of a man. He was also drunk in a dangerous way. Carloboy closed, but Nugawira, eyes flashing, put out a hand and pushed hard into the Marine's mid-section.

'So you like me? So what do you want?'

The Marine was, if nothing, an honest man. 'Want? Yes, want. I want to split your backside.'

Nugawira pulled up the piano stool, climbed on it. 'You wait there,' he gritted, 'can't reach you from the floor.'

The Marine swayed. Then he swayed more as Nugawira swung a bunched fist which smashed into his Adam's apple. He said something like 'Wowk'. A second blow completed the decline and, like Humpty Dumpty, there was a great fall. The man took a table with him as he crashed, poleaxed. Even a glass of gin, dashed in his face with a barman's dexterity, did not revive him. A couple of RN sailors came up. 'Hey, it's Fogarthy. Sleeping again. Now we'll have to carry him to the boat.'

Nugawira climbed down, wringing his hand and sucking at his knuckles.

Carloboy stared. 'Where did you learn to hit like that?'

Nugawira blew on his knuckles. The joint of his thumb had begun to swell. 'Must have sprained it,' he said, 'play something, men.'

The hiccup was over. Now would joy be unconfined.

They sailed for Colombo on the morning of the eleventh. Carloboy sat on deck, admiring his tattoos. Somehow, they had staggered out of the bar, gone gallivanting, bumping into each other and swaying from side to side of the roads they explored. And there was a tattoo artist with his charts and his small curtained sanctum and his gold teeth and his promise to do them proud.

'Anything you want,' he said, 'see the designs. Dragons, eagles, naked girls, hearts, crosses, snakes. Or you show me any picture I do. Colours also. Red, green, black, blue. If black you want only I not charging much.'

Carloboy grinned. 'You put a heart on my arm? With leaves and flowers. Can do?'

'With colours also?'

'Why not? Red heart, green leaves. And put a scroll across the heart and Barbara. Can you do?'

'Easily I can. So come and sit. No pain. Four needles I use. One to do the outline then each colour another needle.'

'How much?'

'Twenty.'

'So do it.'

The man was quick. He placed a tissue over the tattoo

to soak up the welling pinpricks of blood. Carloboy liked it. 'Say, you do another one on my forearm?'

'Anywhere can do.'

Nugawira hooted. 'You can do "Padmini" on my bum?'

'Can, can.'

Able Seaman Outschoon wanted a big eagle, wings outspread, across the back of his body. Stoker Vadergert wanted 'Mother' and Daft said he liked a cobra but no thanks. Another scroll on the right forearm.

'And the name? You want a name, no?'

Carloboy thought a while. 'Write Caryll,' he said. He was thinking of a girl close to Eardley's in Perera Lane. Yes, Caryll. He had not given her much thought but now she came vividly to mind. He knew he had a lot to do when he went home.

An uneventful journey back. The *Vijaya* pushed to 12 knots even around the Basses because Captain Victor seemed anxious to get home too. They took a tremendous beating in the frothy sea and Electrician Panditha was very nearly swept overboard. He clung to the guardrail, one leg dangling over the side, the other hooked round a stanchion and he howled bloody murder. It was a rough two hours before the sea called it a day and mellowed under a glaring noonday sun.

Carloboy leaned over, looked into the incredible sun-splotched blue, felt the thrum of the big engines, heard the hiss of each wave as it swept past, knifed to the heart and bleeding a floss of spume that curdled and creamed. He never imagined that there could be so much colour, subtle colour, in this vast cradle. They were far out, the shoreline having receded to a pencil stroke that the sky had swiftly erased. At the stern, the wake was a gush of white and gold and crushed aquamarine.

Carloboy's skin was near russet, deep-burned in the sun and salt spray. He was never fitter. It was a great feeling, the feeling that, given the slightest provocation, he could lick the world single-handed. As healthy as a young gorilla he was, and the thought of the leave that he would take at the end of the line cheered him.

They swung to starboard and suddenly there was land again, and they saw the distant line of rollers and the fuzzy tops of palms and behind them, the Dondra light cast its long eyes, seeking across the waste of waters, knowing that there would be nothing but water all the way to the Antarctic shelf.

The evening was windy. The ETA had been sent. The *Vijaya* would enter Colombo harbour at 1930 hours and they should be tied up at Kochchikade by 2015 hours. There would be off-duty liberty to the entire red and white watch. Nearly eighty men were readying themselves to go ashore.

In the haze of coming dusk, the silver dome of St Lucia's cathedral told them they were close to port; and then, tauntingly, teasingly and quite sadistically, came the signal. Telegraphist Yusuf couldn't believe his eyes. Indeed, they bulged alarmingly. And he wasn't staying at his post. No, sir! He raced to the bridge, waved the message form before Victor. 'Sir, can't go home sir.' There was the first quaver of a moan in his voice.

The signal put everybody in a tizzy. 'Proceed,' it said, 'to Talaimannar.'

Talaimannar, Carloboy stared. What was this? Some ghastly joke?

It was no joke. Even as the *Vijaya* veered to port, cut out of the harbour roads, turned towards the glow of the Hendala light, everyone knew and cursed the stupid gunboat that had rammed a sandbank and got herself stuck in. Everyone knew that the north-western Pamban Channel was a trial for all good seamen, but why the devil did the *HMCyS Lihiniya* have to get her bottom buried in sand?

Time, the chronicler feels, to introduce the rest of the Royal Ceylon Navy of the time. There was *HMCyS Kotiya* (meaning 'tiger')—a seaward defence boat that was flat-bottomed and rolled in the water like a desperate duck. If one would consider the *Vijaya* a sort of pocket battleship, the *Kotiya* would be in the hip-pocket class.

Even smaller were the gun boats—a single pop-gun on their foredeck mounts and very much the bumble-bees of the waves if only their skippers did not bumble blindly into every sandbar they chanced upon. These boats, used for northern patrols, were the *HMCyS Lihiniya* (seagull), *HMCyS Hansaya* (swan), *HMCyS Seruwa* (cormorant), *HMCyS Diyakawa* (waterhen), and *HMCyS Korawakka* (moorhen). Also, there was *HMCyS Aliya* (elephant) which was a small naval tug.

The gunboats were small, trim, capable of high speeds, very like motor torpedo boats. They were equipped with radar, and their commands were usually entrusted to commissioned boatswains—hardened salts who had risen from the ranks. Trouble is, like most rugged old salts, they had scant respect for protocol. They took their ships wherever their mood dictated. Like the starship *Enterprise*, they boldly went where no gunboat had gone before. The boats, too, were prone to misbehave, very much like street urchins on a Sunday school picnic. They enjoyed running aground, breaking down, swiping each other and chasing illicit immigrant launches into lagoons and salt marshes and places where there was hardly enough water to moisten a blotter.

It was the *Vijaya*'s job to haul the *Lihiniya* off a sandbank and, if necessary, tow her to Colombo. When there, and if it was considered that the *Lihiniya* once prised free, could operate on her own, the *Vijaya* would escort her to Colombo. Well, that was upsetting news, true, but not too much of an imposition. I meant, as Lieutenant Walid said, two days more.

Night seemed to snigger at the general discomfiture and frustration of the crew, as it closed over them. A calm sea, lots of slow rolls and very sullen. Victor cut speed to eight knots. There was no hurry. They would be at the Pamban before dawn anyway. He would anchor, wait for light, radio the *Lihiniya* and ascertain just how much of a stew she was in. He checked course, yawned and nodded to the duty officer.. 'Course change three five seven when we pass Puttalam. Hold her steady. By my reckoning we should be off Talaimannar by zero three hours. But we have a shore wind and some drag. It may be four. Wake me at three. I'm off. Got a good book to finish.'

Lieutenant Naths nodded. 'We should alter to zero zero five nearing Talaimannar, sir.'

'Yes, but not until we see the light. Keep an eye on the log line. Very deceptive, this sea. Puts everybody to sleep.'

Carloboy lit a cigarette. Naths grinned in the green light of the binnacle. 'He's right. Real rock-a-bye-baby this is. Give me a cigarette, signalman.'

They smoked, gazed out over the charcoal and grey water that carried long ribbons of luminescent white as it rolled eastward. A long, lazy night, and the *Vijaya*'s engines were lulled too as they pushed gently on.

Alfie relieved Carloboy at midnight. He brought coffee and a packet of ginger biscuits. 'Have some,' he said, 'where's the navigating officer?'

'Wheel house.'

'Who's his relief?'

'Don't know. Course is 355 now and change two degrees starboard when we pass Puttalam light. Hold 357 until three o'clock and then call the CO.'

'OK. Anything else?'

'Mm-hmm. My canvas in on the flagdeck. I'm not sleeping in the mess. It's bloody hot.'

And hot it was. Even the wind had gone, apparently on vacation, and the stars were as big as egghoppers in the cloudless black. The *Vijaya* took the cross swell from the hook of land at Puttalam and steamed on seemingly undisturbed. The sea had the shimmer of a gently undulating piece of grey silk. With the air murmuring in some sibilant Asian tongue around him, Carloboy slept. He was off watch now, didn't need to muster on deck at five. He even dreamed that he was in Talaimannar, putting ashore to where, from every tall tree, a cassock waved a welcome.

The sound of the steam windlass woke him, and if that wasn't enough of a rude clatter, the yells of the captain. He rose, rubbed his eyes and peered out. Over him, Victor was roaring through a megaphone and waving a furious hand. It was doubtful if Sub-Lieutenant Paul heard him, for the latter was over eight hundred yards away and perched on the sharply sloping foredeck of the *Lihiniya*.

Carloboy rubbed his eyes again. So that was the *Lihiniya*. It was so small. At this distance it was a child's paper boat. Yawning, he went to the galley.

In Colombo, Yeoman Barnett checked the sitreps received from the *Vijaya* and told Patrick, 'It is hard on the liver, hard indeed.'

'What is, Yeo?'

'Why, the dearth, the plight, the deprivation. Our lads are now in northern waters. That is bad, Patrick. See how the *Vijaya* charged off. Did not stop to say hello. Did not even come in to change her panties. Her tanks must be low. Water will be rationed now and there will be less beer and even the cigarettes will run out. Northern patrols are the pits, Patrick.'

'She could have taken water before she went, Yeo.'

'Ah, that Victor is a strange man. Go, he is told, and he goes. And what about this Able Seaman Abeysakes? How can sailors die of typhoid? Is it, I ask, any way for a seaman to go?'

It had caused much consternation on *Gemunu*. Able Seaman Abeysakes had developed some nasty symptoms which necessitated his being warded in the Services Hospital in Colombo. There, the doctors of the Ceylon Army Medical Corps found their whole antiseptic world thrown in a tizzy. The man had typhoid!

Medical staff descended on *Gemunu*. The man had to be checked. Lots of fun and games, and Stoker Mechanic Ryan demanding to know what the hell was typhoid anyway.

'Something to do with your thighs,' Able Seaman Hughes hazarded.

They were each asked how they felt and checked for colour and the state of their tummies. It took a couple of days to give the Navy a clean bill of health, whereupon the

CAMC sent men to Abeysakes' boarding house in Kelaniya where they found, as they said, 'all the signs'—an unprotected well, bad toilets, food from sleazy eating-houses and more flies per square inch than all the people in China.

The problem was that Abeysakes was dead, and the CO *Gemunu* had to do something about his body. Abeysakes had family, but they were in Tissamaharama, which was as good as being on the dark side of the moon. A telegram was despatched, and the Navy waited.

The Service Hospital was not willing to be as patient.

'Remove it,' said the officer commanding tersely.

'To where?' said Surgeon Commander Matthis.

'To anywhere. Try the morgue, or keep it in the camp. The family will come there to take it, no?'

Matthis nodded. 'Yes, I suppose so.'

'You do that. Have to disinfect the ward and get rid of the linen. Can't have the body here. And get it embalmed. It'll be pretty niffy by evening.'

The Army was efficient. Matthis returned to *Gemunu* with the death certificate, having routed the body via Borella where the police mortuary did a bang-up job on the corpse, making it very presentable and laying it in a box, all prim and proper. Why, Abeysakes looked better dead than he ever was alive.

Lieutenant Commander Darley wrinkled his nose. 'The armoury,' he said, 'we'll keep him there and post sentries.'

'With all the guns, sir?'

'So what? He's going to start shooting them off?'

So Abeysakes, his remains that is, if you believe in a soul or an Odic force or whatever, was taken with little ceremony to the shabby little building at the Customs end of Flagstaff Street and dumped, coffin and all, in a space between the racks of .303 rifles and carbines and steel racks that held boxes of cartridges and assorted gunnery appliances. The coffin was not shut down, for sooner or later the family would come and would wish to see the body, howl, carry on, and the Navy would have to give the remains a fitting send-off.

'Drape the box with a flag,' Darley said.

'A white ensign, sir?'

'No, you moron, a national flag. And post sentries. One by day and two at night.'

'Aye aye, sir.'

Meanwhile an equally snappy exchange was taking place between the captains of the *Vijaya* and the *Lihiniya*, most engrossing and full of those words the Navy is so fond of.

'How the fuck do you reverse into a sand bar? That's what I want to know.'

'You're asking me? Took the hump at thirty knots. Suddenly there the bloody thing was. Right across the bows like a fucking dead whale or something. I'm telling you, someone must chart these waters. You think it's easy to run after these *kallathoni* boats? Lift their fucking outboards and go straight for the mud!'

'So you leapfrogged the bank. Then why the fuck did you stop and go astern?'

'Astern my arse! The bloody sand must have come after us!'

'Balls! You must have hit the bank, shot over and your stern must have hit the sand. What the hell were you chasing?'

'Chasing?'

'Yes, chasing.'

'Nothing.'

Victor shook. That the man was flying at thirty knots he could understand. That he took the sand strip in his stride he could understand. But what was it all in aid of? He swallowed and mentally consigned all gunboat skippers to a hell with no women. 'I see . . . well, we will have to pull you off.'

'That's right. I worked the fan blades—'

'What!'

'Thought I could get her out under full thrust.'

'Oh, you fucking idiot. Now the sand must be sucked into every pipe.'

'I know. Made a *barabarrass* noise and whole engine room filled with smoke. Lumps of oil came out and even the oil is full of sand.'

Victor returned to the *Vijaya* full of wrath. He summoned his officers. 'Bloody fool has tried to pull out under full power and fouled his tanks. Even if we pull him out, he can't raise power. Tanks must be full of sand.'

'I'll send a whaler with a towline crew,' said Hamed.

'You do that. And keep some men on the *Lihiniya* to watch the line and signal us. They must have hand flags.'

And, with many lurid oaths and curses, and the sun baking the salt on their backs, the *Lihiniya* was dragged free and wallowed in the swell, swinging on the length of the towline and hauling off in an arc as the sea took her first one way, then another.

The captain of the *Lihiniya* was unhappy. 'We should take in more slack' he complained.

Victor signalled *Gemunu*. He was bringing the *Lihiniya* home. Must be done, he emphasized. Can't trust that bugger with a bucket of water, let alone the Indian Ocean. He wanted to say more, but held peace. Slowly, the *Vijaya* moved south, six knots, with a crew at the steam windlass astern and the *Lihiniya* dipping energetically behind, clouded with the spray of the *Vijaya*'s wake. The stout towlines had been paid out to eight hundred yards and that, thought the *Lihiniya*'s skipper, was a bit too much. He begged that Victor increase speed, at least.

Victor gave him a stubborn no.

'I feel like a bloody duck!'

'Good!'

A tortured journey for the gunboat. It swung to port, to starboard, tottered in the swells and, when Victor told the engine room to make smoke, it was hidden in a haze of black.

'Why are you making smoke?'

'No reason. Like the way you jump sandbars. It just came to me.'

But Victor relented. Also, he didn't like the way the

towline was behaving. It looped too low, and, with each swell, tautened and crooned protestingly. 'Take in slack. Bring it in fifty yards,' he said, 'check the jammer and give the drum an oil bath. I don't want to see smoke when you belay.'

It was in the warmer, rougher seas off Puttalam that it happened. A sound like a pistol crack barked in the air and the windlass crew tumbled back in alarm as, with a wild, keening voice, quite musical had they stayed to consider it, a loop of thick towline hurtled towards them, hitting the stern with a grating thud, then whipping down into the water. The towline had snapped at the *Lihiniya*'s end and catapulted towards the *Vijaya*. Shouts came from the engine room as revolutions stuttered and the engineer thankfully pulled back on the big levers as he heard Victor's sharp orders to stop engines.

Behind, the *Lihiniya*, clutched by the sea, drifted helplessly. It's always dicey when the land grows a crab-claw to hold its lagoon to itself. There is a strong undertow and a lot of cross currents. These currents met, mated, twisted in orgastic fury. They would soon reach out for the *Lihiniya*. It was no real ground for an anchor either, and, in any case, the gunboat's single anchor was an apology for one.

Victor dropped a boat, raced a crew to the hapless vessel. 'Secure her to the jib boom,' he ordered, 'and keep the line slack. Sheet anchor! There will be some stress as she drags.' He called for a report on the *Lihiniya*'s foredeck. Yes, another towline would hold. A long pay-out was necessary to keep the line free of sudden strain.

'What we need is a fucking tug,' Victor said. The *Lihiniya* was secured and her skipper was told that it had crossed Victor's mind to let him drift to Puttalam where he could have spent Christmas eating crab and drinking toddy.

The windlass crew were told to haul in the broken towline and they said they couldn't.

'What do you mean you can't?'

'It won't come, sir. It's caught underneath.'

Leading Seaman Weli leaped overboard, dived, came up with a shout. 'On the props!' he yelled. He swam to the rope ladder. 'The line is entangled, sir. Round the propellers.'

Victor swore. He knew he had trouble. The *Vijaya* was immobilized. It rode haughtily on its single anchor and somehow, as though enjoying the ship's discomfiture, the sea roughened.

'Can you free it?'

'Need more men, two-three more. Have to lift the coils off the blades, sir. Might have to list the ship to get some slack.'

'Clear lower decks!' Victor bellowed. The boat deck swarmed with men. 'Right, everybody stay midships. Now, you, you, you . . . anybody else wants to volunteer? You, you, you, over the side!'

Soon Carloboy, Weli, Binkie, Jacks and several others were under the chopping water, using their small undersea weight to juggle the grassline, shoot up to gulp air, plunge below again. Weli came up, waving a hand to left. Victor ordered the crew to mass on the port side. Their combined weight dropped the *Vijaya* off keel, causing a three-degree list. It gave the divers the slack they needed to raise a thick loop of wire off the right blade.

More men leaped in as Binkie floated, exhausted, his hands puckered with the effort of clinging to and twisting the heavy wire. Carloboy lay on his back, panting, dragging air into his lungs. He then dog-stroked slowly to the rope, clung to the bottom rung and remained there, too tired to haul himself up.

With the crew on board moving in turn from port to starboard, the coil was slowly unwrapped. It took three hours to get the wire off the blades. Finally, there remained a single loop around the main shaft. The metal had been bruised white in that tremendous whiplash. Men hauled the offending wire up top as it came free. Three hours and forty minutes. Four hours. That last loop was a bastard. Finally, it was forced free and the propellers were cleared. The divers came up, shook fists in the air and on board, everybody cheered and ignored Lieutenant Wicks' 'As you were!' Victor ordered two engine room men to go down, check for damage. They came up spluttering, said there was none. Cautiously they tested revolutions. Nothing awry. The evening had made the sky a denser blue and southwards, the sun was making its diagonal race for the sea.

'We have steam,' Victor signalled the *Lihiniya,* 'Stand by.'

They reached the south-west entrance to the Colombo harbour at eight that evening and a tug took the *Lihiniya* in charge, pushing her to berth 10A where she would spend the night.

Victor slowly trundled the *Vijaya* past the Delft Quay to Kochchikade where seamen from the base waited at the mooring buoys. Home at last, and even as the orders were given to shut down steam and the boats took the thankful men ashore, two men with rifles propped against the armoury door of the *Gemunu* were earnestly considering the corpse of Able Seaman Abeysakes. They were also tolerably inebriated.

They were Able Seaman Hughes and Stoker Mechanic Ryan and it seemed sheer folly that the Navy had put them together on duty, and, of all things, to guard a body. They were on an eight-to-twelve. All they had to do was sit in the armoury and keep watch over their dead messmate. They were not expected to take away the flag, open the coffin, hobnob with the dead in any way.

Even the duty chief had groaned. 'What? Those two? Who is the idiot who arranged the shifts? Never, *ever*, put those two together!'

The quartermaster had shrugged. 'Now they're gone on duty also.'

'That's what I'm afraid of. Anyway, I'll check on them at lights out.'

He stomped away, muttering.

42

History—Another Easter, Okinawa and the Divine Wind

Spring 1945, and Germany was just about defeated. This too, is part of the immense battle history, but the writer has let it alone. It was decided that this work should revolve round the Asian scene. The writer sincerely hopes this decision does not take much away from this novel. Even as Germany began to collapse, Japan remained strong, and this strength was very evident to the Americans who were now at Japan's doorstep. There were decisions to be taken. Would the Americans have to invade the Japanese mainland?

To do so, they held Iwo Jima, but they needed a closer base south. Just south of Japan. It had to be Okinawa. Many of the Marine divisions were sure that Okinawa would be their last landing, their last beach assault. But many others shook their heads. Japan would not give up. There would have to be yet another landing, they said—the mainland of Japan itself. Many hoped that it would not come to that.

But for now it was Okinawa. The Americans massed huge land, air and sea forces for the invasion. On the island, Lieutenant General Mitsuru Ushijama knew he was powerless to fight the US troops under the guns of the warships offshore. As in Iwo Jima, the Japanese decided to show no opposition on the beachhead. Let the Marines move inland . . . then wipe them out. It was the same strategy as on Iwo Jima and it was all Ushijama could do. There was no hope of reinforcements. The Americans were supreme in the air and there was little chance of shipping Japanese troops across.

Easter Sunday, April 1, 1945. All Fools Day too. The control craft lay 4000 yards offshore and far out lay the big battleships. Closer in, four destroyers steamed parallel to the beach. In the long line of landing craft, the first wave of the 7th Infantry Division was ready. Each LCI flew an identical red pennant. The men carried the beach markers they would set up as they hit the sand. Objective: Beach Purple One, southern Okinawa.

The bombardment began. Heavy 14-inch shells began to erupt just beyond the narrow beach strip. The destroyers opened up with their 5-inch guns. The beach became a haze of smoke and bursting sand. The Marines streamed in, closing rapidly . . . 1000 yards, 600 yards . . . the boats were 200 yards away when the deafening gunfire ceased. The beach was a havoc of cratered sand and smoking trees, and then the fighters screamed in from the carriers to bomb the beach from end to end, making it a long furrow of flame and exploding sand.

At 8.32 a.m. the Marines landed, pelted to the cover of trees, dug in. Bigger landing craft brought the tanks clanking ashore. The bustle at the water's edge was hectic. The men wondered. Had the naval bombardment and air strike flattened all resistance? There was no opposition. All they saw was a single Japanese plane zoom along the shoreline, wing swiftly away to the north. Oh, the Japanese were there alright, but not a shot had been fired. By eleven the landing was complete. The men looked around, made short forays inland, found the going easy. It was mostly level plain, bamboo clumps and outcrops of weirdly-shaped coral. They spent the day on the beach, spent an uneasy night.

In Tokyo, the Japanese were readying to play their last deadly card: the Kamikaze Corps. They would strike terror into the hearts of the Americans. Japanese flyers would give their lives to knock out the American ships. They would be the *kamikaze*—the divine wind.

The Japanese believed in this wind of God. Long years ago, when the Chinese had sent a huge fleet against Japan, a furious typhoon had arisen, destroyed the Chinese ships. A wind sent by God. A divine wind. Well, now the Japanese would raise their own divine wind. Kamikaze pilots did not need good planes. All they needed was any old crate that could fly, could smash into a ship. And the suicide pilot needed very little training. All he needed to know was how to get his plane into the air and aim it at an enemy ship. And all he needed was the fuel to fly out, for he wasn't coming back.

The Americans knew of the Kamikaze Corps. Reports had reached them of how the volunteers would parade the streets of Tokyo, hailed by flag-waving citizens, then attend elaborate religious ceremonies. They received gifts from schoolchildren and members of their families. They were each draped with a Rising Sun flag before they climbed into the cockpits of their no-return planes. We who are about to die accept your salute!

Yes, the Japanese would launch a concerted kamikaze attack on the US fleet in this Battle of Okinawa. For the Japanese on Okinawa there was little hope. They would have to fight to the end, but meanwhile the divine wind would destroy the American fleet and put an end to America's designs on the Japanese mainland.

Then came another option. Send in the *Yamoto*. Let it go, bite into the US fleet. A kamikaze ship!

The battleship *Yamoto* lay at anchor at her inland sea base—the largest fighting ship in the world, 863 feet long and with a displacement of over 70,000 tons. She carried 18-inch guns which could hurl shells to a range of $22^1/_2$ miles, each shell weighing more than $1^1/_2$ tons. The Japanese were not anxious to have this behemoth lie uselessly in port, only to be destroyed by American fighters. Also, there would be no use for a battleship of such size ever again. She could move fast, true, and she had immense hitting power, but her very size made her a costly liability.

The Japanese loaded her ammunition magazines and fuelled her for a one-way journey. The orders to her Commander, Seiichi Ito, were terse. Engage the enemy. If you should go down, take the biggest American ships with you. Go down gloriously.

The Americans were told of the *Yamoto*'s breakout on April 6. The huge ship made 22 knots through the Van Diemen Straits, accompanied by a light cruiser and eight destroyers. After what seemed a long time in the Pacific War, there would actually be a ship-to-ship engagement.

The Americans fuelled their destroyers to tank capacity. It would be a terrible surface battle, they knew, and the destroyers would need to make as many torpedo runs as they could to breach the monster. The battleships could do little. None of their guns could come within four miles of the *Yamoto's* range.

But the Japanese had not reckoned on the spirit of the American fighter planes that sped away from the carriers. Long before the *Yamoto* could meet the US fleet, the first US strike planes swooped on her out of the sky. The big ship took two well-placed bombs and a vicious torpedo. More planes closed in like angry bees around a hulking victim. For two hours the *Yamoto* took a pounding. She began to list dangerously, almost 35 degrees, then up-ended. Her deck was almost vertical, her battle flag plunged into the surging sea. Across her ammunition room, shells began to tumble, then crashed into the bulkheads, exploding tremendously on impact. Magazines were torn apart and, as the sea reached up hungrily, compartments burst from the pressure of air. The *Yamoto* died as the biblical Goliath did. It was 2.23 p.m. when she finally disappeared, the explosions of her death raising the water in furious boils and spurting ulcers. Her last battle had been a meaningless one. She could not swat away the angry bees that caused her such deadly harm. With her demise came the end of almost five centuries of naval warfare. No longer would ships fight it out, guns blazing. That would never be necessary again. Nor would Japan ever build another battleship. It was, to many naval historians, the end of an era.-

On Okinawa, the Marines secured the northern two-thirds of Okinawa with little resistance. Lieutenant General Ushijama had moved all his men to the south, near the principal city of Naha. From that point would they oppose the US advance. The US 7th Division's objective was the ruin of the old Shuri Castle in the south. From this castle, Japan had once ruled the Ryukyus.

On May 2, the Marines encountered two Japanese tanks which they quickly accounted for. The Marines were confident now, although advancing with care.

The US ships had set up 16 picket stations around the island, each station manned by two destroyers. They were certain that the Japanese would strike, send in their planes from the nearby island of Kyushi, strafe the landing forces and help their men on Okinawa. The Americans were ready for battle, but they did not expect a roaring divine wind!

The Japanese learnt of the pickets with glee. Why, the US ships were at station, very much like sacrificial lambs.

At picket station One were the destroyers *Bush* and *Calhoun*. They worked their patrol a thousand yards apart, fifty miles north of Okinawa. On April 6, the kamikazes came. They zeroed in on the US vessels all around the Okinawa coat—355 suicide planes, sent to kill and die.

The *Bush* and *Calhoun* were hit time and again. They both sank. So did four other ships and seventeen were badly damaged. And more Japanese martyrs would come in, desperately, fanatically. They were not coming to relieve the men on the island. They were coming in to wipe out the US fleet.

Through April, May and June over 3000 suicide sorties were mounted. The kamikazes sank 21 ships, damaged 66. It was Japan's last hurrah.

On June 21, Lieutenant General Ushijama killed himself. It was all he could do—die for his emperor, as the Marines smashed through all Japanese resistance. The last battle of the Pacific was over.

And no, there would be no US invasion of the Japanese mainland, for in Los Alamos, New Mexico, atomic scientists had put the finishing touches on a new weapon—a weapon so fearsome that it would make all the *Yamoto's* massive guns seem like a child's popgun.

Carrying this weapon, Colonel Paul Tibbets took off from Tinian Island on August 6, 1945. The time was 2.45 a.m. His B-29 bomber was the *Enola Gay*.

At 9.15 a.m. he would drop this single weapon above the headquarters of the Japanese 2nd Army at Hiroshima.

The Atomic Age was upon the world.

43

Of the Unhinging of Bollocks and Converting the Captain and a Porthole to the Stars

The coffin lay on a makeshift bier of wooden boxes, on each of which was stencilled in red: .303 CLIPS 2000—X.

The Navy, as is now known, has its system of watches. A sailor (and two or more if necessary) is given a rifle and told to conduct a routine guard duty for four hours. Earlier that evening, in the quartermaster's lobby, someone had declared, 'Hell, I'm not going to that bloody armoury with that dead bugger in there. Not in the bloody night anyway.'

As we also know, Ryan and Hughes were inseparables. They had only two goals in life which, they said, were all that any sailor needed: sex and booze. They were more so, inseparable in the pursuit of both. They picked up women on the strict understanding that the said woman would do for one what she would do for the other. If they ever argued, it was about who should perform first. Sometimes such an issue was decided with the flip of a coin, and one would stand over and watch the other perform while the other would tell the bemused woman, 'So let him look. Anything I fuck he also fucks.' Being in the same Blue Watch, they got into trouble together, and were punished together. This time they had gone to the armoury together to watch over Abeysakes' remains from 8 p.m. to midnight. They would be relieved at midnight by Stoker Mechanic Bollocks and Signalman Herft.

At midnight, Herft yawned hugely and blinked his way to the quartermaster's lobby. Bollocks was already there, a little fellow with no conversation. A dreary companion in the dreary hours of the graveyard shift.

'Who's there now?' he asked.

'Ryan and Hughes,' the QM said, 'if I know those buggers they would have gone off by now. Anyway, you guys get going. It's after twelve also.'

'You go ahead,' Herft told Bollocks, as he watched the kettle, 'I'll bring a pot of tea.'

'Fine. Bring a mug also,' Bollocks reminded, and dragged off down the road to the end of Flagstaff Street where the armoury stood . . .

It took Herft all of ten minutes to make the tea and cadge a tin mug. Very sweet tea. Keeps one awake, especially when the minutes drag by as though stuck up to the ears in chewing gum. He didn't see Ryan or Hughes. He should have met them since they had to report end of watch to the QM, but plainly, such procedures meant little to them. Chances were they had just dumped their rifles and drifted down road to the port where sundry daughters of the night roamed for custom. Ryan and Hughes always bundled in one of these women after night watch. For some time, however, they had been quite restrained—ever since the night they had brought in a hermaphrodite and discovered that their prize had a penis. The hullaballoo had been quite extraordinary!

Herft heard voices on approaching the armoury. No, one voice. Bollocks. The man was going on about something. Herft paused at the door. It was Bollocks to be sure and he was well inside and his voice was edged with pure terror.

'D-don't you try to get up! Don't! You get up you bastard I'll—I'll shoot you! I will! Lie down! D-did you hear? Don'—don't get up! I'll shoot! I'll-I'll shoot you!'

Herft rushed in and Bollocks wailed, swung his rifle,

blindly squeezing the trigger. It wasn't loaded, of course, and Herft dropped the kettle, grabbed at the gibbering stoker. He received a stinging blow with the barrel.

Bollocks was white, sweat-drenched, utterly ghastly. He hung grimly to his weapon, finger hooked under the trigger guard, and then drooled. Yes, actually drooled.

Herft wrenched at the gun, pulled it free, almost breaking Bollocks' finger. The man screamed and rushed for the door, turning his ankle on the fallen kettle, falling heavily. Herft grabbed a leg and hung on. Bollocks was trying to swim for the road. There was little else he could do. Herft dragged him back, leaned over and punched him hard on the back of the neck. Bollocks subsided, whimpering.

Herft had not really taken note of the armoury. Satisfied that Bollocks would behave, he looked around and nearly jumped out of his skin. There was the coffin. The flag lay on the floor. The coffin lid had been removed. Abeysakes, dead and poker stiff, was not a pretty sight. Also, he had not remained in the confines of his coffin. He was practically half-way out, entire head, shoulders and up to the midriff, and on his chest was a tin mug and on the floor an empty arrack bottle. Hughes and Ryan had had a party and, being congenial souls, had invited Abeysakes to it.

At the subsequent inquiry it was grudgingly admitted that the two incorrigibles had gone on duty with a bottle of hooch and a mug. In the armoury, they had settled down to finish the bottle and midway, had decided to toast the corpse.

'Oi, Abey, you're aksherlly dead? What the hell men, howerbout a small drink?'

'That's true. Not good we are drinking and 'e's just lying there.'

'So—so givvim also a drink.'

'I say—pukka—puk-kah idea. Oi, Abeysakes, you wanta drink?'

'He can't hear, men, inshide that bloody thing.'

'So open, men, openitt.'

They pulled off the flag, found a lid that moved, yanked

it off.

'Bugger is dead? How to put a drink if he's like this flat? Sleeping. Oi, Abey! Gettup, you ol' bugger. Have sum arrack, you want?'

'Nothin' doing. Bugger won't budge. Must be stuck inside or something. Come on, help to make him sit.'

Together they had tried to raise up the corpse. This was not easy, but they succeeded in dragging the body halfway up the box by its shoulders, and it must have looked very peculiar, poker stiff and all.

'If—iffew don' don't wanter drink just say,' said Hughes, getting peeved, 'now becos he's dead mus' be thinking he can't put a shot.'

'Balls,' said Ryan pouring the last of the arrack into the mug. He swallowed a mouthful and gave the rest to Hughes who tossed it down. With some care, he placed the empty mug on the corpse's chest. 'When 'e gets the smell 'e'll quickly get up an' arsk.'

Hughes wagged a finger. 'An' when you ask you won' get. Because bottle finished. Serves you right.'

'Ah, just let the bugger be. Come go!'

'Where?'

'Goan' sleep. Dam' sleepy now. See the way e's sleeping.'

Ryan still had some of his wits intact. 'But not twelve yet.'

'So? Wait an' do what? Come go!'

They had left the armoury at twelve minutes to midnight. Bollocks, coming in, had flipped. There was the dead man, half out of his coffin, a mug on his chest, an empty bottle on the floor. He refused to be convinced.

'He's alive,' he howled, 'an' have been drinking also! See the mug!'

The poor man was shaking terribly. Herft tried to make him stand, but he preferred to crawl. He was bathed in sweat and made queer noises in his throat.

There was little else to do. Hauling him up, dragging him along while he kept sagging like a sack of walnuts, Herft made painful progress to the sick bay. Bollocks was in bad shape. He had a high fever. He was pushed into a bed. He lay there, quiet for a while, kept trembling, then he would suddenly gasp, break into a howl and try to do a bunk out of the window. Eventually, he was strapped down, an icebag plonked on his head and on the advice of the duty PO, a deck shoe kept at hand to be jammed into his mouth the very next time he began to blast off. It was shock, of course, and he sank into a delirium and took three full days to get sensible.

Abeysakes was re-laid and a shipwright summoned to screw down the coffin lid and make things shipshape. Ryan and Hughes were brought on defaulters parade and grinned through the proceedings. It was decided to send them to sea with the pious wish that that they would get sozzled and fall overboard. Bollocks was recommended a change of air and, within a week, was drafted to the *Elara* where, strangely, he got typhoid too and was hurried to the Mannar Hospital. There, the Catholic nursing sisters took him to their bosoms and gave him a Bible and a Devotion to Our Lady of Good Succour and told him how much God loved him and he listened and wept, and did not die.

But he grew stranger with each passing day. CO Gunasakes shook his head. 'Man is round the bend. Can't keep him here. What's that thing around his neck?'

'A rosary sir.'

'And why is he wearing long green pajamas?'

'Won't wear anything else sir. Real basket case, sir.'

'Well, he can't stay here. Call Signalman Krause. Colombo will have to put him somewhere else.'

It was thought that the sea would put him right. 'He can sweat out all his madness in the engine room,' Darley said.

'But sir, we sent Hughes and Ryan on board.'

'So? Send Bollocks also. Look around, Number One. You see any other oddballs around? You come and tell me. Ship them all out. *Vijaya's* the place for them.'

The *Vijaya* had languished at Kochchikade for many months. The men were pleased. Carloboy would go to

Gemunu to meet the rest of his friends, exchange fruity words with Yeoman Barnett and keep abreast of the Navy's many comings and goings. He was pleased with himself. Victor had summoned him one morning.

'At ease, von Bloss. You seem to be the most educated rating I have. Can you type?'

'Yes sir.'

'Good. You will be Captain's secretary. You will work in the cabin next to mine. Type the monthly returns, all correspondence, stores and gunnery reports. Think you can do it?'

'Why, yes sir.'

Victor nodded. 'Oh, also, I want the bulletin board outside the sick bay maintained. Make it interesting. Give the men something to read. Put out a piece every day with something on naval history or of some interest. Terms, traditions, anything. Do you know what a block ship is?'

'Yes sir.'

'You sure? What is it?'

'It's a ship that is scuttled at a harbour mouth to block entrance to a harbour, sir.'

Victor regarded Carloboy interestedly. 'That's right. Who told you that?'

'I read it somewhere, sir.'

'Hmm. I bet there'll be many on board who don't know that. Tomorrow you explain what a block ship is on the bulletin board.'

'Very well sir.'

'Good. I will tell the master-at-arms. You will report to the Captain's office every morning.' Victor nodded pleasantly. 'Why did you join the Navy, signalman?'

Carloboy had wondered about this many times. 'Personal reasons, sir,' he muttered.

'I see. But why the lower deck? Why not as an officer cadet?'

'I—I don't know sir.'

'Well, next year there's the HNET coming up. The Higher Naval Education Test. See that you sit it.'

'Yes sir. Sir, why?'

'If you get through you are selected for officer training.'

Carloboy was silent.

'Dismiss, signalman.'

He clicked to attention, marched out. Captain's secretary! That was something. Above all, it got him out of deck duties. He bumped into Hughes and Ryan on the foredeck. 'So how do you like Kochchikade?' he asked.

Hughes closed one eye. ''S'all right. Have a small hooch place near the docks.'

'You buggers made poor Bollocks crazy, no?'

'Who? Us?'

'Who then?'

'Von Bloss, look at this place. See the quartermaster. Blowing his bloody whistle the whole day. Colours, Captain's guard, duty rounds, saluting the quarter deck, kit inspection, divisions, painting sides, chipping decks, polishing . . . you call all this being sane? All the buggers are mad anyway. You're mad, I'm mad, right?'

Carloboy grinned. 'Well, if you put it like that—'

'That's the only way to put it, my boy. This is a floating asylum!'

'Well, I'm Captain's secretary now.'

'I knew it. Even the captain is mad!'

Carloboy stared out at the lorries lumbering like a procession of fat ladies on the road to Muwal. Below him, as he leaned over the guard rail, the water lapped inkily. He had relished these long months at anchor. He went where he pleased, had upset many applecarts in Wellawatte, Dehiwela and Kalubowila and made Barbara's mother, Mrs Heinz, a very angry woman. His adventures ashore were infinitely more interesting than his watch hours on the *Vijaya* and will certainly bear recounting.

In Talaimannar, Stoker Mechanic Bollocks was waving a Bible and telling all and sundry that lo! there was a plague in the congregation of the Lord.

'Plague? You're the bugger who brought the plague!' Able Seaman de Neys hooted, 'Came and got typhoid.'

'If the land of your possession be unclean, then pass ye over unto the land of the possession of the Lord!' Bollocks thundered, 'Rebel not against the Lord!'

CO Gunasakes snorted. 'You're going to be passed on to the possession of the *Vijaya*, my lad, and that's that!'

'So shall the Lord bring upon you all evil things until he had destroyed you from off this good land,' said Bollocks piously.

'You calling this the Lord's good land?' asked Petty Officer Caldera, 'you're madder than the maddest!'

'You shall perish quickly from off the good land which he hath given unto you,' Bollocks maintained stoutly.

'Oh fuck off!'

Carloboy sighed. They were under sailing orders. The *Vijaya* was to carry out anti-illicit immigration patrols in the Palk Strait area for three weeks. This meant, of course, 21 excruciating days. Water would be rationed to a basinful per man per day. Carloboy tried to console himself. He would be at sea again. That was the credit side. But he was having too much fun and games ashore right now and didn't like to leave. Not now anyway. Not when he had discovered Angeline and the way she had stood thirteen feet above his upraised head, her legs apart, so that he could know how deliciously naked she was under her short home dress.

It had all begun on the day the men in the neighbouring houses decided to help Angeline's father clean his well. This well was a menace to man and beast. It lay smack in the middle of a small coconut garden where boys played cricket and threw stones at Mrs Singaraman's chickens. A calf had fallen in one day and so had Errol Juriansz who was backing up to catch a tennis ball. The neighbours kept insisting that Angeline's father build a wall round the well but he had said, 'Only round the well what for? If building better to do round whole garden. Then nobody can come in and no more any more trouble for me.'

This was not welcomed either. Everybody tramped Jambupathi's garden. So the well remained unprotected, claiming tennis balls by the score. Crows dropped festering tidbits into it. Jambupathi ignored it. He had pipe-borne water. The well was useless, unwanted. Also, it smelled. Too many dead chickens, too much dirt, too many soiled sanitary pads. Sonnaboy von Bloss told the neighbours, 'Let's clean it.'

'Better if we just filled it with sand and closed it up,' neighbour Orville said.

'No, men, all we need is to clean it, then put some sticks round like a fence.'

Mrs Ludekens agreed. 'Every week this damn Dehiwela municipality cutting the water. What they're doing God only knows. Better to clean and keep. Then all can have some water in emergency, no?'

'Enough of buggers here to clean,' another neighbour Winston said, 'where's your bugger?'

'He's at home. Off day. You get the boys together, I'll tell Carloboy to come.'

Angeline could not be shooed away. She was a tall, dark girl of seventeen and she loved mini skirts and her black thighs would glisten when she walked. Carloboy had not paid her much attention—not until he was waist deep in the putrid well water, sending buckets of sludge to the surface where a team of boys hauled energetically. Looking up, Carloboy saw the girl smile down at him. She stood boldly, at the edge and her short skirt swirled, and Carloboy was looking up her long legs, the bush of black hair and the way her thigh dimpled into the roundness of her buttock. She knew where his eyes were. She spread her legs, twitched the bottom of her skirt, seemingly slapping at a fly.

'Hurry up with those buckets!' Carloboy yelled. He wanted to clean that well as fast as he could.

Mrs Heinz had blown a fuse. Her daughter! Her good, quiet, grey-eyed daughter who studied so well and never missed a Mass or an evening of Sunday school. Mrs Heinz had not minded Carloboy coming in, sitting in a corner of the veranda with her Barbara. But it had offended her deeply to see her daughter with a leg cocked over the arm of her chair while Carloboy explored under her dress. It also struck her that her daughter seemed to be enjoying it immensely and this certainly called for a show of maternal wrath. She ordered Barbara to the kitchen, ordered Carloboy out of her house. She then proceeded to execute on her daughter a stinging slap which was followed by another on the cheek of her younger daughter, Rose.

'Told you, no, to stay in the front and not to allow your sister to be alone with that fellow!'

Well could Rose have asked if she were her sister's keeper but the slap rendered her speechless and caused a terrible ringing in her ear. Mummy was in no mood, she thought, and ran to the bedroom to cry.

Angeline was so much easier. Old Jambupathi and his frowsy wife never had time for their children. One boy played guitar in a band. The other spent his days throwing stones at every mango tree in the neighbourhood. Angeline went to the Holy Family Convent in Dehiwela and waggled her backside at every male in Vihara Lane. Carloboy took her to the rice field behind her small house. She told him how Uncle Winston next door had deflowered her when she was thirteen.

And there was Caryll and her sister Heatherine who lived across the canal, and their brother Royston who also wanted to join the Navy. Heatherine had latched onto a simp of a fellow who walked in a spidery way and spent long evenings on the beach where Heatherine masturbated him with gusto. Caryll, the younger, was a bubbly sort of girl, small, round-faced and with her hair fringed on her forehead.

Old man Collum was proud of his brood. 'I'm a bastard,' he would say after his third drink, 'my father had women all over the place.'

His wife, who had a double—no, treble chin, and a beak of a nose, puffed all the time and complained at the heat in their tiny box-like home which consisted of a postage stamp veranda, a single big room, a tiny kitchen and a smelly toilet.

Caryll was really no conquest. All Carloboy had to do was lead her to the room where they sat on a bed, and tell her to shed her knickers. The mother huffed and rose, scratching the underside of her breasts.

'You children behave yourselves,' she said, and went out.

Carloboy fucked Caryll and she was pleased. She said he did it better, much better than Royston. 'He does it every day. On the other bed sometimes Daddy is doing to Mummy and Royston comes and does it to me and Heatherine.'

Carloboy nodded grimly. He wouldn't dream of entering that smelly washroom. He wiped himself on the sheet and buttoned his trousers. He had to get out, go home, or go to Eardley's, bathe. For the first time he began to feel that he was unclean. He never went to the Collums' again.

'You bastard,' he told Royston outside St Lawrence's Church one day, 'you're screwing your sisters.'

Royston raised an eyebrow. 'If not? If my father can do, why I can't?'

And now would come three weeks of northern patrols. Well, maybe it was all for the best. Home was uncomfortable enough. Barbara shot imploring looks at him in church. Caryll would squeeze into the pew and hiss, 'Why you are not coming now? After Mass come go home.'

The Sinhalese girl had taken to bathing at the well, then going to the woodshed to change. All this fence climbing was bound to be noticed . . . and his mother had asked one day, 'What are you doing in those peoples' garden?'

'Nothing,' he said, crawling back.

'I saw what you were up to,' Beryl had scolded.

'So?'

'If those people come to complain or anything, I'll tell your father.'

'Oh shut up. Tell him what *you're* doing, will you.'

Maybe a spell up north would settle a lot of things. He was quite cheerful when he told his father he was sailing on the Wednesday.

'Going to catch *kallathonis*?' Sonnaboy grinned, 'Bring a glass and put a shot.'

The next morning two new men joined the *Vijaya*. Stoker Mechanic Bollocks and Electrician Aubrey Ranasinghe. Captain Victor groaned. Ranasinghe was a handful. He liked to hit first and inquire about one's health and general wellbeing later. He had scrapped his way from recruit to electricians mate and broken Leading Seaman Sena's jaw and Writer Pala's collarbone.

Bollocks stepped on the quarterdeck, very much a borderline case. He stared up at the sky and held a big Bible in his hands and there was a rosary around his neck. He bowed to the QM and swayed to the boatdeck, his long, green pajamas trailing in the dirt. He sang, 'The cross is near, the cross is here, my sins have fallen from me,' in a melancholy voice as though he regretted the whole business from the bottom of his heart. The sound was very like a dog whining to be let out at night.

At least, the men agreed, northern patrols wouldn't be so bad. Not with Bollocks, and Ranasinghe, and Ryan and Hughes.

'Where's that son of yours?' Mr Greyman asked Sonnaboy.

'Gone to Palk Strait. Gone to catch illicit immigrants.'

'I don't know about all that. When is he coming back?'

'Why?'

'What about his illicit immigrating in my kitchen?'

'What?'

'You're asking what? Came creeping in my kitchen when we were in the front. What, men, small girl, no?'

Sonnaboy cocked a bushy eyebrow. He couldn't understand what the man was on about.

'My servant girl, men. Small girl. Came to the kitchen and carrying on.'

'Carrying on?'

'Yes, carrying on. She's sitting on the kitchen table, cloth all tucked up and your one standing and doing and her legs round his waist, Bella saw and screamed and dropped the baby's bottle also.'

Sonnaboy offered Greyman a drink. 'Boys, men, that's the way, no?'

'But small girl men.'

'What to small? If can sit and do like that? In the village must be doing on top of the grinding stone also. Cheers.'

'Cheers. Now Bella wants to send her away.'

'These women are mad. Just tell to keep. Every servant someone jumps if go to send away, nobody will have any servants left in Colombo.'

'That's also true. Cheers.'

On the *Vijaya* Bollocks muttered morosely outside the Captain's office. Carloboy had told him that the Captain was busy. 'Fuck off,' he had said crisply, 'think you can just barge in like this?'

'But it is Sunday,' Bollocks said.

'So?'

'A service on deck. A word of prayer.'

'Oh piss off!'

Bollocks said, 'But the Lord has set me over the congregation.'

Carloboy stared. 'What congregation, you bloody lunatic?'

'I will go out before them for they are as a congregation which have no shepherd.'

'Will you get your filthy pajamas out of here!'

Victor growled, 'What's the bloody row there? Von Bloss, what the hell—'

With a swiftness surely come from the Lord, Bollocks nipped in, Carloboy said 'Hey!' and tried to grab the man but he was already doing his prophet act at Victor's desk. 'Captain, sir, you are an ungodly man!'

'What?'

'Should you not be on deck, telling the men of the wisdom and understanding of the Lord? Lo! He will put words in thy mouth that will give subtlety to the simple and knowledge and discretion to the young . . .'

'Will you get the fuck out of here! Von Bloss, get the SBA—'

'Turn us at my reproof? Behold, I will pour out my spirit upon you—'

'Shut up! Pour out your spirit in the fucking sea! What are you waiting for? *Drag this bugger out of here!'*

'Woe unto you! The Lord has called and ye refuse. He has stretched out his hand and no man regarded—'

Carloboy grabbed the man around the neck, hauled him to the door. Bollocks waved his Bible. 'Transgressors! Walkers in the path of unrighteousness!! Let me go, you of the crooked way!'

Outside, with his knee jammed into the man's spine, his forearm tight around Bollocks' neck, Carloboy called for help. Hughes and Sims seized Bollocks.

'Sick bay,' Carloboy panted, 'bugger is really off.'

'Help!' Bollocks yelled, 'ungodly men—carrion eaters, skulkers in darkness, woe unto you! Walkers in the crooked way—you are all ungodly men! Where are you taking me?'

'Shut up!'

'You may persecute me . . . the Lord is my buckler . . .'

'Here, grab his ankles!'

'You may do your worst . . . throw me in the sea . . .'

'That's a bloody good idea!'

'I say the truth! Truth!' The word stuck as he was borne away. 'Truth, truth, truth, truth! Help! Saracens! Pagans! Let go! Owww!—' then blessed silence.

'What did you do?' Carloboy asked.

Hughes shrugged. 'Only a small tap. Sick bay will keep him quiet.'

Once in sick bay, Bollocks began to pray for the eternal salvation of any who came to mind. As a sacrifice for the sins of the world, he refused to eat, and, fearing he would starve, and because Victor said that a starving prophet was infinitely worse than one with three square meals under his belt, a special ration of biscuits was issued him from the canteen.

They sailed the next day and Bollocks played no part in the departure. He was vastly entertaining, however, and collected quite an audience. Living on custard creams and crackers, he would stand in his cot and wave his hands, sing hymns, belabour the Lord with chunks of the scriptures and tell his chuckling listeners that the Lord was leading them through the deep as a horse in the wilderness, that they should not stumble.

But on the first night he broke out. The monsoon had made sleeping on deck uncomfortable, and Carloboy had decided to kip on a galley table. Over his head, he hard the wash of the waves against the porthole. The gentle rocking soon had him dozing.

He awoke suddenly. The sound of the sea seemed very loud and salt water slapped at his head and face. Above him, on the table, stood a pair of green pajamas. Water kept springing in fitfully through the open scuttle.

Carloboy rolled off the table with an oath, grabbed at the pajamas. They came with the yank of his hands, to reveal in the dim galley light, a pair of spindly legs and a very hairy backside. And that was all. Bollocks—the upper part of him—was not to be seen.

With a shout, Carloboy seized the man's legs, Fernando leaped on the table, grabbed Bollocks around the waist. They heaved, and the water wooshed through the scuttle angrily as they collapsed with a roaring Bollocks demanding to be released.

'Shut the porthole,' Carloboy yelled. 'You bloody idiot! Who said you can open scuttles? You want to sink us?'

Bollocks glared indignantly. He rose stiffly, rubbed at his spine, arched, twisted his shoulders. A spectacular performance, especially because he had on sodden singlet, was dripping sea water and his pajamas were around his ankles.

Daft was most reverent. 'First time I saw a holy cock,' he said.

'What the fuck were you doing? How did you get your whole head out and your shoulders also? Bloody mad bugger! What's wrong with you?'

Bollocks sniffed, rubbed his nose, sneezed. 'I was looking for my star,' he said.

'Your—my God, can't keep this bugger below decks. Will have to lock him up!'

They dragged Bollocks to the sick bay, then informed the duty officer. That worthy wagged an admonishing finger. 'You mean you pulled him inside? What's the matter with you? He was half out, no?'

'Yes sir.'

'Then you should have pushed him out! Pulled him inside . . . your fellows never think!'

It decided Victor. 'Looking for stars? What stars?'

'Said it's his star sir.'

Victor thumped his table. That does it. Send a signal to *Gemunu* We ship him out at Trincomalee. Have ambulance ready to meet ship. Signal harbour master Trinco. Need temporary berth, where is he now?'

'Sick bay, sir.'

'Not good. Paint store. Put him there. Stars through portholes. Next time he will be looking for comets in our assholes!'

Bollocks did them proud. In order to get him away, the *Vijaya* put in at Trincomalee. In Jail Road, Abela took Carloboy's hand, made soft sounds of welcome. It was all very hurried.

They sailed for the northern peninsula at 2200 hours.

44

History—The Cocos Islands Mutiny

Going back in time to early 1942, Ceylon became significantly known and made much mention of in British and Australian war records. Japan's Admiral Nagumo (and indeed, all of the Japanese High Command) were very pleased at the fact that somehow, Britain picked the worst men possible to command the little Indian Ocean atolls. The British deemed it necessary to maintain garrisons and troops on the little islands around Australia. After all, Japan had made it very clear that one of her many targets was Australia. That was the time before America assumed sole responsibility for the Pacific theatre.

The British High Command wanted men from Ceylon and India to police the atolls, and, naturally, they liked to have Britishers in charge—men who the High Command had little use for, actually. Men who had bought their commissions or wrangled their way to wardroom status and who suffered from a lopsided sense of their own superiority. These were the men who could also be relied on to keep the Asians in line.

Indeed, a few months before the outbreak of World War II, the Australian Department of Defence actually sent a team of selected officers to the Cocos-Keeling islands. The atoll was surveyed. The team sailed to the islands on *HMS*

Perth, and expressed their concern for the security of the cable and wireless station on Cocos. They informed the British High Command of the necessity to place two six-inch guns on Cocos and to post a garrison there.

The British picked men from Ceylon. Lieutenant Koch of the Ceylon Light Infantry, a Burgher, was sent out to supervise the installation of the guns. The Cocos islands garrison was picked from India and Ceylon. The British found, among the Ceylon volunteers, some pretty hot stuff—men who could be relied on to fight like 'Ellen B. Merry'. Was there any need to post a Britisher to any of these lumps of coral in the Indian Ocean?

Captain Lyn Wickramasuriya, a Sinhalese, was made Commander, Garrison Artillery. The British High Command were impressed by Wickramasuriya's brilliance as an officer and a leader. As Area Commander, Cocos, it would be his responsibility to organize the defence of the atoll.

Wickramasuriya's first act was to dismantle the cable and wireless tower. 'It is a clear landmark for bombers and naval boats,' he informed Australia and the British in Ceylon.

On Christmas Island, a British officer, Lieutenant Senior, was making life very hard for the men under him. Senior had his worries. The Japanese were closing in, and as the danger thickened, he grew more dense-headed. He turned on his own men with unbelievable savagery. He treated them with scorn, derision, heaped insults on their heads and belittled them to breaking point. Wickramasuriya didn't like it. He was in contact with Senior and knew that on Christmas Island there were all the makings of a mutiny.

The Japanese were increasingly active in the region, but Admiral Nagumo held back. Intelligence had reported the state of readiness on the Cocos atoll. With Wickramasuriya in the saddle, it would not be safe to send landing parties ashore to capture Horsborough and Direction Island.

But the British felt it was time to send in a man of their own stripe. Now that the Japanese were showing decided interest it would never do to have a Ceylonese in charge. This was a British war to be fought the British way. They scraped the bottom of the barrel in sending in Captain George Gardiner. He was to replace Wickramasuriya. He would be the great white hope of the coral isles.

Gardiner took over the Cocos command, inspected his men and disliked them immensely. A most bigoted man, he hated to be among the 'blacks'—and all he had to command were the blacks. Long years later, a prominent Lankan author and journalist, Noel Crusz, interviewed Wickramasuriya, sought his comments on the Cocos affair. No, Wickramasuriya did not, could not, approve of 'mutiny'. As an officer—and one of the finest, too—he could not condone mutiny. But he said that the men 'were badly handled' and remarked that no commander could persistently insult the men under his command and get away with it.

Gardiner, apparently, was the very worst type of British officer, filled with a super-fatted sense of his own 'whiteness' and with a deep suspicion of the 'native'. Perhaps he had reason to look on all Ceylonese as traitors. He had doubtless been briefed on the general atmosphere in Ceylon and India. There was a general uneasiness among many in Ceylon and India about supporting the war.

In Colombo, it was known that two prominent local politicians, Dudley Senanayake and J.R. Jayewardene (later to become prime minister and first executive president respectively) had actually approached the Japanese ambassador in Ceylon and promised co-operation in the event Japan invaded the island. They had asked that Japan help gain Ceylon's independence from the British. This was confirmed by J.R. Jayewardene himself at a Tokyo banquet after the war, where he told his Japanese hosts that at that time Ceylon would have done anything to throw off the British yoke.

So many Ceylonese in Cocos—and one of them, Lieutenant Henry de Sylva of the Ceylon Light Infantry became a King Wenceslas page to Commander Gardiner. Perhaps he thought it was good for his own career to remain true-blue to the white boss man. Some people get that way when the crunch comes. Lieutenant de Sylva took orders from Gardiner. He had to report that all discipline had broken down; that what they had on their hands was a mutiny.

Gardiner was furious. All he wished to do was to show the world that he could do better than the celebrated Captain Bligh of the *Bounty*. He would courtmartial the men. He swore that he would see them hang!

Who were these 'mutineers'? There was Gunner Fernando, a Sinhalese. A few months before the troubles on Cocos came to a head, Fernando wrote to his father in Ceylon, actually apologizing for having volunteered for overseas service. He was concerned about his mother and said that he was hoping, above all, to come back home soon. But, he added, 'everything is a matter of fate'.

There was Carlo Gauder, a Burgher. There was G.B. de Silva and Samuel Jayasekera, both Sinhalese. There was Anandappa and Joe Pieris and Kingsley Dias, also Sinhalese. When mutiny broke out, it was not meant to be anything pro-Japanese, treasonous, cowardly or impelled by greed. Rather, it was a forthright showing by men who had been pushed to the brink—even beyond the brink. There was great hatred for the pompous white man who treated them like the dirt on the soles of his boots. Also, there was a boiling in the ranks as the 'loyals' and the 'disloyals' took sides. Peter Jayawardena, a Sinhalese, actually declared that the Bren guns on Cocos had been loaded with dud rounds. Duty Officer Stephens refused to believe this and adroitly passed the buck. After all, he said later, it was Gardiner who was sole Area Commander. Also, he reminded, de Sylva was Gardiner's aide and under Gardiner's jurisdiction. Everywhere that Gardiner went, de Sylva was sure to go! It was hard to later persuade Stephens to give inquirers the full story. He preferred to remain non-committal, on the fence. Also, in his view, Henry de Sylva was a boss man too, having been given the defence of Direction Island with his own force of men of the Ceylon Light Infantry.

Henry de Sylva in later years actually tried to cash in. He contacted the editor of the *Star*, an evening newspaper of the Independent Newspapers of Ceylon group. Noel Crusz was editor. De Sylva was disturbed at Noel Crusz's serialization of 'The Cocos Mutiny' in that paper. De Sylva even threatened to get 'His Majesty's government' to sue both Crusz and the newspaper.

The head of the newspaper organization, the very famous D.B. Dhanapala, formerly of the *Indian Express*, laughed. 'Let them sue,' he said, 'we will then have a bigger story to print!'

What blossomed on Cocos was raw hatred. It had been made very clear from all evidence and interviews, that Captain George Gardiner was a martinet. He handled his men on the islands with a cruelty that was blatant aberration of British military power. Many believed that Gardiner should have been hung. He was the sole cause of the mutiny—no other.

Gardiner wanted heads. Outraged at the manner of the uprising, he summoned de Sylva and said he wanted the 'criminals' arrested and a field general court martial held.

'I will tell you who the men are,' he said, and arbitrarily named eleven soldiers. Some of them had no part in the mutiny . . . but they were Ceylonese, and that, to Gardiner, was reason enough.

When Colombo heard of the strange turn of events on Cocos, Lieutenant Ivor Van Twest, a Burgher, was sent to the Cocos. He sailed on the *Sutlej*. He was told to investigate and bring back the mutineers. On no account was he to leave them to Gardiner to try them and, as commanding officer, execute them.

But Gardiner was not interested in what the British East India Military Command thought. He had the 'mutineers' arrested. He would try them. Then he would execute them. He had a right to do so. Mutiny deserved death.

Neither he nor his aide, de Sylva, had the slightest idea how to form a valid field general court martial. At the 'trial' the accused had no defence counsel. The malice that marked the proceedings was very obvious. Even before the trial, de Sylva had told Sergeant Ratnam to dig eleven graves.

Ratnam spat and refused. 'I'm a soldier,' he said, 'Not a bloody gravedigger.'

It was Gratien Fernando who determinedly stuck to his guns. He knew his legal rights and even when under arrest, contrived to send a telegram to Colombo, addressed to Bombardier Ossman, a Malay, who could be relied on to alert Colombo to the situation. Ossman rushed the cable to his CO, Colonel Mervyn Joseph, a Burgher, who immediately informed the British Military Command that something was painfully amiss.

Gardiner was determined to execute seven of the eleven 'mutineers' at dawn—the morning after the trial—but when he learnt of the cable sent through the wireless facility on Cocos and under his very nose, he wavered. The situation was tricky. And then came Lieutenant Van Twest who expressed much distaste at the sorry condition of the men.

Van Twest wrote a scathing report on conditions on the atoll and denounced Gardiner and the manner of his command. The report condemned the manner and formation of the court martial and the brutal manner of the arrest of the 'mutineers'. He made it clear that it was Gardiner who deserved to be put on trial. The report worried the British in Colombo. More so, Colonel Joseph had consulted with two prominent lawyers, Dr N.M. Perera and Dr Colvin R. de Silva. Clearly, the 'mutineers' would have to be brought to Colombo. The charge of mutiny would be upheld and they would be tried in Colombo at the Supreme Court in Hulftsdorp.

This became a most debatable issue among legal men and military historians—whether a Ceylon Supreme Court trial was valid in law. Both Dr N.M. Perera and Dr Colvin R. de Silva sensed a complete military bungling of wartime jurisdiction. They prepared a strong and spirited defence. In Colombo as well as in New Delhi, many thought it necessary to summon the previous CGA Commander, Captain Lyn Wickramasuriya. His help and advice was considered vital at that juncture.

In July 1942, Lieutenant Van Twest returned with the 'mutineers'. They would be charged and subjected to a fresh trial. It did not seem to matter much to the British that there were many flaws in jurisdiction and in the conducting of a fair trial. Whatever sort of creature Gardiner was, he was the Area Commander and these Ceylonese had 'mutinied'. They had to be tried.

General Wavell and Admiral Sir Geoffrey Layton were worried. They wanted the British High Command to act quietly. They wanted to save face, and also wanted to placate the mounting reluctance both in India and in Ceylon to support the war. They felt that to make a strong show about the Cocos Islands mutiny was to widen the chasm between the British as colonial masters and the people they ruled. But it was also seen that Captain Gardiner and the East Asia Command had taken up indefensible positions. Mutiny was mutiny . . . and mutiny merited death.

The trial was indeed a mockery. It did not matter to the British that they were compelled to relieve Gardiner of his command. What seemed to matter was that mutiny had to be vigorously punished. Of the accused, Gratien Fernando, Carlo Gauder and G.B. de Silva were sentenced to death. The rest received long prison terms. The three men certainly did not deserve to die and, to this day, no one in Sri Lanka believes that they got a fair trial.

The deputy commissioner of prisons at the time was a Burgher, R.J.N. Jordan. He declared that there was clearly a lack of proper relations between superior and subordinate. 'All the upheavals in this country could be traced to unfair or indifferent attitudes to one section or another,' he said.

The prisoners were held, after sentencing, in the Hulftsdorp prison which was then a military detention barracks. Major Whitelow, the Provost-Marshal, was to supervise the hangings.

The trial caused a huge stir. For one thing, there was growing concern in Wavell's New Delhi office that Gardiner's 'court martial' was poorly constituted. At that trial it was revealed how Gratien Fernando had accepted all the guilt, claiming that the 'mutiny' was his only and no other's. But, as Dr N.M. Perera pointed out at the Colombo trial, Gardiner had made up his mind to execute eleven men even before he had found them guilty. It was sheer premeditated murder.

An Australian legal and military writer, Peter Hastings, was certain that there was a conflicting array of events at the court martial on Cocos. He was of the opinion that this was a kangaroo trial and that there was no elementary natural justice. This was upheld by many of the legal luminaries of the Australian Military Academy. It was also seen how wartime cables to Horsborough on Cocos were contradictory in nature. Lieutenant Van Twest said that there was confusion over reports and eyewitness accounts.

Colonel Mervyn Joseph and Dr N.M. Perera fought hard to upset the Crown case. Dr Perera said that the Supreme Court had no jurisdiction to try the 'mutineers' and that Admiral Layton's and Wavell's decision to bring them to trial in Ceylon was bad in military law.

Also, Lieutenant Van Twest's report on the actions of Gardiner and his command was not presented at the trial. It seemed that the British military apparatus was moving inexorably, sticking grimly to its sense of military discipline and ignoring the extenuating circumstances. Also, it was wartime. Quick decisions had to be made. Some observers felt that the British had to have a few heads. It would be a signal to all other colonies and to the locals who served in the ranks.

Layton, obviously prodded by his own conscience, actually indicated that he was prepared to grant a reprieve and a pardon to Gratien and his colleagues. If only these Ceylonese would grovel . . .

But Gratien would have none of it. He sent Layton a stunning rejoinder: 'Take your reprieve and your pardon and wipe your backside with it!'

Gratien's father and Carlo Gauder's brother appealed. Execution dates were delayed, pending appeal, but Gratien's reply to Layton dashed every hope of commuted sentences. Now, he, Gauder and G.B. de Silva would hang.

They took Gratien to death row at 7.45 a.m. The British authorities kept the families of the condemned men in the dark about the dates of execution. Gratien was taken to the scaffold accompanied by two chaplains, Father Claude Lawrence and Father Brennan. With them was Prison Superintendent, M. Crowe. Provost-Marshal Whitelow supervised while other prison executives looked on and provided the hangman's service.

In their cells, other mutineers, Joe Pieris, Kingsley Dias, Anandappa, mumbled a prayer. Gratien went to the noose with a courage that was unfaltering. Deputy Prison Commissioner Jordan said later, 'Gratien Fernando's indomitable courage on his way to the gallows was on everybody's lips for weeks, both among prisoners and staff . . .'

They asked Gratien if he had anything to say.

The condemned man's eyes flashed. 'Yes,' he said in a ringing voice, *'give me a revolver that I might shoot that bastard Gardiner!'*

The hangman pulled the lever of the trap.

'I have been witness to scores of executions but never did experience a disposition of such a nature,' Jordan said.

They hanged Gauder on his 21st birthday. His sister Totsy stood outside the Welikade jail, hoping to claim the body, but wartime regulations forbade this. Eventually the three 'mutineers' were buried in Colombo's Kanatte General Cemetery in unmarked graves.

For many years, journalist Noel Crusz, who is now in Australia, hunted for the court martial records of the Cocos. The quest took him to the Public Records Office in London, then to examine the wartime naval records in Singapore and London. In 1976, Lieutenant Koch, who placed the six-inch guns on Cocos, was thought to have the records, but it was strongly believed that Gardiner, on being relieved of his commission, took the records away with him.

Cannily enough, it was Gardiner's aide, de Sylva, who cashed in. In 1983 Noel Crusz did interview him and he kept offering the 'inside story' of the mutiny . . . for a price. Crusz found that he had nothing really new to say, but de

Sylva hinted at being in possession of vital documents which he was prepared to sell.

When payment was made, all Crusz received were newspaper clippings about life in Cocos. There was nothing even remotely alluding to the so-called mutiny!

A sad and quite weary aspect of the war. If, as one man told the writer, the British had won the Pacific War, defeated the Japanese, Asia and the Pacific would never have been really free.

Who knows . . . we may have continued to be under the colonial power—and a victorious colonial power would have been pretty hard to stomach!

45

Of Northern Patrols and Schoolgirls in the After Steering and Drinking at The Sydney

Somehow, northern patrols were not so bad. Not when the *Seruwa* was reported missing by a hysterical signalman on the *Elara* and the *Korawakka* had run aground three miles off the Pungudativu causeway near the island of Delft.

Victor was not happy. The *Vijaya* was simply pancaking around in a sea that was on its best behaviour. The waves were so insignificant, the swells so like punctured boils that the ship simply seemed to glide on oiled runners. Carloboy would stand at the portside lookout, gaze at the sun setting a blue oilcloth ablaze and feel that there was something unreal about the cruise. It was like moving in a mess of blue-green butter.

They spent a couple of days tracking down the *Seruwa* and reporting back to *Elara*: that all was well. Apparently the gunboat had developed a battery condition that had affected gyro compass and transmitter and other apparatus.

'So you should have taken a star reading!' Victor bellowed, 'and what about azimuth?'

The captain of the *Seruwa* grinned. 'What? And not have you come after us? Why do you think I hung around here? I told the middy there'll be some good whisky and cigarettes when you come.'

Too true, and the wardroom of the *Vijaya* grew quite mellow while the men watched a 16 mm film, *Black Narcissus* on the boatdeck. There were a goodly stock of films on board. Mostly Westerns but some real oldies too with such vintage bombshells like Dorothy Lamour, Esther Williams, Lana Turner and Maureen O'Hara.

The *Korawakka* was refloated before they dropped anchor off Kankesanturai for ships stores that had been sent for collection. It was no problem commandeering a pontoon raft to haul the stuff to the ship and it gave opportunity to many of the crew to roam the pebble beach and stray inland where they soon sighted and followed a man with his pingo barrels of palmyra toddy which they knew, tapped and drawn so early in the morning, would be as refreshing as the finest lemonade. And so it was. So fresh that a few bees floated in the nectar, having opted to die deliciously.

They then rounded the Peninsula and dropped anchor off Talaimannar Pier.

To Carloboy, these patrols were extremely interesting. Hard to imagine they were anywhere near a familiar Lankan coast. The seas were different too and the water would glisten at night with its speckles of phosphorous. The *Vijaya* had a pattern to follow—Eluvaitivu Point, Kovilam, Kakeraitivu, Trincomalee for fuel and water, Delft Island. The days passed swiftly as the ship beetled on, threaded its grey and determined way among the islands . . . Eluvaitivu, Pungudativu, Kakeraitivu, Kovilam, Palaitivu, Mañditivu, Delft, Mannar, Kayts, Velvettiturai, Kankesanturai, Trincomalee . . . in and out and round about the scores of islands and anchorages that clustered like barnacles around the peninsula.

There were many weird happenings too: like the day the *Diyakawa* hove to, hauling a long string of hapless fishing boats.

Victor leaned over the side, watching the approaching procession. Within earshot, he yelled, 'What the fuck are you doing?'

'Caught these buggers off Kayts.'

'So what are you doing?'

'Taking them to Mannar. Bloody *kallathonis*!'

'Those are fishing boats, you bloody idiot!'

'That's what they all say. But one boat has twenty bags of *parippu* (pigeon pea of dhal) and another bugger has six cases of Lactogen!'

Victor scratched his head. Of course, there was smuggling. The smugglers operated mostly out of Velvettiturai. Men took boatloads of stuff across the Strait to India.

'Can't stay to chat,' the captain of the *Diyakawa* hollered.

'Carry on,' Victor shouted and grinned. 'Like a duck pulling a flock of pelicans. By the time he gets to Mannar half those buggers will cut loose and vanish.'

They did find a flock of illicit immigrants on a tiny white-stone island off Delft. It was pitiful, rounding them up, transferring them to the *Vijaya*. Their story was just as pitiful. They had given much to a launch operator to bring them to Jaffna. They were twelve—eight men, three women and a child. The launch had put them on the island eight days ago. As they waded waist-deep to the shore the coxswain had yelled to them to hurry.

'You are in Ceylon,' he had said, 'don't stay on the beach!' and with a hoarse cackle, swung his nose about and sped away.

The group had panted ashore, the women's wet clothes heavy on their bodies. This was Ceylon. Here they would drift inland, go somehow to the interior, trudge the back roads. Someone had given them a contact address in Jaffna. Soon, they would be sent to the hills, the tea country. There, among thousands of other Tamil labourers, they would disappear.

But they had been cruelly dumped on a tiny thumb-nail of land where the bushes were prickly and the stones cut their feet. All they had were small, tightly wrapped bundles holding all they possessed. They had starved. The child, a dark-eyed scrap of a boy who said he was thirteen and was more like nine, was dangerously ill. None of them could talk in their normal voices. Their throats burned with thirst. They had eaten large hermit crabs cooked in brine. They had eaten leaves and yellow wild flowers and the milk of the leaves had burned their tongues.

All over the patch of sand were the signs of feverish digging. They had clawed desperately into the earth for water. And they had gazed imploringly at the clouds, for they knew that soon there would be the wet days of the north-east monsoon.

The women had to be carried to the whaler. One of the men purged horribly and another found it difficult to walk. In the sick bay, they were each given a saline drip to combat acute dehydration.

'Why do these buggers keep coming, I don't know,' said Lieutenant Jello (who had joined ship at Trincomalee because he wished to be as far away from Colombo as he could for purely personal reasons). Only he knew why, thankfully, until the night a signal put everyone in a tizzy. It was from NHQ and it ordered Jello to Colombo immediately. Deanna, it said, had attempted suicide. Deanna, it said, was very pregnant. Deanna's father, it said, was buying a box of 12-bore cartridges. Deanna, it also said, was in the General Hospital, and Deanna's mother was stalking the NHQ with her hair undone and in a kimono with three buttons also undone. Who, asked the signal plaintively, is Deanna, what is she?

Jello paled and had words with Victor. Victor swore prettily and told Jello to take the train from Trincomalee. Jello expressed a desire to be let off at Delft. There he would spend the rest of his days, an island recluse, he said grandly.

Victor was unimpressed. 'Even the wild ponies won't be safe,' he snapped. 'Go to *Gemunu*, Lieutenant, and that's an order.'

With Jello's departure came better news. Patrols were over.

On November 9, with a wild wind taking each wave by the scruff, they left Velvettiturai and headed for the open sea. The coast resounded with cheers. Goodbye for now, you blighted islands, heavy with smugglers and skulking *kallathonis* . . . they were going home . . . no, correction, they were going to the southern port of Galle, for, as Victor twirled his forelock and told his men, the Mayor of Galle had asked the Captain of the Navy to send the *Vijaya* to his city. It would be such a honour, he had said—a short stay, a chance to let the sleepy people of Galle come to grips with a real warship.

Victor gazed bleakly at his crew. 'The mayor has asked us to honour him with a four-day visit. When off port, this ship will be officially open to visitors, so I want you to be in number ten rig and on your best behaviour, is that clear?'

Open for visitors! The men looked at each other and each knew what the other was thinking.

'Hey, PO, what are the girls like in Galle?'

'Like everywhere else, you idiot. What do you think? They've got horizontal slits?'

Hughes grinned. 'Must find out,' he said, and Koelmeyer seconded the motion.

They rounded the Basses just as the first north-easter dropped its calling card, swooping out of the Bay of Bengal with a yo-ho-ho. The monsoon would soon make the northern seas most agitated. There would be depressions in the Bay and the waves would swipe the coast with great rage. The *Vijaya* took a pounding as it swept round the south-east hump and ran, with a racing sea, until the Tangalla light buoy. Then the wind dropped and the waves gentled. Victor frowned. Calm seas and ships as steady as Gibraltar were not his idea of fun.

They couldn't enter Galle harbour either because of their draught. Victor squinted at the palm-girt coast, the rising hump of the old Dutch Fort, the streaks of gold-white beach and the small breakwaters that seemed to enclose a toy harbour for flat-bottomed freighters and sailing vessels. Picturesque enough, he thought. He checked soundings and bellowed, 'Let go number one anchor!'

With an incredible clanking, the hooks shot down even as the *Vijaya* stopped engines. Victor checked the drag, dropped a sheethook and called for tide signals. The *Vijaya* turned like an uncertain corkscrew, then held as the anchors lodged themselves.

'Four days outside harbour,' Carloboy said, 'and they call this an official visit!'

Lieutenant Wicks smiled. 'So what were you expecting? A red carpet?' He then went below. Time to tog up. The *Vijaya* was no longer a messy little refuge for maniacs, drunks, malingerers and perverts. To the good people of Galle who would soon come a-calling, it would be the proud man-o-war of the Royal Ceylon Navy, with its able, intelligent, good and true men.

First came the Mayor of Galle, the government agent and an assortment of city fathers who were more like city grandfathers. They were hustled to the wardroom and dosed liberally, then taken around.

The men squatted moodily on deck. Galle seemed to be full of old and ugly men. But as the afternoon wore on, they perked up. More and more boats kept coming, and they kept shovelling in parties of schoolchildren, convent girls, groups of civilians and bevies of young girls who were convinced that a ship of any sort was the place where they had to simply lose their virginity. All this talk of sailors and girls in every port had to mean something.

Even the offshore wind seemed to enter into the spirit of things, swirling their skirts up around their waists as they tottered to the gangway with squeals of embarrassment much to the quartermaster's glee. The wind chuckled and moved on to make more mischief. The girls blushed and looked coyly about them and kept squealing each time the *Vijaya* heaved on her anchors. It was, to the men, showtime!

It may be, as the dormouse said, too much of a muchness to undertake a clinical record of all that transpired. The duty watch was asked to show the visitors around and Carloboy found himself shepherding a gaggle of tittering schoolgirls who were senior students of the Sacred Heart

Convent. He found them very enlivening company and somehow, too mature for words. Naturally, they wanted to see the bridge and did not seem to mind at all that lots of sailors lolled around the flagdeck to look up their white school uniforms as they climbed.

The wheelhouse had never been designed to take twenty sweet sixteens. Neither was the tiny signals office that could hold no more than two and that with extreme tolerance. But the signals office had its steel door and piped air and a slab across the bulkhead that served as a table but was more like a long cell bunk.

By the time the girls had ooh-ed and aah-ed at the masts, the binnacle, the signalling lanterns and quivered excitedly at the Bofors that were being swivelled around for their benefit, Carloboy knew that it was time to cut one out of her herd. The girl in particular was a sweet-faced, big-eyed thing who kept clutching at his hand as he explained the intricacies of navigation. He had enjoyed their obvious interest. They were most interested in signals and he began to feel like Yeoman Louis in the instruction room.

'V/S is visual signalling. Okay, let me explain. You are walking down a road and I see you. But you don't see me. And you are now some distance away. I want to communicate, so what do I do? I clap. So that's a signal. But it's not a visual signal. You don't see it, but you hear it. That's a sound signal.'

Lots of giggles. One asked, 'So if a boy winks what is it?'

'A visual signal.'

More giggles.

'And when you hear the clap you turn to see who's clapping, no?'

'I won't turn,' one miss said.

'Why?'

'If anybody claps I must turn to see who?'

'Never mind her,' said another, 'too proud, *anney*, she is. I will turn to see. And then?'

'Then I put a wave. You can see me waving. So that is a visual signal.'

'Ah! First the clapping, then the waving.'

'Exactly. Sound signal, visual signal.' His hand squeezed hers. She did not pull away.

'I want to see the wheelhouse again,' she said.

The others said no. They had locked out over the bridge and seen much action around the foredeck gun.

Carloboy ran his thumb on the girl's wrist. 'So you go down,' he told the others, 'I'll show her the wheelhouse and come. And mind your step. Don't fall.'

The girls chattered brightly as they dropped away to the boatdeck. Carloboy led his prize to the little signals office. She hung back at first but his hand was round her waist and his fingers kneaded her hip then moved to her stomach. All they had to do was close the steel door but it would be dark and cramped and he could sense her unease.

'We'll go to the quarterdeck,' he said, 'what's your name?'

She drew a deep breath. 'Ranjini,' she said.

His lips touched her forehead. She reached for his face, kissed his cheek awkwardly.

'You like me?' he asked.

The colour rose in her face. She nodded. His hands moved over her small breasts. Outside, he heard the clatter of many feet on the gangway. 'Let's go down. There are some more people coming.'

Nobody paid much attention to the stern where the depth charge racks and minesweeping gear stood. The trap to the after steering was open and to that rude compartment they went and Carloboy made sure the hatch was secured. It was smelly in there. There was the big ship's wheel, piles of cordage and coiled grassline, belaying pins, the overflow from the shipwright's store and drums of paint. They sat on a nest of new rope and held each other close and, for no reason at all, spoke in whispers. She took off her white uniform, worried at the oil and how it might soil the dress. Her petticoat was flimsy and low-necked and he gently pushed his hand under the elastic band of her knickers, feeling the soft down of her mount.

'Can you lie back on the rope?' he asked.

She was holding his cock, running a finger on its head in a small circling motion. 'Will you put it inside? I'm—I'm afraid.'

He rolled down her knickers. 'You haven't done it before?'

She shook her head. 'Wait a little . . .' and raising herself, shook off her knickers. She sat back, spread her knees as his finger found her clitoris, felt it throb as he pressed into the little ridge under it. He was wet and very hard. He knew she would be very tight, and his knees trembled at the thought. She was wet too and made little sounds between her teeth as he massaged her.

'Will it—will it pain?' she asked.

'You actually haven't done it before?'

'No. Only between my legs. At home my uncle does it like that.'

'But there's no feeling for you then. Only I will enjoy it.'

'But I'm getting a nice feeling now,' she whispered, 'when you touch like that.'

He pushed her back gently. He had to have her. He had keyed himself to a pitch he could no longer deny. What had northern patrols yielded—a hurried encounter in Trincomalee and no opportunity to go ashore at Talaimannar where Carmencita would have made him very welcome. He lay over the girl and gently rubbed the head of his penis against her. She gasped. Up and along the cleft, and he felt her hips jerk as he kept masturbating her. Suddenly her eyes widened and her body arched. He knew she was coming, and with a swift movement, kneed her legs wide apart, put his forearms under her thighs, raising her up as he thrust down, he entered her almost effortlessly and she gave a sharp cry, and he put his weight on her, covered her mouth with his. She lay pinned, and a tear began to trickle from the corner of her eye.

He raised his head. 'Did it hurt?'

She nodded.

'It won't hurt for long. Just lie still.'

They lay together for a long while. He did not move. He was encased, sheathed in firm, tight flesh that gripped his cock and he wanted to keep it that way.

'What will happen?' she asked breathlessly.

'Shh,' he began to move.

She hissed slightly. He moved slowly, gently, and he felt the warm stickiness cling to the bottom of his stomach. She was so tight. He did not have to work hard over her. Every movement was so delicious, almost Tantric. He knew he was fucking her in her own blood . . . and then he felt a bursting within him and withdrew, dropping a blob of semen on her thigh. There was blood on his stomach, his bush, blood rich and red issuing in a thin streak from the lips of her vagina, running down to the cleft of her buttocks.

'It will soon stop. Is it still paining?'

'A little,' she said, 'how to clean?'

All he could find was a sack of clean cotton waste. She cleaned as best as she could and he made a thick wad of the waste and told her to place it between her legs. When she put on her knickers he pushed more cotton waste into them, packing it tightly around her, 'Even if it bleeds a little now, it won't come on your dress.'

She nodded.

'How do you feel?'

She smiled. 'You liked it with me?'

He embraced her. He had to get her out, for he knew he wanted her again.

'Most of the other girls have done it. I'm the only one. I used to tell lies sometimes that I did with a boy but they just laughed and asked who. Now they won't laugh.'

It seemed to be a sort of badge of honour for the senior girls of the Sacred Heart. To be unfucked was to be unaccepted.

'How are you feeling now?'

'All right. Must go now, no? Don't know if they're looking for me, even.'

They emerged, and found the rest of the girls on the

boatdeck where a buxom teacher was calling names and looking quite sheepish. She had been invited to view the sick bay by Warrant Officer Rodrigo. She, too, had lost track of time, since Rodrigo was a very good performer and liked women who were fat.

Ranjini smiled, held Carloboy's hand as he helped the party down to the launch. 'It was lovely,' she whispered.

Carloboy winked. 'Same here. Can you come again?'

The girls giggled. One said 'Ah-hah, Ranjini, what were you doing so long with him?'

Ranjini kept smiling. The little minx would undoubtedly tell all. She would enjoy that very much.

The master-at-arms was not in the best of moods. Civilians had no idea how a warship needed to be run. There was a lot of cleaning up to do. This was carried out good-naturedly enough. The men had things to say. Nathali had scored in the heads, of all places. Hughes and Ryan had taken a brace of women under the canvas of the big gun. Peculiar things had happened in the wireless cabin where Yusuf had found relief with a portly Muslim woman old enough to be his mother. The shipwright's stores, the electrician's office, the galley, the sick bay had all witnessed the many frantic moods of sailors on the make while the wardroom, too, had had its moments. Chickera got full marks for his performance on the bridge. He had actually used the tiny signals office, sealing himself in with two sisters. 'They are twins,' he said casually enough while many stared and said, 'Go on, you're lying, you short bugger.'

But Chickera wasn't. The twins, Malay girls, simply had to do things together. They agreed that Chickera was 'cute'. He admitted it was uncomfortable. The girls had stood against the slab in the bulkhead, side by side, their shoulders back against the steel.

'Had to fuck them standing. In the dark also and not easy men, because I am short also. Everytime I had to say, come down a little, come down a little, but I managed. My God, we were sweating buckets when we came out.'

Carloboy went to the Captain's office. Someone would find the lumps of bloodied cotton waste and raise eyebrows. He sat, put his feet up. Tomorrow was an off day. He would go ashore, post some letters. He thought of Ranjini. Girls. This attraction for girls; the attraction they had for men . . . a peculiar thing, he thought. You look at them, note the way they are, admire their legs, their bodies, their features. But all this is lost in the act of sex itself. You don't even see the hole you invade, you cannot admire the body you take. You just lie over it, use it, drive into it and spill yourself, propelling your passion into a hole made for the purpose. And then it's over and you can go back if you wish to that beautiful, fanciful occupation of admiring those fine lines of thigh and the way the smile touches the corner of the lips and the upthrust of breasts and the roundness of the bum. 'It's a fucking trap,' he murmured and smiled to himself. A sailor's philosophy, maybe, but to Carloboy the realization did come that a man in his rage could fuck anything. 'Even a bloody letterbox,' he said to himself and grinned.

They went ashore the next day with two weeks pay burning a hole in their pockets. Chickera, Aubrey, Hughes, Ryan, Daft, Carloboy, Arnie . . . and it was decided unanimously that nothing would be more pleasing than a monumental booze. They skirted the esplanade, the public bus station. The hotel they chose was the largest they could find. The Sydney. A genteel watering hole much frequented by southern planters and gem merchants and known for its excellent food and its well-stocked bar.

It was the fifteenth of November. In the arched foyer, a weedy girl in a saree of shocking pearl was having her cuticles for supper. The airy restaurant-cum-bar had its fair share of locals, mostly the beer and cutlets variety who scorned rice and curry whenever they had the opportunity to show how civilized they were. The boys opted for a long table and told the waiter that all he had to do was keep the arrack flowing.

'And some chillied potatoes and devilled beef,' said Aubrey who ate like a *T. rex*. He it was who had stolen a twenty pound slab of smoked gammon from the wardroom galley and devoured it in one sitting. Cooks wilted when he came for his meals.

A few tables away sat a spivvy looking character with a real silk tie and cuff links and a moustache that would have given Errol Flynn second thoughts. He was not alone. Around his table sat three women, each built like a steamer trunk. They were Borahs or Parsees or something, Carloboy hazarded, and Arnie told a story of the midget who had married the circus fat lady.

'You know what the bugger did on the wedding night?'

'Wore a lifebelt and dived in?'

'No, men, he put the woman down, then began to walk all over her, hitting his chest like Tarzan.'

'For why?'

'Wait, I'll show you—' Arnie rose and began a circuit of the table. He beat at his chest and howled, 'Acres an' acres of arse. An' all mine! Acres an' acres of arse—' and he had still to take his first drink! The boys roared and the three fat ladies crimsoned and muttered to the spiv who glared.

Soon, pretty soused and very voluble, everybody wanted to say something, sing something, tell a dirty story, shout for more arrack. Carloboy rose to squint and declare that the Ceylon Navy could drink any bugger under the table—that's right—any Galle bugger under the table, so there!

Hughes was singing while Ryan kept tune with a fork on a tumbler:

I'll tell you a story
That's certain to please
Of a great farting contest
At Shitters-on-Tees;
Where all the best farters
Paraded the field
To win for their own
The Fartingale Shield . . .

An interesting song, although they had no idea in what pub

they had picked it up. It told of sundry fat-assed ladies who had vied for honours and how eventually the parsons's wife had to be carried away by men in gas masks because her effort produced a lot more than wind.

The spivvy character was suddenly upon them. 'Don't you know there are ladies present!' he shrieked. He also quivered. So did the fat ladies. They couldn't help themselves. Each had a derrière as big as a grand piano.

Good sense, even decency should have prompted them to move to another table. Or their escort could have taken them upstairs where the main dining hall was. As for the boys, they were drunk, getting bawdier by the minute and had no excuses to offer.

'Ladies?' Aubrey burped. 'My God, I thought they were whales. I wanted to ask also why whales were wearing sarees.'

Ryan never favoured arguments. He banged down his glass. 'Fuck off!'

The spiv curled a lip. Then he reached out and took up a chair. The waiter fled, which was a very wise thing to do. In the next moments, the fat ladies were streaking away, others rose in aid of the spiv. Aubrey had swung a mean fist, breaking the spiv's nose, and two men who had appeared as if on cue at a Punch and Judy show, were running blindly into the wall, their faces plastered with devilled beef.

The management had its bouncers—very necessary in any place where arrack was served. These worthies closed in and that was their mistake. Oh, they had this reputation. They were thugs. They were paid to remove any threat to the peace and good order of the hotel. They wore nylon shirts and broad belts around their sarongs and favoured Indian film star moustaches.

Carloboy did not pause to make selection. None of the boys did. The idea was that anyone approaching them had to be swatted. They had despatched a forward guard of waiters and Ryan had pushed a man's head into the piano keyboard and slammed down the lid. The lid it was that broke and the manager had screamed and telephoned the police. He screamed again when Hughes drove a fist into an ornate wall mirror which had been a proud Sydney Hotel possession for many a year. The receptionist ran to the washroom and locked herself in.

The bouncers bounced against the furniture. The Navy was now in full cry. Everything that moved was pummelled into immobility. Suddenly, they realized that there was nothing more to destroy. Ryan grinned. Aubrey sucked his knuckles. Carloboy tested his shoulder. Chickera was eating devilled beef. There were a few pieces in the dish.

'Better if we go,' Carloboy said, 'can you see the crowd at the door? Whole of Galle must be outside.' He knew they might have to fight their way through the mob. It could turn very nasty. There were street thugs who carried knives. And then the police strode in—three policemen who pushed through and waved their batons and shouted to the boys to come with them. This, to the boys was wholly unacceptable.

Hughes grabbed the first policeman by the tunic. 'What did you say!' he roared, 'go with you where?'

Aubrey and Carloboy closed on the other two.

'Here! You let off! You come go station!'

'No. You come go ship!'

Aubrey cackled. 'Shall we take the buggers to the ship?'

With a vicious heave, Hughes tore open the policeman's tunic. Brass buttons popped like corn. Then he gave the man a butt on the chin with his head that almost snapped the man's jaw. He dropped with a croak, and even as the other two policemen leaped, two well-placed body blows stopped them in their tracks. It was like running into the edge of an open door.

Carloboy had fists of iron. Even as a schoolboy he would split open wooden lockers with a blow. When he struck his prey it knocked the wind out of the man. He fell without a sound and rapidly grew purple. Aubrey found his policeman easy meat. Outside, the crowd sucked back. These sailors were devils!

'Let's go! Now!' Carloboy yelled, grabbing a bottle.

'Take bottles. Anybody gets in the way, split his bloody head!'

They strode to the door, eyes glowing. The loafers dispersed. The mob broke. They walked through an honour guard of gaping men and not a voice was raised in challenge. They found that they were also very sober. Somewhere a clock was striking ten.

Aubrey peeled split skin off his knuckles. 'Damn! We missed the last boat!'

Chickera said something like 'Yowgh'. He had his fingers in his mouth. When he could make sense he said a tooth was shaking.

Stuck ashore, they looked at each other helplessly.

'What to do now?'

'We'll go to the jetty. Must be having a boat we can hire even.'

'Good idea.'

They went.

46

History—Disloyal Politics and the Anti-British Mood

The Ceylon Communist Party did its damndest to fan the anti-British flames in Ceylon in the 1940s. The Ceylon National Congress went about it in a most Gandhian manner. At a meeting of the CNC's Working Committee on March 31, 1941, it was decided that:

(a) Congress members and the public be advised to support locally made goods and stores, and foster the use of Sinhalese as the mother tongue.
(b) That members will refuse to accept imperial or local titles, honours and ranks emanating from a foreign ruler.
(c) That they refuse to attend imperial functions, levees and parades and other functions when the British governor is present.
(d) That they will not support Britain's war effort.

The loyals, mostly of the planting community were appalled at the unrest being spawned on the estates. An organization in Kandy, which called itself the Comrades of the Great War, decided to send a memorial to the Secretary of State. This is what was sent:

To the Right Honourable Lord Lloyd, PC, GCSI, GCIE, DSO, etc.,
His Majesty's Secretary of State for the Colonies

My Lord,

The committee appointed by a meeting, of Comrades of the Great War and their supporters in Kandy, Ceylon, on 4th June, 1940, beg to state the following facts and make the following submissions and requests:-

(1) The complete loosening of the reins of government by, and the *laissez-faire* attitude of those in authority in the government in the past three years has allowed the communist party in Ceylon to stir up strife and disaffection among His Majesty's previously contented subjects until the labour unrest which commenced in April 1939 has, since the commencement of hostilities, reached a critical and alarming stage.

(2) The following are only a few of the instances of labour trouble which has been stirred up among contented labourers since the war started.

(a) January 10—A major riot on Mooloya Estate where the police were called in and after having their car damaged had to fire and kill one man in self-defence.

(b) April—Seven hundred excited and rioting labourers armed with clubs and sticks surrounded the bungalow of a married superintendent on Ramboda Estate. The superintendent was stoned and hit with a stone.

(c) April—On Vellai Oya Group, the labourers rioted and injured an estate conductor.

(d) May—Strife occured between two lots of

labourers on Naseby Estate. Five of the injured were admitted into hospital.

(e) May—There was serious trouble on Needwood Estate and the police were attacked, one being seriously injured and others less seriously.

(f) May—In a riot on Weywelhena Estate a large number were injured, as many as forty being removed to hospital.

(g) May—The Kangany (labour supervisor) on Uda Radella Estate was injured and removed to hospital.

(h) May—The police were assaulted by armed labourers on Wewesse Estate and the superintendent was asked to leave the estate as the police would not be responsible for his safety or that of his wife.

(i) May—The superintendent of St Andrew's Estate was assaulted by labourers and both his arms were injured—one arm being fractured.

How the trouble is increasing will be seen from the above instances, and it needs no imagination to see that a far more serious state of affairs is likely to occur in the near future if strong action is not taken immediately by the government. Bloodshed and rioting will become prevalent with undoubted repercussions of the utmost seriousness in India.

(3) The members of the Ceylon Planters Rifle Corps have been allowed to retain their arms, but all ammunition has been removed from them and sent to headquarters, Colombo, so that these members, divorced from their ammunition, are rendered powerless to defend their wives and children.

(4) Members of the state council who have taken their oath of allegiance have forsworn their allegiance by making subversive and anti-British speeches, of which we submit some extracts as examples:

(a) *Hansard 12-12-39.*

'But British imperialism is a unique kind of imperialism which is smeared with the loathsome slime of hypocrisy in order to deceive the misguided among us.

'I would call upon the House which was misguided enough to pass a vote of loyalty, even at this moment, in the face of things like this, of insults, not to ask us to pay money to get those kicks.'

(b) *Hansard 15-3-40.*

A member states the fact that 'it was a common platform on which the ex-ministers of His Majesty the King stood (A member: some of them) and they are a homogenous board and ranted with the rest of them, "Long live revolution. Down with British imperialism".'

(c) *Orders of the Day April 2nd.*

A member moved 'That this council . . . urges the people immediately to prepare for a nation-wide mass struggle against British imperialism.'

(d) *Times of Ceylon* 29-5-40 (relevant *Hansard* not yet published):

The chief cecretary asked for a supplementary estimate for Rs 100,000 to meet the cost of acquisition of land for an Air Force base for the RAF.

A Communist member opposing the vote said . . . 'Was the RAF retreating East? They were always clever at retreating according to plan.'

Another Communist said they could not see any useful purpose in such expenditure. 'What the British need is not equipment or money but courage. The British are running away, retreating.'

The Speaker—'Order, Order.'

'These are facts appearing in the newspapers of this country. If they are not facts, the government should stop such news. The British are a declining and decrepit empire.'

(e) A minister of the government said in council: 'Ceylon would be a hundred times better off if the Englishmen did not set foot on our shores.'

(5) Seditious pamphlets have been broadcast in Tamil, Sinhalese and English throughout the island of which the following extracts are examples:

(a) 'If all unite together and strike with help of the union the cruel and exploiting planters will feel stifled.'

(b) 'The strike started by the estate labourers against the white planters is the most powerful fight today against the imperialist system.'

(c) 'O comrades, if we fight united and unfurl the red flag all the exploitations will cease from today.'

(d) 'It is revolutions that are wanted in order to secure freedom.'

(e) 'The real war the British are fighting now is in Ceylon. For them, the remaining theatre of war, with any chances of success, is the plantations against the unarmed plantation workers.'

(f) 'Workers of the world unite. Down with the police cruelty. May revolution spread.'

(g) 'We should not support in any way this mastery over colonial people. Rather we should seek to overthrow this system and work for the day of our freedom that must arise from the downfalls of the contending forces.'

'Don't support this imperialist war!'

And there is a sinister addition of a verse by Shelley, the last few words of which are underlined in black: 'Forge arms—in your defence to bear.'

(6) The Sinhalese and Tamil Press publish sedition unchecked of which the following extracts from one paper of 8th March are typical.

(a) 'John Bull (England) who is under the strong grip of war is unable to extricate himself and is strangled.'

(b) 'Just as the Russian labourers did, the imperial war should be converted into a internal war and we should array ourselves to fight for freedom.'

(c) 'The day has approached when your uncontrollable thirst for freedom should gush out from your strong heart, your eyes should redden with rage, you should beat the war drum and line yourselves for the fight.'

(d) 'Boycott English goods. Effect general strikes. Bring deadlock in council.'

'With such awful weapons, we will make the empire choke and bring it to a standstill.'

'Down with war.'

'Let the empire die off.'

(7) The Hammer and Sickle Flag has openly been flown in Colombo and to make the insult more galling, it was flown near the foot of the Victory Column—our largest War

Memorial. My Lord, it was not so that this flag should be allowed to fly in Ceylon that those of us who are comrades fought.

(8) On the day of the national prayer the walls of the town of Moratuwa were plastered with posters saying:—
'Down with the British' and 'Don't pray for the Allied Forces.'
In one instance a poster was exhibited on a church.

(9) On the day on which flags were sold for the Gloucester Fund, Communistic literature containing such remarks as 'To Hell with the Gloucester Fund' were distributed freely in the streets of Colombo by women in red shirts.

(10) 'White dogs' has become the regular expression used by some of the agitators when referring to planters and the police are frequently referred to as 'dogs'.

(11) Field Marshall Lord Birdwood is well aware of Ceylon's effort in the war of 1914-1918, and it is to be deplored that, owing to the present state of misrule in the island, it is practically impossible to allow any loyal men to proceed overseas.

(12) We all anticipate that, unless we have in the very near future a strong government that will take strong action to prevent this canker of unbridled sedition from spreading, we will soon have bloodshed and rioting throughout the island.

(13) In view of the foregoing facts we would respectfully request you to use your powers, with the least possible delay to prevent what was, and still is at heart, a peace-loving and intensely loyal population from becoming, owing to slack government and unbridled

seditious leadership, enemies of our empire. My Lord, we think that we all, and especially those of us who are comrades, have the right to make this request.

(14) In closing we should like to express our appreciation of the loyal work of the Ceylon police force who have acted splendidly throughout, but whose hands have been tied by the weakness of those in authority and who all, officers and men alike, are well-nigh exasperated at the lack of backing they received.

Colombo, 8th June, 1940.

It wasn't long after this that many of the 'disloyals' were arrested and some of them sent to prison. But the British could not quell the tide of disaffection. When the disloyals were released after their terms, they were feted by state councillors and given grand lunches and dinners. In Kandy, these 'Martyrs' were garlanded by the mayor and taken in procession through the streets. In Galle, the municipal council gave them a civic reception. The message to the British was clear. We don't want you!

Within weeks of their release, these nationalists were at it again. In November 1945 a pamphlet was seized in the plantation district of Kandy. It urged the people 'to cut the throats of all white people and those blacks who work for them.'

In 1943 a local minister had said: 'We are told in the incomparable language of Winston Churchill that England is fighting for decency, for freedom, for democracy, for all these things that make human life worth living; that she is the outpost of civilization. Great heavens, what an outpost of civilization! . . . We have given them such assistance as we have been asked to give in this fight to preserve civilization which is fraught with hypocrisy and one which seems largely to consist of nothing but humbug . . . (we) must request the state council as well as the general public to cease giving further assistance to the war effort . . . already the local administration has decided to inform all local bodies that contributing to war funds will be banned. Why should we sacrifice our blood and money for a nation which is trying to ruin the existence of the Ceylonese?'

Another minister said, 'The British started the war with very noble and pious protestations of fighting for equality and democracy. Democracy meant equality, but to them equality meant only equality for white faces.'

It is easy to see how resentment ballooned. It was well accepted that the British were absolutely out of sympathy with the people of Ceylon. In a way, this was painfully evident. There was, for one thing, a tremendous superiority complex that the British wallowed in. Many of them had been leading lives in England far below the type they became accustomed to in Ceylon on inflated salaries. Furthermore, the type of Britisher sent out to occupy various positions in government service was not the best of the litter.

Things got so bad, so vituperative that there was a motion to give notice to the British government that Ceylon would be functioning as an independent state. A member of the state council demanded that they no longer recognize the British government and no longer recognize the governor.

Things had come to a boil. Peculiarly, Japan today has really extended its economic sphere within which Sri Lanka is a most dependent member. Ceylon was never really asked to stand up and be counted during the Pacific War. The British left that to the Americans, and the Americans did not come to rule Asia. The Americans simply wanted to bring Japan to her knees. What Ceylon thought or did not think mattered little in the awful events that marked the onset of the nuclear age.

Only one thing really mattered. Britain had to pull out. Just as Japan's Rising Sun was humbled, the sun over the British empire also set. It was proudly claimed that this could never happen. But it did.

Asia plucked the reins from the white man's hands and kicked him off the driver's seat!

47

Of Illegal Boardings and Parading for the Police and the Fouling and Flying of Flags

The duty officer was very annoyed. 'Charges for all of you!' he bellowed, even as the decrepit bumboat pulled alongside at seven in the morning with its bunch of awful-looking sailors.

In Galle, the police, the postmaster, the Army camp Commander, the harbour master and the chauffeur of the official car provided to take Victor wherever he wished to go, were exchanging notes. The police said that three constables had been severely beaten. The manager of the Sydney simply moaned and wrung his hands. He wanted to give the Navy a bill. There were damages, he said darkly. The postmaster urged the police to count the windows of his post office. The harbour master was miffed. Maldivian seamen had rushed to complain. They had been boarded, they claimed, by pirates who had huffed at them like manatees. The CO's official driver kept saying, 'and what about me? What about me? Just minding my own business. Came and hit me and threw me in the sea.'

The Army camp Commander growled. 'Came to ask to sleep in the barracks. Who are these fellows? When the sentry said to go, said they'll fight the whole Army. Pah! Scoundrels! Pah!'

There is nothing more frustrating than being a sailor with no ship to go back to at night. The boys had spent too much time wrecking, as best they could, the Sydney Hotel. They had hoped to hire a boat. Chickera had said that there was no real harm in even stealing one and Ryan had complained for the sixteenth time, 'Why the fuck can't the *Vijaya* come in and berth instead of lying outside, I don't know!'

They had found no boats, but they did find a dark Standard Vanguard—Victor's official transport sent from Colombo to take him on his visits to town, return calls on the mayor and other dignitaries. The driver, a stoker mechanic named Bala did not like his assignment at all. He had to stay with his vehicle day and night. He had to park on the pier and be ready to chauffeur the captain and other officers who came ashore and said, 'Let's go.'

Bala had smoked his umpteenth cigarette and was dozing off when there were several rude thumps. He saw a mob of uniformed men who had no business to be ashore. He opened the door and swung a leg out.

'Hey, can we sleep in the car?'

Bala pulled his leg in, made to slam the door, but Ryan held it open, leaned and poked a beefy face inside. 'We missed the last boat,' he said.

'But you're drunk. And how to sleep inside this?'

'Buddy, we're not asking. Simply telling. We have nowhere to go. Now past eleven also.'

'But—but this is the CO's car. How to sleep inside this? Go and sleep in the town.'

Ryan hauled the man out. 'One thing,' he said chattily, 'useless asking anything from anybody these days.'

It was only a short punch. Even the sound was decidely a crisp *biff!* and Bala spun off the jetty, hit the water with a wail.

'You think he'll be alright?' Carloboy asked, 'Can't see him.'

'Better find and pull him out,' Aubrey said, 'some buggers cannot swim with shoes on.'

Daft was peering over anxiously. 'He's there alright. Can't understand a word he's saying. Have a rope or anything?'

'Where rope, men, tell him to go near those steps where the boat landing is. There, near that bollard.'

Bala made for the steps and Chickera hauled him up. The man dragged himself to the car and plopped down beside it. He was a palpitating bundle of wet clothes. 'I'll report you,' he croaked.

'Up yours,' said Hughes pleasantly and they wandered back to town.

Carloboy said, 'There's an Army camp somewhere here, no? Let's go and ask for a place to sleep.'

'Good idea,' said Arnie.

They were run out by an enraged sergeant-major. 'Out! Out! No coming inside here looking like that!'

'Like what?'

'Like you! That's what!' The man blew a whistle. Sentries marched up with rifles. 'Go away!'

The men stood at the concrete and barbed wire. 'Come out!' Ryan invited, 'You and your bloody Army! Come out!'

'Go away!'

'Just come out! We'll show you what the Navy is!'

'Go away! Otherwise will come and arrest you!'

'So come and arrest! Break your bloody heads! Come an' arrest if you can!'

After more pleasantries, they made several obscene gestures and drifted away. They had nowhere to go, and all they could think of was the port. It was, at best, a gateway to the *Vijaya*. They regarded the Maldivian sailing vessels that lay, bunched together, then, as if on signal, plunged into the water, swam the short distance to the first of the buggalows.

Pandemonium ensued as they heaved themselves on board. The Maldivian crew jabbered in Maldivian and the boys said 'Oh fuck' and there were no interpreters. Carloboy tried mime. All they wanted was to stretch themselves on deck, go to sleep. They were wet, tired and sleepy. What was more, they were no longer drunk. Oh, they were drunk, but not any more. The Maldivians did not understand. One of them actually brandished a firebrand. They had been cooking something on the fo'c'sle and skipped agilely around saying 'Shoo!' in their lingo. Others from other boats also leaped in and joined the dance.

'Oh come go,' Hughes spat. 'Buggers all look mad to me.'

Carloboy sat on the grimy deck. 'What? Swim again? For what? Just sit and wait.'

Chickera sat. So did Arnie. The Maldivians began to gibber.

'Ask them for something to drink,' Hughes said.

'How? They don't know any bloody thing we are saying.'

'So you're just going to sit and wait? Buggers might cut our throats if we fall asleep.'

The rumpus was extraordinary, and it went on even after the boys slipped back into the water and swam dejectedly to the pier. Hughes clobbered a customs guard who had no business getting in his way, and they were back in the street.

They were disturbed by a stray dog at four in the morning, having gone to beddy-bye on the pavement. Aubrey glared around. 'Let's go to the post office.'

Carloboy found some of his senses. The sky above had a sickly look. He yawned, then patted his pocket. Yes, he had letters to post. He pulled out the crumpled, wet and pulpy mass of what were three letters and looked at them. 'You think they will deliver these?'

'So first must get stamps, no?'

Aubrey said he wanted stamps too. 'Where—where's the bloody post office?'

Naturally, the post office was closed. Only a watcher dozed on the steps. He took one look at the boys and fled with a yell of alarm.

Aubrey banged at the shutters. 'Oi! Open up! I want some stamps.'

But answer there was none, and this wasn't very odd because post offices are not staffed at four in the morning. Not even in Galle. This infuriated Ryan who never liked windows. He shattered a pane with a blow. The effect pleased him. It encouraged the others to show their prowess too. Soon, they were trotting around the building smashing every window they could reach. Carloboy had angry slits in his wrist and Hughes had criss-cross cuts from knuckles to forearm. They then returned to the jetty where they found an early bum-boatman bailing his boat.

It looked flimsy, the boat, but he was a cheerful soul and assured that he could take them all if they promised to sit still and not stand up to make speeches or anything. They piled in and the man rowed with a will. He wanted twenty rupees from each, but on being pronounced mad, settled for ten.

'Place them under close arrest!' the duty officer snapped. 'Six months jail for each of you! We have had enough police already!'

Nathali was also under guard. He gave a whoop and a wave.

'What the hell did you go and do?' Carloboy asked.

'Nothing. If do nothing these buggers get so excited, how if I really go and do something?'

Nathali had decided to explore. He had taken a hired car outside the Dutch Fort and told the driver, 'Go to house that have girls.'

The driver took Nathali to Hikkaduwa, up coast, to the home of a most respected schoolmaster who had three daughters. The house was on the Baddegama road, beside the railway station. 'There have nice girls,' he had said, 'can do jiggy jiggy.'

Nathali had walked in. He had been run out. He had, it was said, assaulted a porter on the railway station platform although he hadn't the foggiest why. He had then done a John Gilpin through Hikkaduwa with half the populace at his heels, schoolmaster leading.

This race was conducted in two phases. On the second

leg, the populace was chased by Nathali and the schoolmaster was found under a coconut tree with a broken front tooth and a very tender jaw. A police jeep gave chase to the hired car Nathali had leaped into but the driver was a sport. He grinned and stood on the accelerator. They had gone off the road past the big bridge and wandered along the beach to a small wadi where they drank toddy and ate prawns and Nathali had found his way back in time for the 10 p.m. boat, sans cap, sans left shoe, his pockets full of sea sand and his trouser buttons undone. He also told the quartermaster to stuff his standing load and this, to the duty officer, was wholly unacceptable.

'So what were the girls like?' Ryan asked.

Percy shrugged. 'Now can't remember. And the Hikkaduwa police are also coming.'

'And the Galle police also,' Carloboy grumbled.

Victor listened impatiently. 'Coming to identify men? What sort of policemen do they have in these parts? How are they going to identify?'

'They got hammered, sir,' said Hughes.

'Balls! That's an occupational hazard. Policemen always get hammered!'

Charges were framed the next day. Carloboy listened to Wicks rather dazedly. Use of illegal water transport; assaulting police officers whilst in the discharge of their duties; creating a disturbance of the peace; damage to public and private property; assaulting the CO's official driver; urinating on the CO's official vehicle—

'What! Who pissed on the car? I didn't!'

'Well, somebody did!'

—illegal boarding of vessels in harbour; assault of civilians; boarding ship in a state unbecoming a seaman; battery; attempting to effect entry into Her Majesty's Army establishment; failure to salute commissioned officers of HM Service; 'and there's a huge bill for damages from the Sydney Hotel!' Wicks blared. 'Jee-sus! How can you buggers do so much in one night? Now the police are coming. Will have to hold an identification parade on the boat deck.'

Victor scowled at Carloboy. 'Now you'll go to jail and I'll have to find another secretary.' He twirled his forelock furiously. 'Wear your cap well down on your head.'

'Sir?'

'You heard, didn't you? Cap square. Clean number tens.'

'Sir, why sir?'

'For police identification, you fool. You had your cap on in the hotel?'

'No sir.'

'Then do as I say. Good God, man, sometimes I think you want to go to jail!'

The policemen and a sub-inspector who accompanied them waved their hands helplessly. They declared it was easier to identify Chinamen who all looked alike anyway. Size varied, true, but from where they were standing, a sailor was a sailor and no more or less.

'So who split your chin?' the sub-inspector fumed.

'How to tell who? Mus' be all.'

The men of the *Vijaya* stood, innocence writ large on their faces. Policemen shuffled, paused, spent painful moments thinking, shuffled on. No, they had no idea who had hit them; who had destroyed their tunics; who had deprived them of teeth, breath and dignity. Those were demons. These were lily-white sailors with caps pulled down to their eyebrows and looking as harmless as unused condoms in their shiny film wrappers.

The post office watcher had also been brought on board. He had the least to say. He reminded the police that he had run. It was the act of a wise man, he said devoutly.

When the police launch pulled away, everybody cheered. They cheered some more when they upped anchors. They cheered when they steamed into Colombo and surged ashore *en masse*.

Victor said, 'Not a bad trip. See that everything's ready for docking tomorrow at thirteen hundred.'

'Usual bottom cleaning, sir?' asked Walid.

'Yes. Will be at NHQ in the morning. We have a good

cruise ahead. Get all working parties ready. Painting, scraping, davits to be checked, stays greased, we move to Guide Pier at oh nine. Oh, and arrange for a shore telephone. We can shut down signals watch.'

'Aye aye sir.'

It was the twenty-first of November. At home, Carloboy rummaged and found his old Crucianelli piano accordion. Long time since he had played on it. With its 120 bass buttons, it was a powerful instrument. He found home agog with his father's latest venture: a shop!

'What's this?' he asked, 'Beverley Stores?'

There was the big sign over the front door. The sitting room had disappeared. There were counters and shelves and merchandise of every sort. He stared. His father sat behind a counter. Neighbours flocked in to buy all manner of things. Sonnaboy beamed.

'With my commuted pension, started this,' he said.

'But a shop? Are customers coming?'

'Everybody is coming. Whole family is coming. Even Wellawatte people are coming.'

Sonnaboy was happy. He would go to the wholesale merchants in the Pettah and come back laden with goods. He had bought a refrigerator 'to store butter' he said and he had arranged to stock sugar and flour and other oilman goods. He was as merry as a sandboy, and he also kept his arrack in the fridge 'for evening customers who also come to put a drink and chat.'

'You can go and bring a bag of sugar?' he asked.

Carloboy nodded and took the bicycle. The stores at Dutugemunu Street had never sold a sack of sugar to a man on a bicycle.

'How taking and going?' the man had asked in Sinhala.

'On the bar you put, will you.'

Sixty-five pounds of sugar were heaved onto the bicycle bar, pressed against the fork. 'Right, now receipt give.'

The man scratched his head as Carloboy rode away, one hand gripping the fold at the top of the sack, steadying it as he swept down the road by the canal.

His mother complained that Sonnaboy was giving goods to the family on credit.

'So why are you telling me?'

'So tell your father to be careful. If they don't pay he'll go to fight and unnecessary trouble for all.'

His mother was right, of course, but Carloboy shrugged. He wasn't going to start advising his father. He bathed and strolled down the garden. Angeline gave him a shy hello. What he gave her was far from shy.

He was very refreshed when he went on board to find the ship a flurry of activity. The master-at-arms was in his element. He had more work parties than he had ever dreamed of: painting parties, scrubbing gangs, chipping parties, scuttle cleaners, mast and funnel painting parties, brasswork gangs, squads to holystone the decks . . .

Carloboy was summoned to the Captain's office where Victor handed him a sheaf of reports. 'Everything must be ready before we leave,' he said. Outside, the QM was hailing for the captain's launch.

'Leave, sir?'

Victor ignored that. 'Get busy, signalman.'

'Yes sir.'

They tied up at the Guide Pier under half port engine and waited for the dock boom to be raised. Slowly, with the wheelhouse keeping 30 port to 30 starboard, they inched into the basin while divers checked the lie of the hull and the chocks. Everything needed to be perfectly aligned before the boom was lowered, the sea pumped out. Gently, the minesweeper lowered, then came to rest on the broad angled chocks that embraced her hull. The water began to lose itself and from over the side came the musty odour of stale sea and dead crustaceans. Soon, the *Vijaya* was high and dry, gangplanks slung to port. Sentries stood at the open rails. The quartermaster moved to portside and servicemen brought in cables and a telephone to the quarterdeck. Below, gangs of dockers waited to move in with their ropes and donkey platforms and big scrapers and chipping hammers.

Carloboy had little time to watch the *Vijaya* being decrusted. The hull was heavy with limpets and barnacles and so many other molluscs that had made their home there. Even goose barnacles, hanging grimly on by their stalks. They would all be scraped away and the docks would begin to smell as the creatures inside them died and rotted in the sun.

That day Carloboy put up a piece on barnacles on the notice board. The more barnacles, the slower the ship. With a clean bottom, the ship goes faster, he said, and reminded all and sundry that that went for them too. Make sure you wash your bums well, he advised, and Lieutenant Walid was not amused.

That evening Victor announced that they would not be returning to Kochchikade. The men listened eagerly. Leading Seaman Weli was sure they were going somewhere. Daft was morose. 'Must be bloody Talaimannar again,' he sniffed, 'where else to go?'

Dock cleaning took time. Also, as Victor insisted, 'I want this ship to come out of here like a new pin. Why are the foredeck guard rails not painted? See to it!'

On the third of December they were ready to leave dry docks. Lieutenant Wicks introduced the signalmen to a new arrival, Yeoman Rana, who had been drafted from the *Gemunu*. He told Carloboy, 'von Bloss, hoist the ensign on the starboard yardarm and stand by the flagdeck.'

They watched the boom rise, the sea swirl in. Carloboy was careless. He did not check the butterfly clips when he transferred the ensign. The flag rose, and even as he cleared the halyard he felt the line go slack. The flag, free of one clip dashed against the halyard and fouled. The breeze whipped it around the yardarm guys and an end of rope hung, beating back and forth with the weight of the clip.

'Von Bloss, you bloody idiot! What have you done? Clear that flag!'

The *Vijaya* was ready to move. On either side of the dock, men were slipping lines, the boys at the sides tending the big fenders. The engine room stood on orders. Outside the dock, the tug *Samson* awaited. She would give the necessary nudge and help in 360 degree swing as the *Vijaya* came out stern first.

Carloboy jiggled the halyard desperately. The flag was too enwrapped to be jerked free and the end of rope and clip were beating at the stays. From the boiler came a whiff of white smoke.

'It won't give, sir.'

'Well get up there and clear it. Hurry up! We have way on!'

There was no other choice. Swarming up the Jacob's ladder, Carloboy reached the struts of the yardarm. He knew the frill. Twenty-six feet to the yardarm, eight feet more to the crow's nest, six feet higher to masthead. Well, he wasn't going all the way. He had hoped to hold on to the cross stays, walk the yardarm, free the flag and pop the clip back, male to female. That was the way to do it. But the stays had been newly greased. He checked.

'What's wrong?' Wicks yelled.

'Grease,' Carloboy shouted. 'Can't hold onto anything. I'm going on the yardarm.'

'Be careful.' Wicks called to Daft for a rope net which was strung over the flagdeck.

Carloboy inched his way along the yardarm on his belly. The halyard had twisted round the flag. He reached down for the loose rope end. From the stays and brace wires, grease had dripped on the end of the spar. His hands slipped even as he strived to bring the clips together, the male into the female. He was sweating and his knees began to tremble. With the clips mated, he was able to ease the halyard. The wind made the trapped ensign balloon, struggle to be free and it cracked like cardboard in his face. He kept nudging the halyard while below, Daft eased one end of the rope to give slack. Soon the ropes moved easily on the runner. The flag was free.

'Secure,' Wicks said.

Carloboy began to bellycrawl backwards until his feet touched the main. Slowly easing himself upwards, he reached for the stay. Grease or no grease, he had to cling to it to get to the wire ladder, and then, with a deep exhalation of relief, he was on the Jacob coming down. The sweat stung his eyes. His hands suddenly refused to function. They were daubed with grease. He slipped, tried to cling on but found no hold. He was twenty feet over the deck when he fell.

48

Operation Downfall—the Olympic and the Coronet

The Americans wanted, above all, to break the will of the Japanese. General MacArthur looked eagerly to this downfall. He planned and shaped it, poured every ounce of his tactical expertise into it. In fact, there could only be one code name for an exercise that would be mounted for the large-scale invasion of Japan—Operation Downfall.

For the Americans, the very planning of such a massive amphibious operation was sweet revenge. They had come to hate the Japanese fiercely. They also knew Japan would never surrender. It had to be a fight to the death. Downfall was a good name for so massive an onslaught. It must hit hard and the death blow must follow. Downfall and Destruction, Disaster and Death.

All this was long before the atom bomb. The first fierce face of Downfall would be Operation Olympic. It would be launched under the joint command of MacArthur and Admiral Chester Nimitz. It would involve 650,000 troops, 2,500 ships and 5,000 planes. The troops would constitute 13 divisions of the US sixth Army. The assault would open three fronts on the southern coast of Kyushu island and from here, the US would push northwards to seize a third of the island, forming a line from Sendai in the west to Tsuno in the east. The operation was scheduled for November 1, 1945. It would be X Day.

The attack would be supported by an air and naval blitz, with Nimitz storming in east of Kyushu to what was called Town Car Beach. The veterans of Iwo Jima, the fifth marine amphibian corps would concentrate on Taxicab Beach on the west coast. It was surely slated to be the largest amphibian effort of the war and its sole purpose was to force Japan to cave in.

As a plan, it was worked out to frightening precision, Kyushu held Japanese infantry divisions almost equal in number to Tokyo. The Japanese sixteenth area Army was based at Fukuoka with four divisions. Nagasaki had a single division. Four divisions surrounded Sendai and the western littoral. Five divisions were spread across the east coast at Tsuno and the Bungo Strait. There were no armoured divisions, and the Japanese knew that the taking of Kyushu, even the southern sector, would put the Americans too close to the Japanese Army headquarters at Hiroshima.

The Americans sectored the beaches of the southern part of Kyushu with specific assault orders for each. Town Car Beach was the eastern stretch from Tsuno to a point over Kanoya Bay. The sharp-toed boot of land below the bay was Station Wagon Beach; the big inlet with Kagoshima on its west bank was Convertible Beach and the other southern head was Limousine Beach. Roadster Beach would lead to the assault on Kushikino, while Taxicab Beach would give access to Sendai, looking out on the East China Sea. Delivery Wagon Beach was the toughest, being at the top of the big Kagoshima inlet where two Japanese divisions were known to be.

The US leaders knew that they would be sacrificing many, but they also knew that the American public was war-weary and demanding an end to it all. They wouldn't mind a final thrust, wouldn't really mind the loss of life, provided the agony wasn't prolonged. The harsher realities had to be faced. There would be a fierce engagement, no doubt about that. The Japanese would defend fanatically. At best, Operation Olympic would take ninety days and casualties would be high. Washington was told to expect up to 20,000 dead and 75,000 wounded.

And that was one end of the Japanese islands. What about Honshu where Tokyo was, and what about Shikoku where the Japanese Army headquarters at Hiroshima was? This would be the second face of Downfall—Operation Coronet. A drive towards Tokyo.

Washington was still not satisfied. Victory had to be assured. Japan had to surrender. Professor J.R. Skates, in a book on Operation Downfall said that even poison gas was considered a necessary weapon. It had to be the final death blow.

Meticulously planned, Operation Olympic would see the US first corps under Major-General Swift and comprising three infantry divisions, storm Town Car Beach, driving inland into Tsuno, Miyakonojo and Kobayashi. The US eleventh corps with two infantry divisions and an armoured division would enter through Station Wagon Beach, run down the end of Kagoshima inlet, take Kanoya and establish a support line for the blitz on Delivery Wagon Beach. They would also link with the First Corps at Miyakonojo to secure the line from Tsuno to Sendai.

The fortieth infantry division would fan out between Sendai, Kushikino and lend beach support at Taxicab, Roadster, Convertible and Limousine, moving in four waves. Three marine divisions under Major-General Schmidt, comprising the fifth amphibian corps would hit Roadster and Limousine, driving to Delivery Wagon. The infantry would mop up on the island of Tanegashima and the smaller islands off Sendai.

But the second stage of Downfall was also considered necessary in case Japan stubbornly fought on. This second phase—Operation Coronet—was to be the knockout blow. Honshu's Kanto Plain would be the main target, a 120-mile stretch of Japan's industrial heartland with Tokyo in its clasp. This blow, it was certain, would bring Japan to her knees.

Operation Coronet was scheduled for March 1, 1946. Three marine and three infantry divisions of the US First Army would advance on Tokyo. They would be under the command of General Hodges. Also, the US Eighth Army under General Eichelberger would unleash six infantry and two armoured divisions to sweep up from the south-east. Target: the Japanese Twelfth Area Army. Fierce fighting, much loss of life was expected. It would be, Washington said, a much larger operation than Olympic.

Such a lot of planning—and all to appease a war-weary, disgruntled American public. And then, Harry Truman succeeded President Franklin Roosevelt and learnt with some consternation that there was a Manhattan Project and that he had to decide.

He had to give the order . . . to drop the atom bomb! There would be no need for Operation Downfall. There would be no need to sacrifice so many American lives. One man and a bomb could end it all.

49

Of Another Kind of Flag and a Murderous Cook and Rowdy Nights in the Lap of the Buddha

Carloboy fell twenty feet. Not much. Also, he had the sense to throw himself outwards even as he lost foot- and hand-hold, and he fell on the back of his shoulders, missing the deck mount by inches. As shipwright Silva swore, he actually bounced.

Silva had only the one cry for such ungodly situations. Sailors falling out of the sky were not everyday occurrences. 'Man overboard!' he yelled, and pointed at the hatchway leading to the sick bay. 'There! There!' At least he knew where to point, for Carloboy had bounced off the deck boards and rolled down the gangway, coming to rest at the sick bay door.

Wicks rushed down from the flagdeck. 'Did he fall in the sea? Where? Where?'

Silva stared wildly around. A man had dropped out of the blue, bounced at his feet, then bundled into a ball, had rolled below deck. 'There!' he said, a shaking finger pointing to the dark throat of the stairs.

'Bloody fool! He went below? That's overboard?'

'Anything like that is overboard,' Silva maintained, recovering quickly. Nothing like being called a bloody fool to pull a man together.

Victor yelled from the bridge: 'What's going on? Where's von Bloss? Throw out a lifebelt.'

'He's here, sir. Somewhere.'

'Well find him. And stand by with berthing crews. Get a signalman up here.' 'Yes sir.'

The sick bay attendant popped up. 'What happened? Found von Bloss outside the door.'

'Where is he?'

'In the sick bay. Big swelling round the back of the neck. Will have to X-ray.'

'How's he feeling?'

'Don' know. Almost unconscious when I pulled him in.'

Victor signalled *Gemunu* for a surgeon lieutenant.

'Send sick man to base hospital,' came the crisp reply.

Victor swore. He didn't like it one bit.

They tied up alongside the Queen Elizabeth Quay where a special pavilion had been erected and decorated with tender coconut fronds. Navy vehicles crowded the jetty and all sort of bumptious types with two and three bars swaggered around. There were trails of bunting and flags and railed enclosures.

'How are you?' the SBA asked Carloboy.

'OK I think. What the hell happened?'

'You fell from the mast. Can you walk? Feeling giddy or anything? Head is hurting?'

Carloboy stood up. 'Back of my neck. Hell of a pain.' He moved his shoulders back, hunched them gingerly, 'Mmmff! Shoulders also.'

'You're lucky. No bones broken but have contusions. Try to walk slowly. Any spine pain? Can you climb the steps? Must take you to hospital.'

The fresher air of the upper deck cleared his head which was throbbing dully. Carloboy looked around. Guard rails on the port side had been removed, the canvas stripped. He noted the almost festive air on the quay and all around him. 'What's going on?'

'You don't know? We're going to Burma.'

He was still too dazed to take it all in. At the *Gemunu* sick bay doctors shone lights in his eyes, prodded his back, made him raise his arms, cross them, walk, bend, try to touch his toes. 'You're OK,' said Leading SBA Senavi, 'God knows why. Should have broken your spine. Here, take these pills and drink this. Light duty for a week. If you feel any giddiness or get even a headache, you report to the sick bay.'

On board, Sims was worried. 'Bad sign,' he told the back of Hugo's neck, 'even before we sail accidents are happening.'

'Push harder, men,' Hugo said, 'aaah, that's better.'

Victor did not show that he was pleased. 'So you are alright? What is this? Light duty? In the Bay of Bengal with a north-east monsoon? Oh, very well. No morning muster. Report to the bridge.'

It was all a part of the Buddha Jayanti celebrations, signalling two thousand years of Buddhism. The government had decided that the Navy should also do its bit. The nearest Buddhist country was Burma, and to Burma would the *Vijaya* go, bearing gifts. Not just the Navy, but the Army and the Air Force as well. Marching snappily came a contingent of the Ceylon Army under Colonel Sepala. Also, an equally smart cohort of fly boys of the Ceylon Air Force. Two journalists of the local press were also on board.

Carloboy stood at the guard rails, looking down on the quay where a large number of Buddhist monks had assembled. There were gung-ho military and naval types. There were citizens of many stripes. Some waltzed around as much as to say, 'See how important I am', while others wore that cosmetic confidence that said, 'I am also here,' and sidled this way and that to get into the frames of the cameras. Far east, the north-east monsoon was howling its head off in the Bay of Bengal and forty-foot waves were the order of the day. It was a greyish morning with a bad weather smell and a whippy wind that seemed to threaten, 'Just you come out of harbour and see what I'll do.'

Sri Lanka's only warship was ready to make its first voyage to Burma. Victor addressed the crew and quite fiercely too, saying that they were henceforth ambassadors of their country and would behave themselves as such. A pugnacious little squirt of a man, Cook Steward James, was drafted on board. He went berserk somewhere between the Andamans and the Nicobars and had to be locked up in the shipwright's stores.

Behind the wardroom curtain, Sims was washing a blob of shit off his penis. 'If you're gong to do this I won't come again,' he grumbled. Hugo said he was sorry.

Yeoman of Signals Rana trotted between boat deck and signals deck in shiny white. He was quite taken up with the whole ceremony. He was also an ardent Buddhist and knew how to swear in Sanskrit.

'We are taking a statue to Burma,' he said with great awe.

'A statue?'

'Yes. Lord Buddha. A gift to the people of Burma.'

So that's why the port side guard rails had been removed.

On the quay, oil lamps were lit and the covey of monks began a sonorous chant. On deck, the men of the *Vijaya* adopted demeanours of rapt attention. They, the sea, the captain, the ship, even the barnacles no longer on their bottom, were subject to a carpet blessing of sorts. A crane trundled up on parallel rails and readied itself to swing on board a most important passenger. Lord Buddha himself. Bronze, heavy, lotus-positioned.

Nineteen fifty-four was special. It was the year to knit some good wool between neighbouring Buddhist lands. The Ministry of Culture and the Ministry of Foreign Affairs came up with the idea. Carry across the Indian Ocean a special gift to the people of Burma. Let's make it big. After all, we are a small country.

The statue was, indeed, huge, must have weighed a ton. The heavy bronze was swung aboard amid rising chants of praise from the quay. Over the deck . . . between the lifeboat davits . . . Victor supervised the soft, precise landing. The statue was steadied, then carefully lowered, inch by inch to the deck, slap against the vegetable locker which was the only large structure in sight. It looked secure enough.

Able Seaman Jackson creased his brow. 'So where do we show the films?' he asked.

A chief petty officer sniffed. 'No films on this trip.'

'Why?'

'Why, can't you see the locker can't be used?'

Painfully true. The canvas screen used to be slung on the locker. Now the statue was in the way.

'So no films?'

'How many times have I to tell you, you idiot!'

Exit Jackson, swearing foully.

No one knew that the devout Yeoman of signals had brought a Buddhist flag on board. He had tucked it into the flag locker and breathlessly bided his time. No sooner had the statue touched down than the harbour sucked back in wonderment. From the flag deck, rising on the main mast halyard, tautening on its butterfly clips, was a strange flag. A flag that no naval or international signal book had any answer for.

Oh, everyone's proud of a flag. Hoist the colours and it does something to one. It gives one a sort of lift; puts one's soul on an escalator, makes one's mind swell. In Sri Lanka, many flags are honoured. Colours, too, are of significance and of all the flags, nothing is more striking than the Buddhist flag with its many stripes and patches of colour. All these colours must mean something, but when this flag was jacked up on the main mast of the *Vijaya* the skipper of *HMCS Okapi*, a Royal Canadian destroyer, blinked and blinked again. True, he was in the exotic east where strange things usually happen, but never had he seen such a peculiar signal.

Yeoman Rana was well pleased. He had honoured the arrival of the statue of the Buddha. The flag slapped cheerfully in the morning wind.

From its berth, the *Okapi* sprang to action. A ten-inch visual signalling lantern was turned on the *Vijaya's* bridge and began to flash its concern. 'What is the trouble? We are ready to slip moorings and come alongside. Do you need assistance?'

Victor tore at the forelock he liked to twirl with his finger. The Yeoman blanched as the skipper's roar knifed the air. Without waiting for more he ducked out of sight, then bent in two, crept down the gangway.

'Von Bloss! What the fuck is that!'

'Sir, what sir?'

'That, you fool! Up there! What's that flag up there? Who hoisted that? *Get it down at once!* Is this a fucking warship or what? Who hoisted that? *Who?* I want to know who? And here—come here! I haven't finished. *Where the fuck are you going?'*

To take the flag down, sir.'

'Signal the *Okapi* and say no trouble.'

'Yes sir.'

'Pull that flag down!'

'Yes sir.'

'So go!'

Carloboy went. Of Rana there was no sign. But he didn't get into any really hot water. It was dismissed as a serious bout of Buddhistic fervour.

Despite the assuring signal, the *Okapi* had put out a boat and a Lieutenant and a leading seaman came abroad, quite anxious. They were also most intrigued.

'So what is that flag?' the hookie asked.

Carloboy explained.

'Never saw one like that before.'

Few naval vessels in the world have. Navy signals are mysterious. Anything that cannot be read, identified or interpreted is considered a distress signal. This includes any flag hoisted upside down or the raising of a bucket and a blanket or, as in this case, a totally unidentifiable flag.

Rana was unrepentant. He declared it his Buddhist duty to signal to the world the importance of this Buddhist cruise. 'This is a religious mission,' he said grandly.

'And this is the Navy,' Carloboy said.

'You wait and see,' said Rana darkly, 'we will have trouble on this trip.'

The *Vijaya* was grossly overcrowded. The wardroom with its additional Army and Air Force officers was ready to burst and the mess system was shaken out and stood on its ear. The seamen's mess was turned over to the Air Force and communication mess to the Army. This latter was a grave mistake. The mess, slap against the bows, was the worst place to be in if one were a landlubber. It's the bows that take the pitch and toss. The Army, let it be said, groaned and vomited and wept and those who could talk declared that they were dead.

The seamen's mess had its own comforts. The Air Force men were convinced they would never see Burma.

The men of the *Vijaya* decided to spread canvas on the boatdeck but wet weather put paid to that and there was a rush for the galley tables.

The *Vijaya* sailed past the pilot station proudly enough, then took the first big sea like an overfed duck. They were in for a terrific beating. The December gales had their own mixer-blender operation going, whipping the sea into a rare tizzy. The *Vijaya* also had this disconcerting habit of poking her nose under like an inquisitive puppy. The sea would swirl over her breakwater and dash angrily on the holystoned decks. Then, well satisfied that all aboard were convinced that she wasn't coming up, she would do just that, rising clean out of the water like a grey ghost, sending thousands of tons of Indian Ocean to sweep clean her boat deck, wash the feet of the Buddha and gurgle down to the quarter deck. Guy ropes had to be slung. The lines holding the statue creaked alarmingly and the mast shook as the ship tried for a ten-knot average in the face of forty-foot waves that kept rising up and acting like wayward battering rams.

The Army died several times. Face and uniforms were of the same khaki hue. Carloboy took to going on duty with a bucket. Even the duty officer of the watch vomited. And then, in a fury that could only be attributed to the foul weather, Cook-steward James wrenched off the head of a brass tap in the galley and with it, split Percy Nathali's head. He had no real reason. There was the tap, there was Nathali. It seemed like a good thing to do.

Yeoman Rana muttered a Buddhist prayer and rocked on his heels. 'Nothing but trouble; you wait and see.'

With James locked in the shipwright's store and declaring his determination to fuck everyone's mother no matter how old she be, Victor was told that the man had to be insane.

'Good. A mad cook is just what we need. Hold that course! Zero one seven it is. Where the hell do you think you're going?'

And then the sea seemed to whoop and hurl the ship any which way with much malice and on the boat deck, Able Seaman Rodney, making slow progress with decks awash, heard a crack and a thud and saw Lord Buddha advance on him, he later swore, at fifty miles per hour. The statue had snapped its ropes. The pitch of the ship hurled it across the boat deck.

Rodney screamed, let off the guy rope, slipped and was flipped towards the guard rails. He hung on, and inches from his shoulder the huge bronze slammed the rails like a runaway train. It took three men to pull Rodney to safety and up to fifty swearing sea drenched men with winches and ropes and blocks and pulleys to secure the statue first, using the mushroom ventilators to take the strain.

The guard rails had cracked outwards and it was a period of savage desperation, fighting every sickening lurch and toss, keeping the statue from plunging into the sea. Forty searing minutes, and then, satisfied that the guard rails would not collapse, the frenzied haul-in began. Every man was rushed to the deck and the waves rushed in to welcome them. Muscles bulged, neck veins swelled as the bronze was manually dragged back and lashed down. A Buddha in chains. It looked on the men, the fury of the sea with softly smiling eyes and a look of great tenderness. The only island of serenity in a millrace of grunting, griping men who blasted the black air with their oaths.

And then, as if acknowledging that it had done its worst, the sea settled. Victor clamped his cap on his head, inspected the damage on the boat deck. The statue seemed none the worse. 'Will it hold?' he asked.

Walid nodded. 'Some slight scratching, but it's OK.'

'Good. There'll be better weather now. We are off the Andamans. I'm going to take a nap.'

The Nicobars lay like bright jewels in the morning light and the sea was an incredible blue turning green and cream. Nathali, with a bandage round his head, emerged asking after James and expressing a wish to do murder. He was persuaded that there were, after all, more days than years and that James was crazy and had taken to throwing his food into the big barrel of nails. The ship, too, settled. Even the Army emerged and began to muster on deck and show some interest in the things of the living. Carloboy found that he could handle his accordion. His shoulders and back had completely healed. With no films, evenings were spent merrily enough on the boat deck. The familiar sea shanties ripened the air, and as for comfortable playing, the statue was an ideal support.

Yeoman Rana panted up to the bridge. 'Playing and singing all the filth in the world,' he said brokenly. 'And the Army and Air Force men also listening. Disgrace, sir, disgrace, that's what it is.'

Walid calmed the man down. 'So they're singing. What's the matter with you, Yeoman, don't you like singing?'

'But sir, round the Buddha, no?'

'So? Where else can they be? No harm in a little singing, Yeoman.'

'But sir, that von Bloss is too much. With that music thing . . . sitting on the statue, sir. Not good to do like that.'

Walid sighed. 'Yeoman, when that statue almost went into the sea these men hauled it to safety. Don't come to me with your head full of shit, do you hear? I didn't see you doing anything that night.'

'I-I was also there, sir.'

'Bullshit! Can you hear them? Muslims, Sinhalese, Hindus, Burghers, Malays—all nearly killed themselves dragging the statue. Did Yusuf say I'm a Muslim I won't pull? You are becoming a bloody pain in the arse! Keep your bloody beliefs to yourself. Hoisting Buddhist flags! Should have court-martialled you! Where is von Bloss sitting? On the statue—what do you mean on the statue? Is he sitting on the shoulders?'

'Sitting in the lap, sir,' Rana muttered.

'And what is the statue doing?'

'Sir?'

'What is the statue doing?'

Rana gulped. 'N-nothing, sir.'

'Then fuck off! If the statue doesn't like it, it will tell von Bloss to get off!'

'Y-yes sir.'

'Don't want to hear another word out of you, do you hear?'

'Yes sir.'

On the ninth of December they picked up the pilot at the mouth of the Rangoon River and dropped anchor six miles out of Rangoon. At 0715 on the tenth they tied up to a pontoon in Rangoon harbour.

The voyage was over.

50

History—The Testing of 'Little Boy'

'My God,' wrote Lieutenant Colonel Paul Tibbets in his journal, 'What have we done?'

This may be a question still asked, still not fully answered fifty years later. It is a question of morality, of politics, of America's domestic and geostrategic policy, of anxiety, of haste, of an utter weariness of war. All these could have been part of the answer: why America chose to drop that first atom bomb on Hiroshima in the summer of 1945?

There is much uncertainty and regret today and many Americans seem to think it was a wrong act, even a totally unnecessary act. An act of sheer mass murder even. Japan, they still argue, was collapsing anyway. In ten days in March 1945, General Curtis LeMay had led the 20th Air Force to methodically destroy the major cities of Japan with concerted firebombing raids. There had been 11,600 sorties by B-29s that had erased 32 square miles of Japan's four largest cities. Over 150,000 people had been killed. On May 25, 1945, an air raid on Tokyo had raised a firestorm so fierce that bomber crews later said how they had smelt burning humans from over a thousand feet up.

There had always been this thing about bombing civilian centres, but the Allies no more had such scruples. Not after Hitler's blitz on London. There had to be retaliation. Thus came the day and night raids against Germany, the terrible firestorm of Essen and the huge loss of civilian life. In its issue of March 19, 1945, *Newsweek* proclaimed that LeMay's firebombing of Tokyo had made about one million persons homeless.

Still, the Japanese made no indication of surrender. At best, they were looking for a negotiated settlement. They had to save face. It was what they were best at doing. Indeed, upon learning of the US plans for Operation Downfall, the Japanese marshalled 540,000 men to defend Kyushu and made provision to send out 5,000 kamikaze planes against the gathering US forces. They were determined to force Washington to accept a negotiated settlement.

But the Americans would not play. They knew that Japan would not bow. There had been fights to the death in Okinawa and Iwo Jima. No, there would be no 'terms of surrender'. Unconditional surrender was what the US demanded.

Oh, the Americans knew that Japan was collapsing. They had set up a code-breaking operation which was known as 'Magic'. This Magic told US intelligence that Japan had begun to put out peace feelers through her ambassador in Russia. One cable intercepted by Magic told of the Japanese Emperor's desire to see a swift end to the war. All Hirohito wanted was to be allowed to keep his throne. He, too, simply had to save face.

So why the bomb? This is what some historians demand to know. If Japan was crying out for peace, was not there the opportunity to end the war without the bomb? Let Operation Downfall be the *coup de grace*. People even made strategic surveys. Japan was bleeding. She would have doubtless surrendered by November.

Looking for reasons, it has even been said that the dropping of the atomic bombs was not really done to finish off Japan but to put the wind up on Russia. Others say that it was all a test and nothing more. Even the scientists were not really sure what they were producing. President Truman hadn't a clue either. General Leslie Groves was the man in charge of the Manhattan Project. They called him the Atom General. He had 200,000 people working on 'Little Boy'—a 20-kiloton atom bomb—in 37 secret plants and laboratories, and he, too, was worried. What if he was producing a dud?

Also, other officers were sceptical. Even the White House Chief of Staff, Admiral William Leahy had opined that Groves' 'damn thing' would never work! Groves couldn't abide this negativity. He had spent over two billion dollars of State funds and consoled himself that the atom scientists were at least confident that there would be a big bang.

But how big a bang? All the military planners expressed their reservations. Also, what would be the target? With LeMay pounding and wrecking Japanese cities, Groves considered Hiroshima. The boffins were enthusiastic. Hiroshima was a city of 280,000 people. It was surrounded by hills. Situated as though in a basin. The bomb would be better concentrated, produce a focussing effect and much blast damage.

Then Groves switched to Kyoto. He seemed to like the idea of wiping out that ancient capital. Kyoto, with its many Buddhist and Shinto shrines, was an intellectual centre.

It would make the thinkers of Japan appreciate the significance of the attack. He had one problem—Secretary of War Henry Stimson, who abhorred the way the war was going.

Stimson was wholly ethical. He believed that civilized man must make civilized war. He hated LeMay's firebomb tactics and now here was Groves with some sort of diabolical weapon no one had a clue about.

He summoned Groves. 'What is the target list for this A-bomb?' he asked.

Groves did not like this at all, but Stimson insisted. 'Kyoto,' he said.

'No! Not Kyoto. How would you like it if Japan destroyed the Lincoln Memorial?'

Groves fell back on Hiroshima.

Stimson had his reservations. In his diary, he would refer to the A-bomb as 'Frankenstein', and also called it 'the thing', and peppered his entries with phrases such as 'the dreadful', 'the dire', 'the awful', 'the diabolical', and 'the terrible'.

All the while, America was mustering over one million men from the Pacific and Europe for Operation Downfall. To meet it, Japan was drafting suicide bombers who would wear belts of high explosive and hurl themselves at US tanks. Even Japanese schoolgirls were issued with chisels and awls. Their teachers told them how they should stab American soldiers in the abdomen.

Stimson was old and weary. He felt like an old, gentle-minded dog among a pack of vicious pit bulls. He advised Truman to use the carrot-and-stick. 'Let the Japanese keep their Emperor. And tell them that if they don't surrender, we will use a terrible new weapon which can wipe out whole cities in a single blow.'

The pit bulls would have none of it. Why warn the Japanese of any such attack? Wasn't the A-bomb top secret? And what if this A-bomb did not work?

Stimson was stubborn in his views. On July 2, 1945, he wrote to Truman, urging that the Japanese be given timely warning. 'Japan,' he wrote, 'is not a nation composed wholly of mad fanatics.'

But Stimson's critics would not be budged. What of Pearl Harbour, they asked, and what of the Bataan death march? And what of the tortures? They called Stimson's attention to a newspaper photograph which showed a Japanese soldier about to behead an Allied P-O-W with his sword.

Truman weighed the matter carefully. He had come to dislike Stalin very much at the meeting of the Big Three at Potsdam. Stalin had not minced his words about his postwar ambitions in Eastern Europe. It would not be long, Truman knew, before this particular ally would turn enemy. Russia would be more 'manageable' if it knew that America had the A-bomb and was ready to use it.

Also, it seemed that trying to make peace with Japan was like flogging a dead horse. Japan did not want to deal, he was sure, despite the feelers intercepted by Magic. In fact, the Japanese War Minister, General Anami was actually advocating national suicide rather than surrender.

Again, Truman was convinced that the A-bomb would actually save lives. There would be no need to keep up the murderous firebombing of Japanese cities and there would be no need to sacrifice as many as 20,000 American lives in Operation Downfall. But there was one snag. Would the A-bomb work? How confident could one be, how brash, if one did not know what this much-vaunted bomb could do?

The scientists were ready. The test would be conducted in the New Mexico desert. But they were still hazy about the bomb's yield. Some thought it would incinerate New Mexico, others that it would ignite the very atmosphere. Others were more pessimistic. One man had even written a ditty which was painfully true of their doubts and notions of failure:

> From this crude lab that spawned a dud,
> Their necks to Truman's axe uncurled,
> Lo, the embattled savants stood,
> And fired the flop heard round the world.

July 16, 1945. When the bomb exploded at zero hour, it filled the sky and sent a column of green, blue and red fire 10,000 feet up, to billow like a huge umbrella. Shock waves broke windows 125 miles away. Groves said it was like several suns at midday. The yield had been up to 20,000 tons of TNT.

So they had it! The most terrible bomb in the history of the world, as Truman noted in his diary. Now he was the most powerful man among the Big Three. Even Churchill noted that Truman became bossy and was filled with a new confidence. Stalin received the news coldly. He had to stay in the race. He secretly ordered his people to press hard on the Soviet Union's own A-bomb project.

There was little else left to do. On July 31, Truman gave the fateful order. On any day after August 2, weather permitting, the A-bomb must be dropped over Hiroshima. Let military objectives and soldiers and sailors be the target. Not women and children.

Which shows how much he really knew about the awesome power he was about to unleash.

51

Of Sandalwood Paste and a Convent Bolt Hole and Going Home for Christmas

'What's so interesting about Rangoon?' Aubrey demanded. The men were being 'organized'. There would be specially arranged sight-seeing trips, a programme cordially offered by some cultural affairs something or another with slim, slightly-built guides who looked like well-sucked mango seeds.

Ergo, the boys were not happy. They were taken to visit the Schwe Dagon, the Golden Pagoda, which was very big, very airy and very Buddhistic in tone and flavour. They were told in very hissy tones of the tremendous war damage compounded by Communist uprisings that had left the city looking like a well-punched paper bag. They were told not to wander into the narrow side streets and to stay on the main thoroughfares where there were people. Elsewhere, there were vile men in sarongs who cut throats for the price of a cheroot. They were told to visit the Merchant Club and stay clear of the Green Café and not roost at any roadside dive.

The boys listened and changed their money to kyats and bahts. Poor rate of exchange, too, but what the hell, a man and his bahts are soon parted.

The Ceylon ambassador to Burma insisted that the Ceylon Navy entertain and be entertained, and that turned out to be an altogether nice evening where a little stage was erected in a corner of the embassy garden and on which Leading Telegraphist Gibbs sang, and so did Telegraphist Roberts and others who were tone deaf, making several ladies blanch and complain of benumbed teeth.

Amazing, Victor thought. Sailors were not worth their salt when chaperoned ashore and made to feel in advance the weight of sins they couldn't commit. Also, he thought of the voyage home and knew that a lot of pent-up feeling would doubtless explode. As it was, Nathali had been overheard telling an indignant Hugo that he hadn't come all the way to Rangoon (and with a broken head, too) to go on Sunday school picnics. 'So we sail back in two days, no? So I'll just stay on board and get drunk. Or I'll go to the pontoon and wave my cock at the girls on the road. I'm not going anywhere else!'

Yes, all things considered, it would do the men good to be let out on their own. This wasn't Galle. They had to consider that they were strangers in a foreign land. So it was that Carloboy and Aubrey fared forth to see how quickly they could get into trouble.

'The Green Café. That's where there are all Burmese waitresses,' Aubrey said, 'Never fucked a Burmese girl. Shall we go there?'

They had found the Merchant Club vastly uninteresting, but the Green Café had its charms. There was this door, and beyond it a flight of steps leading to the upper floor and there, in a long row of rooms were the youngest looking whores they had ever encountered. They clasped their hands in greeting and said in piping, flute-like voices that they liked foreign sailors. Satin-skinned and narrow waisted, small in stature and delicate of movement, they looked like fragile porcelain figures. Even as the girl stripped, Carloboy, his penis rearing uncontrollably, wondered at her seemingly youthful innocence. She knelt at his feet and held a bowl of jasmine water in her hands. With a soft tissue, she sponged his cock and ran long-nailed fingers along it. 'You like I suck,' she said.

Her lips closed around the head and he felt her tongue dart, curl around the glans while her cheeks narrowed, then enlarged as she drew on it. He ran his hands down her head, to the nape of her neck and along her shoulders. She held the root of his penis and her head began to move down, engorging it. He took her by the sides of her cheeks, raised her face to his.

'Is very big,' she said.

He clasped her around the waist, drew her to the bed.

'You wanted to go soon, soon?' she asked.

'No. Why?'

'You don't like to play. I thinking you in hurry.'

'No hurry. Why do you say that?'

'All come and go like this. Inside outside finished. You like me I think.'

'Of course I do. But when you are like that what can I do?'

'So I am pleasing you I think.'

'Of course you do,' and he spread her legs, traced a finger on the mount of her small cunt. He smiled, 'You know what some buggers said on the ship?'

'Please. Fast you are talking, what is buggers?'

'It's not a nice word. Men on my ship. They are saying mad things.' His finger worked under her clitoris. It was small and very red. 'They said Chinese girls have cunts the other way. And Burmese and Korean girls also. Like mouths.'

She smiled uncertainly. 'Still you say fast talk. I not understand.'

'Never mind.' He found her hole moist. At the juncture of her thighs there were lines of powder. She had hardly any bush, just a slight shadow of down. He was tumescent, dripping a long line on the sheet. Gently he placed his cock in her. She raised her slim legs onto his shoulders. He lay over her unmoving, told her to lower her legs.

'Now what can you play,' he asked softly and repeated the question slowly. 'Can you play with me now?' He rested on an elbow, squeezed her small breasts.

'How I am thinking to play, but how I can?'

'So suck it now.'

'To suck? How I can do that like this?' Her lips glistened with his tumescence.

'Try. Suck it with your cunt. Make it tight.'

She smiled. 'Ah, you are not hurry, no?'

Overhead the fan whirred. She began to contract her vagina, found it easier to do so when she slipped her hand down between his stomach and hers, massaged herself. The feeling was slow, delicious.

'You like it,' she murmured, 'I also like. Everytime this I do after gentlemans go. Hurry hurry for them. You I like. You also like?'

Carloboy began to move. Very gently. He pushed in, pressing her fingers, against her cunt, then withdrew very slowly, almost to the entrance, then plunged in again. She made a soft sound and her tongue washed her lips. A ballet of slow motion. And all the while her fingers moved between the hairs of his bush, round the head of her clitoris until suddenly, she jerked her hand away, put her arms round him, pressed them into his buttocks. He knew she was ready to explode. With a savage thrust he began to quicken, moving in, barely withdrawing but grinding into her, feeling her pelvis hard against him, the softness of her mount crushing into him. She lay, eyes turned up, panting, her fingers tight, pressing, pressing and even as he spent himself, she gave a sharp cry and he felt her labia grip him, felt her tighten, slacken, tighten convulsively. Her hips jerked as though with a life of their own and her hands came up to hold him tight, embrace him, force his whole self into her.

'From you no pay to me,' she whispered in a voice husky with spent passion, 'You stay more time, I thinking you stay long long.'

Carloboy couldn't. He couldn't imagine what Aubrey was doing either. He simply lay over her until her breathing eased.

'You like? I like very much. You want going?'

He shook his head. 'I like to stay. But I cannot.'

Her eyes were soft, doe-like. 'Nothing you pay then. More than ten baht you give me. Here, you move and I give money. You come again? Don't want you pay. You come?'

He moved off her, flopped on his back, watched her rise, go to a little curtained niche. 'I clean you nice nice,' she said, sponging him gently and with much tenderness. Dipping her fingers into a smooth cream salve, she began to work it into his skin, all along his shaft, on his upper thighs, the pit of his abdomen.

'What is that?' he asked.

'Is sandalwood. Make you nice nice. You like?'

'Mmmm.'

She took scented powder, pinches of it between her fingers, rubbed it in. She bent her head, kissed his glans. 'Good man you are. You come again, no?'

Carloboy stroked her cheek. Of course, he wouldn't come back. They sailed tomorrow. Maybe he would never come back. And she was so lovely, so, so desirable. But she was a whore, and this was her whore's business. She rose to place the notes he had given her in his hand. He shook his head. Somehow, he felt that this hour had been different, special for her. She was thanking him in the way she knew best, giving him back his fifteen baht. He pushed the notes into her hand, refused to accept them.

'But you I like,' she protested. Such a childlike simplicity. He embraced her, felt her breasts warm and soft against him. Then he kissed her, long and hungrily and she pressed herself against him and he felt himself hard against her stomach. She smiled, well satisfied. He had paid her a tribute. He had kissed her as a lover would. She watched him dress, then touched his face gently. He could have sworn that the stars in her eyes were shining through a mist of rain.

'Oh what the hell,' he muttered as he found Aubrey pacing the corridor.

'What the devil, men, you're taking so long. What were you doing? Pukka girls, no? No hair even on the pussy.'

Carloboy nodded. They went into the street and suddenly decided to get reckless. They walked into a little dive and drank saki—colourless and lethal. It burned all the way down and Aubrey, who had no qualms, ordered a second dram and eyed the woman in the corner with interest. She smiled and came up. Then she fished in her jacket, pulled out a long black cheroot and asked for a light. Her face was a peculiar colour, daubed heavily with a thick, creamy substance.

'That's sandalwood,' Carloboy said.

'How the hell do you know that? Saw lot of women like this. Like white shit on the face. What for?'

'Makes them fair. And makes the skin smooth. In the night they wash it off and go out.'

'The girl told you? The one you screwed?'

Carloboy nodded. 'How was yours?'

'Pukka.'

No other details were really necessary. They strolled along Merchant Street, moving deeper into the town. Then they saw the girl.

From fifty yards she seemed very nice. She swayed invitingly, like a windjammer in a high sea and she was different. She wore Western dress, trim high heels and carried a large handbag—not those Burmese sling bags. Aubrey declared that there was a wench worth knowing in all senses including the Biblical. Carloboy agreed. When on a formal visit to a strange country it was very good policy to win friends and exercise that Carnegie influence.

Then, out of the indecent blue came a startling development. Their quarry was mincing past a typical Burmese suburbia—a row of little houses with latticed windows and iron-grated gates. Suddenly, a man in a heavily coloured batik sarong and light slippers darted out of a gateway, pushed heavily at the girl. She staggered, nearly fell and the man seized her handbag.

Aubrey gave a whoop. As the bag-snatcher hared away, he leaped in pursuit. His cap flew off as he changed gears and Carloboy stood, astonished at the way the evening had changed. Pursued and pursuer were small dots on the horizon.

Retrieving Aubrey's cap, Carloboy swung on the girl who stood white-faced, against a railing. 'Don't worry, we will get your bag back.'

She simply stared, her mouth working soundlessly. She really was good-looking, but she didn't seem to have much wits.

'Where can we bring the bag? Do you live close by?'

No answer.

'What is your name? Shall we give the bag to the police?'

'Poliss,' she said. The colour rushed to her face and her eyes widened. 'Poliss!' she said again, then waving her hands at him, she scurried away.

'Hey! What about your bag?'

'Poliss!' she cried, and darted into a small alley.

Carloboy scratched his head. Things like this were always rather complex. There was Aubrey running around Rangoon sans cap, which, if one considered the Navy, was an offence of the first magnitude, guaranteed to merit fourteen days Number Ten. To cap it all, Carloboy had two caps and felt rather foolish. There was nothing to do but charge on after his madcap friend who could be across the border into Thailand by now.

Navigation through a maze of side streets brought him to the Rangoon market square and wriggling through, he saw in one corner, the bag-snatcher. He was in animated conversation with a crew of cut -throats. Then, a fair distance away, Aubrey rounded a stall where an old man sold some hideously-painted glass vases while an older woman turned a crusher into which she was feeding sticks of sugarcane.

Aubrey seemed to recognize the bag-snatcher too. There was no mistaking the man. His sarong was like a sunset gone mad and the handbag was distinctive enough. He raced up, clamped on the man's shoulder and pointed to the bag.

Carloboy closed rapidly. It was a high-pitched argument—Aubrey in choice Sinhala and breaking into English and the Burman in nasal Burmese. Both were convinced that the other was mad while a crowd swarmed round and began to give freely to their nastiest thoughts and looks.

The mob hemmed Carloboy out. Many seemed anxious to contribute to the argument. Carloboy waved both caps, semaphoring wildly.

Aubrey turned, caught his eye, turned again and caught the bag-snatcher's eye with a powerful right. Then he tore the bag from the man's grasp and punched another who pushed his face in to say how.

Carloboy had to create a diversion. It was nice to know that these people favoured sarongs. He beaned a man who had begun to edge away and swarmed upon another, yanking down his sarong. There is nothing a like a falling sarong to hamper the intents of the best of men. They concentrate on the falling tube of cloth, leaving other bodily parts to be pounded. Carloboy pounded.

Aubrey was in his element. He had this terrible habit of roaring 'Hah!' before delivering a blow and these yells were most demoralizing. Between them, they cut through, met, and while most of the opposition were dragging up their sarongs, decided to make a break for it. They ran madly down the cobbled street.

Those immediately behind flourished knives, anything that could serve as a club and picked up stones.

'Very in-in-inhos-damn-inhospitable,' Aubrey panted, 'run!'

'I'm running,' Carloboy puffed, 'Come on!'

Stones whizzed uncomfortably close.

'The whole bloody market is behind.'

'Don't talk—run!'

They took a bend, raced up a narrow street and there, a large gate loomed. Beside it was a board. In neat white letters were the blessed words,

GOOD SHEPHERD CONVENT, RANGOON.

'In there!' Carloboy shouted.

They wheeled. Aubrey swung shut the gates and looked curiously at the red gravel drive. 'Now what?'

'Don't just stand there. Come on!'

They pelted up the drive and were soon hidden from the gates behind a tall, boxed hedge. A long building, steps, a broad corridor, evenly-spaced pillars. In the wall, a big door of rose-coloured wood. They checked, looked around. The door was open and from within came the sound of sweet music. They walked in. They were in the chapel.

In a shaded corner, six nuns round an old bellows organ stopped singing 'O Sanctissima'. They were rather flustered. The organ died with a sucking gurgle. They knew that twelve eyes were on them and Aubrey, who wasn't a Christian, stared at them in a manner wholly disconcerting. The nuns stared back. Aubrey shrugged. Men who stared at him he could clobber, but nuns? He felt that life was becoming more difficult by the minute.

Carloboy grabbed his arm. 'Come and kneel,' he hissed.

'You're mad? What'll they say?

'They' were speechless. They simply stood and stared.

Carloboy hurriedly genuflected, made the sign of the cross. The nuns gave a relieved sigh and a foot was placed on the organ's bellows pedal, Slowly the music began to issue, and the nuns rustled as they turned to their sheet music.

'Kneel down,' Carloboy gritted.

Aubrey knelt heavily, looked warily round him. 'What the hell is this place?' he asked hoarsely.

'Shhh. Pray.'

'Pray?'

'Just be quiet.'

After a while the singing stopped and the sisters of the Good Shepherd trooped gravely out, Indian file. They did not look at the boys.

After a few moments, Carloboy said, 'Let's go.'

They rose, went out, looking to right and left. The nuns were nowhere to be seen. Just the long corridor, the screening hedge.

'I think we can get back now. Know the way?'

'But what about them?'

'Who?'

'Those women in the blue things.'

'Don't worry about them. They will understand—I think.'

The streets were quiet. They walked away soberly enough, checked the setting sun, used their seamen's bump of direction and found themselves on the Pagoda road. They returned to ship.

The quartermaster grinned. 'What? Went to buy a ladies handbag?'

Aubrey scorned reply. He wasn't in the best of moods. Girls, he said, were, what was the word?

Carloboy smiled. 'Open the bag. Might find her name, or address even.'

'So why didn't you tell that earlier? Could have seen in the convent.'

'Convent? You buggers went to a convent?'

'Where else to go?' Carloboy said cryptically, 'What's in the bag?'

'Bloody hell! Cigarettes. Whole bag is full of cigarettes!'

They emptied the bag on deck. About four hundred cigarettes, sealed in wraps of ten. Carloboy broke a pack, sniffed. 'Funny, smell is like tobacco but the colour is not right.'

The QM took one, eyed it distastefully. 'And not in real cigarette packs. Don't know if its dope or something. Where did you get?'

Carloboy said quietly, 'That bloody girl. Must be a carrier. I spoke to her. When I said police, she bolted. These must be what they call joints. That's how they smoke it. Put marijuana in cigarette wrappers.'

Aubrey whistled. 'Let's light one and see.'

'You're mad? You'll get into deep shit. Throw the damn thing in the sea.'

'Then that bugger we hammered . . .'

'Must have known she was coming. Grabbed the bag and ran. And you also ran, and I had to run behind.'

The QM was very interested. 'To where?'

'The bloody convent! That's where. With this!'

'And half of bloody Rangoon chasing!'

Carloboy stuffed the packs into the bag, then hurled it over the side.

Aubrey had the last word. 'I hate convents. All bloody virgins playing organs.'

He cheered up when he was told that there would be a film show on the boat deck. The vegetable locker was free. The statue was safely ashore. The *Vijaya* was very much back to its old self again.

They sailed at dawn. The monsoon practically blew them back as they caught its full fury and the seas boiled around them. The Army and Air Force wept on each other's shoulders. Great oaths were made between protracted bouts of bringing up whatever they did not eat. After all, they moaned, they were soldiers, not bloody turtles.

Past Barberyn Light, within sight of Colombo roads, the whitecaps were fewer although the swell was tremendous. The *Vijaya* wallowed, was shoved mightily, seemed to stand still, then plunged on. The motion caused havoc in many khaki-clad stomachs.

Mission accomplished, the *Vijaya* tied up at Kochchikade on December 23. Carloboy asked for leave and got it. All Christians did. At home, he found his father admiring a big fir tree.

'Ah, so you came? How was the trip?' Sonnaboy von Bloss asked.

'Not bad. From where did you get the tree?'

Sonnaboy was in his merriest of moods. The shop was doing well. Oh, very well indeed. He had stocked lots of Christmas goodies and even cylindrical boxes of crackers that were guaranteed to burst every eardrum for miles. They were venomous triangular crackers with long wicks which gave the man who lit them the opportunity to run for the nearest wall and scale it before the cracker exploded. Sonnaboy said he had tried out a few. The next-door dog had gone crazy. It broke loose, ran to the canal, swam to the other side and then bit a man who was minding his own business. 'Battas they are called. Like to try one? Your mother dropped the pot of hot water in the kitchen when I threw one near the bloody window.'

Carloboy grinned. He emptied his bag. NAAFI whisky, cigarettes, wine. He had gone to the Fort for little gifts for his brothers and sisters. Home for Christmas. He didn't realize how tired he was until he sagged into a chair, sipping whisky with his father.

52

History—Hiroshima and Nagasaki

At 8.15 on the morning of August 6, 1945, men, women and children ran screaming into rivers in Hiroshima, the skin hanging off their bones much like tattered kimonos. In midair, birds burst into flames.

Ringing the islands of Japan, the American troops preparing for Operation Downfall, danced between the rows of their tents, fred into the air, cheered and whooped and yelled themselves hoarse. They drank all the beer they could in a mad celebration. Some sat to weep in relief and joy. They were going to live. There would be no invasion, no '20,000 soldiers dead', as the planners had made allowance for.

What were they celebrating? Were they celebrating the instant death of about 70,000 civilians—men, women and children of Hiroshima? Months later, 130,000 more would die to radiation poisoning and burns.

They were celebrating the dropping of the first atom bomb over Hiroshima; Truman's most terrible bomb in the history of the world.

Lieutenant Colonel Paul Tibbets was the pilot of the B-29 *Enola Gay*. His co-pilot at his shoulder kept thumping him as they climbed away after dropping their terrible capsule. 'Look at that!' he kept exclaiming, just look at that!'

A bright light had filled the plane making everything on the instrument panels glow like antimony. They could not see their target. All they could see with eyes unbelieving, was a huge cloud, boiling up, spreading like a massive flower. Below, the city, as one described it, was nothing but a cauldron of boiling oil. What no one knew was that Emperor Hirohito had already decided to surrender. This decsion had been made before the devastation of Hiroshima.

Truman was giddy wth happiness. 'This is the greatest thing in history,' he said. American newspaper headlines screamed: THANK GOD FOR THE ATOMIC BOMB. And Truman later told reporters, much later, 'I didn't have any doubts at the time.' In 1956 he said, 'Why, I'd do it again.' And in 1965, repeated that he would not hesitate to use the A-bomb.

In *Newsweek* of July 24, 1995, we have the account of a young ensign, Osborne Elliott, who was on board the heavy cruiser *Boston*. He was steaming towards the coast of Japan with the US Third Fleet, a part of Operation Downfall.

Then came the news of the incineration of Hiroshima. Osborne said later how his ship 'erupted with whoops and shouts of joy'. There was no feeling of pity even when, not many weeks later, he and some other officers toured the city. They could not feel pity. Remorse, maybe, but not pity. In his view, the atom bomb had saved many lives—'Quite possibly including our own.'

Standing in the middle of Hiroshima he found nothing rising above the level of his knees, 'except for the shell of a building or the grotesque skeleton of a tree . . .'

Everything was oxidized by the heat beyond recognition. With gratitude and acknowledgement to *Newsweek*, the writer quotes Elliott:

> How anybody was left alive, I do not know. But here and there, women and children were sittng on the rubble that was once their homes. We didn't see many wounded—just a few on crutches or with bandages on their heads. Many people had sores on their faces. We stared at them and they gazed blanky back at us.

But why the follow on? Indeed, the Americans were all for it. Groves was most eager to show what he could do. The second atom bomb, an implosion type missile was exploded over the largest Roman Catholic cathedral in the Far East. It killed 70,000 people including many Allied P-O-W's held prisoner in Nagasaki.

Maybe there are some feelings of shame and remorse on both sides now. As the gruesome details of Hiroshima and Nagasaki emerged there was a queasiness among the American public. This is evident in the number of new books now being written about the end of World War II. And no, the world will also not forget the infamous Nanking massacre, the terrible Bataan death march, Japan's vicious medical experiments on Allied prisoners. Much barbarity was inflicted by Japan on her neighbours. There were the 'normal' crimes of a 'normal' nation fighting a 'normal' war: colonization, killing of civilians, ill treatment of prisoners. But the Tokyo War Crimes trials showed much worse.

It's all over now, but Japan still struggles to confront her wartime past.

Somehow, it will not go away.

53

Of an end to a Beginning and a Sailor's Diary and the Best That's Left Unsaid

Home. Chapter one began at home, and not long ago, we brought Carloboy home. Home for Christmas. And there, the writer wishes to leave him. This, many will say is but the beginning, and if so, it is time to bring this beginning to an end. Carloboy spent a merry Christmas indeed, and a boozy Christmas evening at Eardley's where he tried hard to remember the name of the Burmese girl—the only one, he said, who washed and powdered his prick.

'Mylord, I think . . .'

'My Lord?'

'I don't know, men. Sounded something like that.'

'What? She took one look at you and said "My Lord"?' Eardley guffawed. They laughed heartily. They had both relished the 'Oh brother' story and chortled some more.

'You thought I'm like Pedro?' Carloboy asked.

It was a nice story, actually. Seems there was this Mexican boy named Pedro who married Juanita of the smouldering eyes and who walked as though her tail was on fire. But early the next morning a worried Pedro was beating on the padre's door.

'Padre Juan, Padre Juan, wake op! I theenk I have made terrible meestake!'

The padre tried to calm the agitated Pedro. 'Why Pedro, what ees the matter? Happy you should be, with your new wife, no?'

'But padre, I sure I marry my seester!'

The padre stepped back amazed. 'Your seester? How this can be? Is it that so early you drink the cactus juice?'

'No, no, padre. You must help me. I marry my seester!'

'Nonsense. You are taking the loco weed, my poor Pedro. I know Juanita. Her family. Her oncle on the other side of the mesa. All good people when not dreenking. How you can say like this? You no marry your seester. What seester? You no have seester.'

Pedro frowned. 'Then padre, last night when I ondress to go to bed . . .'

'Yes, yes?'

'Why, she look at me. Look at me in the place . . . you know, padre?'

'Yes, yes?'

'So why she look and say oh brother?'

It certainly was a very liquid evening and Carloboy slept late and rose and yawned hugely and went to the 'shop' where his father was addressing a sack of New Year cards to people who had sent him Christmas cards.

'Buggers you send cards to never reply,' Sonnaboy grumbled, 'and buggers you never think of send cards and you have to wish them back.'

It was all too complicated, so he drifted to the kitchen for breakfast which was a stack of leftovers from the 25th night celebrations. His mother was washing a stack of tumblers.

Being the season to be jolly, we will leave him full of the Christmas spirit. The writer could take him back to the *Vijaya* but rather, if only to hint at the best that is left unsaid, we could skip a few years and take a peek at Carloboy's diary. Many dramatic entries, to be sure, and most enigmatic.

Item. *Minesweeping exercises in Bombay*. And the startling information about being drunk and disorderly in the Eros

Cinema and a night in the Bombay jail. He makes a note about the largest cockroaches in the world.

Item. *East African cruise.* Some pithy remarks about a French girl in Seychelles and how he had used his raincoat to cover them for the sake of decency until a policeman had become over-inquisitive. Note of a cracked rib in Mombasa. The African girl had no idea of her crushing powers when having her orgasm. Illuminating details about the red light district of Crater, in Aden and the smell of cloves when approaching Zanzibar.

Item. *Signals course and examination on INS Vendrurthi, Indian Navy shore sation in Cochin.* Dhal and bread for breakfast, bread and dhal for supper, he writes. Also falling into a disused well and wearing a gas mask before being hauled out. Mention of an angry cobra in the old brickwork, four feet over his head.

Item. *Far East cruise.* Many entries here. Basket girls of Hong Kong and much about Banda Street, Singapore and playing piano at a nightclub and *HMS Terror* and tidal wave at Banjerinasin in South Borneo. Some high jinks on a rubber estate too.

Item. *Going with Eardley to the Good Shepherd Convent in Hendala, Sri Lanka.* Meeting Karina, the girl he is determined to marry.

Item. *Drafted to HMCyS Rangalla as a signals instructor.* Some strange entries to be sure. Cobras in waste paper baskets and giving his flannel trousers to a viper. One needs to know more about this, to be sure.

Item. *Wriggling out of the Navy.* Another operation that was done wih some regret, naturally.

One wonders what one could make of all this. Oh yes, there's Mauritius and the Maldives, too, and as these chapters have seen, Carloboy breezed through, taking the lumps and bumps, the pleasures and pressures as they came. Perhaps some day, the writer will try to put the rest together. But for now, begging your pardon, the best is left unsaid. Perhaps it's the worst. That too, is a matter of interpretation.

Sonnaboy poured himself a drink. 'So what did you do in Rangoon?'

Carloboy smiled. Sandalwood paste and soft lips around his cock and small hands pushing, pushing, pushing at his bum. He smiled.

'Nothing much,' he said.